THE SELF-MADE MEN

THE SELF-MADE MEN

MICHAEL CURTIN

THISTLE
PUBLISHING

First published in 1980 by André Deutsch Ltd

This edition published in 2015 by:

Thistle Publishing
36 Great Smith Street
London
SW1P 3BU

www.thistlepublishing.co.uk

ISBN-13: 9781910670552

For Anne

CONTENTS

CHAPTER ONE
BILL JOHNSTON

Ten years earlier Billy Whelan had twelve hundred pounds on deposit with Barclays and yet managed to starve on Christmas Day. He did not usually breakfast – a pint of milk on the site cured him. But he felt the lack of it on his way to Christmas mass. The great breakfasts of his youth on top of the rigid communion fast, rashers, sausages and eggs, taking care not to allow a morsel of yolk stain the good suit, needled him. As did the guilt of staying in London over the holiday. In other respects he had done his duty. He wrote home well in advance paving the way for his non-appearance. His mother replied with entreaties. He sallied by way of registered letter.

According to Father Moriarty – after a lifetime on the missions now grassing in the Quex Road, Kilbum nerve centre – it was a day to think of loved ones. Billy Whelan thought of food. Hogan had turned to him the night before in the Falcon and said: 'You don't cook at all do you?'

'No. I eat out all the time.'

'Are you invited someplace tomorrow?'

'No. But I'd prefer just to have the few scoops and nip in someplace and have a steak or something. I'm not a man for turkey.'

'And where will be open?'

'I don't know. I usually go home at Christmas. There's bound to be someplace open. Will the caff be open?'

'Not at all. I couldn't find a place last year. Twas the one and only time no one invited me. I went to Mackey's a couple of years. Tommy Cook had me once. Martin. I used to go to Maurice and Connie till they broke up. Maurice is worse than ourselves now. Last year no one invited me. The first time. I traipsed the High Road as far as Smiths Watches. I went back as far as Marble Arch. There wasn't a Wimpy, a chipper, nothing. I ended up in the room putting on the bacon and cabbage I had in for Boxing Day. No one's invited me this year either.'

A phrase of Father Moriarty's hooked Whelan:

'. . . the Black Hole of Calcutta. The Black Hole of Calcutta, an apartment in New York, a pension in Paris, a room in London . . . a stable in Bethlehem . . . not a place but a state of mind . . . true Christmas is the clean feeling of a stainless soul, not the replete materialism of a stripped turkey. . .'

Neither Whelan or his mother liked turkey. Aunt Molly sent two chickens every year into which Mrs Whelan sank a bloody elbow and plucked entrails on to a bed of newspaper. Christmas was not a state of mind: it was the shipwreck silhouette of chickens on the table and a book by the fire and a clandestine cigarette while Mrs Whelan was lying down.

'. . . live is no more than a geographical quirk. True home is not in the lap of the gods but rather in God's lap . . .'

After mass Whelan idled outside the tube station a hundred yards or so distant from the Falcon; he had a distaste for being seen idling outside pubs. He did not normally drink in company; not having hands like shovels or a shorehole of a mouth he was unable to keep up with his fellow labourers' pace not to mind Hogan and his three swallows to the pint. But it was after all Christmas morning and Hogan had said the night before 'unless I'm asked yet' and the strategy of buying Hogan a drink was obvious. At a minute to twelve Whelan strolled towards the Falcon but before he reached it the opening time maw swallowed the crowd and Hogan was in the process of buying for himself and Tom Mackey, Whelan's landlord.

'Happy Christmas.'

'Many Happy Returns. Will you join me?'

'I'm with Mackey. I'll get you one. Sit down and see that I'm in the cast out.'

Tom Mackey and Hogan and Whelan, Tommy Cook, Martin, and Maurice of Maurice and Connie all had red faces and wore blue suits; all were originally from the County of Limerick except Billy Whelan who was from the City of Limerick; all worked on the buildings; all were settled emigrants of various times served; Whelan, in his fifth year, did not have roots apart from his twelve hundred pounds with Barclays and lodged with Tom Mackey whose colours were so prominendy nailed to the mast that his two grown daughters thought of themselves as English, which they were. But Mackey of course was Irish.

'And how's Billy? What's keeping Hogan with the porter? Who's in for the cast out? Hogan. We'll have to deal him in or the skin and hair will be flyin'. Hogan, Tommy, meself, Billy, no sign of Maurice, down in Chelsea up to his nose in red biddy, the Lord love him, Martin, sure we haven't a quorum, we've only five. Corkey. Corkey, will you make up the rubber?'

Hogan struggled down from the counter with two pints and went back for the third. He returned and took out his glasses from a case shinily denuded of cloth covering. The counter had been six deep with the red and black faces of Ireland and the third world.

'I was safer with Wingate in Burma,' Hogan chuckled and Whelan grinned sheepishly. For two years Whelan had sat beside Hogan listening to the wonderful old man's reminiscences, believing every word and chafing at the bit of his own dull life until Hogan's eyes tired early one night of his *Evening Standard* and he put away his glasses and said: '"Wingate, you flogpot," I said. I was the only one he allowed to call him flogpot. "You flogpot," I said. "Now look what you've landed us into." We were surrounded by about a hundred of them, yellow men

4

with machetes, Wingate with the ferrule of his cane and Hogan with nothing. "You and your we'll go for a drive," I said to him, "you big flogpot. I might be your batman but you must think I'm Batman." Anyway, one of the yellow men threw a rocker and Wingate's out for the count. I looked around. I picked up the jawbone of an ass and said here goes . . . '

'Hi.'

'What.'

'Getoutofit. I'm a right eejit. And all the other yams. You were having me on all the time. Next thing you'll tell me that you had your long hair at the time.'

'You don't believe me? When Wingate came to and saw all the yellow bodies . . .'

'Hogan, stop. I'm not listening.'

'. . . you did it again, Hogan, the flogpot says . . .'

Whelan loved him that night more than he had ever envied him his supposed experiences. It did not matter that Hogan had not been with Frank Ryan in Spain or Monty in Alamein or stood Ike a pint in Berlin. Whelan was not as hopelessly behind in life as he had thought.

Corkey made up the rubber; he was Denis O'Leary of Cork and as the only non-Limerick man at the table had to be called Corkey. When they cast out knaves Whelan drew him as partner, Tom Mackey was paired with Hogan and Tommy Cook with Martin. Whelan concentrated neither on the cards or the drink. The talk was of turkey, particularly from Tom Mackey, who as a settled man was naturally obsessed with the trappings of his station. To a bystander, red-faced and blue-suited, observing the school he said: 'Happy Christmas, Pat. Buildin' up for the turkey.'

Whelan discerned no association of ideas flicker on Hogan's lined face. He might have indeed weathered yellow men, such was his stoicism in the face of two hours away from no dinner. The invitation certainly would not come from Corkey. It would stem from Tom Mackey, Tommy Cook or Martin. Whelan hoped it would be Tom Mackey. With Hogan to preside over the table talk and Whelan's familiarity with Mrs Mackey the two English daughters might not succeed in making Whelan uncomfortable. Hogan roused him.

'A club led flogpot. Wake up. You must have had a cut last night.'

Hogan's sexual conquests, à la Wingate, consisted of widows and landladies who rewarded him with sums varying from half crowns to fivers. It struck Whelan that they must have been trumped up.

Tom Mackey ordered three pints through the bystander who was building up for the turkey. Hogan savaged his and said: 'Flogpot, would you take long and immediate steps to the bar and purchase the porter.' Whelan let the bystander play his cards and went to the counter. Alone among the black men and his fellow Paddies it struck him that there would be no invitations to dinner. One did not roll in with company on Christmas Day without prior warning to the woman of the house. Mrs Mackey was an economical

6

woman and would not be equipped to deal with two extra labouring mouths suitably oiled with liquor. He told himself at the counter that it was Hogan he was thinking about. He could not think of what he could do on Hogan's behalf. An enquiry at the card table would be insensitive.

'Lads, would there be anyplace open today where I'd get a bit of nosh?'

That would hang translated in the awkward silence: It's Christmas Day and the landlord sitting on my left has not invited me down from my room to share his dinner and the society of his wife and two daughters. Tommy Cook or Martin, whoever had the quicker wit would jump in: What? You mean you've no place to go for your dinner? For God's sake why didn't you open your mouth. You're coming with me. Tom Mackey would have no choice: What? I thought you'd be going – I didn't think – how do I know what young fellas do be up to, Margaret will have a fit if she thought, why didn't you let me know, you'll have turkey with us and no more about it. Hogan. Where are you going today?

The thought of sitting down to Christmas dinner with Tom Mackey and his family or with anybody and his family became distasteful to Whelan at the start of the second round of drinks. He played the cards mechanically, nursing his flair to brush stroke the prospect of an invitation to Hogan's den; that would be some Christmas dinner, bacon and cabbage from the plate on his lap squatting on Hogan's concave bed, the detritus of bachelorhood and forty years' exile crashing the etiquette barrier. Afterwards, primed with bottled stout, Hogan might admit the inadequacy of his own innings as a spur to Whelan making something of himself.

A pint and a half of Whelan's reproached his full gill when Hogan again reminded: 'Flogpot, art is long and time is fleeting, would you ever take long and immediate steps to the bar and purchase the porter.'

Whelan did not buy for himself; he struggled through the remaining drink until closing time; dimly he accepted two half crowns for the rubber he had won thanks to Corkey's singlemindedness and his own narrow avoidance of a disgraceful play.

'It's Mackey's house tonight so,' Tommy Cook was saying, 'where are we meeting?'

They were meeting in the Falcon, a select band possessed of the secret knock. Whelan was pleased that they planned in his presence as though he was made of stone. He needed their collective rejection as further proof of their individual lack of concern for a young man alone on Christmas Day. Higgins, Murphy, Mark Brown and Nicky – they had prepared him well. He downed the dregs and left without exchanging the season's greetings; the five and a half pints slowed his walk and a clatter of tipped heels pre-cursed Mackey catching him up.

'Ah that was grand porter. You'd eat the cross off an ass's back as the fella said.'

At the door, as he was turning the key, Mackey said: 'Where are you having your dinner?'

'I'm going to a mate's house in Milman Road.'

'Grand. Well, happy Christmas to you, Billy.'

'Many Happy Returns.'

He sat on the bed in his room, listening. He wanted to hear footsteps on the stairs. Mrs Mackey would have said to her husband: Did I hear Billy come in with you? She would force him to run up and check and double check that Whelan was going to a mate in Milman Road. Her maternal instinct would rescue him. To the face of a woman — a mother — he was capable of admitting need. He listened and heard the sound of his electric fire click off. Five hours lay ahead of him until the Falcon would open at seven to the secret few; and he did not know the knock. He would have to wait on the alert till he heard Mackey going out and follow him and bump into him and hang on to him to gain entry into the pub and afterwards to the gathering in Mackey's house where there would be, surely, turkey sandwiches. It was cold. He did not have a single shilling. He searched his old suit hoping that he would not find one; cold went well with rejection. Cold, hungry, alone. Among the pot-pourri there was no sign of a single shilling but in a tobacco-crumbed underground map there was a dollar and a penny ballad sheet. The dollar. It was better than not finding a single shilling, better than hunger, better than being alone. The Lord have mercy on you Mr Ryan, he whispered.

His relationship with Mr Ryan owed nothing
to any degree of consanguinity. It began the night
Billy pressed his nose against Lil Dwyer's window
pane dreaming of what he would select if he had his
choice of anything from the display – a haphazard
jumble of toys flounced amid empty detergent boxes
and cardboard chocolate effigies. His mother would
chastise him for not having the kettle on and for
not putting a match to the fire; she did not understand that he was afraid of the house and that the
November starry cold under the light of Lil Dwyer's
window comforted him. Contributory negligence,
he had heard his mother say, had been established
and whatever damages there would be the company
intended to establish their gratuity thereby avoiding 'dangerous precedents'. A butt had fallen from
his father's ear and the man had foolishly stepped
to retrieve it; he was crushed between the reversing wagon and the wall of the packing plant. The
company's money was put away, earmarked towards
Billy's education; Mrs Whelan got her old job back
in the clothing factory. Lil Dwyer's lighted window
was preferable to the lonely kitchen from where up
to a month before he had bolted from his tea when
he heard the footsteps in the passage and leapt into
his father's arms. His father was waiting for them all
above in heaven alongside holy God but until they
would all be together again the house was lonely and
not as warm as Lil Dwyer's magic window of water
pistols and cranes, custard packets and *Beanos* and

Dandies and a self-supporting placard of two sisters, one with the perm and the legend: Which twin has the Toni?

'What are you doing out in the cold?'

'I'm waiting for my mother.'

'You'll get your death without a coat on.'

'I'm all right Mr Ryan. I'm not cold at all.'

'Nonsense. I can see you shivering in front of me. Run up home and stay there by the fire till your mother comes. Like a good boy.'

Mr Ryan called to the house later in the night; the following morning Mrs Whelan told her son: 'Mr Ryan says you're old enough to join the altar.'

Ad Deum qui laetificat juventutem meam, Billy Whelan chanted running to school or on errands; Lil Dwyer accused him of cursing and threatened to report him. Within six weeks – it was a record at that time Mr Ryan assured Mrs Whelan – Billy made his debut as an acolyte at a midweek early morning mass attended by his mother and Mr Ryan and the regular matutinal communicants. The moment did indeed bring joy to his youth, patriarchal contentment to Mr Ryan and took the sting from the hole in Mrs Whelan's purse after the purchase of vestment material. But it was nothing to the euphoria of serving the American priest. Any old giddy garsun would not do for an American priest and afterwards in the sacristy the legends of American largesse bore fruit: Billy was presented with a dollar. He ran home.

His mother said: 'Go down and tell Mr Ryan.'

Mr Ryan consulted the financial page of his newspaper and divined the dollar was worth seven shillings and a halfpenny. He cashed the dollar from a cup without a handle on the top shelf of the dresser.

'When you are older and working you can buy the dollar back. I'll mind it for you as a souvenir.'

Mrs Whelan gave him the halfpenny and a three-penny bit and minded the rest of the money till he would need it.

Sometimes, at Sunday mass with his mother when he was not serving, Billy occupied himself with her voluminous missal. It was not the content sanctioned with the bishop's imprimatur that engaged him. An In Memoriam photograph of his father that grew more youthful as Billy aged chilled him. A few pages on held a desiccated autumn leaf; at titillating intervals throughout the prayer book were to be found a newspaper cutting of the examination prayer, Code 12/21/29/40 of the Rehabilitation Pools, a blood donor's card, a registered parcel receipt and an uncharacteristic piece of memorabilia, a penny ballad:

> Alone, all alone,
> By a wave-washed strand,
> All alone in a crowded hall;
> The hall it is gay,
> The waves they are grand,
> But my heart is not there at all.

It flies far away,
By night and by day,
To the times and the joys that are gone;
But I never will forget
The sweet maiden I met
In the Valley of Slievenamon.

Mr Ryan's spirit lived on while the dollar was preserved;
Mrs Whelan was not permanently abandoned by her
son while the words maintained their legibility on the
creased octavo sheet; and the stack of *Screen Monthlies*
piled on the floor of the wardrobe were a chronological
rejection of Higgins and Murphy and Nicky and Mark
Brown. He had told Higgins of the advertisement in
Screen Monthly and Higgins guffawed his disbelief and
added, which made them all laugh, 'Go way you dirty
bot Whelan reading the ads in movie magazines.'

Whelan had coloured and not brought in *Screen
Monthly* to show them the advertisement because it was
surrounded as Higgins insinuated by bust developers
and unwanted hair removers. For six years Whelan had
never failed to buy *Screen Monthly*. He put the dollar
and the ballad on the bed and went to the wardrobe;
he opened the latest issue. There it was in its little box

Fart International
Box 13
SEND NO MONEY

Because it was Christmas Day and he was alone, all alone, not in a crowded hall or by a wave washed strand, but alone with a dollar and a ballad and over seventy *Screen Monthlies* and his heart full of hatred for Higgins and Murphy and Nicky and Mark Brown, he cried for the first time since his father died. Now he had everything: Cold, Hunger, Solitude, Tears. It was definitely the best he had ever felt in his life. He plucked up the courage of the anonymous and wrote:

Fart International,   14 Burlington Avenue,
Box 13   Queens Park,
SEND NO MONEY   London NW6
c/o Screen Monthly

Dears Sirs,

I enclose no money. I have money – twelve hundred pounds on deposit with Barclays Bank. It is Christmas Day. I have had no breakfast and no dinner. I hate this world. I love my mother and I loved my father but he died for the butt of a cigarette when I was eight. The wagon of a train crushed him while he was stooping down. There was a neighbour lived near me called Mr Ryan. I loved him but he's dead too. There's only my mother now at home. I was driven away from home by Higgins and Murphy and Mark Brown and Nicky. Nobody knows that but me – and you, whoever you are. A rumour got about that I was emigrating to become an actor and it

THE SELF-MADE MEN

was reported to me that the teacher franced the plausibility by remarking: I don't see why he has to go anyplace to become an actor, he already is one. Typical magisterial snidedom. Every time I long to go home I imagine Higgins sneering: Well, Gary Cooper, when's the next picture coming out. I went back on holidays every Christinas for the past five years ducking from pub to pub with my shoulders hunched in case I'd bump into Higgins. I can tell you I never had any notion of becoming an actor. I can't go into a kiosk for a packet of Embassy without a bird struggling at my accent: Youwahdearie? That's how far from ever being an actor I am.

For the past three years I have been working on the buildings – as a labourer. It's built me up. Instead of being tall and stringy I'm tall and full of muscles and I have a great appetite, a thing I never had. I used to be finicky about food. My father was a labourer in the production end of a cement factory. The money we got as a result of his death saw me through school and it was a great consolation to my mother that with my education I would never have to work in the open. I have her heart broken.

The only person I met in the past five years whom I can remotely understand or feel is – is right – is a maintenance man in a Swiss Cottage hotel by the name of Hogan. He told me dozens of stories that I was simple enough to believe in

15

which he was caught up in great moments of history. It wasn't until he told me he killed a hundred yellow men with the jawbone of an ass protecting Wingate in Burma or someplace that I copped on. I began to feel all the more that he was – was right – when I realised he was making it all up.

For all I know I could be writing to an eccentric millionaire with a heart of transatlantic gold who will adopt me and send me home dripping dollars yet somehow I don't think, whoever you are, that you'd pull a lousy trick like that on me. The electric fire has gone out on me and I've no shilling for the meter. I'm cold, alone, hungry and a few minutes ago I was crying. At least I'm not rich, apart from my twelve hundred pounds on deposit with Barclays. Imagine being really rich and crying. Mr Ryan, a neighbour, was nice to me when I was a child. He didn't shackle me with rules or anything. He took a detached interest in my welfare. I wish I could tell you about Higgins and Murphy and Mark Brown and Nicky. You'd probably think it's childish and in a way it was, but – then – it was serious then, it was – but no matter. And what would be worse than you turning out to be an eccentric millionaire landing out of the blue here in Burlington Avenue would be your eccentrically, millionairely, manifesting yourself with a bronzed and slim golden-haired daughter who would quiver all over exposed to my jangled personality. Please do not do that to me.

It seems like yesterday that the fire was lighting in the kitchen before I came home from school and the room was warm and the tea was on the table and I was on my father's lap while he was reading the Hopalong Cassidy strip out to me from the *Independent*. I'll admit it, it's maudlin. But everything happened so fast, just like that, and here I am at twenty-five years of age writing rubbish to a box number in Los Angeles. I suppose it could be worse. I could be a box number in Los Angeles.

Whatever it is you're floggin', if it has to come wrapped in plain paper, I don't want it.

Yours sincerely,
Billy Whelan

Taking off only his blue suit he went to bed in his shirt and tie and socks and underpants; he had lost the habit of wearing a vest by achieving an all over tan on summer sites astride pneumatic drills. He lit an Embassy and placed it on the ashtray on the table beside the bed where he had put the dollar and the ballad and the letter. After each pull of his cigarette he withdrew his hand and his nose under the blanket and peered coldly at the letter he had composed. He was puzzled by the author of the letter; the Billy Whelan who had written with such honest detachment was not himself; that man did not have his head full of Higgins or inhospitable landlords. The man curled into the foetus position under the bedclothes had no authority. Yet they were one and the same. The so far unrequited communion with a film magazine box number an ocean and a land mass away was a source of strength; what must it be like to have a pal, a rock of a father, a girl friend or a wife.

He woke, hungry, at half-past five and went to the communal bathroom on the landing taking care to make as much noise as was natural. He had the hope that he might be heard and invited for tea. Back in his room, refreshed after the splash of water, he noticed the cold and went downstairs in search of a single shilling from his landlord. Mrs Mackey answered the door and wished him a Happy Christmas and shook Tom Mackey awake from his somnolent television vigil; between them they managed two shillings in exchange for his florin. The room warmed quickly with the two bars on and for a while the heat and his cigarettes were a comfort. But then the hunger returned and by way of idly taking his mind from it he read the letter. Written three and a half hours and five and a half pints earlier in the day it appeared the issue of a madman; Fart International might be a journal that printed letters, names and addresses and all; someone would see it and tell someone who would tell someone until it reached his mother; worse, until it reached Higgins. He would never be able to go home again as long as he lived. Instead of putting it in the dustbin where Mrs Mackey might find it and afraid to bum it – Mrs Mackey had reprimanded a like deed on the evidence of ashes – he put it with the dollar and the ballad in his old suit.

It struck him now that Tom Mackey would certainly not leave his house at seven o'clock to go to the pub. The landlord's capacity for drink at a sitting was exactly eight pints. Hogan had once said of him, you could set your watch by Mackey. He caught the six fifty-seven tube every morning without fail and hit the pub every night two hours before closing time. He completed a pint every fifteen minutes. Whelan set out for the Kilburn High Road in the faint hope that an enterprising alien might be patrolling in a chip wagon. The High Road was deserted save for a distant figure approaching. It was a man in a blue suit with a red face whom Whelan did not know. Not knowing the man Whelan was not shy of enquiring: 'Excuse me. You wouldn't know by any chance if there's any restaurants open today?'

'To tell you the truth I'm after searching high up and low down myself for one. Nothing. There's no place open. Are there any pubs opening tonight do you know?'

'I think the Falcon is. I heard someone saying it.'

'I had nothing since my breakfast. This is the third year in a row that I keep forgetting there's no place open. You'd think there'd be someplace open, wouldn't you.'

'I usually go home for Christmas but I didn't bother this year.'

'I haven't been home in ten year. Where are you from yourself?'

'Limerick.'

'I'm a Galway man myself. How long are you here?'

'Just over five years.'

'I'm twenty-five year here now. I used to go home twice a year one time. But you'd know no one. It's fuckin' awful not having someplace open Christmas Day. You'd think there'd be even one place open. Get a steak or a few chops. I was in a pub last Christmas in Maida Vale – what's the name of it – I asked the barman had he any sandwiches. He had no sandwiches but he said he had crisps. I was just going to buy a bag of crisps and something stopped me. Do you know what I mean? You'd be out of place eating crisps in a pub on Christmas night. You'd be tellin' em all that you had nothing to eat that day. There I was starving and I wouldn't eat crisps in case I'd upset people. Fuckin' mad isn't it.'

'I know. I may as well keep on. You should try the Falcon. See you.'

'What I was going to say. Five year you're here. Is it true things are picking up over. I heard there's loads of factories going up all over the country. In Shannon Airport there's supposed to be a lot of them. Japanese and Americans. I often go into a factory for the winter sometimes. When the weather is really bad. I must have worked in every factory in Harlesden and Willesden. Walls, GKN, Indestructo, MacVities, the lot. It gets harder to get in though. Some fuckers wouldn't believe you when you'd tell em you're thirty-nine. What age would you take me for now?'

'To be honest I'm useless as guessing people's ages but I'd have placed you at forty-two.'

'I'm fifty-eight. Fifty-eight last February. You'd get into no factory in Ireland I'd say at my age. Unless you got in as a sweeper. No matter how much experience you had. When I was in GKN twas nearly all wogs. There was this cunt there he was supposed to be over me – August was his name – can you imagine that – from Nigeria or someplace. He'd stand up looking at me while I put the nuts and bolts onto the pallet he'd walk in front of me then while I was pushing and he'd point to the ground and grunt: Har. Here he meant. I was rolling a fag one day at tea-up and he says to me out of the blue: Ou cum you say English so good. You'd have to laugh. I told him how everyone in Ireland learns English from the time they're in the cot, his head nodding up and down all the time: I see I see I see. I have a grand chat anyway with him and then after the break we go back to work and here he is ordering me around and not doing a tap himself only sending me up ladders and filling the pallet and grunting: Har. Not dur. Har.'

'I know. Well I must be . . .'

'I've a sister still alive all right, she never married either, she lets the house out for most of the summer and the races, she manages like that, I couldn't see myself really going back, I mean you know the way single women have everything just so, spotless sheets on the bed, everything shining, meals on time, I couldn't see myself fitting in, when you're used to goin' and comin' when you feel like it, I'll hang on for me pension anyway. That's one sure thing.'

'You're right. I might see you later in the Falcon. I've to see a fella first. Good luck.'

'Yeah. See you Limerick.'

The stranger's resilience, Mackey's, Hogan's, his own refusal to knuckle under irritated Whelan; he excused the uncharitable ear he had lent to the stranger by blaming the Higginses – tenuous whip-crackers and detonators of delayed action misery in others; the lunacy of tearing himself away from even a stranger who only wanted someone to hold his coat while he told himself lies struck him; he should have been thankful for small mercies on a cold Kilburn High Road on a deserted Christmas night. He reminded himself that he had become hard and decided to forget the plight of the descendants of earls. There was getting in to the Falcon to be achieved.

Whelan took the long route back to the Falcon in case he might bump into the stranger and in the hope that he would bump into Hogan who always travelled that way coming from Swiss Cottage. He enjoyed mixed fortune; neither the stranger nor Hogan was on the road and it was quarter past seven when he reached the pub. The blinds were drawn and all lights cunningly concealed but he could hear the comforting murmur of illicit voices. He tapped on the window. The fourth, sporadic knock was rewarded with the drawing of a bolt and the query: 'Who is it?'

'Billy Whelan and Tom Mackey.'

A second bolt and the appearance of the tenant's face later brought admittance. The tenant looked up and down:

'Where's Mackey?'

'He won't be down for a while. He sent me on ahead.'

The tenant appraised Whelan silently and nodded him in. Without taking a deliberate head count he noticed the morning custom in full attendance with Tom Mackey yet to come so that those who set their watches by him might not be confused. Whelan's pint was served with alacrity; he took it to the card table around which sat Hogan, Tommy Cook, Martin and Maurice of Maurice and Connie. The drink was running out of both corners of Maurice's lips. After his day on the red biddy he bought pints of light and bitter two at a time and placed them under the table; it was not unknown for him to pick up someone's pint of Guinness or glass of whiskey and drink it. The gentle and firm hands of those on the alert stopped him on the way to his mouth and re-routed him to his own cache. He was a comfort to them all. Hogan affected, by way of explanation to Whelan, not to understand the tragedy of Maurice.

'You'd think getting rid of an oul whore like Connie he'd be offering up masses.'

Maurice, Whelan was informed, had been a Christian Brother. At the time and in the part of the country from which he hailed, which could have been any part of the country at the time, dropping out did not constitute a social grace. Maurice took the boat and married Connie, the first barmaid to succumb to his slurred advances. Because he would have been seen to be, looking at it from his own point of view, festooned with scholarship Maurice depicted himself in the Oxford Street agencies as fit fodder for office work in the managerial line. It was so far from meeting the case that only golden hearted employers took him on – as a junior but with a salary commensurate with his twenty-nine years of age. They reasonably expected that he would grasp the essentials and go on to reward them with the broad view.

'The flogpot got bogged down in trivia. He used to come in here, Connie wouldn't come in here with him because she'd worked here and, well, Connie knew us and we knew Connie if you know what I mean.'

'I don't.'

'No matter. Naturally from the first day Maurice took one look at my high forehead and he could see I was a man of breeding, education, taste and so on. The flogpot latched on to me. Night after night he squashed me into a corner and bored me with his silly worries. Paper clips. He went over three people's heads over something to do with paper clips. The physical stock of paper clips didn't match the stock on the ledger cards. The man thought he was Sherlock Holmes. To make a long story short he went from one job to another and then he couldn't get a job for a long time. I think he stopped trying. Connie was full time in the King's Arms in Acton and she started doing part time at bingo in Fulham Broadway. A job came up at the bingo and Connie got it for him. Keeping track of the books or whatever it is. I had to listen to that then. His bingo problems. He used to get a taxi from the bingo in here when he was working. That'll tell you how mad he was. He cracked up on a New Year's Eve. He had to work two sessions. He was drinking all day knowing he wouldn't be finished in time after the late shift. He was already pissed going on for the first session half seven till half nine and he made a cock up of it. He had some job going from one side of the stage to the other with books for the sellers and of course all the ould ones spotted he was on it and they got up on him: Oi Pat, who's been avin a couple then. Up jumps Maurice onto the stage and opens his fly and drowns the front row.'

'You're joking me.'

'As sure as I was with Wingate in Burma.'

'That's what I said. You caught me again.'

'No. This is the truth. Connie herself told us. Ask Mackey or Tommy Cook. That was only the end of it. All along before this he used to beat her. His mind was occupied with large problems. It must have been a vacuum created by paper clips. The Albigensian heresy often cropped up. He was on about that one night to Mackey. Can you imagine Mackey. He thought twas the name of a picture. Maurice told me one night, when I was the only one knew he was mad, he told me Connie had started giggling when he tried to tell her of the Albigensian heresy. Hogan, he says, what could I do, I thumped the bitch. Naturally I agreed with him. The heel in the throat, I said, anyone who won't listen to the Albigensian heresy should get the heel in the throat.'

'Hogan, you should get the heel in the throat. You're the greatest liar . . .'

Hogan's account stopped there. They went playing cards and in a hiatus between deals Hogan chuckled and said: 'Mackey, what do you think of the Albigensian heresy.' Mackey frowned and said: 'The knave up to me? Hogan let me alone with that thing. We got enough of that from Maurice.'

Whelan had to beg the rest of the story from Hogan the following night. Connie left him. Maurice had disgraced her. For years after Maurice followed her around London trying to get her back until finally she was driven to calling in the police; by then she had anyway taken up with a man who wore a moustache and a brown waistcoat.

Whelan was forced to admit that he believed Hogan: 'Only don't expect me to swallow the one about Wingate.'

Whelan had long since come to accept the inevitability of a Maurice or a stranger with a red face and a blue suit popping up on a deserted Kilbum High

Road. It was no phenomenon that a man would buy two light and bitters and proceed to drink out of his neighbour's whiskey. Maurice was not always allowed to play forty-five because of his habit of concentrating fiercely in order to win the rubber and be paid two half crowns and of developing amnesia of the pocket when he lost.

The first time Whelan played forty-five in Maurice's company he won the first two rubbers after each of which Maurice leaned towards him and whispered: I'll see you again. That night ended with Maurice owing him the two half crowns. But when next they played and Maurice won the first rubber Whelan, not wanting to have it supposed he had a neurotic memory of debts, pushed a half crown towards him and waited dutifully for Maurice to push it back with one besides. Maurice put the half crown in his pocket and said: Thanks. When Maurice went to the counter for his two pints of light and bitter Whelan mentioned the incident to Tom Mackey.

'Did you not know about his system? He has a great system. He can't lose. You have to pay him when he wins but when he loses he pays no one. Except Hogan. He sometimes pays Hogan.'

'Why does he pay Hogan and – and not me for instance.'

'Hogan asks him for it.'

'Well, I'll ask him for it.'

'Ah, don't now. Be nice. But you shouldn't have paid him that half crown. That's three he owes you now. The next three games he wins don't give him anything. Except that he doesn't carry over what he loses to another night. If you lost to him say tomorrow night and told him he owed you for three rubbers he'd say that was last night, let the dead past bury their dead.'

Whelan tasted his Christmas night porter. He was not a judge of drink as Hogan was but he detected a tang. Not being a judge of drink he did not comment until Hogan said: 'Schemery porter. Tis Donie's night.'

'He filled my pint very fast. Funny taste of it.'

Tommy Cook claimed that their drink could not be as bad as his whiskey. Martin offered his bottle of Mackeson around for anyone to taste because he had no words to describe the contents. He had no takers. Whelan asked: 'How come everyone's drink is bad?'

Hogan explained that Donie, the tenant, not being obliged by law to open Christmas night, had once confided in him that he would be fucked if he would make illegal profits for the brewery; and that if he did open it would be on his own account. '"Hogan," he says to me, "I'll water the whiskey, slop the porter and colour the beer." I said it to Mackey. We thought he was joking. Every penny he makes tonight goes into Donie's hip pocket and the stocks won't be down a gill.'

In spite of his hunger Whelan began to whiff the glow of comradeship. He was drawn with Hogan

in the first rubber and when they won it Hogan
turned to Maurice on his left: 'That's that Maurice.'

'What's what?'

'It's finished. We were twenty-five coming in Billy
got the first two and I had the five last day.'

'Was that your five?'

'It was my five. And one has paid me. Cough up.'

'I'll see you again.'

'You won't floggin' see me again. Come on you're
drippin' doubloons. Pay the man. Pay the man or
leave the bed.'

It was, as Tom Mackey often said to Whelan, easy
to start a heated engine. Now on his first drink since
the morning Whelan was tipsy and inclined to senti-
ment. They were comrades all, gathered together out
of the loneliness, united in the face of bad porter,
and staunch with the leg up for poor Maurice without his Connie. Hogan particularly conveying on the
wretch dignity by demanding payment. In a foggy
way Whelan would have liked to rescue them all,
including the blue-suited, red-faced stranger of the
deserted Kilburn High Road.

Later in the night finding himself beside Hogan
in the toilet he was drunk enough to ask: 'Did you
chuck on the bacon and cabbage today?'

Hogan was suddenly just an Irish mottled face.

'And I going up the road last night Tommy Cook
ran after me and insisted I go to his place. Did you go
to Mackey yourself?'

'No. I went to a mate of mine in Milman Road. I wasn't that hungry really but, ah, he's a bit of a poor eejit, gets lonely, I said I'd cheer him up.'

Whelan struggled through the rest of the night nourished with the thought of food to be had Boxing Day. Hogan was no longer a god, having singularly failed to produce the neck to inform Tommy Cook that turkey would turn to ash in his mouth at the thought of poor Billy Whelan alone in his room. What they had done and were doing to Maurice outraged Whelan. They would never look in any mirror or invite any Billy Whelans to dine while they had Maurice to cloud the perspective with manifestation of their charity. Maurice was not enough for Tommy Cook. At the low point in his low enough cycle he needed Hogan suddenly at his dinner table. Martin was a mystery man and as such beyond respect. He listened and gave nothing. Tom Mackey was the archcriminal. England had done it to him, not that that was an excuse. Asleep the man had been in front of a television when a lost soul called for a single shilling to warm the desolation wreaked by Higgins, Murphy, Mark Brown and Nicky.

'Flogpot, did you not see him rob the ace?'

'Sorry. I'm dreaming.'

It would be a mercy to see them – Higgins, Murphy, Mark Brown and Nicky – if only that they might torment him.

It was closing time. Hogan and Tommy Cook and Tom Mackey were hatching a plan to bring a crate back to Mackey's house without Maurice horning in on the act. They plotted as though Whelan did not exist. Whelan angrily decided not to make it easy for them. He timed his departure with theirs not, he knew by now, that Mackey was likely to be embarrassed. But at the door of the house Mackey said: 'Billy, the cut of him. You'll sleep tonight. But you'll be able for a few bottles an' a few oul sandwiches. In ahead and tell the missus we've a few drunken flogpots for guests. And where's the flogpot himself. Hogan. Hogan will you come on outa that.'

As Tommy Cook had needed Hogan at his dinner table, Mackey now gave recognition to the infirmity of his lodger. Billy Whelan did not know whether or not he cared; the plucking of clanking bottles from the crates punctuated the wait for the sandwich; when it came Whelan had to grip his chair to prevent himself from leaping on Mrs Mackey before she got round to him. Between his thumb and forefinger he daintily lifted one off the plate. Mrs Mackey pressed a second and a third on him. He was disappointed to discover the three sandwiches filled him. Inevitably they reached a stage in the night when someone said: Someone give us a song. Tommy Cook sang 'A Letter Etched in Black'. Tom Mackey sang 'Lovely Leitrim'. Martin sang 'Are There Angels in Heaven Like Little Black Me'. Mrs Mackey sang 'Doonaree'. Her two daughters were out at a disco. Billy Whelan sang:

> Alone, all alone,
> By a wave-washed strand,

All alone in a crowded hall;
The hall it is gay,
The waves they are grand,
But my heart is not there at all.

It flies far away . . .

Each song was listened to attentively and rewarded with applause.

Tom Mackey said: 'God be with long go.'

The remark drew memories of creamery cheques, days in bogs, buttermilk in summer. Whelan fell asleep. He woke as they were trying to lift him upstairs to bed. In his room he was driven to read the letter. The emptiness that was upon him and that he could not identify made him promise that he would post the letter in the morning and so that he would be reminded he put the letter under his watch on the table by the bed. He was hungover in the morning and grateful for the renewed hunger. On his way to the workman's caff for breakfast he put the letter without a stamp into the post box. A week before St Patrick's Day, when the nostalgia was gathering momentum, shamrock in a green and white box arrived from his mother. In the same post was an airmail letter from the United States of America.

My Dear Fellow,
I notice you did not send any money. Fair enough.
But no stamps! If that is your idea of cricket then

I am forced to conclude you are a man after my own heart. To take a leaf from the book of the Mr Ryan of your letter, Fart International does not propose to shackle you with rules except for Rule Number One, which is unwritten, and states: There are no rules. Except those of the heart. For instance I like to feel it would not be white to advertise in other than *Screen Monthly*. If my wonderful homeland – dear England – can purr along without a written constitution – then F.I. has no notion of climbing down from trees and getting uppity. (You are entitled to the attached biography in return for your own succinct cri de coeur.)

As the zombies (who abound) are wont to say: Fire away your gun is your own. But I would advise, no, not advise, I would give it as my opinion that you return to wherever you came from and conduct your ministry from there. England has no need of thee at this hour. *Screen Monthly* forwards the mail direct to me here in New York. Rather than send the fools further – so to speak – I can arrange to have all correspondence re-routed to wherever it is you have been driven from by the mysterious Higgins, Murphy, Mark Brown and Nicky. (I would not be at all averse to hearing further in that vein.) As I said, your gun is your own but my method of dealing with enquiries is to carefully slit open the envelope – I detest torn dollars – extract respectfully the

lucre and plop any superfluous accompaniment
into the nearest shredding machine. Callous?
No, my dear fellow. No one – no one – is worthy
to join Fart International. It was not always thus.
Believe me I tried. In the early days I logged
the Fart International accounts with Dickensian
probity – but people! Would you credit that one
chap actually suggested regular meetings, election
of officers and committee including president,
the keeping of minutes, agenda, the wearing –
and my left hand is clutching a racing heart as I
write – the wearing of credentials on lapels! How
you deal with correspondence is your own gun.
I pocket the money and shred the hypocrisy. In
this regard I cannot speak too highly of *Screen
Monthly* as distinct from, say, the *Manchester
Guardian* or the *Skibereen Eagle*. The testimonial
is between you, me and the wall. Good people,
Screen Monthly, and it is not that I want to do
them out of what I think their going rate should
be, but one must bear in mind the feelings of
those other good people who provide toupée,
siliconed tit and Charles Atlas muscles for the
needy. At any rate, you will of course from
here on bear the advertising costs, and I will so
instruct *Screen Monthly,* but so that you will be
overwhelmed by my bona fides I will forward the
next response to the advertisement complete
with donation. You therefore will be in pocket
before you begin.

All subject to your reaction to the foregoing and attached biographical details.

Good luck to you now my dear fellow.

Bill Johnston

Without preamble the Bill Johnston biography staccatoed:

My folks were religious. Never be ashamed of it. I can still feel the vicar patting me on the head. Both dead now. Three years my mother is gone. Faversham. In Kent. You know it? I've had them both to New York a couple of times but it wasn't really fair of me. For instance I remember we used to go to Margate and Broadstairs on the train – before the war – they used to sit in the shade. An hour in the train to sit in the shade. Of course they married late. Had only me. But they were puzzled when I brought them to America and showed them my wife. My wife is All American in those respects where one would be better off being All Serbo-Croat peasant. It was worse when we went to visit them. Honey – that is my wife's name and it must be true if I'm admitting it – Honey had the folks fourth on the list after the Palace, the Tower and Westminster rising out of the morning fog.

And that list was a secondary list after the list that began with Killarney and went through Madrid, Rome, Paris, Hamburg. We managed four wonderful days with my puzzled folks. Honey gave them both Aran sweaters bought in the duty free at Shannon airport. They would be ideal for sitting in the shade – of your peak cap while you were mending your net. My folks did not understand our taking in Europe. Neither did I. But Honey had said in that way of hers: Godalmighty whoever heard of spending six weeks without doing Europe and I know it's cute you have folks over there but Chrissakes. They were very gentle and I understood when Mam wouldn't fold her tent and come to New York after Dad died. But where was I? The war. He hated it although he did join the reserve. He gave me a Russian hug and she just cried. They were reticent that way. They were never very confident about being parents and I never got to know them – really know them – the way people do today. Maybe people know too much today. I was very excited at the time and I'd made one friend by the time leave came. An American – Al Guerrini – he was in London trying to become a writer. He never did but we'll come to that. He was five years older than I and he said we were going

on the town. We went to this whorehouse – a
pub really with loose women and the cost was
minimal, after all we were heroes. That was
my first time and Al ribbed me a lot. Being
C of EI didn't have too much remorse, my
parents had not come to stress that part, they
hadn't banked on a war. Well, there was the
war. Trying to stay alive and watching people
being killed. That's war for you. It ended.
Now that was a good time for a while. I'd say
you'd have liked that time. Making love to a
woman then you really felt you were doing
her a favour. Anyway, the war ended and the
euphoria died down, so did the bulge in my
wallet, there was nothing doing in Faversham
bar hop-picking, even Dad couldn't get me
into the brewery, not that I wanted that, and
besides I was jittery. I dossed on in London,
Al Guerrini said we were getting nowhere
fast and hawked me over to the States with
him. Al had connections and we got into
advertising. Now let's skip a few years. Al's
people had a few bob and we started our
own agency. But before we did something
had happened to Al. He'd been some years
in Paris and London and then there was that
war. It wasn't his States when he went back.
America got at him. He was way ahead of me –
in years, oudook; I expected Americans to

be savages collectively and naturally I wasn't
disappointed. But on his own your American
is a delightful fellow. So I said to Al Guerrini.
He agreed with me. That, he said, is the
problem. When is an American on his own.
Never. He's terrified of being on his own. To
prove it, Al wrote out on a slip of paper: Fart
International, Send No Money, Box 13 and
said he was going to put it into *Screen Monthly*
which was the lowest form of publication he
could imagine. He insisted on my paying half
the subscription so that I would be obliged
to share the returns. That was an instance
I think of Al not wanting to be on his own.
To show you how far ahead Al was in his
thinking, he registered Fart International
and kept in touch with the registration
office who were happy to inform him, why,
yes, there have been enquiries trying to
register the name. Back to our agency. I
discovered I had flair – could encapsule any
situation or product into a snappy caption,
also, I took to administration like a duck to
water. The long and short of it, a big success
for Guerrini Johnston, Inc. We married and
settled down. Al never made it as a writer
though he kept trying. When I say he never
made it I mean he never wrote anything
that satisfied himself enough to send to a
publisher. He kept trying until this night

we were working late. He always wrote for a
couple of hours after work. But this night he
said fuck-em-all and sent out for a stock of
Jack Daniels; we polished it off and sang 'The
White Cliffs of Dover', 'We'll Meet Again',
'Lili Marlene', and that. The songs made him
sad. He told me he was never going to write
again. It was like Fart International, he said.
They'd never understand that application
for membership automatically incurred the
black ball. Fart International aimed at purity,
he said, and so did Al Guerrini's writing.
There was only Fitzgerald, he said, and
there never was that gobshite Hemingway.
He used to say that gobshite would shoot
himself before he'd ever make a writer. Al
said he couldn't take the business any more
either. Told me to make some arrangement
that would leave him enough to go on. We
made a fair deal. Lump sum that with the
interest from the lump sum he wouldn't have
to touch the lump sum but one condition:
he couldn't take Fart International any more
and he insisted I was to perpetuate it. There
I baulked. I didn't want to be on my own
where Fart International was concerned. He
made me promise to keep it going until some
outrageously suitable person should turn up
to take over. I'm banking that you might be
that OSP if you'll pardon the initials (initials

incur an avalanche of black balls I hope you agree). Al drank himself to death, fair play to him. As for me, I'll continue in American: Honey, my wife is a shithead, we've two daughters who are mother-fucking cunts of whores they're so cheap they'd give change out of nothing. And I was a boy who played in the sand after an hour on a train while two gentle people sat in the shade.

Bill Johnston,
Outgoing President,
Fart International,
SEND NO MONEY,
Box 13.

Chapter Two
Nicky

Now, ten years later, with Declan and Eddie in tow, Billy Whelan traipsed O'Connell Street while his wife Breda rifled Dunnes Stores for bargains on a wet July Saturday morning, eve of the Cork v Limerick Championship Hurling Match. It was not in his line to mind the children but he had given Breda an opening and there was no better woman than she to take her chances. It was too important a fixture to risk shoving off with a slow puncture and no spare wheel; he had sent young Cyril off to Pete O'Mara to supervise the overhauling. Whelan had bought the van second hand from O'Mara who maintained the vehicle with second-hand parts. O'Mara had established a reputation for dishonesty, shoddy workmanship and mechanically disapproved transplants. Whelan loved him.

Breda had jumped in: 'Since you're not working so you can look after them for me while I do a bit of shopping. Twill be an ease to me not to have them dragging out of me.'

Though ten years married and the father of Declan, eight, and Eddie, two and three quarters, Whelan did not understand the language of motherhood. He thought the exercise of elementary discipline on the part of his wife should preclude the likelihood of children dragging out of her and, worse, he said so and continued when Breda accused him of not taking Eddie to the toilet with him to show him how it was done: 'Breda, I have hardly time to piss myself without holding seminars on the subject.'

Whelan bought two ice pops and planked the children on a window ledge. There was a smell off the younger boy. The father eased himself a dozen yards away from them and, leaning against the wall, put two fingers in his top pocket in pursuit of a nobber. He kept nobbers in his top pocket or in his matchbox but never on his ear. He knew of a man, his own father, who died because of a nobber on his ear. Out with the stump of a cigarette came the circular. Breda had it opened and reigning on the mantelpiece the day he came home from Listowel Races. She opened all his mail except the ESB bill and including Fart International correspondence. At the races Whelan had cleared over ninety pounds and brought to the circular an easy mind. It incited him with a vague curiosity that they knew his address but later he decided that he should not have been surprised. Donal O'Sullivan seemed to have nothing better to do than keep tabs. As far as Whelan could make out from the biographical scraps that filtered through to him Donal was a dutiful plodder, as he had been at school, who ground his way to the managerial seat of the department store in eighteen years. Whelan had read in the *Chronicle*: 'Pnikerettes have announced the appointment of Donal O'Sullivan . . .' There followed a brief eulogy worthy of an obituary to the effect that Donal O'Sullivan was a keen sports enthusiast. The only enthusiasm Whelan could recall in him at school was an inclination to be punctual, have his exercises done in neat handwriting in covered copybooks, a tendency to smile ingratiatingly when Higgins tossed his quiff and a retention of the official school match song composed by Cahill. Now Donal O'Sullivan was President of the Union and sending circulars to Whelan summoning Whelan to dinners.

A half hour had passed since Breda went into Dunnes Stores for a pair of underpants and a t-shirt for Declan. Whelan had told her to walk up to the assistant and say: Could I have one pair of underpants and one t-shirt for a child of eight please. But he knew in his heart and soul that she had not followed his instructions. He imagined his wife lifting this and that up and putting them back in the wrong place. He sniffed and moved another yard away from his offending son. A voice confronted him: 'Well, for Jaysus sake, Billy Whelan! '

He trailed the nice language to the face smiling at him and was not surprised so much by the fact that it came from a priest but that that priest was so recognisable after eighteen years.

'Nicky! I beg your pardon. Father!'

'Don't mind your "father". How are you? It's seventeen years.'

'Eighteen. I didn't stay the distance.'

'Yes. But how have you been getting on? You went to England. Donal O'Sullivan mentioned you have your own business. Donal certainly got on well, didn't he, and no one would have thought it.'

'You met Donal? He can't be laughed at. What about yourself. Every time I pick up the *Chronicle* you've survived a coup or you're under house arrest or what not. Where are you, Nigeria? Or the Congo or what?'

The priest shook his head. 'It's not the Congo now. I was in Zaire up till a year ago. I haven't been too well.'

'Oh. I'm sorry to hear that.'

'I'm all right now. But they're grounding me for a couple of years. Giving missions. They tell me there's no religion in Ireland these days. Is that true?'

'It depends what you mean.'

'People don't go to masss. I hear tales of wife swapping.'

'I wouldn't know about that. I keep my end up. Although if you come across anyone that's interested I might swap my one. Ha ha.'

'Ha ha. Nice kids. Yours?'

'They're not too bad. Say hello to Father Nicky. Declan, say hello to Father Nicky. Eddie, say hello to Father Nicky. They're shy.'

'Listen. Are you going to this thing tonight?'

'What thing?'

'The dinner. Donal was telling me. All the lads will be there. All that's still around.'

'Hardly.'

'What? I think it's a great idea. To concentrate on the class of '60. Donal says the PPU is all old fogies every year. Higgins is going. And Murphy is coming. And Mark Brown is coming down from Dublin. You'll have to come.'

'Ah, I don't think so.'

'For God's sake, what's the matter with you? We'll have a right crack.'

'I don't dance.'

'Dance? It's stag for fuck sake.'

Whelan could not stop himself glancing at his children. He was in the habit of a morning to admonish: Eat up your porridge or I'll send for the priest.

'Anyway, I'm class of '59. Heh heh.'

'Yeah. Rubbish. You must come. I'll call for you.'

'Nicky. . .'

'Where do you live?'

'Nicky, there's no need to call for me. I'll go. Promise.'

Whelan began to sweat. The idea of Father Nicky calling to the house and being invited in and seeing the state of the house was more terrifying than a stag dinner. Father Nicky was wearing a yellow check shirt and light grey slacks. Whelan's clerical trousers were unfashionably narrow, ill- creased and stained with spatters of every variety of fruit and with semen – he was given to sudden urges and paid his wife occasionally to oblige him in the clothed, standstill position, racing against the appearance of Declan from the street. His shoes were mildewed from the want of polish. A ten year old once fawn gaberdine that he brought back from London hid the rest of him.

'You say you'll go but I know you. You won't turn up. I'll call for you.'

'Nicky, I swear on the Bible. I'll be there. Once I know it's stag.'

'You swear?'

'I swear'

'Good. I'm really looking forward to it. I was in the seminary for seven years and the wilds for ten. I haven't seen anyone in ten years. And not yourself for seventeen. How's Higgins? You must see Higgins a lot.'

'I don't see him that much. But I see him around. Higgins is grand. I'm away a good bit.'

Whelan saw Breda coming out of Dunnes Stores. Because he was ashamed to introduce her he guillotined.

'Listen, I have to rush. I'll see you tonight then. You can buy me a drink.'

'You're on.'

Whelan was proud of his wife. She was wont to turn up the radio volume and on coming out of the trance answer: 'Liebestraum.' She had a quirky sense of humour that, unfortunately, did not extend to Fart International. She was beautiful. Whelan admired her taste in the clothes she managed to buy out of what she wheedled out of him. Her family were respectable. And her occasional rebellion against the drudgery he had visited upon her gave meaning to his life. But for some – chemical – reason, he did not want to stand over her in the presence of a cowboy priest.

CHAPTER THREE
THE CAMEL

In those days a ten year old child was considered too long in the tooth to be taken to school by his mother. Billy Whelan was one of the very few so escorted apart from the children of bookmakers who were dropped off out of cars on wet days. Mrs Whelan meant well in her role of dual parent. The school route through the park was fraught with no more danger than that of geriatric conkers shaken by the late September breeze yet the woman sped on with a maternal grip on her son's hand, the son coated and scarfed and helmeted against the temperate climate. At the gate she took off his wrappings. She was afraid he might not hang them up properly or that they might be stolen. And she kissed him. Higgins witnessed the tender scene but did not comment, Whelan had to admit, but at the same time thought he detected a circumstantial sneer. To an extent there was consideration for a child whose father was dead or gone into voluntary disappearance in England. Beyond that it was dog eat dog.

Brother Dalton held an audition. He banged the tuning fork on the desk a few times until he was satisfied his own ear was in and then he banged it once more and said to Mark Brown: 'Did you get the note?'

'Yes, Brother.'

Brother Dalton banged the tuning fork again, this time allowing out of his own mouth by way of accompaniment and to lend clarity to what was going on: Doh. Mark Brown took the cue and sang: Doh. Mark Brown was in. In the firsts. Murphy and Nicky dohed their way into the seconds. Higgins, whose singing voice was so deep that Whelan was reminded of him every time he heard Paul Robeson on the radio, became the anchor man of the thirds. There were borderline cases, in one day out the next, depending on the whim of Brother Dalton. Billy Whelan tried his best to connect with the clue from the tuning fork and the Brother's doh but though the Brother gave him five chances Whelan ended up at the back of the class with his English book where he shared a desk with Cahill, the prodigy. Cahill's trial run had forced Whelan himself to laugh.

'Doooohaaaa.'

'Doh. Not caw.'

'I sang doh, Brother.'

'You did? Go back and get your English book and sing dumb in case your talent is contagious.'

During the last hour of class every day for five weeks the choir practised for the impending Feile. Most of those reading their English books giggled behind their hands. Whelan sat in a quiet rage of exclusion. He nursed the injustice of having lost his father and not having a singing voice. Beside him Cahill read, wrote, listened, smiled, shook his head in disbelief and, in general, appeared oblivious to the ignominy of their position. Walking out the yard with Cahill after school Whelan heard him sing: Speed bonny boat like a bird on the wing, Over the sea to Skye and then add, perfectly: Doh. Whelan stopped.

'You can sing?'

'I can sing a lot better than some of those crows. That's certain.'

'But what happened to you the day he was testing us?'

Cahill did not answer but kept walking. It was a known habit of his since he had come to the school from the country at the beginning of the year. He was given to reverie, but when aroused showed by his answers that he was away ahead of the class on all subjects.

Whelan persisted: 'Do you mean you sang bad on purpose?'

Cahill stopped and looked at him, Whelan imagined, with tenderness. Then said: 'You should be in the choir. You sang perfectly. Brother Dalton doesn't know what he's doing.' Abruptly Cahill walked away.

Whelan knew it wasn't true. He couldn't sing. But he was comforted. From then on he looked forward to sitting at the back of the class with Cahill during choir time. He wouldn't have liked to sit beside Cahill all day. Cahill was secretive, quiet, clear-sighted, frozen-faced to ridicule that emanated from the Higgins, Murphy, Mark Brown, Nicky axis. Whelan shared a desk with Nicky and was protected from the flak.

'Jesus,' Cahill said one afternoon.

'What's wrong?'

'What's wrong? Nothing. I want to make you a promise. Let me promise you that as long as I live I will never hate anything as much as that song. Tell me a tale of a lad who is gone, Over the sea to Skye.'

''Tisn't as bad as Brahms' Lullaby, is it?'

'You don't like Brahms' Lullaby?'

'Well not the way they sing it anyway. That lu lu lu, lu lu lu business, that's like sissies.'

Cahill smiled, but did not comment. Whelan left it at that; he was not friendless at the back of the class; that was enough for him.

There was a dress rehearsal a few days before the Feile. The money for the uniform had been collected in dribs and drabs, only Higgins and Mark Brown bringing the lump sum of twelve and six. The uniform consisted of a white shirt with a maroon pocket; a maroon tie; grey trousers and grey socks; and the pupils' own black shoes (polished and shined). Brother Dalton was a practical man. He cut cloth according to the parents' measure. Without the maroon pocket the uniform was suitable for everyday wear. During the final rehearsals Over the Sea to Skye and Brahms' Lullaby both sounded beautifully rendered to Whelan. He prayed to the God he so firmly believed in that the choir would lose and disgrace Brother Dalton who might be relied upon to take it out on them collectively and individually for the rest of the year. But as sure as his father was in the grave and as sure as he had no voice himself, he knew they would win.

Whelan would have foregone all the half days in the world for a different result but once the result was in and they were back in class and the shield was on display and the miniatures were passed around he did not mind any more not being part of the choir. It was over. Higgins, as Whelan examined his trophy, said: 'Don't paw it' and while other teachers came and went to offer their congratulations the choristers plotted. Nicky sat on top of the desk facing Mark Brown and Higgins in their desk with Murphy and Donal O'Sullivan hovering about the nub. Whelan listened to *Treasure Island* v *The Red Badge of Courage*. Opinion was divided until Mark Brown said: 'I think *Treasure Island* would be better.'

Outside the Lyric at half two, where Whelan knew they had arranged to meet at twenty to three, he was confused with a shame he did not understand. He had seen *Treasure Island* the previous Saturday. When Nicky and Murphy and Donal O'Sullivan arrived he was no longer confused.

'Are you going to this Billy?'

'Yeah, Nick, are ye going?'

'Yeah, we're waiting for Higgins and Mark.'

Whelan smiled at Higgins when they arrived and by way of reciprocation Higgins asked: 'Where are you going?'

'In here.'

Higgins left it at that and led the way into the seats. He stood up at his own seat and told Nicky to sit on his left and let Whelan pass in three seats explaining: Mark's sitting here and Murphy's sitting there. When it was warranted Higgins led the laughter or waited for Mark Brown to lead the laughter and joined in uproariously. Whelan, especially on his second viewing, did not find the picture funny He thought it sad but once when the pirate said: I'll give you my solemn affidavee I'll not lay a hand on the boy, Whelan laughed and was checked by Higgins: 'Shut up Whelan, you hyena. Do you want to get us all thrown out.'

Mr Ryan tackled him when he saw the photograph of the choir in the *Chronicle*.

'Why are you not in it?'

'I can't sing.'

'Who says you can't sing.'

'Brother Dalton.'

'What do the other boys do who are not in the choir? '

'We read our English book at the back of the class.'

'You must tell me a story from your English book.'

'You see there's this camel out in the desert and it gets freezing cold in the desert at night time and he was frozen this night and he asked his master if he could put his head inside the tent to keep his nose warm and the master said all right and the next night the camel asked him could he put his legs in, his first two legs, and the master said all right and then the next night he asked him could he put his hump in and it went on like that till the whole of the camel was in and he was all warm. But then the camel said the tent wasn't big enough for the two of them and he asked the master to sleep outside. The master got angry and threw the camel out for being ungrateful. That's all.'

'That's a grand story. What other stories do you know?' 'There was this king had horse's ears. . .'

'That's a grand story. Wait till I see if there's anything in the stone jug. Here you are. There's thruppence and don't spend it all in the one shop.'

Chapter Four
The Dinner

Breda Whelan had no need to draw from her litany of aggressive apologies, amassed down the years in proportion to her husband's collection of feminine imperfections. In Dunnes Stores her eye had fallen on a blouse; Declan's underpants and t-shirt would have to wait a week or be smuggled out of the housekeeping money. She admitted her purchase and waited expectantly for him to threaten to wash his hands of her and the children and go to a public house. But he had no comment to make. By way of reward Breda said: 'Will I get black puddings for the tea?'

'What? Oh. Yeah. Do. Get black puddings.'

'Dunnes is getting very dear. The blouse was an awful price. You'll have to give me another pound.'

Whelan handed over the pound. His wife could not contain herself.

'You seem preoccupied.'

'I'm just after bumping into Father Nicky.'

'Father Nicky?'

'Higgins, Murphy, Mark Brown and Nicky. That Nicky.'

'Oh.'

'He tried to drag me along to the dinner tonight.'

'He had some chance.'

'I said I'd go.'

'What? I don't believe you.'

'I don't believe it myself.'

'Well, go and enjoy yourself and then maybe you'll take me out to something some night.'

Breda walked on ahead clutching the children by the hand to maintain unity against die Saturday after-noon throng. Whelan did not study her. He did not notice the left tight untaut or the hair pulled back from her ears accentuating the growing roundness of her face. His head was a whirl of soup, speeches and a grinning Higgins. When they reached home Whelan went straight upstairs to switch on the immersion. It was supposed to be switched off first thing every morning but again Breda had forgotten. Something of his normal self propelled him to the landing to shout: 'Breda! '

'Yes?'

'Squandermaniacess.'

He put the thought of another ballbreaking account from the ESB from him and began to strip as the bath filled. He laid clean socks, underpants, shirt, tie and his suit on the bed. In the bath he was disgusted with the dirt on himself. He had got out of the habit of cleanliness by working seven days a week and trying to compress work, drink and an obligatory presence as a husband and father into a short day.

He dried himself in front of a naked mirror and took stock of his slender frame. Higgins and Nicky had guts and presumably Murphy and Mark Brown – no. Mark would be in shape. Whelan could not imagine him otherwise. Whelan shouted down to Declan to bring up the polish box and hairbrush. He did not want to present himself in stages to Breda. When he did descend the stairs Breda did not let him down.

'Well. If it isn't Rudolf Valentino. It just goes to show you should clean and dress yourself now and then. Do you want one or two eggs?'

'One will do.'

Whelan felt good – clean and spruced. He felt good because Breda was admiring him the same way he would find her desirable if she were all togged out to the knocker and he was scruffy. He took off his jacket and rolled up the sleeves of his light blue shirt and loosened the wine tie at the neck and sat down to his tea of four sausages, three rashers, half a black pudding and one fried egg.

'When I think of all the times I begged you to take me to a dinner dance.'

'Breda, this is stag.'

'Am I a black?'

'C'mon Breda, you know I don't dance. And I wouldn't go tonight in a fit only for Father Nicky. *Father* Nicky! He said fuck in front of the children.

I don't know how I'm going to stick it. Showers of drips with sideburns.'

'What do you call those things growing down your jaws?'

'I grow them because I like them. They do it because it's fashionable. That's probably Cyril.'

Whelan pronged a sliver of rasher atop a slice of black pudding dipped in yolk into his mouth and answered the door, chewing. Young Cyril leaned on the gate smiling.

'Someone die belong to you?'

'I have to go someplace. A dinner.'

'A dinner? You?'

'It's stag. The Past Pupils. I got roped in. Suppose you go to the dance and I meet you after, we could load up then. Would you mind?'

'All right. Although it might be the very night I'd do business. Are you using the van?'

'No. You take it. I'll see you in the Wimpy for a coffee. If you're there before me hang on. I'll definitely be there before two.'

'Okay. See you. See you Breda.'

'Hello, Cyril.'

Cyril drove off in the van, one half of the fleet. The chip wagon/ice cream wagon was parked outside the next door neighbour's. Whelan had a shed rented in a lane at the rear of an O'Connell Street Georgian building where he kept his stock of non-perishables. The two vehicles and the shed were his total assets.

It was too early for Whelan to pretend he was setting out for the dinner and he did not have the excuse of seeing to the van. He found no way out of sitting with the children, Eddie on his lap, watching The Little House on the Prairie. It struck him that to pass away the time he would prefer to make love to Breda.

'I think Eddie's foundered. I'll carry him up on my back.'

'Hurrah!' Eddie shouted, though he was far from tired. Whelan carried him upstairs to the cot where he discovered the child did not know any prayers. When he came back down, before he could attack, Breda got in: 'He should be in a bed by now.'

'I know, Breda. I know. Give me a chance. I know a fella . . .'

'A fella, a fella, a fella. You always know a fella. Why can't we buy a bed in a shop like everyone else?'

'Because I'm not everyone else. How many times do I have to tell you that?'

'You don't have to tell me at all. Too bloody well I know you're not everyone else. Do you know any fellas who sell washing machines?'

'Don't start.'

'Don't start, don't start, don't start. I will start. Is there something so terrible about wanting a washing machine. Everyone, everyone I know has a washing machine, my own sister is on her third, she wanted to give us her old one, what did you say, No, we're not going to become stampeded into the acquisitive society. A fucking washing machine.'

'Must you talk like that. You know how I feel about swearing.'

'I know how you feel. We all know how you feel. If you're too mean to spend your own money on a bed for your child and a washing machine for your wife, take the money out of that crazy organisation.'

'Leave Fart out of it. I told you a hundred times I've never taken a farthing of that money for myself and don't ever destroy yourself in my eyes with a suggestion like that again.'

'That's rich, that is. Destroy myself in your eyes. You'd think you were a Knight of Columbanus. My brother-in-law said eleven years ago, I could have you committed. You could be put into the mental home and I could have my marriage annulled. Where's your husband tonight Mrs Whelan? Billy? Oh, Billy's gone to his meeting. His Confraternity is it Mrs Whelan? No, actually the meeting he goes to . . .'

'Declan, bed.'

'Aw, Dad.'

'Come on. I'll give you a piggy back although you're getting heavy for me.'

After Whelan put his eldest son to bed he came down still in a rage.

'Breda, you talk again like that about Fart International and I'll kick you from one end of the room to the other.'

'Back to the wife beating again. Hurrah for the brave man.'

'Breda, I've never laid a hand on you . . .'

'Huh . . .'

'. . . I never touched you since we were married first, when the two of us were at it. You know that. We talked about it. We laughed about how stupid we were. You admitted you nagged me over nothing and I admitted I should never have struck you and I was ashamed of myself after. We've been through all that. We put it all behind us once we knew what marriage was . . .'

'Marriage is not having washing machines, marriage is knowing fellas, the cot arrived in the dead of the night, it only needed a lick of paint, you said, and guess who had to do the painting, I said to you that cot might have come from the North, you said we've no proof of that. We would have known where it came from if we'd bought it over the counter in Roches Store where they pay their rates and taxes and employ people . . .'

'Breda, please. Rates, taxes. Think of my heart condition.'

'Don't try to be funny.'

'The kids are in bed. I've half an hour.'

'Shove off for yourself.'

'I need you, Breda.'

'I have to wash up.'

'I'll pay you.'

'You can't afford me.'

'I must be mad. Okay, no need to say it. I've been in a knot all week with the tenth AGM of Fart tomorrow night, and Bill Johnston about to turn up. That's how Nicky got to me. I wasn't myself. And Thurles tomorrow. No chance to – to recover.'

'Recover from what?'

'You've never understood. I'll be well drunk before I go near the Sarsfield Arms I can tell you. At least it's on in the Sarsfield Arms. That's something. This is an ordeal, Breda. You could help me. Knowing that somebody thought something of me, that someone loved me, thought I was someone, that's the type of thing that would help me tonight, Breda.'

'You'd think twas into the valley of the shadow of death you were riding. It's a stag dinner, Billy.'

'That makes it worse.'

'And by the way. That Bill Johnston. Keep him away from this door.'

'Bill Johnston. What a man. You needn't worry. As a matter of fact I might stay in the Sarsfield Arms myself tomorrow night. All human life is in that Sarsfield Arms. Higgins tonight and Fart International tomorrow night. I wonder what made him decide to come.'

'You've been wondering that for three months.'

'America might have got him at last. The way it got A1 Guerrini. What a man he was! His wife, Honey, might have kicked the bucket. He's well off, he might stay here. He could take over again. I could resign.'

'If that happens Billy, you can bring him to the door. He can sleep between the two of us. Imagine to wake up in the morning knowing your husband was not President of Fart International. Some women don't know how lucky they are.'

'Oh, Breda, I'm randy. A quickie.'

'No.'

'Please Breda. I'm serious. I'll pay you.'

'How much?'

'Breda, you should be hanging out of windows. I'll never get drunk before this thing if I don't hurry. Double the rate. Two quid.'

'A fiver.'

'You're joking.'

'A fiver.'

'Ah, no. Be serious.'

'I'm deadly serious. First offer of five pounds.'

'You are serious, you bitch. Okay. Venue?'

'Upstairs.'

'No. Back room up against the wall.'

'I don't buy a pennyworth of food out of the five pounds mind. And payment in advance.'

'Don't you trust me? I've always paid you. That's one thing. Admit it. I'm a man of my word all my life. Admit it.'

'All right. Hurry on. The table isn't cleared yet.'

The back room was cluttered with tricycles, clothes, brushes, footballs, old shoes, toys, Breda's bicycle, a pram and a go-kart. They cleared a space where Breda stood with her back to the wall. Whelan kissed her, part of an old routine that they were as loath to put out to grass as the old shoes.

Breda said: 'Get it over with.'

'You're very romantic.'

Breda laughed:

'So is this.'

Quickly Whelan lifted her apron and pulled her denims far enough below her knees for her legs to part; he unzipped his fly, entered her, ejaculated and, because neither had kissing her on the neck been sent to the knacker's yard, he kissed her on the neck and said: That was lovely.

They were silent while Breda cleared the table and Whelan combed his hair. They were incapable of civilized exchange after intercourse because each felt they should exchange civilly after intercourse. What they knew they had learned from each other and Whelan knew that she loved him but could not tell him. If he bought her the washing machine she would say she loved him but then she wouldn't mean it. He was proud of the way she had managed without a washing machine (and carpets), managed not to drive him to buy a washing machine. He loved her. She went so far and no further. And he felt for her. It must have been annoying when she visited the sister who landed the accountant for the unveiling of the cow or the sheep in the deep freezer. But he could not tell her he loved her or that he sympathised with her.

There was a seven day old elliptical butt in the top pocket of Whelan's suit that he extracted and smoked while he stood at the hall door casting a gifted eye at the weather. There would have been no question of taking the van; he imagined Higgins leading a gin and tonicked gang out to circle it: What do you run her on, firewater? The bon motif of the night called for the entire fleet out earning and Whelan forced to shank's mare, relishing the simpler pleasures of the poor. It would do for Nicky and for Donal O'Sullivan who was cursed with politeness. Whelan did not like the look of the clouds. He took grim consolation from the fact that Higgins worked in the met office. He could not bring his raincoat but could always step in a doorway.

'I'm off Breda.'

'Bye. Enjoy yourself now.'

'Breda, will you promise me you'll say a prayer for me before you sit down to the television.'

'Billy, go on. Don't annoy me.'

'Promise me.'

'Billy!'

'Promise.'

'All right. All right.'

The Sarsfield Arms was an old, grey building, not at all unlike the old, grey school. It was only five minutes walk from where Whelan lived and the route was liberally punctuated with small pubs. Whelan decided to crawl a few of them while he got his bearings. Father Nicky, he did not mind too much. Nicky would be as lost as Whelan himself, despite the shield of the collar. Higgins was the danger. Not that Higgins ever tousled his quiff and got away with it. In Donie O'Sullivan there was little harm even if he was the Union head bottlewasher whose arse could not be seen for dust in Pnikerettes. Whelan did not know what Murphy was doing. The *Chronicle* was not keeping him informed. Murphy, now that he thought of him well down on his first pint, Murphy was all right. He wasn't the worst of them. Mark Brown. He did not like to think of Mark Brown. Mark was a big nob up in Dublin but that was not the entire issue. It was all the same to Mark Brown – over the bar or under the bar, history or Latin, poetry or applied maths, apologetics or current affairs or who'll sing a song as its the last day before the holidays. Good man Mark. Without sweat or a hair out of place Mark cruised through deviating only between eighty-five and ninety per cent. Given the nature of the school that had turned them out, Mark's mark in property development was a feather in all their caps. Success that could be seen to have been achieved without the taint of nepotism or a handy start.

Mercifully, thanks to rather than despite the nature of the school, there would not be in evidence as much as the hint of a solicitor, doctor, dentist, quantity surveyor or merchant prince (himself excluded). There had not been an awareness of 'the professions'. At the thought that he had really little to fear Whelan became morose. He wondered if by any chance they might have produced a poet, a scruffy fucker without the price of his round who might bear the brunt of the laughter and jibes graciously donated tonight by that other fucker Higgins. Whelan steeled himself against ordering the fourth pint. Dos never started on time and there would be stoking up before the meal. It was inevitable and desirable that he get drunk but not before everyone else. And he wanted to clear his head of having thought of anyone in terms of fuckers. He had long ago forsworn bad language. He went to the toilet where he stood on the bowl and combed his hair into the reflection of the water tank. It was all there, the hair. Admittedly the water tank was not merciless, but all the same the hair that was all there was black. Using a strip of the multipurpose newspaper wedged between the wall and the pipe he administered a last polish to his shoes. He coughed, cleared his throat and set out for the Sarsfield Arms Hotel.

CHAPTER FIVE
ALVIN T. BRINE

The advertisement

Far Tinternational
Box 13
SEND NO MONEY

appeared in the Limerick *Chronicle* as regularly as the
Chronicle itself appeared, Tuesday and Thursday nights;
the Monday, Wednesday and Friday *Leader* in Whelan's
eyes representing too much value for money. It was his
aim to find the lowest possible readership and in this
he was successful notwithstanding such nuggets as the
succession stakes in Pnikerettes. In the advertisement
itself, the juxtaposition of the 't' and its elevation of
case to upper was not the work of the gremlins; the
small ads supremo was holder of a thirty year confraternity medal and was a man of much morality and little
humour.

He said to Whelan: 'I beg your pardon?'

'Fart International.'

'I'm afraid the *Chronicle* is not the type of newspaper that would accept an ad like that. I suggest you try the *Echo*.'

Whelan had been prepared for the reaction and followed the man very clearly, so clearly that he put it so: 'I don't quite follow you.'

'That word is not accepta . . .'

'Oh. I know what you mean now. No, no. It's not that. Sorry, that's my poor diction. It's Far. FAR. FAR TINTERNATIONAL.'

'What does that mean?'

'Is it necessary that you should know what it means for the acceptance of the ad?'

'No. At the same time this is a reputable newspaper. We like to cover ourselves.'

'I understand. The unfortunate thing is I can't help you there. You see, I don't know what it means myself. Somebody in New York picked me at random, I think by computer, and sent me funds to place the ad specifically in the *Chronicle*. I have to send all replies to an address in New York. As a matter of fact I'm going to reply to the ad myself to find out what it's all about. I'd say it's one of those bullworker yokes.'

The man excused himself and returned fortified with the second opinion of the manager. The ad was accepted. The man was covered. Whelan, he was exhilarated to realise, was also covered, from himself.

The gremlins were not found wanting. After a month the ad appeared as Fart International. Whelan called to the offices to complain.

'I don't find it at all funny.'

'Mr Whelan, I can assure you neither do I. The compositor insists it was a genuine mistake and I've had words with the reader. It won't happen again.'

'All right. I'm making a few shillings out of placing this ad and I don't want to lose the commission. I presume you're not going to charge me this time.'

'Of course not.'

Whelan's twelve hundred pounds transferred from Barclays to the Bank of Ireland, O'Connell Street branch, took the drudgery out of repatriation. He had returned with a miscellany of cross channel occupations successfully behind him, including his three years on the buildings. He had the idea that there were few jobs he could not satisfactorily undertake. For his mother's sake he applied for jobs in the clerical line and all of them precluded to applicants without a Leaving Certificate. He could have found work on the buildings as the country was moving again but he would have been ashamed to be seen doing this kind of work. During his first year in London he worked part time helping a Cockney on a chip wagon route until the romance of the occupation palled. For a month at home he allowed the idea grow inside him that he go into business in that line for himself.

He did not discuss the idea with his mother knowing that she would have preferred the buildings. His father was dead and would not anyway have been the man to discuss the project with. Had his father lived Whelan would not have left school and would now at the very least be in the civil service. He felt the want of Mr Ryan; it was too cruel to have lost Mr Ryan. He was drawing niggardly from his Bank of Ireland deposit trying to make up his mind when he received the letter from New York. He had written to Bill Johnston, c/o Fart International, Screen Monthly accepting the position of Outrageously Suitable Person and informing that worthy that he was returning home in a month. Exactly nine weeks later came Bill Johnston's reply. The air mail envelope was brought to his bed by his mother on the breakfast tray.

'Who could that be from?'

'I've no idea.'

'Aren't you going to open it?'

'I'll have my breakfast first.'

Reluctantly his mother left the bedroom. Whelan knew she would be back up the moment it could be reasonably supposed that he had finished his breakfast which in Whelan's case was two minutes. He invented Cahill writing to him from New York, Cahill unknown to Mrs Whelan and whose whereabouts were unknown to Whelan. After Mrs Whelan left with the breakfast tray and her son's foggy notion of what Cahill might be doing in New York if he were in New York, Whelan opened the letter.

It contained a short note from Bill Johnston to the effect that all future Fart International mail would be routed through *Screen Monthly's* London office and no longer through New York and a request that Whelan keep Bill Johnston informed (if Whelan so wished) through London who would forward Whelan's letters to Bill Johnston in New York. There was also a cheque for fifteen thousand dollars payable to Fart International signed by Alvin T. Brine. The only explanation of the cheque was the postscript to Bill Johnston's note:

> My Dear Fellow, you are certainly off to a good start assuming the cheque does not bounce. His last one didn't. A word to the wise: Alvin T. Brine is persistent. Expect to hear from him. You are at liberty to propagate the Guerrini Johnston genesis of Fart International but you must keep to yourself the LA/Big Apple/London imbroglio. If you'll pardon the expression, the trail of the buck stops with you.

The teller behind the nameplate G. Ellis smiled and said: 'Good morning. Lovely day, sir.'

'Yes. I'd like to open an account.'

'Yes sir.'

Whelan was privy to the ramifications from his Barclay experience and his lodgement of twelve hundred with the Bank of Ireland. He knew the stock questions and answers would not carry him through this particular transaction. He was relieved when they reached the bone.

'Correct me if I'm wrong here, Mr Whelan. Your own account is a deposit account and you say you have no need of a cheque book. But now you want to open a company current account for which you also say you will have no need of a cheque book. Fifteen thousand dollars is a considerable sum. Think of the interest that would accrue on a deposit account. That's if you're positive you don't need a cheque book.'

'No. I don't need a cheque book. I don't mind my own account gaining interest but it's against the rules of the company for the company account to gain interest.'

'You're kidding me now, Mr Whelan.'

'I'm not.'

'You're not? What is the name of the company?'

'Fart International.'

'Pardon?'

'Fart International. F-a-r-t I-n-t-e-r-n-a-t-i-o-n-a-l.'

G. Ellis chuckled. Whelan saw no harm in smiling back.

'Is the company limited?'

'No.'

'Have you a copy of the memorandum and articles of association?'

'The what?'

'You know – the rules, constitution of the company.'

'The company doesn't have any rules or constitution.'

'But you said it was against the rules for the company account to gain interest.'

'That's right.'

'How can it be against the rules if there are no rules.'

'The rules are unwritten.'

'I see. I mean, to be honest with you, I don't.'

'Look,' Whelan pushed the cheque through the grille, 'can you cash that or put it into an account or what can you do with it.'

While G. Ellis scrutinised the cheque Whelan continued: 'Or do you think I should go to Allied Irish?'

'I think you should see himself.' G. Ellis indicated the manager who at that moment was throwing one hand back at his office and the other in the direction of a priest. Whelan was reminded of D'Artagnan.

'Himself?'

'The manager. I'm new here, really.'

'I don't mind.'

'I'll check his appointments.'

G. Ellis returned with the news that the manager would be free after dealing with the priest.

'I wouldn't say he'd be long. About ten minutes. Turned wet again.'

'Yes.'

'He's usually not very long. Would you like to sit down. Over there.'

For twenty minutes Whelan watched G. Ellis nervously performing at his grille, at intervals stealing a look over the shoulders of his clients in Whelan's direction. The priest emerged shaking hands with the manager who said: 'Not at all, Father. Any time.'

G. Ellis scurried into the manager's office via the staff door and a minute later the manager came out again. He swivelled his gaze around the vestibule. Whelan rose.

'Mr Whelan?'

'Yes.'

The manager adopted the musketeer stance and Whelan led the way into his office. He was given a comfortable seat, an ashtray and a meteorological observation and then: 'Now. How can we help you?'

'I placed an advertisement in a magazine. In reply to the advertisement I received a cheque for fifteen thousand dollars. Here's the cheque. I want to negotiate it.'

'Fart International.'

'Yes.'

'Alvin T. Brine.'

'Yes.'

'Please understand I have no wish to pry into your affairs but what exactly is Fart International?'

'I don't know.'

'But you placed an ad in some – where?'

'*Screen Monthly.*'

'You placed an ad in *Screen Monthly*. What was the ad?'

'Fart International. Box 13. Send No Money.'

'I don't know why Mr Whelan but for some extraordinary reason I believe you. Now tell me about Fart International.'

'There's nothing to tell. I haven't got any further than placing the ad.'

'But what sort of service do you offer? Or what business is it?'

'I don't know what service I have to offer. If any. All I committed myself to was a request for no money.'

'Excuse my smiling. I can't help seeing a comical element in this.'

'Neither can I. To an extent.'

'Who is Alvin T. Brine?'

'I have no idea.'

'The cheque is drawn on the Chase and Manhattan, Des Moines, Iowa. Mr Ellis mentioned the company is not registered, has no rules, no directors. Do you follow me, you might have found the cheque in the street.'

'I didn't. It was forwarded to me from *Screen Monthly* as per my instructions.'

'All right. Accepting that, do you not see I certainly can't cash the cheque and to negotiate it via an account will involve investigation.'

'Investigation?'

'I'll have to contact Des Moines. Presumably they'll get in touch with Alvin T. Brine.'

'You'll telephone them?'

'Telephone? Telephone?'

'Why not?'

'Why not indeed. The whole business is unusual enough to take to the telephone. Suppose you come back – wait, we're five hours ahead of them. Come back at four. We might have an idea where we are then.'

'Thank you, Mr . . .'

'Harnett. John Harnett.'

'Thank you Mr Harnett.'

Whelan had to ring the bell at four o'clock. G. Ellis conducted the admittance as far as Mr Harnett's office where the manager himself took charge.

'Mr Whelan. Make yourself comfortable. I'm expecting a call any minute. I've been on to the Chase. They do have an Alvin T. Brine. He's an established client – man of substance. They contacted him while I was on the fine. He dropped whatever he was doing. He wants to speak to you himself. There's no problem with the cheque according to Chase. But the man is apparently delirious at the prospect of talking to you himself.'

'Delirium is the word. I don't want to talk to him.'

'Mr Whelan. I told them you'd be here at four. They might ring any – Jesus – I beg your pardon, that must be them now. Hello?'

After the telephonist's Limerick accent was superseded by the American connection, Mr Harnett, because it was a transatlantic call, raised his voice to a shout.

'Yes. This is Harnett. Yes. Mr Whelan is with me now. Right. Certainly. Hello. Yes Mr Brine. Yes, Mr Whelan is with me. Just a moment. Alvin T. Brine wants to speak to you.'

'He can't.'

'But what will I tell him?'

'Tell him I said he can't speak to me.'

'I can't just tell him that.'

'Suit yourself.'

Mr Harnett uncovered the receiver.

'Hello. Mr Brine. Mr Whelan says you can't speak to him. Pardon? I don't know. Par – what?'

Mr Harnett put his palm over the phone and cleared his throat: 'Mr Brine says who does the fucker think he is.'

'Ask Mr Brine to apologise for that remark. Tell him bad language is against the rules of Fart International.'

'Mr Whelan, are you sure of yourself. You're not giving this any thought.'

'Thought is against the rules of Fart International.'

'Hello. Hello Mr Brine. Mr Brine, Mr Whelan would like you to apologise for your bad language. He says it's against the rules of Fart International. Pardon? All right.'

'Mr Brine is asking us to hold on a moment. You know what you're doing?'

'Mr Harnett, you won't hear a lie after me, I'm playing by ear.'

'If this keeps on I'll end up asking you to pinch me. Hello. Yes. Yes. I understand. Just a moment.'

'Mr Brine says you have ten seconds to get on the phone or else he'll cancel the cheque.'

'Tell him he has nine seconds to get off the phone or I'll tear up the cheque.'

'Mr Whelan, it's fifteen thousand dollars!'

'Tell him.'

'Hello. Mr Brine. Mr Whelan says you have nine seconds to get off the phone or else he'll tear up your cheque. All right.'

'Mr Brine wants us to hold.'

'No matter what he says next tell him I said no one is worthy to join Fart International.'

'Would you oblige me? In the cabinet behind you. Pour me a tincture like a good man. And help yourself.'

'Yes. Still here. Mr Brine, I understand. And I sympathise but I can't force the man to speak to you. And Mr Whelan says no one is worthy to join Fart International. I don't know. I have no idea. You know as much about Fart International as I do. All I know is your cheque is in front of me for fifteen thousand dollars payable to Fart International. I beg your pardon? Just a moment.'

'He wants to know can I describe you.'

'No.'

'Hello, Mr Whelan says no.' And a minute later:
'Now he wants your address.'

'17 Wellington Avenue.'

'Mr Brine, 17 Wellington Avenue, Limerick. Just a moment Mr Brine, Mr Whelan wants to say something to me.'

'Tell him that you are going to process that cheque and that I said this is far, far from constituting an acid test.'

Mr Harnett ran his tongue over his lips and stared at his odd customer.

'And then drop the phone.'

Mr Harnett finished his brandy. He carried out his instructions and forced his hand to let go. He recognised what had just happened as being ridiculous but nevertheless luxuriated in the commendation: 'Well done. Thank you, Mr Harnett. You might let me know – know the – the dénouement? Please don't get up. I'll see myself out. G. Ellis will wave me into the street.'

CHAPTER SIX
ANNA ROCHE-REILLY

L ess than a year after his return home Whelan made his first public appearance at Clonmel racecourse motivated by the reasonable hope that he might operate unrecognised by his neighbours or by the likes of Higgins. His entire fare consisted of glasses of milk and ham sandwiches. He made one hundred per cent profit on the milk and eighty per cent on the sandwiches and was ninety-five per cent confident in his new occupation. That ninety-five per cent stemmed from his having met Anna Roche-Reilly and Alvin T. Brine; from G. Ellis having been appalled at the notion that a client would withdraw from deposits to purchase a van, so appalled that he ushered Whelan into John Harnett who initiated him into the world of the term loan; from the fact that Pete O'Mara was not at all flustered at that stage of the negotiations where it emerged that Whelan could not drive, O'Mara taking him out the Dock Road and teaching him in one hour; and from the smooth negotiation of the Fart International cheque of Alvin's.

'Free glass of milk with every ham sandwich purchased,' Whelan bawled at intervals on his first day at
Clonmel racecourse. The price of his ham sandwich
was dearer than the norm by the price of a pint of
milk and each pint of milk yielded two glasses. He
sold two hundred sandwiches and gave away one
hundred pints of milk, a net profit (excluding petrol,
depreciation and the atom to be taken into account
to appease the baying of the term loan) of sixteen
pounds which was a phenomenal return by any
reckoning. When he got home Whelan rang Anna
Roche-Reilly to tell her his good news. She was happy
to meet him for a drink in the Sarsfield Arms.

Two months earlier Whelan had made Anna
Roche- Reilly's acquaintance through the medium
of the Fart International advertisement in the
Chronicle. She had chanced upon the gremlin version and wrote succinctly for details enclosing the
requested No Money. Whelan was human enough
to respond to her signature – Dr Anna Roche-Reilly.
He invited her to a meeting in the Cedar Room of
the Sarsfield Arms after negotiating the use of the
room from the proprietor T. A. Dufficy. It was one
of the smallest function rooms in the hotel catering
in the main for poetry readings. T. A. Dufficy made
out a receipt to Fart International without comment.
Whelan requested and was granted the use of a small
table and chair that he sat upon outside the door of
the Cedar Room until diffidently approached by a
woman of thirty-eight who stood five feet and eleven

inches high, who was thin, had jet black shoulder length hair and the hint of a moustache under a long narrow nose.

Dr Anna Roche-Reilly said: 'Excuse me – am I – is this – what's on in this room?'

'Dr Reilly?'

'Yes.'

'Billy Whelan. Shall we go inside?'

Whelan folded the table and withdrew to the meeting. He seated himself at the table at the top of the room and indicated to Anna Roche-Reilly her choice of seats in the front row.

'Dr Reilly, what exactly can I do for you?'

'I was about to ask that.'

'You probably want to know what Fart International is?'

'Yes.'

'That's a bad sign. As if your being a doctor did not hinder your prospects enough as it is. Nothing against doctors per se. At least not too much against them. But they are part of – part of – (Whelan gestured hopelessly) – part of everything – and Fart International would scarcely be in favour of – of everything. If you follow me?'

'I'm very much afraid I don't. If you follow me.'

The good-natured twinkle in her last four words encouraged Whelan.

'All right. In the magazine *Screen Monthly* for many years now has appeared the ad: Fart International, Box 13, SEND NO MONEY.'

Whelan then read from Bill Johnston's letter. Over the years, as he deviated from its credo he was capable of inducting without recourse to notes. Now, when he finished reading, he made a show of stacking his papers to camouflage the fear that Anna Roche-Reilly might think him insane as the contents of the letter certainly entitled her to think. When, after a digestive interval, Anna Roche-Reilly did speak, she said: 'I think that's very beautiful.'

'Good. Now, what can I do for you?'

'Tell me what it feels like to be an Outrageously Suitable Person?'

Again the twinkle. Whelan gave up.

'To tell you the truth I don't know whether I'm coming or going. Let's establish one thing. You don't think I'm mad?'

'I'm not that kind of doctor . . .'

'. . . please. Be serious.'

'No. I don't think you're mad.'

'Good. Because I'm not. I know, I'd be the last to know and so on. But I'm not. No. Fart International is a crutch for me – and anyone who needs it. Miss – is it Miss?'

'Yes.'

'Miss Roche-Reilly, you don't strike me in need of a crutch.'

Defiantly and without twinkle Anna Roche-Reilly replied: 'Everyone needs.'

'It's a small town Miss – damn it I can't call you that long name – Miss Reilly, it's a small town.

Take the weekend *Leader*. The results from the two
golf clubs, Stablefords and words like that, Bridge
notes, Soroptomists, Lions, Rotary, Toastmasters of
all things, they're all out Miss – they're all out Anna.
How are you faring?'

'I play bridge at the 99 Club. Three months ago I
won the mixed foursomes, handicap eleven.'

'And that name of yours. That two names.'

'I'm Protestant.'

'Roche? Reilly? Protestant?'

'Proselytism way back. Land. The professions. All
the family. My brothers are doctors. I never practised.
Believe it or not too squeamish. My uncle FitzGeorge
made up a fourth with Maugham in some jungle.
He put Fitz in one of his stories. So Fitz used to say.
He's dead. I'm thirty-eight. Five foot eleven. There's
hair on my lip. I've been living off capital for fifteen
years. I can't ride a horse. What the hell have you got
against golfers anyway?'

'If you have to ask . . .'

'Listen. We marry our own . . .'

'. . . pardon?'

'Our set. The medical. There was nobody suitable
for brother James, he had to marry the daughter of
a racehorse trainer. They've had all sorts of trouble
with me. The lip. The height. This is the truth – a
jockey, with the blessing of my parents – a jockey proposed to me at a hunt ball – and he wasn't even over
the jumps, a bloody flat jockey! Now what can you do
for me?'

'I don't know what I can do for you. You'd be the first member apart from myself if – if I admitted you. Do you know I was driven out of Ireland? Driven! Not by your "set". Would that it was. God be with those days. I was driven out by Nicky, Higgins, Murphy and Mark Brown. You don't know about them. If I admitted you I'd tell you about them. All right, you're in. You're a member. We'll start the meeting. There's no rules only anti-rules but I'm appropriating to myself two luxuries. See if you can stomach them.'

Whelan took from his pocket the dollar presented to him by the American priest and minded by Mr Ryan as a souvenir. He made a tender knot around the dollar with strong twine and tied the twine around his neck.

'My chain of office. I'll explain that some other time. Do you know "Slievenamon"?'

'The mountain?'

'The song.'

'No.'

Whelan handed her the ballad sheet.

'These are the words. I'll give you the air. At the start of every meeting one verse must be sung. Are you ready?'

Anna Roche-Reilly read the words slowly, looked up, nodded.

Whelan sang quietly:

> Alone, all alone,
> By a wave-washed strand,

All alone in a crowded hall;
The hall it is gay,
The waves they are grand,
But my heart is not there at all.

It flies far away,
By night and by day,
To the times and the joys that are gone;
But I will never forget
The sweet maiden I met
In the Valley of Slievenamon.

Anna Roche-Reilly managed to join in with him on the last three lines.

'Good. What happens now?'

'You tell me – Mr President.'

'I have no idea. I suggest we adjourn. The next meeting in a fortnight. Same time. Same place. Which reminds me. This room cost three pounds. Since there's only two of us – have you thirty bob?'

'Yes.'

'And do you know why you're in? It's not the hairy lip. That might have got you in if you were a lonely bird cooped up in digs. And it's not the height or thirty-eight. It's your uncle making up the fourth with Maugham in the jungle. That's what. I bet I know who the other two were.'

'How could you?'

'Hogan and Wingate.'

'Who?'

'I'll tell you about Hogan some time. If we progress.'

At the second meeting of Fart International in the Cedar Room of the Sarsfield Arms Hotel Whelan stony-faced produced his chain of office and sang with Anna Roche-Reilly the first verse of 'Slievenamon'. He had booked the room over the telephone and again T. A. Dufficy noted the booking with a poker voice. Whelan sat outside the door with his table and chair. T. A. Dufficy passed by and asked: 'Are you expecting a crowd?'

'I don't think so.'

'The reason I ask, the Fountain Room is available if you needed more space.'

'Thanks. No, the Cedar Room is quite adequate.'

Anna Roche-Reilly arrived at that moment and placed a pound and a ten shilling note on the table. Whelan matched the amount and handed the proceeds to T. A. Dufficy saying: 'It's gone time. I think we should go in. It doesn't look as if anyone else is coming.'

They took the same positions as at the first meeting. After the song they sized each other up and Whelan said: 'We're here again.'

'Yes. Who would have believed it.'

'I must tell what I spotted in the *Chronicle*. There was a photo of this flogpot with waders up to his neck. He had a fishing rod in one hand and a salmon in the other. There was a grin on his face to describe which would pain me. It was the first salmon of the season. The man revealed to whatever thick interviewed him that the bait he used was a silver devon. What do you think of that?'

'What do you want me to think?'

'I don't want you to think anything. But if you felt, as I do, that that man should be stoned with black balls if he ever tried to join Fart International, then we'd have a consensus on which to build. Don't you think?'

'All right. I'll go along with you.'

'Did you spot anything?'

'In the Chronicle?'

Whelan extended his palms to embrace the world of Anna Roche-Reilly: 'Anyplace. *Tatler, Horse and Hound*, walking down the street, listening to the radio. But not the television.'

Anna Roche-Reilly bent her head in thought. She giggled.

'I overheard a woman in Pnikerettes saying she was holding a Tupperware party.'

'Yes?'

'That to me is much more dreadful than your chappie with the bait of silver devon.'

'I'm with you. I think we should write this down. Number 1: Silver Devon. Number 2: Tupperware Party. What do you think? And build on it?'

'What would you do if that very woman wrote to Fart International?'

'Well, and I know this is unlikely, if she under-stood the evil of the Tupperware party and wanted to be saved from it, then she would be given consideration. She could have her Tupperware parties seven nights a week just as long as she saw them for what they were – as bad as golf and bridge for smothering the individual – yes, Anna, this isn't a game, bridge itself is not at fault, golf itself is not but they're contributory factors to your ending up being proposed to by a jockey. A flat jockey. It's just come to me – Independence – that's what F.I. is all about. The Individual. Don't you see?'

'I don't know. I do and I don't. You have it all worked out. You must give me a chance. Give me time. What about morality? Sex? Where are we supposed to stand on that?'

'I don't know. I don't know anything about sex. Where do you think we should stand on it?'

'I haven't a pat opinion. What do you mean when you say you don't know anything about sex?'

'I never kissed a girl in my life. Have you experience of sex?'

'I'm not a virgin. Hunt balls, don't you know. How is it that you have never kissed a girl, if I may ask? And why shouldn't I ask, the way you carry on?'

'I don't know how to go about it. I know, you go to dances, ask a girl to dance, buy her a mineral, walk her home, make a date. But I don't know how to go about it. I'd die. I tried it a few rimes in the Banba in Kilbum. I'm no good. I'm too shy.'

'You're shy?'

'Yes.'

'Whatever else you are, you're not shy. I never met anyone so sure of himself.'

'There you are: the first, unsolicited testimonial to Fart International. And from yourself. You're right. I'm not shy now. I'm confident, sure of what I'm aiming at. But in half an hour I'll go back to the world and I'll be pitiful. A fortnight ago I said I might tell you about Nicky, Higgins, Murphy and Mark Brown. I never will. Not here, not within – within this glow. They don't come at me here, I'm protected, by myself. If our social paths cross and I knew you and I was down, then I might open up on Higgins and the rest. But I'll never need to here. Do you see?'

'What are you going to do about a girl? I take it you're not – incidentally where do we stand where they are concerned – ?'

'No. I don't think I am. Them? Everything else being equal, assuming they don't catch salmon with silver devons or say "uptight" or "no way", I don't think we should point the finger. Agreed?'

'All right. What are you going to do about a girl? Marriage?'

'If it happens it happens. I can't go through that dance thing. Anna, give us another contribution. Tupperware was good. One more for tonight.'

'Lesbians are out.'

'No.'

'Yes.'

'No, Anna.'

'Yes, Billy.'

'I'll toss you for it.'

'All right.'

Whelan tossed a coin, lifted his palm and said: 'Well?'

Anna cried: Heads. Whelan looked at the coin: Tails. He said: 'You win. Lesbians are out. We'd want to recruit another member fast.'

'How do I know I won?'

'Pardon?'

'The toss.'

'You said heads.'

'Yes.'

'And heads came up.'

'How do I know? I can't see from here.'

'Don't you trust me?'

'No.'

'Do you want me to toss again and you can come up and witness it?'

'No.'

'What do you want?'

'Let lesbians in abeyance. Cross the bridge when we come to it.'

'You're right. Anyway, there are no lesbians in Ireland.'

'Billy. . .'

'Yes?'

'I'm sorry to say this . . . but I can feel it in me . . . it's not going to work. Not with the two of us. We need at least a third . . .'

'Your uncle FitzGeorge might stagger out of the jungle . . .'

'Listen to me. I'm thirty-eight. For all your flippancy you're innocent. You don't know what's happening.'

'What's happening?'

'I'm sitting here growing attracted to you. I'm not a virgin. I get re-charged now and again. I don't want to take you.'

'Fart is working wonders. You're beginning to feel like Marilyn Monroe.'

'I'd love to do it to you, you smug bastard. Sitting there thinking you're protected by my hairy lip. I could go up to you with a bag over my head and make you sweat. Some day you'll understand. Good night.'

Whelan did not have a third when he rang Anna Roche-Reilly from a call box to tell her of his successful day at Clonmel races. She agreed to meet him but not in the privacy of the Cedar Room.

'I'll see you in the lounge. See how your good news stands up to being seen with a thirty-eight year old hairy-lipped giant.'

Whelan was deflated by her bitterness. When he reached home to change he discovered the third waiting for him in the parlour.

'Billy,' his mother introduced, 'there's a gentleman come all the way from America to see you. Mr Brine.'

'So this is Bill Whelan. Alvin T. Brine, Bill. How are you?'

'Pleased to meet you, Mr Brine.'

'Alvin, Bill. Just call me Alvin. I was just saying to your lovely mother here, I heard of these cute little houses, first time I've ever been in one. Real nice.'

Whelan was proud of the house. His mother was celebrated among the neighbours for her industry in cleaning and dusting and painting and papering. She was constantly tipping around with the paint brush. Modestly she accepted compliments with the simple explanation: a little a day, every day. The house did not have a bathroom but it was far from the shambles Father Nicky threatened to visit ten years later. Whelan discovered that Alvin had had tea from Mrs Whelan and had enjoyed it, thanked her and said: I'd like to wash my hands. Mrs Whelan boiled the kettle and poured the water in a pitcher that she placed beside a basin in the back room. Alvin said the pitcher was real cute but he still needed to go so he came clean and further confused Mrs Whelan by asking for the john. Eventually, after Alvin came cleaner still, he was directed to the lavatory in the backyard after using which he ran out of cute comments. He was a squat man of about forty-eight years old, with close cropped hair, a bit of a belly and jaws navigable by a razor in its sleep.

'Alvin, I'll just change my clothes. Make yourself comfortable, I'll be with you in two minutes.'

'Sure, Bill. You do that. And don't hurry. Fine boy, Mrs Whelan.'

While Whelan changed he heard footsteps on the stairs. His mother, as he expected, had torn herself from her guest to satisfy her curiosity.

'Billy, who is that man? How do you know him? What does he want?'

'I'll tell you later Mam. He's a friend I met in London. I'm taking him for a drink.'

On their way to the Sarsfield Arms Alvin pointed out the lovely houses and the cute little shops. Whelan stopped and said: 'Alvin. Can it. They're small, smelly, claustrophobic and there isn't room to swing a cat in them and most of the people have cats and they shit all over the place. The coal is thrown any old way in the corner of the yard, ill-covered with a bit of tarpaulin, you go out for a shovel of coal and you get a shovel full of cat shit. All right, Alvin?'

'Sorry.'

'Do be. But you're wrong and I'm worse. I should have let you off. Fart would never forgive either of us.'

They walked a few yards in silence; Whelan was in the grip of the exciting presence of his first American. All very well to look down his nose at the idea of them but in the flesh the goddamners were exotic. He reminded himself of his authority and so was confident he could continue to bully the American as though they were both still at the safe ends of the transadantic call.

'Fart International. You know that's why I'm here,' Alvin T. Brine almost whined.

'I know.'

'Nine seconds to get off the phone. I said, Alvin, you go see that man. And here I am.'

'What do you want, Alvin? Your money back? It's all there. Untouched.'

'Of course I don't want my money back. I want – I'm not sure what I want. What exactly is . . .'

'I don't know. I don't know, Alvin. Here we are. You're going to meet a lady. Anna Roche-Reilly. She's the only other member besides myself and maybe you. You want to join?'

'I guess so. I mean . . .'

'What do you drink, Alvin? Bourbon, Martinis, whiskey?'

'I don't really go for liquor, Bill.'

'Oh Jesus, Alvin. You're not serious. And it's Billy. Not Bill.'

Anna Roche-Reilly was on a stool at the small bar of the big lounge. Whelan performed the introductions and noted that Anna copped on immediately to the name, Alvin T. Brine. She accepted that it was no longer a social gathering when Whelan said he would go and see T. A. Dufficy about the Cedar Room.

T. A. Dufficy was sorry but it was booked.

'There's a poetry reading there tonight. How many did you need a room for?'

'Three.'

'Three?'

T. A. Dufficy could not restrain the corner of his mouth at the increase.

'Good for you. A three way split of the rent. Let me see. You could have the Blue Room. It's smaller than the Cedar Room but twill hold three. And there's a hatch. It's back of the lounge bar. Very popular with the French Circle, the Patricians, a chap booked it for T.M. once. He got such a crowd I had to give them the Fountain Room. Luckily I had no dinner dance booked in the Fountain Room that night.'

'The Blue Room will be fine. What'll that cost?'

'The Blue Room? For an hour. Let me see. Say three pounds.'

'It's smaller than the Cedar Room?'

'It is. But there's a cachet about it.'

'Yeah. Will you make out a receipt to Fart International?'

'Certainly.'

'Mr Dufficy?'

'Yes?'

'Why don't you ask me what the hell is Fart International?'

'I couldn't do that.'

'Why not? You must be wondering?'

'I'm certainly not wondering. You see, I have absolutely no curiosity.' – T. A. Dufficy beamed and added confidentially – 'Knowledge is pain and knowledge comes to one soon enough without sending out invitations for it.'

'Mr Dufficy, I'm at liberty to reveal one facet of Fart International that may interest you: it does not solicit membership.'

'I see.'

In the Blue Room, indistinguishable from the Cedar Room except for a drop in acreage, Whelan sat at the top table and chair while Anna Roche-Reilly and Alvin T. Brine occupied two seat of the front row. Without a word, but with a little ceremony, Whelan took the twine and the dollar from his pocket and placed it around his neck.

'Are you ready, Anna?'

'Yes.'

Anna sang from the ballad sheet in accompaniment to Whelan who had the words engraved in his heart. When they finished Whelan said: 'Alvin, you'll forgive me. I haven't got around to having copies of the ballad printed yet. What do you think of it as an anthem?'

'That's a cute song. Yeah, I like that.'

'What do you think of the chain of office?'

'Isn't that a dollar?'

'Yes. This is a piece of twine. I'd better fill you in.'

Whelan began with his father's death in pursuit of a cigarette end; he went through Mr Ryan; his early days at school; Higgins, Murphy, Nicky, Mark Brown; particularly Higgins' disbelief of the advertisement in *Screen Monthly*; he jumped to his being driven out of Ireland at seventeen by Higgins, Murphy, Nicky and

Mark Brown; he told of Hogan and Co., including Wingate, and he told of being hungry on Christmas Day and writing the fateful letter to Box 13. He told of Bill Johnston and Al Guerrini.

'That's why my first cheque didn't have Bill Whelan's endorsement.'

'Billy.'

'Sorry, Billy. Johnston cashed the cheque for five grand and sent me a note regretting my unworthiness. I upped it to fifteen. And here I am.'

'And here we are, Alvin. Now what can we do for you?'

'You don't give a guy a chance, hey. No rules. I like that. So you're the president, and Anna is . . .'

'Anna is Anna. And I'm not so much the president as the OSP, the Outrageously Suitable Person, but initials are out so to be shortwinded okay president will do. Alvin, here is what we have so far. A woman running a Tupperware party: Out. A man catching the first salmon of the year with die bait of a silver devon: Out. Mention something, Alvin. Something you don't approve of.'

Alvin T. Brine might have been in love with the world, so long did he take to summon an object of his distaste.

'I'm trying to think . . .'

'Take your time, Alvin. I think I'll give a tap to that hatch there and get a pint. Anna?'

'G and T please, Billy.'

'Anna, if you weren't in you'd be out, do you know that? Such language. Have a gin and tonic water. Alvin?'

'I don't . . . well I'll try your black beer, all right?'

'No. I'll get you a pint of Guinness.' Whelan tapped at the hatch which slid to reveal the incurious visage of T. A. Dufficy. He ordered the drink and returned to his seat.

'How are we doing, Alvin?'

'I was thinking: I've no time for America bashers. You know? I mean you take guys . . .'

'America bashers? As far as I'm concerned Alvin, you're in. Anna?'

'I'll accept that coming from Alvin. But it shouldn't go in the book with the silver devon and the Tupperware.'

'Agreed. It's not that strong. Here's the nectar. And the gin and tonic.'

T. A. Dufficy gave Whelan his change out of a pound and seemed reluctant to close the hatch. Whelan said: 'That's all, thanks.'

T. A. Dufficy closed it.

'By the way, Alvin. The room cost three pounds. I've already paid so you and Anna can cough up a quid each. There's another thing. Round buying. Round buying is in. Anna?'

'In.'

'Alvin?'

'Yeah. In the States we've rounds, include the barman. The barman buys every third round.'

'We'll leave out the barman. Preserve some tit of class. Right, Anna?'

'Most certainly. The Empire might have gone but that doesn't mean we drink with trade.'

'Well said. I think we could nearly pack it in for tonight. Where are you staying, Alvin?'

'A place further down town, funny name for a hotel, the Percy. That's it, the Percy Hotel.'

'You would pick the Percy. That's the only union-ised hotel in the city. What's a hotel without lackeys? Where's the atmosphere when people are standing on their dignity? What do you think Anna? Unionised hotels: Out.'

'Out.'

'Are you staying long, Alvin? You should move in here.'

'I might do. How long am I staying? Who knows. Maybe for ever.'

'Pardon?'

'Yeah, I've had the American Dream. This is a nice little country. I thought I might get me one of those cottages. Near a river, you know? I mean, Jeez, Elks, Country Club, Rotary. I've had it up to here. Compromise, compromise, compromise. Yeah, I made it. For what? One kid, gave him everything. What's he at? Into revolution! Can you believe it. One of them hippies. Me and Sooky are all screwed up. Sooky's my wife. My dad built up a business. Not big but something I got my teeth in. The Alvin T. Brine

Construction Company has five hundred men leavin'
out casual. And I did it all by myself with my tongue
out the whole way, compromisin'. Billy, what do you
say? I could come here and really get Fart moving?
No hassle. No sweat. I'll put it to Sooky: I say, Sook,
we're going to buy us a little country house in Ireland
and retire, if she's not on she can live on goddam
alimony.'

'Alvin, don't be precipitate. There's no law against
you selling out and moving to Ireland. That's your
own business. But you can't do that on Fart's account.
Think of the good you could do in Des Moines, working in the field, spreading the gospel from the inside;
it's a simple message, we may as well get that clear,
the fundamental.

'Here's a story, Alvin. Tell me what you think. You
ready? Right: There's this camel out in the desert and
it gets freezing cold in the desert at night and he was
frozen this night and he asked his master if he could
put his head inside the tent to keep his nose warm
and the master said all right and the next night the
camel asked him could he put his legs in, his first two
legs, and the master said all right and then the next
night he asked him could he put his hump in and it
went on like that till the whole of the camel was in
and he was all warm. But then the camel said the tent
wasn't big enough for the two of them and he asked
the master to sleep outside. The master got angry
and threw the camel out for being ungrateful. That's
the story. What do you think of that story now?'

'Well. The moral is obvious. The camel should have been thankful for small mercies. Instead he got greedy.'

'The moral isn't obvious. It never is. The master's reaction was predictable, fashioned by the mores of his time. The herd instinct. No individuality there, Alvin. The brute reaction of a rational but unfeeling beast. I'm not saying he should have moved out and slept on the cold sand. But he could have let the camel down gently. He should have reverted to the status quo acceptable to himself: both of them in the tent. But no. He had to rub the camel's face in it. That's Fart: letting down gently where there has to be letting down. This twine, the dollar, the song and the camel: that's the bedrock. I stood up in Clonmel racecourse today and I shouted my head off peddling sandwiches and milk and I was programmed for an office job. But I could do that today thanks to twine, dollar, song and camel. You go back Alvin and revert, to probity, honesty, deep sleep at night. The twine, the dollar, the song and the camel will be your talis- men.'

Whelan's pulse quickened as he noticed the look of rejection on the American's face; on the chair beside Alvin the black beer was headless from neglect.

'Alvin, I don't think you're in love with that Guinness?'

'Well, it is a bit heavy.'

'Don't drink it, Alvin. Don't drink it if you don't want it. I'll finish it. Now what do you say, we'll pack up the meeting and go outside and have a sociable gathering. Anna? But. Outside of a meeting Fart International cannot be discussed.'

Whelan poured the remains of his drink into Alvin's glass and took it to the hatch where he asked T. A. Dufficy to transfer it to a table in the lounge. T. A. Dufficy was so vigilant in his availability that Whelan was prompted to say to Anna Roche-Reilly: 'A pound to a penny T. A. Dufficy for Fart International?'

'You think so?'

'His ear's been cocked there for the past half hour. I'm nearly sure.'

Chapter Seven
The Dinner

Not that the product of St James' Gate Brewery was in need of it, but it's efficacy was heightened by a confident Billy Whelan pushing open the door of the Sarsfield Arms lounge; and no reflection on the same divine black brew, but he was also sucking restoratively on a Gold Flake cigarette. The lounge was crowded, punctuated with navigable roundabout tracks to the bar and groups in gaggles here and there. Whelan stood frozen, seeking a direction. After a moment all the strange faces melted and yielded up the recognisable Father Nicky in his vestments of red pullover and white slacks. Whelan began to walk in their direction; a voice hailed him from behind and presently there was a hand on his shoulder.

'How are you, Billy? Welcome.'

'Donal. Thank you. Congratulations by the way. I saw you in the *Chronicle* recently. Big promotion.'

'It's not as great as it sounds but they like to publicise these things. It's free advertising for the firm.'

'I know. Still, fair play to you.'

'I hear you're going great guns altogether. You can't beat working for yourself.'

'Donal, I'd swop with you any day. There's a lot to be said for packing in at half-five and leaving the job behind you. Although I bet you can't pack in at half-five. Being the manager.'

'You can say that again.'

Whelan was almost tempted to say it again because it seemed they were at the end of their conversational tether. They had scarcely as much to say to each other at school so they were not doing too badly after eighteen years.

'Are you with the lads?'

'Not yet. You go on over. I have to stay here and do the honours. Would you ever think of joining the union, Billy? We need younger blood . . .'

'. . . with my job . . .'

'. . . I know. You don't have to tell me. But if you only managed to make an odd meeting . . .'

'. . . I'll think about it. Listen, I'll see you later, okay?'

'Mr Roberts. Welcome.'

Jovial Timmy Roberts, the one-handed chemist, at seventy-eight a thrice past president of the PPU and indefatigable in support of all activities under its aegis, proffered his good left member to be shook, the sleeve of the right stump lodged limply in his pocket.

Whelan could see Nicky, Higgins, Murphy and a few unknown to him occasionally glancing in his direction while he spoke to Donal O'Sullivan.

Naked, without a glass in his hand he strolled in their direction.

'Hello Billy.'

'How are you, Billy? Long time no see.'

'How's the banana business, Whelan? Whelan's in fruit.'

'Nicky, Murph, Higgins. I saw Nicky. I see Higgins and Donal around. It's donkeys' years, Murph.'

'Yeah, but you're looking incredible.'

'You're not exactly going around with a stick, are you.'

Even as he spoke, Whelan could do nothing to prevent Higgins rising and deftly lifting the few camouflaging strands from Murphy's pate and exclaiming: 'Jesus, Murphy, you're going bald.'

Whelan blushed on Murphy's behalf and was gripped with admiration for Murphy's spartan defence: 'We're getting on, you know.'

Whelan had no drink and there was no sign of any offers.

'I'll get a pint. Be back in a moment.'

Still no offers. As he quashed in at the bar he thought bitterly: this is not happening to me. How can it be? I'm a madman. T. A. Dufficy manifested himself by Whelan's side and muttered: 'Good luck. We're all with you tonight. You know that.'

A surge of gratitude flowered into confidence.

'Thanks T.A. I know that.'

Though fortified with the glass in his hand and T. A. Dufficy's timely encouragement, Whelan sat beside

Nicky for protection. Murphy's anecdote recalled an anaemic experience in third year and was addressed to Nicky. Murphy said: You must remember, Father?

Whelan did not listen; he concentrated on an analysis of Murphy addressing Nicky as Father. He decided Murphy was harmless. He had thought earlier in the night while stoking up and here was the comforting corroboration: Murphy was next door to being an assistant bank manager, it was now being revealed. In his outpost in West Cork he played poker for daring stakes with one of the two local doctors, an accountant, the parish priest, a publican and a chemist. But they had to keep the activity quiet, Murphy explained, not for the sake of the parish priest, as Whelan supposed, but for Murphy's own sake. In his position. It was sad: Murphy was moulting aloft, he had a paunch that could not have been envisaged in those days when he had the hurley in his hand, and he did not have the wit to buy Whelan a drink or be offended by Higgins' wounding observation. He had to rouse himself from pitying Murphy. Murphy was asking him: 'What did you say you were at, Billy?'

'I have a little catering business. Nothing elaborate. Keeps the wolf from the door.'

'Any man who can keep his door open today is doing well. Take it from me. If you're small, stay small. The bigger guys are in trouble. Things are bad in England and what happens in England today happens here tomorrow.'

'And happened in America yesterday.'

'Correct. I'd say catering is a good business to be in, is it?'

Whelan was disappointed in Higgins. There was an unmistakable cue for Higgins to chime in: Catering? It's a fuckin' hawker he is, Murph. He decided Higgins was keeping his powder dry.

'Well, catering is rather a grandiose term for it. I'm by way of being more of a hawker. My fleet consists of a van and a convertible chip/ice cream wagon and I've a staff of one casual.'

'I see. I bet you're making the money though?'

'I'm making a few bob.'

'How does the tax situation affect you?'

'Tax? What's tax?'

He drew a round of laughter. Higgins' mirth was genuine and pleased Whelan. He did not think now of Higgins of the leering mouth under the slit eyes dotting the fat face; he did not reflect bitterly on the large brandy in Higgins' paw courtesy of the long-suffering taxpayer who received in return skies full of pissing rain when Higgins forecast sunshine for the two weeks away from the factory bench; all right, they had not bought him a drink but that was a collective oversight, probably happened among the best people; take Murphy, Whelan had said: 'And happened in America yesterday' and Murphy had not reacted to the slur on his originality, it was the same with Higgins really, when it was all boiled down, superficial probing and pleasantry, a patch of banter among friends, it was ridiculous hating them all those years, they had really made it up to him, whatever it was, by laughing at tax? What's tax?

Donal O'Sullivan was among them.

'Now Gentlemen, don't let me down. That's the third bell. Ye can bring the drinks into the meal.'

'Donal, wave your chain somewhere else. Half the crowd aren't gone in yet.'

'Higgins be fair. It's not me. It's the waitresses. It's not fair to the waitresses. Waitresses have homes to go to the same as any workers. Come on now, lads. There'll be plenty of time for booze afterwards. The speeches will be short.'

Whelan panicked in the direction of the bar where his right eyebrow was rewarded by a fast pint from T. A. Dufficy. He returned in time to hear Father Nicky: 'Donal, are you sure Mark Brown is coming? It's almost half nine.'

'Definitely. I was on the phone to him yesterday. He might have got caught up coming down from Dublin. Keep a seat for him.'

There was something fishy about the night: Mark Brown's absence. It was not the same without Mark Brown. Whelan trailed after them into the Fountain Room thinking: Mark's all right.

Whelan was thankful to be among a group as he strode into the reception with a pint glass of Guinness in his hand; everyone else carried a short or at least nothing more vulgar than a glass of lager. To cater for the sixty-odd guests two tables were laid in the form of a T. Higgins led the way to the top table where there were a few seats unappropriated by dignitaries.

Higgins said: 'Here's grand. Father Nicky, you sit here. Murph. We'll keep this seat for Mark.'

Whelan stood with the pint in his hand, nowhere to sit unless he took the seat reserved for Mark Brown. Reddening, he excused himself: 'I'll go back down the other table. I'll see ye after the meal.'

Not Higgins or Murphy or Nicky took a blind bit of notice of him. He walked the length of the body of the T, discovering this seat and that seat reserved till the voice of Timmy Roberts, the one-handed chemist rescued him.

'Youngfella. Here you are. Sit down here.'

Whelan loosened his tie; his hands were shaking and sweat was copious on his forehead though the Fountain Room if anything was ill-heated. In front of him was a confusing galaxy of cutlery; he had been to two dinner dances before with Breda but he had had Breda to confide in, to help him choose the correct spoon for the soup. The old chemist was saying: 'And what's your name?'

'Whelan, Billy Whelan.'

'What Whelan would that be? I know a lot of Whelans.'

'I come from Wellington Avenue, off Wolfe Tone Street, off O'Connell Avenue.'

'I know it. I never heard of Whelans there though. How are you, brother?'

The aside, tossed in the direction of a geriatric was not a whit of a decibel louder than his jovial enquiry of Whelan's ancestry; and there was no need for it to be as Timmy Roberts' joviality was a booming breed. Whelan could not ask Timmy Roberts which spoon to use; the reply might travel in Higgins' ear and out of his laughing mouth.

'That's Brother Hennigar. Brother Hennigar taught me. A great man for his age. He's a hundred and four or a hundred and five.'

Whelan smiled appeasingly.

'They're serving now.'

The observation was roared at no one in particular. Whelan realised that the chemist, struck with thought, did not believe in keeping it to himself. It was a straw that relaxed Whelan to an extent. Donal O'Sullivan had his presidential chain around his neck and was seated amid a presence of Brothers. Whelan, despising himself, craned to watch Donal's choice of spoon; the effects of the preliminary stoking up were beginning to wear off and Fart International might never have existed. The soup approached. The old chemist stuffed the serviette into his shirt collar. Whelan copied him and immediately felt ridiculous as all around placed the serviette in their laps. Whelan picked the correct spoon and bent his head inches from the plate to minimise the shake. At the top table, to Donal O'Sullivan's right, the laughter of Nicky, Murphy and Higgins joined the babble. They were splitting their sides at him, Whelan was sure.

He said one of his rare prayers: Jesus Christ, stop cru-
cifying me. He resurrected Fart and almost closing
his eyes he got through the soup thinking of the sym-
pathy he would receive from Anna when he related
the ordeal. After the soup, he was full.

Given ideal conditions, Whelan's favourite
breakfast consisted of tea, bread and butter, rashers, sausages and a fried egg; for his evening meal
he liked his breakfast plus a dash of black pudding.
When he was at home to dinner top of his list was
breast bones and skirts and kidneys and potatoes. He
also savoured spare ribs, bacon and cabbage, packet
and tripe, in fact any meal about which there might
be a lack of decorum to be observed. He inherited
the dishes from his mother and the vulgarity of his
appetite was a cross Breda made no bones about letting him know she bore. His spirit was in revolt at
the gentility of heads slurping almost in unison and
the deft tilting of plates scooping die last few dregs of
soup. The sixty spoons put on sixty plates, handed to
sixty waitresses with sixty smiles (including his own)
affronted him: we are well got, we smile at waitresses.
He held a brief, mass blackballing.

Whelan ploughed heroically into the turkey and
ham and potatoes of quaint nomenclature on the
menu: Jesus Christ, spuds are fucking spuds. The
turkey reminded him of Hogan. He wondered if
Hogan was dead. He had often thought of nipping
over to London for a weekend to tell Hogan about
Fart International. He had procrastinated even as he

procrastinated now in vaguely determining to go in the future. Timmy Roberts shouted for an extra helping of potatoes. He was a veteran who could distinguish between solecism and a healthy appetite. Whelan's own meal, spoiled by the restriction on burping and wiping of the mouth with the cuff, he pushed aside and took out his cigarettes, behaviour that drew from Timmy Roberts the stentorian rebuke: 'God, boy, what you ate wouldn't feed a hungry blackbird.'

Whelan smiled sheepishly and lied that he had mistakenly taken a big meal earlier in the evening. He thought he lied; rashers, sausages, black pudding and only one fried egg did not constitute a meal big or small. That was only what he had for his tea. He drifted into Fart International. Small appetites are disgraceful in Ireland. If you were in wherever it was you'd eat it. As though reading his thoughts Timmy Roberts intoned: 'They'd ate it in Germany.'

Germany? Timmy Roberts was old. It had been Germany when Whelan was growing up. The waitress was not pleased with the large remains on Whelan's plate, nor with his refusal of the sweet. He did not eat the sweet on the grounds that he was not a gourmet and in fact skipped pages of a writer he admired – Condon – for the same reason. In reparation he had tea and brought the smile back to the waitress. There was the tintinnabulation of a spoon against a glass: Donal O'Sullivan was on his feet.

The speeches would end and Whelan would have the comfort of Higgins and Murphy and Nicky and

Guinness; anything was better than being alone, surrounded by the one-armed chemist who could not mind his own business. The speeches were short, as had been vouchsafed to Donal O'Sullivan by a reliable authority. They were short but many. During the first – Donal's – Whelan stood and raised his cold tea to Ireland. He was afraid to clutch the headless pint lest he draw comment from Timmy Roberts. Whelan was up and down like a yo-yo toasting the School, the Guests, the Order, the Old Boys, the Winning of the Cup, the Future. Mercifully, Donal O'Sullivan called on the last speaker, Brother Hennigar, an orator, apparently from Donal O'Sullivan's introduction, of no portfolio save that of his great age on whom not to call for a few words would be to let the night go. Brother Hennigar rose slowly and spoke slowly at great length and practically inaudibly. The gathering almost held its breath to allow something of Brother Hennigar's intelligence to trickle through.

'. . . the boys of today are the men of tomorrow. It should never be forgotten . . . I cannot stress that enough . . . It is something we should keep to the forefront of our heads at all times. The boys of today are the men of tomorrow . . . We would do well to remember that. I feel it would be a great tragedy were we to forget that. When I first came . . .'

Whelan's chin began to veer towards his chest.

'. . . into each and every one of your fat heads: Wednesday is not a half-day, repeat *not* a half-day. Wednesday differs from the other afternoons in that the subject is *games*, not what's on at the Savoy or the Lyric or the Royal and by *games* I mean *games*, Gaelic Games and not that sissy's kiss – not that relic of the garrison element, soccer. Any of you with delusions of non-attendance may only be excused with a letter from your parents. And if you manage to inveigle your mothers to write that you are not up to the rigours of the national pastimes you won't be rewarded with a visit to the cinema. You remain in class, studying . . .'

Under the haphazard supervision of the lay teacher next door Whelan read his English books. He had made one appearance at the field where a corner back, ambidextrous at mowing meadows or forwards, convinced him that he was not up to the rigours of the national pastimes. Higgins had made the team. Cahill, who had felt no compulsion to put his finger in the wounds, welcomed Whelan to Wednesday afternoons with the consolation: 'That fucker Higgins is too ignorant to know fear. What's the comp?'

'Haven't you done it yet?'

'No. What are they?'

'A House on Fire/A Day in the Life of the School Clock/ Autumn. I did a house on fire.'

'I think I'll do that too.'

The composition was given out on Friday to be accomplished by the following Thursday morning. Whelan had written his, the mandatory offering of two foolscap pages, one tortuous paragraph at a time over the weekend. He sympathised with Cahill having to write his that night on top of the usual homework.

'Yeah. Let me alone. I'm going to write a house on fire.'

Cahill wrote for an hour: six marginless pages liberally blobbed. When he finished he read over what he had written with – it seemed to Whelan – admiration.

'I don't know how you write so fast. Can I see it?'

'I'm not handing it up. But you can see it.'

Whelan struggled through the first paragraph, knowing he had not a hope of negotiating six pages if it was all going to be like the first paragraph which began without warning:

Cahill among the crowd. Hands deep in pockets. Shoulders hunched to frame arsonic leer on lips. Awed spectators. Susceptible to conflagrations. Voicing I wonderhowitstartedness. Todds roof gone. Cahill volunteering: discarded cigarette butts. Getting looks. Moving again. Peter Lorreing. Night before petrol splashing on all floors. Among new crowd of sad to see a building like that go liars. Cahill muttering: only one em, fuckem. Pardons? Move back in here for safety. Fine Wimpy doorway for firewatching. Cromers jewellers tucked under facade. Cromer mopping shiny brow. Praying. In all religions. Aaah. Todds wall. Sergeant McDangler rising at flame-sights. Cahill fingering Searge to truss spot under shorts.

And there was great happiness among the
crowd who awed: Look at all the jobs that'll
be lost now.

'I can't follow this at all. You couldn't hand it up
anyway. Sentences without verbs. What do you mean?'

'It's supposed to be a parody.'

'What's that?'

'D'you ever hear of Donleavy?'

'Who's he?'

'He wrote *The Ginger Man*.'

'That was the filthy thing there was trouble in
Dublin about. That's banned.'

'Show me your comp.'

Cahill read the composition beginning: 'I will
never forget the night of Todds Fire,' and ending:
'never to be forgotten spectacle.'

Cahill said: 'You should read the editorials in the
Sunday Times. Pick out all the words you don't understand. Look them up and build sentences around
them no matter what you're writing . . .'

The bell rang. They scrambled to their prayer feet
and Cahill's advice would have been lost only that
Whelan every Sunday collected Mr Ryan's *Times*; the
old man no longer had the use of his legs. Mr Ryan
was very happy indeed to encourage the quarrying of
new words. Whelan discovered Affinity, Dichotomy,
Détente, Entrepreneur and *Laissez-faire*. In his next
essay – A Day in the Country – he wrote:

tremendous affinity between the mare and the farmer behind the plough . . . the fundamental dichotomy raging in the rural son – the yearning for factory wages and the distaste of where they are earned . . . the shaky *détente* between industry and agriculture . . .

Whelan could scarcely believe how quickly the composition wrote itself, quickened by sporadic reversions to type: We reached our appointed destination . . .

Brother Crowe daubed each essay with red pencil and flung it at its owner. He paused and announced: 'At least one of you is beginning to learn. Mark, come up here. Read out that composition.'

Whelan recognised his copy-book. As Mark Brown read, Nicky turned to Whelan and said: 'Whose is it? Is it Cahill's?'

'It's mine.'

'But whose is it really?'

'It's mine.'

'It's like your scrawl from here. Really? Is it really yours?'

'I could swear.'

Nicky craned his head back to confide in Higgins: 'That's Billy Whelan's.'

'What?'

'It is. He says it is.'

Mark Brown finished reading. Brother Crowe said: 'All right Mark. Now that is an example of how a composition should be written. With imagination, vocabulary, diligence.'

Brother Crowe wrote ninety-seven out of a hundred in the margin and flung the copy-book at Whelan.

'Well done. See that you keep it up. Cahill, you're malingering. Ninety out of a hundred is not good enough where you're concerned. We'll have to buck you up.'

They descended upon Whelan at the break. 'Give us a look, Billy. Ninety-seven! Ninety-seven! How did you do it?'

'Where did you get that word? Dich whatever it is?'

'Daytenty. That's not an English word, Whelan.'

And then Mark Brown said: 'Congratulations, Billy.'

Whelan followed them out to the yard but at the door he was drawn to look back at Cahill. Cahill stared at him frankly; Whelan saw a smile in Cahill's eyes for Whelan and contempt all over his face for everyone else.

In the yard Whelan idled over to them, as he always did, but now he was not greeted by Higgins': What are you doing there listening? Now Mark Brown said: 'I never knew you had it in you, Billy. You had some right jawbreakers in there.'

'I get the *Sunday Times* every week and read the editorial. Any rime there's a word in it I don't understand, I write it down and look it up. You'd be amazed what help it is.'

'Good idea.'

'Huh. Anyone could do that.'

Whelan did not even hear Higgins. Mark Brown was talking to him. Mark Brown was talking to Whelan. He was as important now to Mark Brown as Nicky was or Murphy or Higgins. Who would have thought when God made the world that he would have put so much happiness into it.

After this Whelan suspected an increase in the local sales of the *Sunday Times*; words began to crop up in Higgins' compositions that had no right to crop up in Higgins' compositions. Usually they were disastrously ill-used and invited and received Brother Crowe's derision. There was more talk of the comp now vis-à-vis algebra or latin or science. The Mark Brown essay, never with much of a foot wrong, assumed a taut verbosity. But Whelan had got the drop on them. Apart from the *Sunday Times* there was the dictionary and apart altogether from the *Sunday Times* and the dictionary, the chrysalis of conflagrations was suddenly as far behind him as cowboys and Indians: there was hair now on his output. But now that he was ready to be taken by Cahill, Cahill fell in love with science. . .

'. . . if we never forget that simple dictum we will be doing a good day's work . . . the boys of today. . .'

Chapter Eight
T. A. Dufficy

When he expanded to that stage, Whelan broke himself and the convertible in touring the ghettos. In the same way that he felt he reached his majority – that one hundred per cent efficiency – by graduating to die local race meeting with his sandwiches and milk, now he forced himself away from the housing schemes and out to the suburbs. He throttled majestically into a Roses Avenue that was splendidly gardened front and rear and that was tree-lined on that fateful fall evening with leaves of russet where they were not auburn and reddish brown where they were not russet. It was almost a crime to pierce the mature serenity with his Mr Whippy jingle and the guilt was compounded by the lack of response; there did not seem to be any children about the place.

'What are you doing?'

The child's effortless command of the 'ing' pricked Whelan's nostalgia for that other end of town where the homely hordes of snot faces pushed and shoved and cried: I'll break your fuck in neck

I was here first and left him short a penny. This child had crept around the blindside and startled Whelan by his mild manner. The child had a tennis racket and something Whelan had never handled before – a lawn tennis ball that wasn't bald. A sallow-skinned child with black trained hair that sensuous adults love to fondle.

'I'll allow you one guess and if you guess right I'll reward you with a cone. Now would you say I'm selling turf?'

'No. You're selling ice cream.'

'Giving it away I am. Are there no children around here?'

'Not during the summer. They go to their summer houses in Kilkee.'

'And you have no summer house in Kilkee? Here.' And he gave him a cone.

'Thank you. Oh, we have a house. We're going down again tomorrow. I came up with my sister Breda to check. In case it was robbed. I usually come up with my dad when he's checking but Breda had to come up for more clothes.'

'I see. Do you like Kilkee?'

'It's all right.'

'I was never in Kilkee.'

'How were you never in Kilkee?'

'I don't know. I never got around to it.'

'I never heard of anyone who was never in Kilkee.'

'Chris! Chris!'

'That's my sister.'

She was already half-way out the path, walking slowly with her arms inquisitively folded for action, and when she again spoke she looked directly at her brother; Whelan was able to take brief stock. Her long hair was as jet as her brother's, and hung loose.

'Chris, you didn't have any money?'

Hair that could not possibly ever need to be done; a maroon ribbon kept it from her forehead but otherwise the hair had no leash and swished gloriously as her head asked a question. The grey cashmere shirt with the top button opened was a subtle contrast, not only to the ribbon, but also to the triangle of exposed tanned flesh where a tidy medallion reposed; her mini-skirt – now all the rage in Ireland though dying a death where it was born – was also cleverly grey.

'He gave it to me for nothing.'

The insurable legs grew out of maroon sandals but Whelan's inventory was abandoned before he reached them.

'That's nice of you, thank you.'

'Don't mention it.'

His voice might have been what was left over after a day shouting at the races. He realised he was in the presence of the most beautiful woman in the world. Even the way she now prised open her purse and fished in it with two dainty fingers was beautiful.

'I think I'd like one myself. How much are they?'

'This one is on the house.'

'No. Please. You've just given Chris one.'

'Take two, they're small, as the man said.'

'No listen. I insist on paying.'

It had worked with Alvin T. Brine. Whelan tried it again:

'You insist? How's this for insistence. If you don't take this cone for nothing, not only will I not sell it to you, I'll take his back. Now would you do that to a child? Your own brother?'

The girl coloured and went slightly rigid in defeat.

'All right. Thank you.'

'That's all right.'

'Chris, come in soon. It's changing.'

To her back, a pace and about to be a second pace out of his life, Whelan bade: 'Enjoy Kilkee.'

She stopped, turned and glared at her brother: 'Chris. . .' 'Excuse me. Don't blame the child. There's one thing you can be sure of, surer than anything you were ever sure of in your life, I won't rob your house.'

'I wasn't. . .'

'You were. And you were right. Chris, pay attention to your sister. You shouldn't tell every Tom, Dick and Harry that your house is idle. You can tell me because I'm not any Tom, Dick or Harry. But no one else.'

'Thank you again for the cone. I didn't mean to suggest . . .'

'I know that. That's all right. Will you marry me?'

Whelan immediately regretted the four words. Now he was the one colouring but he was saved by the laughter. Chris could not stop himself and in the process drove his sister to giggles. Whelan was able to cloak his confusion by pretending to be hurt.

'Am I really so pathetic that you laugh at me?'

This made the girl worse but she stopped as quickly and said: 'Chris, you be in in ten minutes. We have to be up early tomorrow.'

She ran up the path. The child remained, gazing at Whelan with awe. In the silence Whelan listened to the music; it had been playing all along but he had been listening to a different tune: the sight of a girl who thrilled him.

He asked Chris: 'Is that the radio?'

'That's the record player. She's weird like that.'

It was Liebestraum.

'Weird?'

'She doesn't even like the Beatles.'

Whelan could scarcely believe what the boy was saying. Whelan did not know Liebestraum from Put Another Nickel In – but – she didn't like the Beatles. The only noise Whelan hated more than that of the Beatles was that of Mick Jagger. Tom Mackey's English daughters had been Beatle fans; they wore Mary Quant print dresses that looked as though they cost tuppence ha'penny a dozen from a slot in an off-licence durex machine; their hair was cut short and boyish. Any time Whelan came upon them they were giggling – at him, he was positive. Well, now he was talking to this Chris who had a sister who had hair, clothes, skin and a detestation of the Beatles and asking her brother: 'What's your second name?'

'Matthews. That's my sister's second name too.'

'I wasn't asking your sister's second name at all. What age are you?'

'Ten.'

'When will you be back from Kilkee?'

'Two weeks.'

'I might see you then. No point coming back till then. No children around. I'll move off and make a few bob. Here, you've finished that. Have another.'

'Thank you.'

'And here. Take that one in to your sister. My name's Billy Whelan. And I want you to give her a message for me. Tell her I love her.'

The child laughed.

'Make sure you tell her.'

'I'll tell her.'

'Tell her if she marries me she'll have free ice cream for the rest of her life. So will you.'

Whelan drove back home and sold the remainder of his ice cream in his own neighbourhood. He did not have the heart for work. He rang Anna Roche-Reilly and was pleased and disconcerted to locate her at home. The woman did not seem to have any life.

'Anna? I must tell you what happened to me. I met a girl . . .'

'. . . good for you . . .'

'. . . wait till I describe her first. Wait till I describe her. She has long, jet black hair, her clothes. . .'

'. . . stop. I don't want to listen. If you've found a girl, congratulations. But spare me.'

'Anna, I'm sorry. Forget what she looks like. Forget about her. Let me tell you about me. It's the way I behaved I want to get across to you. What Fart International did for me. Remember I told you how I was trying to pluck up the gall to move out of the ghettos.. ?'

When he finished Anna Roche-Reilly said: 'That's grand if you've only progressed that far. I'm happy again. Matthews. That must be Bob Matthew's daughter. He's the manager of Todds . . .'

'I was there the night Todds burned down.'

'Who wasn't. We haven't had a decent fire since. People have lost their fibre. No one to fight the insurance companies now. I must think of that. Arsonists – in. What do you think? Arsonists in?'

'Definitely. Anna, have I a chance? Will she marry me?'

'I'd say you have a chance. I think I remember hearing somewhere Bob Matthews had an older brother, had to lock him up. . .'

'Anna, please.'

'Anna please, Anna please. You're in love. Good luck to you. Now leave me alone. Do you hear me? Leave me alone.'

Whelan mused into the dead line. What had she been doing? Reading a book? Watching television? It was once a town house, the Georgian building in Barrington Street. Above was let out to a variety of

aged spinster sisters on a long lease. Anna Roche-
Reilly had the ground floors and basement servant
quarters which were short of nothing bar servants. At
the next meeting Whelan would revive the woman.
Until then, it was a tough world for all outside
Fart International. For instance now – outside Fart
International – Whelan acknowledged the impos-
sibility of the situation: she was a daughter of the
manager of Todds, the Harrods of the city compared
to Pnikerettes where he had half a notion Donal
O'Sullivan worked at something or other; Pnikerettes
had a social pigeon hole way below Marks and
Spencer and a bare tit above Woolworths. He tried to
reason: She's a girl, I'm a boy, a cat can look at a king,
and concluded: Says he. It appeared to him that he
would have to pay court in his Fart hat. So be it. He
did not make the world.

Every day he went to a race meeting peddling
sandwiches and milk and sold ice cream in the ghettos
at night. On Sundays he attended the Gaelic Athletic
Association parish matches where he dispensed kiosk
produce. Though he was alarmed at the amount
of money he was earning or because of that alarm,
he lived frugally. He was not obliged to contribute
much money to the household as his mother was still
in her old job in the clothing factory. Because of the
nature of his occupation he patronised neither hat-
ter nor tailor; his tattered rags from the building site
– shorn of alluvia in his mother's breast bone pot –
blended well with the raiment of his fellow hawkers and

proclaimed him innocent in the eyes of the experienced gardai and stewards of any tendency to pluck from his person a folding table, the queen of diamonds and the ten and nine of spades. His gross and net profits might have been indistinguishable were it not for his maintenance of the habit of drinking between six and ten pints a night, every night, seven days a week. Naturally he smoked. There had been Mr Ryan – he would never forget that – there had been Hogan, there was Bill Johnston and A1 Guerrini but though it might have been sacrilege to think it, he thought it, there was above all Arthur Guinness and W.D. & H.O. Wills. As the cursed hour of closing time loomed in public houses the drunken Whelan scooped Breda Matthews up into the passenger seat of his van and chugged off into the – the house in Wellington Avenue where all three of them lived happily ever after.

If Whelan spent little, he maintained a comparatively large pocketful at all times; he setded his purchases in cash. At the end of a week he lodged what he considered weighed down his trousers. G. Ellis tried again to press a cheque book on him but Whelan would have none of it. He had already confounded G. Ellis and banking practice in general by refusing to have the term loan repayment taken from his account in the normal manner. He presented himself at the hatch dutifully on the first of every month and from his back pocket withdrew the repayment and handed it to the cashier.

G. Ellis said: 'It's much simpler the other way.'

'But wouldn't you charge me a bob for a transaction like that?'

'Well a bob isn't exactly . . .'

'To you it mightn't be. To me it is.'

Whelan would not accept a receipt and refused to allow the bank to post him a statement either of his deposit account or the term loan account. But once a month he demanded to see his money; his initial request had been to see the cash physically. G. Ellis directed him to the manager. John Harnett, Whelan was forced to concede, produced a stroke.

'You want to see your money in a drawer with your name on it? As though it were your cake in the Home Crafts Exhibition?'

'Exactly. You're a very understanding man.'

'Well, what about you showing us our money – the balance on the term loan – in a drawer with our name on it.'

John Harnett did not smirk. He waited as though the hawker might make him draw again from the deck. Whelan could not top him.

'Well done. But I won't accept receipts and you can't send me statements. You may show them to me. I won't handle them. You hold them up so I can see them.'

John Harnett thought. Whelan waited for the manager to fall into the Catch 22 situation where Whelan was prepared to fool's mate him.

But John Harnett, to Whelan's delight, said: 'As you wish.'

Only once did the manager refer to the fifteen thousand dollars lying fallow in the Fart International current account.

'You still intend to let that money just lie there?'

'Yes.'

A postal order to the value of one pound was sent to the box number in the *Chronicle* from a subscriber whose address was another box number c/o the *Chronicle* and sought details. Whelan did not reply. By-passing G. Ellis, he lodged the pound through John Harnett. The Manager's acquiescence in cheering the coach and four through procedure led Whelan to the conclusion that battle was joined. John Harnett asked no questions about Fart International and Whelan offered no information. Both of them were under siege and no man's land was the silence between them.

On the first Friday night in September Whelan forsook the flush pastures of the ghettos to minister to the children now in winter quarters in Roses Avenue and to try and shift the fabulous bird. That was how he could not help thinking of her, his vocabulary and thoughts not entirely free of the vulgar influences of the pre-Fart world. Well-bred, freckled, tanned, groomed and polite, the children queued and paid top price for their cones. Chris Matthews brought up the rear, his money in a tentative grasp. Decisively Whelan accepted the coppers.

'Now, like a good boy, bring this cone in to your sister, compliments of Mr Whippy.'

'She said I wasn't to.'

'She did? Excellent. Tell her I threatened to cut your head off if you didn't. Remember, when Breda has the good sense to recognise what a lovely person I am, you'll be on the free list. Off with you.'

Whelan poised his toe on the accelerator. When she appeared at the door with the cone unlicked he drove off. She had been expecting him and anticipating his ploy of the free cone had warned her brother.

Billy Whelan of Fart International would not have returned again the following night; he would have rested between rounds, given the horse a breather. But it was the other shambles who was in love and on Saturday night when his peal rang out Breda Matthews came to her gate and waited with her arms folded. Whelan concluded: 'Thank you Chris. Now if you'd present this as a token of my affection to your lovely sister.'

She hesitated a moment and glared at her brother's tendering of the cone. Angrily she took the cone from the boy's hand, took two steps towards the wagon on the counter of which she planked the price of the cone and them stormed in to the house. Whelan took a pound note from his pocket and said to the boy: 'Here. It's the policy of Mr Whippy to present a pound to every nine hundred and ninety-ninth customer. Why don't you trot in and tell your sister of your good luck.'

Whelan held his ground. In the doorway appeared Mr and Mrs Matthews, Breda and her sister and Chris and his pound. Whelan began to redden. He was not able for any Mr Matthews who, presumably, would now come out acting his part. But to Whelan's relief it was Breda who emerged from the conclave bearing the rejected pound. He plunged home the advantage before she could get her words in.

'You think now I'm going to congratulate you for not sending your father out to hunt me. Well, I'm not. You get no medals for fighting fair. It's the least I'd expect from a girl I deem worthy of me.'

'It was wrong to give the child that money. Now take it.'

'It was wrong of you not accept the gift of a cone. Take back your cone money and I'll take back my pound.'

'All right. But you'll have to stop this.'

'Stop what?'

'This pestering me. It's not fair.'

'Are you joking? Think of your family. They're peering at us from the doorway. Think of the fun they'll have. "That's Breda's hawker" when they hear my jingle.'

'Please . . .'

'You don't like me. That's it, isn't it? You just don't like me.'

'I don't know you.'

'I don't know you.'

'But . . .'

'But, but. It's the truth. And you'll have to admit this is the truth also: I arrived out here a few weeks ago selling ice cream. The children were on holiday. The one child here, I gave him a present of a cone. I had never seen you or ever heard of you. What did you do? You deserted your classical music to gatecrash your way into my life. And what crime did I commit? I gave you a cone and asked you to marry me. Even after you insinuated I was going to rob your house.'

'It's hopeless. I don't know what to say. No matter what I say . . .'

'I'll have an answer? No. Not necessarily. If you said: Okay, I'll meet you outside Todds tomorrow night at eight, I'd be speechless.'

'And if I don't you're going to come along here every night and send me in free cones.'

'Don't jump the gun. Do you think I have no imagination? The weather's getting chilly. I'm switching over to burgers and chips. By the way, are you with or without onions? Sauce?'

A thousand Christmases alone, hungry in a cold room; a father pulped against a packing plant wall; Higgins, Murphy, Nicky and Mark Brown ignoring the vociferous yet mute appeals of the beggar in soul's garments. What were they? Scratches beside this transfiguration. She could not stop laughing. And she did try to stop. When she almost succeeded she looked at him looking at her lovingly and she laughed again. Whelan had the sense to remain silent. He did not move. His heart was pounding but his apparent calm quietened her. She folded her arms and contemplated the pavement. The smile was still about her lips as a horse is not stopped directly at the winning post. When the smile disassembled she chewed her lower lip meditatively. She did not, as she had already said, know what to say. Whelan did.

'Don't renege on your instinct. Todds. Eight o'clock. Tomorrow night.'

He waited. She cleared her throat and became businesslike.

'Are you a man of your word?'

'Dictum meum pactum.'

'It's far from the stock exchange you are.'

'My God. Are you real there in front of me. You went to school!'

'I'll meet you at Todds at eight o'clock tomorrow night. On one condition.'

'Hey, you're not bringing a pal?'

'One condition: one date. That's all. And you don't sell cones here again.'

'You're on.'

Whelan leaned out of his wagon and raised his clenched hands in the direction of the family in the doorway. Suddenly, not daring to look at her, he muttered good night to Breda and drove away.

Later that night, before he went to the public house to get drunk, Whelan rang Anna Roche-Reilly. They had not had a Fart International meeting since he last rang her and he decided he may as well pile on the agony as he would be reviving her anyway at the next meeting.

'Anna, I have dreadful news for you. Are you sitting down?'

'What's wrong?'

'I have a date with old man Matthews' daughter tomorrow night.'

'Well done. Congratulations.'

'Are you not upset?'

'Why should I be?'

'You know why. You sound positively in good form.'

'Well the truth is, there's a cousin I don't think I mentioned to you. He's not too happy about Smith. He's on his way from Salisbury at the moment. Morgan. I remember him as a child. We've had word that he might stop over in Ireland a month or two while he's taking his bearings. Billy, I have a feeling. Listen, you're the very man. Isn't there some cream or stuff for lips, you know? Would you enquire into that for me . . .'

'Anna, you can't marry a damned cousin!'

'Why ever not?'

'The madness department.'

'Don't be commonplace. Our blood can stand it.'

'But it's giving up. A cousin. Anna think of Fart International. There was no contemplating cousins when you were admitted. But now that you're in your behaviour is subject to strictures, anti-rules. We'll talk about it at the meeting. Do you want to hear how I managed the date?'

'No. Goodbye.'

After four pints the impending date with Breda was no problem. He would charge in and be himself, whoever he was, the mixture as before would do the trick. He tackled the Anna Roche-Reilly/Morgan prospective misalliance. Windy Rhodesians were out. No one should marry them. Flat jockeys were less distasteful. Whelan did not know anyone in the bar. Or in any other bar. He did not have any friends. Murphy and Mark Brown worked out of town, Nicky was God knew where, Higgins and Donal O'Sullivan were ludicrous to contemplate on their own. He had not ever formed an attachment with any of the neighbours' children. It struck him that he must possess the glamour of the orphan, which in a sense he half was. Poor Mr Ryan. Even if Mr Ryan was still alive Whelan could not tell him about Fart International. Mr Ryan would bring the priest around; priests were brought around for less. Whelan had left all his friends behind him in London. Hogan was a friend, long in the tooth for a friend, but a friend; it was not Hogan's fault that he did not have the insight to look out for the dinnerless. He had his own problems. All Whelan's capacity for giving and receiving affection could now be concentrated on Breda Matthews. His thoughts raced ahead of him; the date, the courtship, the honeymoon in a hotel, a hotel like the Sarsfield Arms, T. A. Dufficy. T. A. Dufficy! They had sent Alvin back. They needed a third. Apart from the fact that Whelan was convinced T. A. Dufficy was a ripe candidate, Whelan would have a bar to go to, where he would not be reduced to staring at the ceiling. It would not be breaking a rule to tout T. A. Dufficy for Fart. There were no rules and what there were of anti-rules Whelan made up as he went along. On the sixth point he decided to try and enlist T. A. Dufficy before the next meeting.

The block-long shelter that abutted from Todds' first storey was a contributory factor in the store's posses-sion of a hallowed name as a trysting spot for those of a certain class – the earless. He would have preferred to haul up in the van and take Breda for a drive out the country where they might stop in a quiet boreen where somehow it might happen that he would end up with his arm around her and get a court. But in the matter of transport he was a realist on his first date. He joined the throng respectably distanced from each other and assumed an interest in the window displays. It was five minutes to eight. He was wearing the blue suit in which he had been dressed on his return from London and at eight o'clock he had a red face to go with it. At five past eight, as his fel-low suitors were picked up, linked and had umbrel-las thrust at them and were forced to walk on the outside, Whelan had the feeling that he was being watched and that those who watched him thought: Stood up. At ten past eight he suspected agonisingly that he was indeed stood up. He walked to the next window which was now without a vigil. The female dummies were naked. Whelan crossed the road and slunk in the doorway of Burtons where the dummies wore modest executive suits. His own suit began to feel tight under the armpits and his shirt tight at the neck; a drop of sweat fell from his forehead. He extended the fingers of both hands and was not at all surprised to see them tremble. He began to prepare every kind of vengeance in the event of her not showing up. Go out there on Christmas Night with ice cream. He would be set upon. Find out where she worked, send a youngfella in there with chips at ten in the morning. It was twenty past eight. He crossed back to Todds where he was now the lone sentry and where, at twenty-five minutes past eight, he decided he could not stomach further humiliation and thought of her with old fashioned hatred as he departed. And then from the top window of a bus she called him: 'Billy!'

Flogpot, Hogan had used to call him; his mother and Mr Ryan of course called him Billy; he was Whelan to Higgins, Murphy, Nicky and Mark Brown except when they had wanted something from him – like the *Sunday Times* key to his development as an essayist. That was something to be mulled over a dark pint. He had been walking in a different direction than the arriving bus. He walked back to where it stopped and from out of which emerged a girl who had called him Billy. She was no more beautiful than the night he had first seen her but tonight, she was going out with him, had called him Billy, and it might have been raining angels' caresses so velvet-cushioned and silver-spooned did he feel. Not that the feeling could do anything to prevent: 'Have you no manners? I'm standing here for half an hour.'

'It's a woman's privilege.'

'I beg your pardon?'

'Look, smile. It's supposed to be a date. We're not married yet.'

'Yes, that's in the future. I might be saying the wrong thing but I'll say it and if you think it's the wrong thing tell me; what I'm going to say is: Why are you wearing slacks? You've beautiful legs.'

'I like to wear slacks now and again.'

'And this is either now or again. I see. Where would you like to go?'

'I don't mind.'

'Well, thanks to your privileges we're late for the pictures. What do you usually do when you've had a date and you're late for the pictures?'

'Who said I usually do anything?'

'Let's go for a walk.'

'All right.'

The blue-suited Whelan walked by her side down the town; her hands were thrust into the deep pockets of her three-quarter length slate grey raincoat; she wore a white head scarf and a shoulder bag; the effect was casual, not the type of dress a girl wore to a dance. Whelan had his date and did not know what to say. He did not blame himself, he thought it a fault in the system. Strangers setting out together was a lunatic asylum. There should be some other way, a way that would come easy to him. She was obviously at ease within the system. Qute happy, she appeared to him, to stroll in silence taking in die shop windows, windows with tailors dummies, windows with butcher's meat, windows with novelty toys. Whelan was forced to say: 'How did you know that I don't like dancing?'

'I didn't know.'

'Do you go dancing.'

'Yes.'

'But you didn't want to go dancing with me tonight?'

'I didn't say anything about not wanting to go dancing with you. Where do you get your ideas?'

'I don't have to be Sherlock Holmes to notice that you are premeditatedly dressed after a fashion that precludes the possibility of going to a dance.'

'Tell me two things. First: do you want me to go back home?'

'No.'

'And tell me: how did you become a hawker?'

'Is there something wrong with being a hawker?'

'There is nothing wrong with being a hawker or an undertaker or a gun runner or a priest or a bus driver but it seems to me that's something wrong with you being a hawker.'

'What do you work at?'

'I'm a private secretary.'

'That is a euphemism for work of what nature?'

'It's not a euphemism. I'm secretary to Mr Baggot the gas company engineer if you must know. I'm his only secretary, his private secretary.'

'Do you type?'

The girl did not answer immediately.

'Of course I type.'

'Then you're a typist.'

Now she stopped and faced him with rage in her eyes. But she was immediately disarmed by his pugnacity. She laughed and resumed walking.

'All right. I'm a typist and you're a hawker. So that's setded.'

'No it's not. You're not a typist, I'm not a hawker, your father isn't manager of Todds, you've let yourself be labelled all your life. But there's no need to worry any more about that. I'm here now. To the rescue. Have you gone with many fellows?'

'Hmm. Some.'

'I bet every one of them was a bigger eejit than the chap before him, or after him.'

They were already past the last city bridge. She stopped again and leaned on the parapet.

'You hate yourself.'

'I don't. I love myself. Smoke?'

'No thank you. I don't smoke in the street.'

'What? You don't smoke in the street? Just how much reclamation do I have to do with you. Come on. Tell all. Look, there's people coming. Show us how above the street you are. Kiss me.'

'I'm not in the habit of letting myself be kissed on a first date. If you must know. And definitely not in the street.'

She walked on, Whelan catching up with her, letting the cigarette smoke down his throat to warm his lungs. Soon they would reach Corbally and the river, and the walk by the bank of the river, where there were trees.

'This isn't our first date. It's our last date. By right you should give me all the kisses now that you usually ration out over all your dates with the one chap.'

'How many girl friends have you had?'

'None.'

'Listen, I've answered your questions honestly. Don't cheat. Remember?'

'I have never been out with a girl in my life. I've never kissed a girl, I've never held a girl's hand, no girl has ever called me Billy, the way you did out of the bus. And I thank you for that. Could I hold your hand. Please?'

'You have a novel approach.'

She was gone half a dozen paces when she realised that he was not in step, that he was half a dozen paces behind, standing and gushing from the wound, though he was not as badly cut as he managed to make out.

'I don't have approaches, hackneyed or otherwise. Now look, I don't know what – people – you've known or know, but I'm like that, I'm like the way I say I am, I don't want to sound like a saint because I'm not a

144

saint, I mean, I don't know what I mean, that's the way you have me, what kind of a world is it when you ask to hold a girl's hand – a beautiful girl's hand and the gesture can't be accepted in – in its simplicity?'

Without discussing the itinerary they turned off the road on to the red path that wound with the river towards the swimming baths.

Breda said: 'Sorry.'

'Don't mind me.'

They walked a hundred yards in silence during which Whelan told himself: take her hand, she won't object. He might have been contemplating putting his fist through a jeweller's window such was the knot in his stomach. Awkwardly he touched her hand, held it, and in heaven he walked on with her in silence.

When they reached the swimming baths Whelan said: 'Let's sit down. You can have yourself a cigarette.'

Breda opened her shoulder bag saying: 'I smoke tipped.'

The river was at its widest; the bank at both sides had been municipally tiled and the result christened an open air swimming pool. Whelan remembered being taken there as a child when the river itself was as populated as the Serpentine on a July Sunday afternoon. Now the dressing cubicles were without doors, there was graffiti on the walls, the tang of stale excreta hung in the air.

'This would have been a really beautiful spot if it had been left alone. Or if it had continued to be patronised. I used to live here as a kid.'

'I was never here before.'

Because he had held her hand his enquiry was gentle.

'Were you not? That's strange. How come?'

'We weren't allowed to swim in rivers.'

'Why?'

'Oh, dead dogs and cats. My mother said the river was polluted. Anyway I was practically reared in the sea at Kilkee.'

'I was swimming out in the middle once; and a dead dog did sail by. Funny, I didn't think of the river as being polluted. You don't hear of people swimming here now. It's all indoor. They pay money to swim. They have to take a shower before they swim and after. And wear hats. I've never had a swim in the sea.'

'You serious? Were you never in Kilkee?'

'No. I was very nearly in Kilkee once. I'm glad I wasn't there. Do you know why? If I had gone to Kilkee I wouldn't be here now with you.'

'I don't know how you make that out.'

'I do. I know exactly how I make it out. Higgins, Murphy, Nicky and Mark Brown. Instead of going to Kilkee I went to London. I don't know you well enough. To tell you. It's something I could never tell to a girl whom I wouldn't be taking out again.'

It was the first time he had spoken to her in a tone of voice recognisable to her as that of a human being. He was quiet beside her, his mind obviously wandering, drawing deeply on his cigarette and exhaling through his nostrils as he gazed at the river. She asked him: 'Are you in – in trouble?'

Whelan stood up and ambled to the edge of the baths. Idly he kicked an abandoned mineral can into the water. He had difficulty choosing words to reply.

'Trouble? No. I'm not in trouble. But – wait for this – this is a phrase I bet you never heard before – I'm trying to find myself. How's that for originality?'

'You seem to be mocking yourself when you're not mocking everyone else. Why is that?'

He walked back towards her and sat on the step beneath hers. He pawed the dirt on the tiles with his finger. The dirt was his sand.

'How did you get to like classical music?'

'I've always liked it.'

'Are your parents classical?'

'No. Daddy thinks he is when he recognises Sousa on the radio. I suppose I was no different to anyone else, it was probably the Pathétique.'

'What's that now when it's at home?'

'The Pathétique Symphony. Tchaikovsky. You must have heard that.'

'I haven't. Hum a bit for me.'

'I can't.'

'Why not?'

I'd be embarrassed.'

'I understand. But go on. Hum it. There's no one here but me. I won't laugh. Please.'

She did not so much hum as da-da. Whelan recognised the tune.

'Hey, I know it. I've often heard that.'

'Yes. It's popular.'

'Who's your favourite composer?'

'It depends. On the mood I'm in. Sometimes Chopin, sometimes Wagner. Sometimes it might be Holst.'

'I never even heard of the last chap. It must be wonderful to be able to appreciate classical music.'

'It is. What music do you like?'

'Me? My taste isn't great. I like things like Richard Tauber, Nelson Eddy, I haven't any records, but if they come on the radio I listen. John McCormack. I keep it all quiet of course. I hate the Beatles. I heard you don't like them. Chris.'

'I don't exactly hate them. They're light. And you don't like them?'

'It's their faces I hate. I hate all groups. I can't see how it takes four people to sing a song.'

'Did you never hear of a choir?'

'Did I hear of a choir? Did I, Billy Whelan, hear of a choir? Not that we are accusing the Beatles of constituting a choir. Let them be innocent of something. I'll tell you about choirs. When I was a kid the Brother made us all sing one note: doh. Just doh. He put me to the back of the class with my English book, myself and a few more, and turned the rest into a choir. They won medals and shields for singing, they did. Because I couldn't sing doh and I couldn't even get into the choir let alone win a medal, and a boy

who knew, a boy named Cahill, he said I could sing
better than any of them.'

'Aha. So you have a voice!'

Whelan chuckled. 'I haven't really. I could sing a
ballad now, if there were no high notes or low notes
in it. But I wouldn't want anyone watching me. Or I'd
have to be drunk. I'd start blushing, tears come in my
eyes, my throat just goes dry. Let's face it. I can't sing.'

'Your friend Cahill wasn't a good judge then?'

'Cahill? He was a good judge. A lofty judge. He
was kind to me, Cahill . . .'

What Breda took to be a sob escaped from him.
'What is it?'

'Sorry. I was working in London. With a builder.
Sisk. I was just after collecting my twenty-five notes.
That was fantastic money. No tax, no insurance. I
was on the lump. I went into a workman's caff and
ordered three pork chops, mash and chips and a pint
of milk. When I went there first I couldn't keep down
scrambled eggs. I was thrilled with myself. I'd roll up
my sleeves at night and feel my muscles. I took the
Standard out of my pocket to read while I was waiting
for the order. I was sipping a glass of milk, nursing
it to wash down the food. I can't forget the details.
There it was buried in a small filler column on the
bottom left of the front page. It leapt out at me.
Man Found. A twenty-four year old Irishman, originally from the County of Limerick, believed to have
committed suicide. The reason it was believed he

committed suicide was because the police ruled out foul play and because there was a bullet in his brain and a gun on the floor with his fingerprints on it. In a Chelsea flat, that had a Royal typewriter and four completed manuscripts; and a box of rejection slips, some with the word "sorry" written on them, and a dozen letters all saying the same thing . . . "very much afraid there is a sense of being out of Donleavy" . . .'

'That was Cahill?'

Whelan had his head bent and was rubbing the two indexed fingers of his cupped hands along the sides of his nose into his closed eyes. The gesture was by way of reply as was his nod, his standing up and breathing 'aaah' and walking again to the edge of the baths where he suddenly screamed: 'Jesus! Why Cahill! Jesus!'

He stayed there for a minute; she watched him take out a handkerchief and wipe his eyes. He returned and sat, not on the lower step, but along-side her. He said: 'Forgive me.'

'Forgive you for what?'

'That was uncharacteristic of me.'

'Well if it was, it was delightfully uncharacteristic of you.'

Whelan was at last able to turn and look at her while he spoke. Up to now he gazed over her or at her entirety but now he could look at her eyes. He said: 'Thank you.'

They both turned and fixed their eyes upon the river; the moment, lengthened, ripened, into conditions that could not have been more favourable. He reflected on his outburst and was in an introverted way proud of himself. All he had to do was slowly lift his left hand and bring it smoothly behind her back, gently turn and kiss her. Even though he had managed to grope her hand in his coming out the red path it was too big a step for him to make the inevitable, evolutionary move. Breda waited and waited for him. It was getting dark. Soon it would be so dark that they would not be able to see each other without striking a match. She did not want it to be that dark. She waited. But it was Whelan who said: 'It's getting dark. We better start making a move.'

He stood up and with the cordiality of a bus conductor aiding an old lady on to the vehicle he put out his hand and helped her to rise. He did not retain her hand. They walked slowly along the red path without talking. Whelan crazy with love, Breda unsure.

The red path was bounded on their right by a shoulder high stone wall and on their left by the river and across the river the new houses, some not yet completed, Shannon-banks. Inside the stone wall trees grew protectively screening the grounds of the diocesan college and their branches formed a canopy over their heads. The dim light on their side of the river helped them to spot the low branches; they stretched their hands out in front of them to keep the overhung growth from their eyes. They did not speak until the path turned with the river and they were directly opposite the houses the lights from which flickered in the water. Whelan stopped and bore witness to the scene.

'You know, there are people who probably consider that scenic.'

Breda had been considering the lights in the water scenic. An odd fear drove her not to take issue with him, a fear not so odd when suddenly there came another outburst, an angry roar, not a plea for an explanation:

'VANDALS!'

The cry was not out of the same stable as his agonising wail for Cahill; it was self-indulgent. He knew it and knew from her silence that she probably thought it so. They were back on the road leading to town. The night was proceeding fitfully, the surges of happiness within him alternating with panic-stricken groping to find some way of impressing her. It was no more than the time honoured brittle détente of any romance at its preliminary best and worst. Breda had been there before. Not each and every one a bigger eejit than his successor or predecessor, as Whelan had, typically, she now realised, maintained but all much of a much. Norman had – after three months during which she had been unable to clarify her feelings towards him – Norman had suddenly put his hand underneath her dress while they kissed near the ESB pole less than ten yards from her house. He rang her and rang her afterwards, sent her notes, accidentally-on-purpose bumped into her on the street; she remained obdurate. Now, as it was brought home to her that the totally unsuitable hawker by her side was beyond contemplation of indecency, she forgave all the doubts that had lingered about the righteousness of what she thought was her prudery. Norman was not an eejit; neither was he for her. There was a time and a place for everything, her instinct advised, yes, she had lain awake in bed dreaming ambivalently of what intercourse must be like, she traded speculations with the girls in the office – the way he had latched on to the private secretary appellation, she would tell him if it ever came up again that she had to do the corporation exam and come first that year because of the one and only vacancy – there was a time and a place . . . She heard the bus a hundred yards behind him and suggested: 'There's the bus. Will we get the bus?'

'All right.'

They crossed to the bus stop. The 'all right' had been almost gruff. She hoped he did not think she was precipitating an end to the night as she had once done with one of the eejits who had taken her walking in another direction. That eejit had in common with Whelan a total gaucherie in courtship but did not have the redeeming feature of shouting 'Vandals!' Though they sat downstairs Whelan lit a cigarette. He said 'Todds' to the conductor and paid for them both. Breda was at ease; they still had a long walk ahead of them from Todds to Roses Avenue; she would not ask for a second bus. Because of the people and the lights in the bus there was no obligation to talk; only lovers at an advanced stage spoke, whispered on populated buses, she knew from her experience with another eejit. Whelan was angry. But he was done with begging. He might never have been with a girl before, never kissed a girl, but he could interpret demands for buses as well as the most jaded practitioner. He clung to the one hope – that she might not bring down the curtain at Todds and leave him like a spumed uppity camel while she saw herself home. Blushing, and he could not summon the effort to try and camouflage it, he stood up as the bus eased to a halt outside Todds, and allowed her precede him.

'I don't know when I was on a bus last,' Whelan choked as he landed on the pavement.

'I cycle to work when it's fine. I thought by getting this bus if we walked the rest of the way I wouldn't be too late getting home.'

'What hour is Cinderella expected?'

'Unless I'm going dancing Daddy expects me home straight after the pictures; he doesn't approve of going into cafés late at night.'

'Why is that?'

'Daddy says it's cheap . . .'

'My God . . .'

'. . . and you can make what you like out of it.'

'Aha! Temper. You like your dad then?'

They crossed the road and rounded Burton's corner.

'Yes. I like my dad. Don't you like your dad?'

'When I was eight years old my father was at his job; he had a cigarette butt on his ear. He worked in the cement factory, in the packing plant. The butt fell off his ear on to the track. Wham! A wagon plastered him to the packing plant wall . . .'

'I'm sorry.'

'I've heard people say things were bad then. No jobs. Emigration. Before Lemass. But my God when I think of it. That bad! Dying for the butt of a cigarette.'

'I didn't realise, I'm sorry. You were only eight?'

'Yes. But wait now. I won't have you marrying me because I was half-orphaned at eight. If you insist on marrying me do it for my lack of money or for my social graces or the quaint way I cough after a cigarette. Listen, can I hold your hand again?'

They were almost across Sarsfield Bridge. The lighting in the river beneath them Whelan found scenic, the more so when she smiled and ceremoniously extended her hand. As they walked on Breda said: 'So you really never were out with a girl before?'

'No.'

'Well, what's it like for the first time?'

Whelan stopped. 'You have to ask me? Well – it beats – it beats – what – what does it beat – I don't know how to say it – I haven't got the words.'

'You haven't the words?'

The three storied red-bricked houses of the Ennis Road with their poplars and elms guards of honour to the driveways provided Breda with words: 'When I was a kid we used to joke: the Ennis Road, where they

155

can get the dinner in the letter-box, sausages, fur coat and no – no – knickers . . .'

'You're indelicate. I'm surprised at you. But there's a thought: No messenger boys nowadays. When did you last see a messenger boy? There was a shop near me, Lil Dwyer's, all her messenger boys were given this long raincoat, apart from the bike, I remember this character, we used to wait for him to throw his leg over the bike, he had no pants . . .'

'. . . I don't believe . . .'

'I could swear. Today where are they? You know where messenger boys are today? Wearing white coat tops in lounges bringing around trays of drinks to people too lazy to get up and go to the counter. It's against nature, a Celt waiting for drink to be brought to him.'

'You go from one subject to another.'

They were at the Union Cross traffic lights.

'I say the first thing that comes into my head.'

'Like 'vandals'. Or will you marry me.'

Whelan did not have an immediate reply. He decided to maintain an eloquent silence. It would puzzle her, his walking and not talking. She would examine her conscience to see how she might have offended him. She did no such thing. She was totally preoccupied, now that there was less than two hundred yards to the turn into Roses Avenue, with what she wanted to happen. She was not sure what she wanted to happen. She wanted, on the one hand, to have done with the whole business, go in home, her hands washed of the hawker. And, desperately, she did not want to say or do anything that would hurt him. The way he held her hand was foreign to her experience. He did not squeeze it; it was like the prolonged grasp of football captains grimly accommodating a butterfingered photographer. She would have been more relaxed with her hands in her pockets; it was unnatural to be so clinically attached to him. And yet if she withdrew her hand he would take it as a spit in the eye. They turned the corner.

'Landed,' Whelan forced out of a dry tongue.

'Yes.'

Whelan had to reach for his cigarettes. Their hands had become unclasped of their own volition as the gates of Breda's house drew near. Whelan exhaled a jaunty: 'A pity, this lovely road will no more resound to the magical chimes of Mr Whippy, the children's friend. The little children. Learning what a tough, coneless world it is. What?'

'Yes.'

'You had better be getting in. Your father will be tolling the knell or whatever. Long live Dickens. I'll say goodbye.'

'Goodbye. Thank you for the night.'

'Not at all. Thank you.'

'Goodbye.'

'Goodbye.'

He was leaning against the pole, three feet from where she was propped cross-ankled against her own gate. And though they had twice said goodbye he continued to look at her with the hunger of an urchin, an urchin so accustomed to his state that he would stare suspiciously at a proffered cake. Quickly Breda took three steps towards him and planked the hint of a kiss on his lips. She ran along the pathway. Whelan put his arms around the pole and hugged it. He had no idea how long he stayed there or of what he dreamed. He unwound himself as the music began to leak out of the house. It was the Tchaikovsky thing she had da-dahed for him out in the baths. Something gnawed at Whelan as he trotted in the road. He had a girl, of that he was positive, she would see him again, he did not know about peddling his ice cream in Roses Avenue, he would not mind about that, it was not seemly to hawk in his sweetheart's neighbourhood, or was it? That was not what itched him. It was not until he was at home in bed and trying to sleep that he identified the scratch: he had had no drink that night.

He was up at six in the morning to drive to the bakery and intercept a milkman. He was delirious at his good form. They would hear shouts at the races that day unrivalled by all the throaty timbres of the McCarthys and the Sheridans put together. He did have a good day at the races, selling out long before the bumper, and that night sold ice cream to the issue of homes that had doubtful dinners that day and where the fathers were counting the pennies to make up the entrance fee to the pubs. He was in a rare mood to take on T. A. Dufficy. Whelan changed into his blue suit; changing into it so soon after changing into it to meet Breda made him think that he would have to see about another suit or a jacket and trousers. He had been offered everything from a colour television set to a carpet during his hawking at the race meetings. He thought perhaps if he let his measurements and taste in tweed be known that something might come of it. In that regard he had no conscience. He did not make the world.

At half past nine on a Monday night the Sarsfield Arms was quiet. Whelan did not need to ask for a normal pint. He discovered that T. A. Dufficy did not believe in the cooler. An otherwise inoffensive middle-aged gentleman had politely asked in Whelan's hearing: A cold pint please. T. A. Dufficy had said: Certainly sir, drawn the pint and enquired mildly of the gentleman as he brandished the ice cube tongs: One lump or two? Maureen, the barmaid, served Whelan. She was a hefty woman whose hair was probably black originally but was now certainly dyed black. It was difficult to tell from her prominence what was chest and what was muscle. She had the build that gave Whelan bad thoughts. It was in the middle of the bad thoughts that Whelan noticed T.A. idling around, picking up a pair of empties, overturning ashtrays. He disappeared out the door to Whelan's left and reappeared through the door at Whelan's right. He came inside the counter and said goodnight to Whelan and rinsed glasses under the tap. Whelan began: 'Is the Blue Room engaged by any chance?'

'The Blue Room? The Blue Room. I don't think so. I'll consult my diary.'

T. A. Dufficy extracted from his inside pocket a pathetic looking penny notebook and declared: 'You're in luck. The Blue Room is free.'

'Thank you. Would you put my drink through the hatch for me? And I'd like the table and chair.'

'Splendid. Do you anticipate . . . will there be many . . .'

'I'm not expecting anyone,' Whelan declared, achieving a tautness at the corner of his mouth that he was proud of. He went and stood outside the Blue Room. T. A. Dufficy produced the table and chair. Whelan sat and drummed his fingers on the table.

'You say you're not expecting – anybody? Nobody?'

'That's right. The room will cost three pounds?'

'I'm afraid so.'

'I hadn't thought of that. You see, I only decided to hold a meeting on the spur of the moment. If nobody comes – and as I say I'm not expecting anyone – if nobody comes and I decide not to enter the Blue Room – c ould you not see your way to just renting the table and chair for, for ten, fifteen minutes, or till whenever the mood passes?'

'I suppose I can accommodate you in that respect.'

'You know it would actually pay you to sit in yourself; cost you thirty bob, I'd pay thirty bob, you'd get die three quid for the room, you could pay yourself back and have a profit of thirty bob. And it would satisfy your curiosity.'

'But I have none.'

It's against the anti-rules of Fart International to solicit but to hell with the anti-rules. Come on in. Let me get you a drink.'

'I don't know.'

'Mr Dufficy – please?'

'I suppose I don't see why not.'

'Good man.'

Whelan closed the door of the Blue Room after them. He directed T. A. Dufficy to a seat; Whelan might have been the hotel proprietor. He sat at the top and said: 'I forgot to get you that drink.'

'Just as well. I don't drink on duty. When I start drinking I like to stay at it. I'm not a nibbler.'

'Of course. I'll begin.'

Whelan told him everything there was to know about Fart International that Whelan thought he should know. He finished: 'You see my problem. With Alvin returned to the States I'm short of a third – a suitable third – so that Anna Roche-Reilly will not be distracted by my charms, especially now, you see I'm practically affianced. I'm sorry I have not the dollar with me. I know the ballad. But one without the other isn't the same thing. Don't you agree.'

Whelan thought for a moment that Dufficy was asleep. He was a cadaverous six foot three, dressed in a brown suit inside which he sported a beige cardigan limply wooden-buttoned. Whelan was not a brown man but he conceded that Dufficy was at least a brown man of a bygone taste – the shoes were brown brogue and the socks and cardigan beige. Dufficy's chin rested on his chest but his eyes were open; but people were famous for sleeping with their eyes open.

'Ah, Mr Dufficy? Mr Dufficy?'

'Very interesting.'

'You find it interesting? Good. Now tell me. Have you a contribution?'

'A contribution?'

'Tupperware, silver-devon bait, you know?'

Dufficy allowed his chin to drop but maintained a creased forehead. It was obvious that the man was in thought. Whelan waited and was rewarded.

'People who don't open envelopes.'

'People who don't open envelopes?'

'The letter lies on the table. Now I'm talking about an opened letter. They lick their lips, they to, they fro. They are indecisive. Morality gets the better of them. They spend the rest of their lives wondering. I'm not even talking about those people ! But the letter that requires the steam of the kettle – Watt might have laboured in vain – they are out !'

Whelan could scarcely believe his ears. He realised Anna Roche-Reilly or Alvin for that matter would never go along with it, but to Whelan it was magical stuff.

'T. A., brilliant. Am I to take it you're with us?'

162

Dufficy might indeed not have heard. He began to gush: 'I bought this damn place twenty years ago. Didn't know a hotel from an ostler's. I hired a young chap in striped pants; from a hotel management training course. He'd been to Switzerland. I had an incredible touch the year Pas Seul took the Gold Cup. I'd always wanted to do nothing so I bought the hotel. I followed this chap in the trousers around for a year with my tongue out. The little bollix patronised me because he knew one chef from another. I had to keep him for another year. Mercifully an opening turned up in Killarney. He said, the day he was leaving, he said: I'll keep my eye out for a good man for you. The little bollix. The last I heard he was managing the Gresham or was it the Dorchester? Anyway I set to. Now I realise what I was doing was trying to run the place into the ground. If I hadn't stopped short of commercial travellers I would have. But they came and they came and continued to come and some of them said: Nice place, Dufficy. Homely. Keep it up. Every place antiseptic these days. You can imagine them? During Clounanna or is it Clonmel, I'm never sure which, you wouldn't get a straw in here, jodhpured shrieking about brindled bitches, florid brandishing of brandy, only they don't call it brandy, they don't call it Hennessy: Another large Hen, Doris . . .'

Whelan did what was foreign to him in such a situation: he laughed. But T. A. Dufficy ploughed on heedless.

'. . . I hide nowadays. I flit. Maureen looks after everything, the kitchen, the stocks. I make the policy decisions – the availability of the Blue Room, the abandonment of the commercial rate – some people look at me as though I'd gone off the gold standard – but the large Hens love it. Maureen is the nerve centre. I made no mistake the day she said yes. . .'

'Oh. Maureen is Mrs Dufficy?'

'A wizard – a wizardess behind the bar. None better. . .'

'. . . I've noticed. How did you – if I'm not intruding – what was she . . .'

'A barmaid.'

'Oh. I see.'

'I've never regretted it. The large Hens ogle her arse when she turns round and it runs off me. Good filly you have there, Dufficy. But I have my day. The things I know. I see to the mail personally. It only takes an hour in the morning and an hour in the afternoon. They're threatening to do away with the Saturday post I see, as if Sunday wasn't a drag as it is. But we'll motor on. Something will turn up. The postcards of course are no problem, or the bills. Getting up steam is the great challenge. You wouldn't know what you'd find. I hope you realise that I would never touch money. Not that you'd see any of it these days. The postmen are not trusted. I remember as a child reading about a postman who was in the appropriation business. It was front page news in all three dailies. Could you imagine that today? But *then* – the little bollix was just gone. I didn't need him anyway, Maureen had started behind the counter, there was a fiver in this letter, I forget the gory details, enclosed five pounds all I can manage for the moment, there's been so many letters I can't remember, but I do remember adding a fiver of my own to the enclosure and watching the puzzled face at breaskfast. But where does one stop? I had the room next to the bridal suite converted to an office. My office. I made the hole in the wall myself, the wardrobe covers it in the bridal suite and of course it's papered. I remember a couple, they pulled up outside in a car with cans tied to it. I exchanged a few words with them at the register. They were common enough. I would say he was a factory worker. They went upstairs at eight o'clock and didn't appear till lunch next day. You never heard such energy. Even today I can stand upsides with my peers but those two were out of my class. I thought it might have been the changing times, began to wonder had I the misfortune to have arrived too soon, but no, subsequent vigils confirmed that they were champions and cuts above their own generation. But towards the end of the week they began to talk. Talk. Of money. I'd catch snatches: . . . what are we going to do? . . . I don't know. We'll just have to leave a day early. I hate the thought of facing the long get of a manager . . . I don't know how you talked me in to going to Bunratty Castle for that meal. Seven quid. . .

'Oh yes. The early days. For them and for me. I often wondered how they fared. The next day, first of all I managed to persuade myself that I had never seen the tin cans tied to the car or the confetti or the newness of her overcoat or their suitcases. I glided by at dinner and whispered: Pardon the interruption but is it true? The porter informs me that you are on your honeymoon. That's right, grumpily. A long get he had called me. First of all let me offer my congratulations. But you should have told me. Imagine if you had gone off. I would never forgive myself. Of course they're mystified. It's the policy of the hotel to honour newly weds. Now, if you'd be so good, take your time, after the meal, would you join me in my office? For the brief ceremony. It was Maureen's office, naturally. How I managed it I don't know but I managed it. One hundred pounds I managed to persuade them to accept on the understanding, the strict understanding that Mrs Dufficy was not to know, the porter was not to know, it was a tradition handed down by my father and his father. The sum was not significant to many people but was only intended as a gesture – and so on and so on. I tell you love was made that night. . .'

T. A. Dufficy did not so much conclude as peter out. His chin remained on his chest but his forehead relaxed. He appeared to Whelan to muse whimsically.

'Do you know,' Whelan offered, 'that I believe you.'

'Is that a fact. Is that a fact now.'

'Tell me. What were you before you had the click at Cheltenham?'

T. A. Dufficy took his time. 'A draper,' he admitted lamely.

Whelan could not resist: 'I wouldn't have thought you the cut of a draper somehow. Was it in the family?'

'You jest. What was in the family was a desire to eat. I would remind you that a position in the House of Burton was sought after in those days. You could tell an educated man by the tape around his neck. I haven't bought a garment in five years. Luckily I had a decent wardrobe. I look after it. I have to. I dropped into Montague's a year ago with half a notion to buy. I was not encouraged. I found my own way downstairs. There was a drawing of a pop singer on the wall. The lighting was dim. It might have been a picture house. Two girls – *girls* in Burton's – were playing noughts and crosses. The Drapers' Club is still there of course. Staggers on from lease to lease but the end can't be far off. We've had to close the membership. All ex now. If I might so put it. Certainly no o's. But that's neither here nor there. I was, originally, a draper.'

'This horse – Pas Seul – he coughed up enough to buy a hotel?'

'Again I would remind you. We were outfitters to gentlemen and their sons. Pas Seul was the coup de grace. Gentlemen – and their sons – are privy to information, information they are gentlemanly enough to share with their tailors. I was the victor in many skirmishes with the turf up to then. I plunged all on Pas Seul. You see – I wanted to become a class of a gentleman myself. Isn't it odd? I can't shake the habit of being privy to information. When my watch stops and I need to know the time I can't even ask Maureen. I stroll around, my ears pricked, till I hear something of the nature of: Good fuck, it's ten past four. Three quarters of an hour later I might be conjuring: it must be near five, it seems like three quarters of an hour since I heard Good fuck it's ten past four. I'm trying to preserve something and I don't know what it is by receiving information indirectly. . . . So there you have me..

'Mr Dufficy, T.A., for my part, and my part is the only part of consequence, I would be honoured if you would join us. People who don't open letters. Up the covert. I would love to have thought of it myself. I can tell Anna Roche-Reilly – you're with us?'

'I would prefer to become an associate.'

'Meaning?'

'I wouldn't actually come into the Blue Room to a meeting. I'd like to be at the hatch – listening.'

More than Anna Roche-Reilly or Alvin T. Brine, more than Whelan himself, Whelan thought, more than Bill Johnston or Al Guerrini, T. A. Dufficy was so worthy a candidate that it was fitting his involvement would not get beyond the peripheral. Whelan nodded slowly.

'All right. One thing. We'll continue to pay for the rent of the room. I insist.'

'And so do I, Mr Whelan. So do I.'

Chapter Nine
The Dinner

'. . . and so if we never forget that the boys of today are the men of tomorrow . . .'

The collective gratitude at the release was reflected in the volume of applause. There was mild panic then at the sight of Brother Hennigar rising again; but it was only to lead the assembly in grace after meals. This was followed by the shuffling of chairs, the rejoining of groups and repairing to the bar. Desperately, Whelan manoeuvred himself into the driving seat: 'What are you having Nicky? Murphy. What'll I get you Higgins?'

'All right Billy, I'll get it.'

'No. What is it?'

'No, no. I'll get it. I'm drinking brandy. Twouldn't be fair.'

'No matter. Large or small? Have the large. It isn't often we get together.'

'Murphy, grab that corner before it's taken. Come on, Nicky, you can help bring down the drinks.'

T. A. Dufficy allowed his eye to be caught: 'And yours, sir?'

'A large brandy, a Jameson, a lager, and a pint, please.'

Whelan handed the spirits to Nicky and remained at the counter for the draught. Timmy Roberts was shouting to someone – Whelan presumed it was to someone: Drink that and we'll have the crack. T. A. Dufficy raised his eyes in the direction of the chemist who experdy passed drink from the counter with his one hand over the heads of josders. 'Now, sir,' T. A. Dufficy said as he put the pint and the lager on the counter. Whelan's hand shook as he lifted the drink. He looked at the proprietor. T. A. Dufficy was rinsing a glass and staring over Whelan's head. But Whelan was in no doubt that T.A. was aware of the shake in the hand and the dreadful sweat on his brow. The conversation had not yet got going when Whelan joined them in the corner. Whelan sat down, gave Nicky his lager, took a large mouthful from his pint and heard Murphy say: 'What did you think of the meal?'

He's addressing me, Whelan thought. Not Higgins or Nicky. Me.

'I thought it was a fine meal. Especially . . .'

'. . . the soup was cold.'

Whelan's soup had not been cold; certainly not by Whelan's lights. Maybe the soup was cold – as dinners went. Whelan did not know. He was a stranger to functions. What he did know he expressed to himself inwardly: Fuck you Higgins, could you not let me finish. I bought the drinks – in any civilised company that bought respect – you uncivilised fucker.

Higgins recalled the meal at the met dinner while he juggled his brandy and cigar. Nicky and Murphy listened attentively and Whelan might have been listening just as eagerly such was his pose. But he was in fact thinking that he would give the night another half hour and then vanish. The respectful silence that followed Higgins' eulogy to the fillet steak was broken inappropriately by Nicky who had so much to catch up on.

'That was sad about Cahill.'

'It was sad,' agreed Murphy.

'Poor bastard.' Higgins momentarily fooled Whelan. 'But in a way, when you think of it, you could almost see it coming.'

'What do you mean?'

'The way he used to carry on at school.'

'Yeah.' Murphy's ruminative assent outraged Whelan but he managed to hold his tongue.

'What really happened I wonder? Did anyone ever find out? I remember I was in Maynooth.'

'The paper said . . .'

'. . . don't mind the papers. I'd say there was drugs involved.'

'Cahill?'

'Yeah. Someone told me once, I forget who, someone told me he was knocking around with a queer crowd. Poets and fucking eejits like that. Long-haired beatniks. You know the way they carry on. Actually the last time I met Cahill his hair was down to his arse. And that was a good two years before he killed himself.'

'But did he kill himself? The paper just . . .'

'Don't mind the papers.'

'Where was I then? Oh, yeah. I was in the Middleton branch. Wasn't there something about a poetry book he was writing tom to bits beside his typewriter. . .?'

'He was always a nut at writing. Remember he used to write two compositions, one to hand up and a different one for himself. Can you imagine that? And the rest of us murdered trying to fill two pages of foolscap. He had too much brain. Remember, Billy? The way he used to do two comps? Hey! You were knacky at those comps too now that I remember.'

The mounting anger in Whelan subsided. 'That's right. He always did the comp twice. He was brilliant at latin too. And science. He went mad altogether about science . . .'

'Yeah. Still, it's sad. Poor eejit like that.'

'He wasn't an eejit! '

'Well, I know he wasn't an eejit in that sense. Okay, he had brains. But he was odd, right? Can you imagine a fella – remember Murphy, Nick? – we were in the final, the Brother asked how many were going to the match – can you imagine it? – first chance of the Harty Cup in twenty years – there was some-one, who was he? from the country – Hynes – it was Hynes, another oddball, his mother was dying and he couldn't go, but Cahill! Naturally, the Brother asks him why he isn't going and what does Cahill say? Remember? He says: I haven't the remotest interest,

Brother! I don't know how the Brother didn't beat the shit out of him.'

'I thought he was the nicest fella I ever met in my life.'

'Come off it, Billy. I know we shouldn't speak ill of the dead but don't go overboard. Although you did get on with him. Often saw you talking to him. What kind of fella was he really? You know? What was he really like?'

Whelan might not have bothered had only Higgins been in search of truth, which Whelan was sure Higgins certainly was not. But Nicky and Murphy were looking at him with a glimmer of respect. Whelan tried to do justice to a life.

'All right. You remember he was an oracle since he came to the school at ten? English, Irish, history, maths and latin? He had brains. When we came to science he switched – switched faculties as it were. It's as though, I think – I think he was looking for the truth and thought it must have been in science. Because that's what he did at Uni. B.Sc. Now I'm only conjecturing. But first, I remember he showed me a thing he wrote after he had asked me did I ever hear of Donleavy whom I naturally hadn't heard of then . . .'

'Who's Donleavy?'

Whelan loved Murphy for answering: 'Higgins, you must have heard of Donleavy? *The Ginger Man*? The fella in the train with his tool hanging out?'

'So years later, say gone off science, there's these letters from agents found . . .'

'. . . Hey! There's Mark! Mark! Mark! Over here.'

Afterwards Whelan imagined they stood up and cheered but he reasoned with himself that they could not have cheered, not with other people around, not in their mid-thirties. Certainly they were up from their seats shaking hands and thumping on the shoulder while Whelan stared at a bullet ridden head bloodily slumped on a wreck of a typewriter. He did remember clearly Higgins' proxy hospitality:

'What are you having, Mark? Murphy, get a drink for Mark.'

They were standing in a circle of three – Higgins, Nicky and Mark Brown while Murphy went to the bar and Whelan remained seated, his presence shielded by Higgins' back. Mark Brown told them what delayed him:

'. . . just outside the Curragh. Of all nights. I had Ann-Marie with me and Jason and Robert. If I was on my own I could have ditched it but with the kids – Jason's only just over measles – so – hello there Billy, didn't see you there. Didn't see you for years! What are you doing with yourself? You went abroad or something?'

Whelan stood up and gratefully accepted the out-stretched hand.

'Hello Mark.'

'. . . he sells bananas.'

'. . . ha, ha. What are you doing though, Billy? I know what the rest of this shower are up to. How're die pagans, Nick?'

'I'm a hawker.'

'No kidding.'

'If you ask me it's back to the pagans I came. No religion I'm told.'

'Hah, hah! Good old Nicky. I think I owe you a letter. Sorry about that. But what are you really doing, Billy? I haven't seen you since we left school.'

'I'm really a hawker.'

'Like at matches?'

'Yeah. And race meetings.'

'That's fabulous! I bet you're cleaning up.'

'I'm making a few bob.'

'Fair play to you. Yeah. What are we standing up for. Let's sit down.'

Mark Brown sat with his back to the wall, Nicky and Higgins on either side of him. Whelan sat on a small stool on the opposite side of the small table, facing them. Murphy arrived with Mark Brown's brandy.

'Thanks, Murph. Where was I?'

'. . . the car broke down.'

'Yeah. I'm raging over that. Of all the bloody nights. Bastard in the garage robbed me of course. I know, company's worry but still, you'd hate to be done. What could I do? If I hadn't Ann-Marie and the kids I'd have let him have it, thumbed down. Anyway we got here. Better late than never. Higgins, you should see Robert. You'd think the hurley grew out of him. Good crowd here. Well, fill me in. What's happeneing?'

'. . . we were just talking about Cahill.'

'Cahill? Oh, Cahill! Yeah, poor Cahill. I'd almost forgotten. He stabbed himself, didn't he?'

'. . . shot himself.'

'Shot himself. That's what I meant. You know, I bet it happens in every class. I bet if you examined every class from every school you'd find, you know, a bank manager, someone in the Met, a priest and so on, and someone who stabs himself . . .'

'You're probably right there, Mark.'

'Higgins, I think you're putting on a bit. Are you not playing squash?'

'I can't play it as often as I should. They should have closed it years ago. You've to book a week ahead. Are you playing it much?'

'Oh, yeah. Every day. One hour. It pays off. Look, there's Brother Hennigar. I didn't realise he was still alive. I must go over and say hello. Listen Higgins, here, get a round and get me another brandy. I'll only be a sec.'

While Higgins went to the counter and Nicky and Murphy were exchanging: Mark's keeping fit isn't he? He is mind you, Whelan realised that Cahill, as a topic, was dead. He watched the ease with which Mark Brown brought himself to the attention of the old Brother. Mark Brown had not grown an inch since Whelan had last seen him at school. He was still six foot three. His hair was black, combed forward now and without the parting. He wore a dark green pull-over with a patch on both shoulders after the current para-military fashion; it was a neat fit and emphasised that he played squash for an hour every day; if his grey slacks were any lighter they would have been white. His shoes were of a brown so dark as to be mistaken for black in dim light and they were brogue. It was altogether an outfit Whelan could not help admiring, though an outfit he did not have the character to don himself. And from the way he stood Whelan was certain he did not smoke. The thought of Mark Brown smoking a cigarette was as hard to conjure as Higgins in a study wearing thick-rimmed glasses and browsing through his John Donne. 'That's fabulous' Mark Brown had said. 'Hello there, Billy, didn't see you there.' Billy. Billy. Whelan had made a mistake, that summer, in approaching Higgins and Murphy and Nicky. He should have gone directly to Mark Brown. Mark Brown was innocent. Had Mark Brown known . . .

Mark Brown did not rejoin them in the sec he had promised. Whelan watched him shaking hands with the one-armed Timmy Roberts and heard Timmy Roberts': Sure Mark Brown. You were a good one. Ye were great lads. No one came after ye since.

Whelan admired the way Mark Brown knew everyone. Whelan told himself that he too would have known them all had he stayed, known more of them than Higgins. The Met, with that shift work, had not been a decent target. Whelan had the Junior Ex in his sights and was by no means aiming above himself. The Met would have been a terrible come down. Higgins arived with the drinks and Mark Brown's change.

'That's Mark's change. Watch that.'

'Did you get me a pint?'

'What? Jeez, sorry Billy. What's a pint? Here, hop up there and get it out of the quid. Sorry about that. I was concentrating on the spirits.'

The turmoil at the counter had by now eased; the post was manned by T. A. Dufficy alone, Maureen having returned to the lounge upstairs to keep a sharp eye on the part-timers. Whelan said: 'A pint.'

'Who's the big lad in semi-mufti that joined you?'

'That's Mark Brown.'

'Ah! I thought so. I checked in the cloakroom. He deposited a windcheater. What's with this one pint?'

'Mark Brown gave Higgins the money to buy a round. Higgins forgot the pint.'

'Listen. They're all upstairs. Anna and company . . .'

'They're twenty-four hours early.'

'No. I rang them. I told Anna spread the word. Now listen, we're all cheering for you. Higgins and that Mark Brown, their brandy. I can hardly go as far as poisoning them, but what would you like me to do? I could water it.'

'T.A., you have it wrong. Mark Brown's okay. And Higgins – I know he forgot my pint – but forget about that. He really forgot . . .'

'. . . Why don't you duck up to the lounge and draw strength from die crowd?'

'No. I don't need Fart tonight. I must do this on my own. I think I went off on a wrong track all those years ago. Mark Brown is a gentleman, T.A., I could swear it.'

T. A. Dufficy put the pint in front of Whelan. Mechanically he accepted the pound and placed the change beside the pint. He took a cloth and swabbed the counter and, not taking his eyes from his swabbing, hissed: 'Get a grip on yourself!'

Chapter Ten
Paul Tindall

Driving to Mallow races the day after enlisting T. A. Dufficy, two days after being kissed by Breda Matthews outside her house, Whelan felt an acute sense of loneliness, the lack of a confidant. He had so much to report. His brain was awhirl with a kaleidoscope of happy thoughts. It had been such a short time since he was cold, hungry and alone on Christmas Day; now he was making money hand over fist at a job that was derisively unsuitable and he was growing to love the job more and more each day just because of it; Fart International was proceeding beyond his expectations; he was in love with a girl beyond anyone's expectations and he suspected the devotion was reciprocated if not exactly with the same intensity, yet. He decided to pour his whole soul out to Bill Johnston in a missive that night. Having had Fart International to occupy him the day before – specifically the recruitment of T. A. Dufficy – Whelan had been able to tactically refrain from ringing Breda Matthews. Now he decided to ring her from Mallow and the likely effect of his jetsetter's trunk call was not lost on him. She would be tingling as the connecting buttons were pushed and the magical words were spoken: You're through now.

'Miss Matthews?'

'Yes?'

'I love you.'

'Who's speaking?'

'Ah my my my my! Who's speaking! Who do you possibly know, or should I say whom, whom/who would ring you all the way from Mallow with those three magic words. You must say a name. You must say a name. I love the way you say my name.'

There was a pause while Whelan hoped she lost the battle with herself.

'Billy Whelan.'

'Aaaah. Music. Your old pal Tchaikovsky couldn't put it better. Breda, my darling, I'm a busy man. I have wares to peddle. Correct me if I'm wrong. It's outside Todds at half nine. Is it?'

'I can't. I . . .'

'No no no no no no. You're not washing your hair. Todds. Half nine. No women's privileges. I must rush. Goodbye.'

Whelan waited until she said goodbye and then he replaced the phone.

He left Mallow before the last two races. He had not sold all his sandwiches and free milk but the knot of his own excitement got to him. He wanted to reach home early to purge himself to Bill Johnston and to spruce himself for his appointment with Breda

Matthews. To add further to his delirious cup his mother handed him a letter that had arrived in the afternoon post via *Screen Monthly*. It was from a gentleman named Paul Tindall and contained a cheque for five thousand dollars. But it was the content of the letter that staggered him. The gentleman named Paul Tindall was no gentleman, five thousand dollars or no five thousand dollars. He was a true nut as befitted any American and Whelan admired him as such. But the information in the letter, information unwittingly included by Paul Tindall, staggered Whelan. He had to read the letter three times to grasp its enormity.

At once he wrote a long letter of his own to Bill Johnston, not doing proper justice to his own happiness because of his haste in reaching the Paul Tindall development. Whelan imagined that Bill Johnston himself would be confounded.

Because of the Indian summer heat of the October night Breda Matthews wore a light dress that highlighted the tan of her long arms and her legs from an inch above the knee down. She was standing outside Todds at half nine when Billy Whelan arrived. She glided coolly towards him. Whelan felt a hick in suit and collar and tie. Not having thought of anything better to say, he said: 'Hello.'

'Hello.'

'Where to?'

'I don't mind.'

'What about a walk?'

'All right.'

They fell into step and proceeded maidenly down the town. Whelan slipped into a role.

'Now that we're going steady I think we should get to know each other. What do you think? Hm?'

'I think I don't know where you get your ideas.'

'You'll tell me next you didn't dream about me all day yesterday at work? How many typing mistakes did you make? Honest now?'

'Thousands.'

'No. You didn't make any. I know you. You're efficient. Burdened with the weight of love you managed to cope. Am I right?'

'How did you cope? Burdened with the weight of love?' 'Actually, it's an inspiration to me. I was at the races yesterday – and today – there I was with this ridiculous shout on my lips – for a man of my breeding – and I thought of you and how lucky I am – and I managed to shout my shout: The last of the sandwiches! Can I hold your hand again?'

Breda slipped him her hand. She asked: 'How *did* you become a hawker?'

'I'll tell you. I was a bright lad at school when I was seventeen but something happened to me that stopped me staying on to do my Leaving. I didn't want to leave. I was driven away – to London. I worked at a lot of jobs there for six years and then I came home. I couldn't get a job so I started out on my own as a hawker.'

'How were you driven away? If you didn't want to leave.'

'It was my classmates. Higgins, Murphy, Nicky and Mark Brown. They drove me the same as if they had ash plants. They hounded me.'

'You had a bad time at school?'

'I had a great time at school. I can't tell you. Not now. Can I tell you when I – when you know me better? Please?'

'I don't mind.'

'How did you do at school? You did the Leaving? How many honours?'

'Six.'

'Six! Six out of?'

'Six.'

'Beautiful. My target was seven. Seven out of seven. I met Donal O'Sullivan, he was in our class. He got three honours. Higgins, Murphy and Nicky got four. Even Mark Brown only got six. He only passed Latin. Cahill got eight out of seven. At Easter he bought himself a book *Teach Yourself Applied Mathematics*. After only two months he got honours in it. Cahill was a genius.'

Whelan began to tell her his story about the camel. She could recall it from her own book.

'Wouldn't you agree? He could have let the camel down gently. People do that to each other all the time, they don't let down gently, they're rough, they look for the weak spot and wound. I hate that.'

They turned into the red path where the houses shone in the water. Impulsively Whelan let go of her hand and brought his up lightly to her shoulder. Breda allowed her cheek to touch his as they walked on as though the affinity between them was that of two months and not two dates. As they approached the baths they eased contact. They sat down. Whelan said: 'It's true. A dead dog floated past and I did not remotely think there was anything odd about it.'

'Ugh.'

'But do you know what I mean? Today people come along to the freshest of water, sniffing, you'd expect them to pull out a pocket laboratory to do tests before they'd strip off. People should ignore pollution. Or die of it. If enough died those who still lived would bum all the factories. Imagine a country where there was no factories.'

'How would people live?'

'Off their wits. They could become hawkers. Go to race meetings. All the people at race meetings are farmers anyway. We could live off the tourists. We could have beggars quoting Milton outside hotels. We could become a nation of scholars and saints again. Educate everyone and then let them loose on farmers and tourists. That your honour's horse may win. What's the Latin for that? The Greek? If we knew that, they'd flock from all over the world. We need only work in the summer. We could spend the winter in scholarship. The service industries are the new future. Fuck the three cycle shift . . .'

'Please.'

'I'm sorry. That slipped out. But you know what I mean?'

'I don't.'

'Neither do I. It came into my head. I don't have a Checkpoint Charlie.'

Whelan took out his cigarettes and after lighting up, guiltily flicked the dead match into the river. He tried to plot a thread of conversation that would keep what was between them alive until the darkness fell; then he hoped to put his arm around her again and do what now he had an almost uncontrollable urge to do – squeeze her breasts against his body. The alien erection that had visited him from time to time over the years he now understood to be not the work of the devil. There had been no one, his father gone, Mr Ryan unapproachable on that topic as was his mother, Higgins, Murphy, Nicky and Mark Brown no comfort.

'Do you like me?'

'No. I only go on dates with people I hate.'

Whelan stood up and slowly raised his two fists to the sky. He whispered loud enough for Breda to hear: 'She likes me! She likes me! ' and sat down again beside her.

'Breda – I hope you like the way I say your name – Breda, I don't believe in engagements, making rich jewellers richer with rings, let's get married quietly, without fuss. Are you on?'

Breda laughed quietly and drew out a long 'oooh' as she shook her head at him.

'Breda, I'm serious.'

'I know. At least I think you probably are.'

Whelan put his arm around her. She remained looking ahead. She maintained a rigid gaze even as he tried to pull her towards him. She allowed herself to be turned and, closing her eyes, she gave herself up to be kissed. Whelan had both his arms around her as they kissed and he drew her towards him tightly. They were sitting on the top step. It was a combination of Whelan laying her down and Breda yielding backwards that saw her gently at rest on the hard, clinical tiled surround of the municipal baths with Whelan on top of her from the waist up, kissing her squashily and inexpertly on the mouth, neck and cheeks, her breasts rigid under his weight. He put his hand on her leg. She followed his hand and pushed it away. He brought his hand up to her right breast and squeezed. She did not stop him until he tried to put his hand inside her dress. So he ltissed her, lying on her, for a full minute without a word or a groan between them. Then she pushed him off her. He sat up in the merciful darkness. She rummaged through her shoulder bag for her comb. She said: 'We'd better be getting back in.'

'All right. I love you.'

He stood up and lit another cigarette while she combed her hair.

'I said I loved you and you never said you loved me.'

Quickly she closed her bag, smoothed her dress and linked him on to the red path.

'It's not fair,' Whelan began and was cut short.

'I love you too.'

Whelan stopped and turned to her with an honest grin.

She confirmed: 'Yes. Now, let's not talk till we get out on the road.'

The red path was almost a quarter mile long. To shorten the silent distance Whelan concentrated on the letter from Paul Tindall. It was bad enough that Alvin T. Brine was the son of an O'Brien from Mayo who had changed his name in a fit of expediency; it was worse that Alvin – Alphonsus – perpetuated the treachery. Whelan could forgive all that. But that Alvin or Fonsie or whatever the hell he should be called, that he did what Paul Tindall let slip in the letter, that was a reserved sin that Whelan out of the great charity of his episcopacy could just about forgive, but never, ever forget. The water was ablaze with electricity. Whelan stopped but before he could utter Breda said: 'Don't. Please.'

'It's not what you think. What I want to say is: Aren't the fights lovely in the water? Everything – everything is beautiful. Thanks to Breda. Forward!'

Whelan suggested the bus. And the second bus out to Roses Avenue. Outside the gate of her house

Whelan held her two hands and whispered again that he loved her. They kissed and Breda stood at the gate waving to him as he departed.

Whelan had spent many a night in London dreaming of his eventual return to Limerick as a millionaire or man of achievement. He did not long for a precise capacity in which to flaunt himself; he was vaguely content that the likes of Higgins should respect his status. His thinking in this respect was not innate but more the inevitable growth with its stem rooted in loneliness. He was not lonely now but his lack of control over thinking ahead was a relic of those bitter nights crouched by the electric fire. He could not contain the anticipation of marriage to Breda, intercourse with her in the bed in his own room in Wellington Avenue and, far from recognising an incongruity in his mother's occupation of the room across the landing, he saw her in the foreground of his planned ecstasy – teaching Breda how to properly cook his beloved breast bones and how to turn the collars of his shirts and keeping Breda in knitting company while he was late at the races or at a Fart International meeting or, more regularly, while he was lowering seven pints of normal porter in the Sarsfield Arms. He saw his mother minding the babies while he and Breda went to the pictures. He saw Breda and his mother doing the wallpapering and the painting and the spring cleaning and he saw himself inspecting the handiwork as they waited hungrily for his approbation.

He also saw clearly the obstacles he would have to overcome.

There were many girls in Ireland who did not want to move in with their mothers-in-law; and there were many girls in Ireland whose dream did not include domicile in the historical inner cities; many of those girls were themselves from the smelly, back-to-back houses of the historical inner cities. The houses in Wellington Avenue were eighty years old and made no attempt to hide their red-bricked age. Given Breda Matthews' position in society and the modern house and leafy area in which she had been brought up, Whelan imagined her – and saw her point of view – turning her nose up at the prospect of Wellington Avenue. He imagined her – and again he saw her point of view – wanting just the two of them setting out on the road of life. Whelan could have survived without his mother but not without his mother's house. In his Mr Whippy wagon he had toured suburbia and the vast housing schemes that strangled the inner city. He honestly did not know how the people survived. What did they do when they needed a blade at a moment's notice at eight o'clock at night? There was no Lil Dwyer's shop fifty yards away. What did they do when the hour of drinking time struck? There was one pub in each of the various suburbs and ghettos. Whelan had seen pubs like them in parts of London – he had served behind the bar in one of them – they were too big, too comfortable, too dimly lit and did not have the character of any of the dozen pubs between Wellington Avenue and the Sarsfield Arms. What did they do when they wanted to back a horse? Buy chips?

To persuade Breda Matthews that she should marry ringless, marry a hawker, live with him in his mother's house that did not contain a bathroom, turn her back on the utility room, the world of the lawn, the capacious back garden, the plastic receptacle and note for the milkman, would require the eloquence of the Celt at his impassioned worst. Whelan planned to rise deviously to the occasion. They would live in a flat after their marriage – an inner city flat – and Breda would keep on her job while – as she thought – they were getting money together for the mortgage. Whelan saw no difficulty resisting Bob Matthews' offer of half his kingdom to set them up in a manner as befitted his daughter. Whelan heard himself gloriously aghast: Breda, what type of man do you think I am? You'd despise me if I accepted a penny of your father's money. In the flat Whelan could chip away at her, wittily pinpointing the warts of suburban existence, the lack of poetry in the middle class. And they would visit his mother so often – Sunday and Saturday dinner, Sunday evening tea, overnight at Christmas – that the notion of moving in with Mrs Whelan would, when sprung, seem attractive. Whelan did not think of himself as a conniving heel to plan in this fashion because the whole business had a ring about it that was deserving of the blessing of Fart International, a blessing he was happy to bestow from his eyrie of Outrageously Suitable Person. He would write accordingly to Bill Johnston.

Whelan wrote to Bill Johnston when he felt the need. He did not expect or receive a reply but the confessional nature of the correspondence cleared his head.

At a meeting of Fart International Whelan and Anna Roche-Reilly brought each other up to date. Anna's first question on entering the Blue Room was: 'Who is the third you rang me about?'

'Patience. Observe the formalities.'

Whelan produced the dollar and sang the first verse of 'Slievenamon' enunciating strongly, conscious of T. A. Dufficy about his chosen calling. Anna Roche-Reilly sang with him, lamely.

'Now, Anna, what have you to contribute? We're going to have that first at every meeting. What did you notice?'

'Chemists who use brand names.'

'Chemists who use brand names? Anna, you're out of my depth.'

'I equivocated between this euphemism and that and finally decided to charge straight in. And I didn't wait till the shop was empty. In the hearing of a woman who was waiting for a cough bottle I said: "Good afternoon. I'd like some of that cream for removing unwanted hair." I froze the cough bottle woman. But the slut in the white coat brazenly enquired if I preferred Removio to Smoothex. Damn her.'

'Which, in the event, did you choose?'

'Both. A large bottle of each. For all the good they did.'

'From what I can see they worked wonders.'

'Yes. They removed the blasted hair. It needs constant application. But it didn't land my cousin.'

'Ah. Excellent. I would consider that a wonder worked.'

'Morgan turned out to be a drip. Did not notice my existence. Before dinner, during dinner, after dinner he never once shut up about the inefficacy of sanctions. My father loved it. At the ball he didn't ask me to dance. Not that he asked anyone else. He was introduced from group to group, the blasted peripatetic Smith lecture went on all night. And do you know what I thought? I thought in my Wodehousean way that if I got his arms around a woman – me – he'd begin to blubber. Morgan is four inches taller than I am. I'd gone into a chemist and bought Smoothex, I had Fart behind me, so I charged shamefully over and said: Morg, you're neglecting me, I can never resist Strauss. He protested, said he had no leg. But I got him on to the floor and he began to blubber. Did he blubber. Straight over my head in all senses he blubbered – about Smith. It was a disaster. But then who arrived? I didn't ever tell you about Michael FitzHarris? No? Just as well. Michael is a dear. In every way. Michael is – what *do* they call them now? We introduced Morgan and Morgan began to blubber. But not about Smith. Oh no. I watched them going off together after only ten minutes. I prostituted myself in a chemist's shop and shaved my lip for a fucking queer! '

'Anna! Beautiful!'

'Yes.'

'I don't know about brand names. It's a bit weak. But, you've earned it. In with brand names to take its place in the Tupperware pantheon. By the way. Steel yourself. I'm practically engaged.'

'Fuck off. I'll not steel myself. I'll not listen. And where's the third?'

'Language. Please. All right, your blood can stand it. But still. The third.'

Whelan told of his interview with T. A. Dufficy.

'You mean, he's . . .' Anna looked around in the direction of the hatch. T. A. Dufficy waved and withdrew. 'How could you?'

'Now Anna . . .'

'Now Anna. Now Anna. You've something coming to you . . .'

Anna Roche-Reilly left her seat and walked towards him. She was going to strike him, Whelan realised, and raised his elbow protectively. She walked until she was standing directly behind him. 'Put down your arm, child.' She put her hands around his neck, gently and slid them along his shirt front. Her long hair swept off his jaw. 'Oh Billy' she whispered and gradually her hands plunged deeper till they hovered at the top of his trousers. She groaned: 'Oooh!' Whelan, though he reddened, could not restrain his own hand landing on hers and begin to push. Abruptly Anna Roche-Reilly detached herself from him.

'You innocent little man.'

She went back to her seat and took out a cigarette, exhaled and repeated: 'Innocent.'

Whelan nodded repeatedly.

'All right Anna. Point taken. Fair enough. But there's just one thing – just one thing,' Whelan repeated himself while he clawed for the right words, 'one simple thing to remember, you're in the Blue Room now, this is a Fart International gathering, I'm, *I'm* the Outrageously Suitable Person around here – and – and if you don't like the music leave the band.'

The cliché did not emerge with zest, it petered out, as was appropriate. By way of acknowledgement Whelan joined her, put his arm around her shoulder comfortingly and invited her for a drink which they both enjoyed at the bar of the lounge, being served and spied upon by T. A. Dufficy. There was for the three of them no going back on Fart International. Whelan mentioned Paul Tindall and his contribution of five thousand dollars but instinctively kept to himself the awful truth about Alvin T. Brine.

On the last Friday night in October a cold drizzle fell that almost dissuaded Whelan from setting out with his ice cream. But it was, after all, Friday night and Friday night was treat night in O'Malley Park; also, ice pops were sold on Christmas Day. As a child Whelan had not known a shop to open on Christmas

Day let alone one that sold ice pops. He dropped his Mr Whippy anchor in the centre of the ghetto and they approached from all sides, cheering. He noticed, as he filled the cones, six little boys standing respect-fully against a garden wall a half dozen yards away from the queue. They were lined up in the order of their conception, like the proverbial steps of stairs; the youngest would have been about three and the eldest nine, Whelan guessed, but on account of their iden-tical no-nonsense short back and sides haircuts they might have been sextuplets. All the other children buying cones had long hair according to the current fashion – though dreadfully unkempt long hair – and they helped to set off the innocence of the six broth-ers. Whelan was about to serve the last purchaser, whom he realised with shock was a thirteen year old version of the six against the wall when a straggler fell into the queue behind him. The thirteen year old stood back and allowed the straggler to be served first. When his turn came again and he was alone he asked for four cones. Whelan's suspicions were aroused. He remained to watch. The thirteen year old gave a cone each to three of his brothers each of whom shared the cone with another brother. Whelan was transfixed watching them alternately lick the cones. He called the thirteen year old and gave him three free cones so that all the family might have one each.

'Thanks very much.'

'Don't mention it. They're your brothers?'

'Yes.'

'How many are there in your family?'

'That's all. My eldest brother is in England.'

'What age is he?'

'He's twenty.'

'What's your name?'

'Cyril.'

Whelan thought the name Cyril slightly incongruous in the context of a ghetto. But it was not half as jarring as a family aged twenty, thirteen and nine, eight, seven, six, five, four. He was puzzled.

'Why is your eldest brother in England? How long is he there?'

'Four years. He went to earn lots of money to buy the house.'

'What house.'

'I don't know. It's the house we'll be going to when we leave here. My mother isn't sure yet. She says it doesn't matter as long as we get away from here. She won't let me help. She says everyone of us has to stay at school till we're eighteen.'

'Your mother is right. Listen to your mother. Run along.'

A few hundred yards outside the O'Malley Park ghetto Whelan parked the wagon and lit a cigarette. He wanted to plan while the obstacles to be overcome were fresh in his mind, and while he was in the mood to feel proud of himself. Doing good by stealth – that was what Fart International was all about. He would have it enshrined at the next meeting: Anyone who has not covered his tracks, anyone who has been discovered aiding charity – out. Stealth – in. The way the winter was hatching he would have to convert to burgers and chips soon; chips were dearer than cones; he could not give free bags of chips to half of Cyril's brothers; or rather he could, and it wouldn't cost him, but it would do nothing for the children's morale. He planned to enlist Cyril's aid in filling bags and by way of payment let him have seven bags of chips. And no one would know of his good deed. He would not be an Outrageously Suitable Person if he did not set headlines. Unfortunately he would have to let Breda glimpse the light beneath the bushel. There would be no problem in bringing it up: Life can be sad, I was up there in O'Malley Park the other night . . . He needed a full quiver to land Breda. Though he would have to behave otherwise in his dealings with her, he felt, which for practical reasons was the same as knowing, that he did not deserve her. Indulging this low opinion of himself or more accurately his high opinion of Breda Matthews was negatively productive; he foresaw her wearying of his outrageousness. He planned to rush her; he would propose elopement though he shuddered to imagine her going along with it – he had not the faintest idea how to organise elopements. But if he could allow her talk him out of elopement and into an immediate engagement and early marriage . . .

'It's just – it's just so soon,' Breda said weakly. They had been seeing each other on Monday, Wednesday and Saturday nights; it was a dying custom of the time to date with spaced precision, a tradition that instinctively grew from a dread of familiarity. What was surprising – and surely constituted food for the sociologist – was that people married at all given their appreciation of how courtship palled without the element of abstention.

'Don't you know me after three months?'

They walked or went to the pictures and, of late, had taken to a lip service of a walk and then a drink in a lounge bar or hotel, as was becoming all the rage. Outside her gate they kissed hungrily and squeezed each other; it was a sin according to the commandment that forbade the male to have an erection and the woman to be a party to the cause of it. They were the last members of the last generation to commit such a sin. Their successors would have bigger sins to commit.

'You admit you haven't any money – money to put a deposit down – I haven't enough. Where for instance are we going to live?'

They had gone no further than the bridge before Corbally, against which they leaned, chastely close in debate. The walk was now no more than a motion they were going through before they would end up on leatherette with a couple of drinks. The late November air robbed the outdoors of its glamour.

'Breda, you're being practical.'

'Someone has to be.'

'Breda, I love you. You love me. We'll live in a tent. On the moon. What does it matter where we live? Is it my taste in real estate you love? Tell me now before I make a mistake. You intend to be a Dr Spock wife? Do everything by the book? Be indistinguishable from a statistic? I know you Breda. That's not you. I won't let that be you.'

'It's getting cold. Let's walk back in.'

Breda linked him. They were gone from holding hands. Whelan was thrown off track by the realisation that he would have to invest in an overcoat. He had bought the jacket and trousers that he now wore from a fellow hawker whose hunting ground was the North.

'You don't know my parents. They wouldn't understand the idea of getting married after three months. My father would have a fit at an engagement after three months, let alone a marriage.'

'I'll have to give your father a talking to,' Whelan proclaimed as the air suddenly disappeared from his stomach, 'his standards of propriety are not wrong in themselves but his base is hypocritical, narrow, shallow. If the Chamber of Commerce decreed that all marriages should proceed from the acquaintances of three months he'd push you into leading the charge.'

'That's unfair.'

'Certainly. To me.'

'Daddy is a good man. A reasonable man. And he has a mind of his own. Are we going in here?'

They were outside Cruises Hotel.

'Let's walk on up to the Sarsfield Arms.'

'What do you love so much about the Sarsfield Arms. It's so out of our way.'

Whelan was tempted to tell her. He had sufficient conscience to know he would have to tell her before they married. He was not entirely beyond redemption. But he would wait until a date was fixed for the wedding. Then he would tell her. He feared her reaction. In what he had anticipated would be a golden moment for both of them he had told her of his schooldays in detail, cluminating in the abominable performance of Higgins, Nicky, Murphy and Mark Brown during Whelan's last month at school. Breda did not seem to understand. She actually said: But surely you didn't take it that much to heart? I can imagine it must have been a let down but it shouldn't have stopped you going back to school. She had been reminded of an incident during her year in Sister Martina's class . . . Whelan was nauseated that she could see a similarity between what happened to him and the schoolgirlish trivia she dredged from her cushioned education. Nonetheless, he would have to tell her about Fart International.

'The Sarsfield Arms is homely. The manager there doesn't believe in the commercial rate. Breda, I'll take on your father. Set it up.'

Breda smiled. 'That will be some confrontation.'

'Don't worry. I'll go easy on him.'

Breda laughed and hugged his chest. In so far as either of them knew what he or she was doing,

they were in love. Over the drink at the Sarsfield
Arms, drink Whelan insisted on having at the counter
because he claimed a predeliction for high stools, they
continued: 'What night will I tell him you'll come out?'

Ears pricked, T. A. Dufficy was busy with his swab,
Whelan took a mighty swallow for courage from his
normal pint, placed the glass back on the counter
beside Breda's gin and orange, and said: 'Breda,
you'll never get to know me. Your father and I will
meet on neutral territory, here in the Sarsfield Arms,
over a drink. Equals.'

'Billy, be serious.'

'I am serious, Breda. You dragged your father into
this. You're over twenty-one. It's because I respect your
filial quality that I don't suggest we elope. I'm not asking you to let my mother run the rule over you. And
besides, I mightn't think your father good enough
for me. He mightn't have the qualities I expect in a
father-in-law. And if he hasn't. It won't matter. I love
you Breda. You. I want to marry you. You. You stand
alone. Perfect. I'll meet your father here tomorrow
night at ten o'clock. I'll ring you in the morning. If he
can't make it then we'll arrange a night he can.'

Later, while Breda was in the Ladies, T. A. Dufficy
said, having prefaced his remarks with half a minute's
silent cocking of his right bushy eyebrow: 'There are
times when the hotel business isn't entirely dull. You
meet all kinds of people.'

He went cryptically off about his business and
left Whelan, not with the glow he imagined shone

from Whelan's face, but with a sense of shame and dread of the commercial ogre he anticipated in Bob Matthews.

The youngest of five brothers and one sister, and having negotiated a moderate Intermediate Certificate of Education, Bob Matthews joined Todds department store as an assistant wrapper. The eldest of the family, Joe, emigrated to Melbourne via London at the age of fifteen and the proxy experience stood Bob Matthews in good stead years later amid golf club tales of hardship known: Joe had gone off dressed in an aunt's modified overcoat, with a nightshirt wrapped in brown paper, and a florin. Joe was fourteen years older than Bob and by the time Bob started at Todds Joe had already achieved one bitter trip home that culminated in a letter to the *Chronicle* that castigated the city of litter. That was what emigration did to one, was the consensus among Bob and his brothers and his parents; he knuckled down as an assistant wrapper with a will. Even in those days of high foreheads in menial tasks the moderate Intermediate Certificate was an open sesame into the stores. Bob Matthews diligently unravelled the complexities of requisition and ledger control and finally graduated to a striped suit, a drop in wages and the position of shoe salesman. He did some buying; he did relief in carpets, tailoring, haberdashery. After ten years there was little he did not know about the functioning of the entire shop. He attended night classes at the technical school to round off his grasp of the double entry. He was officially appointed buyer. In three managerial succession stakes he was not even mentioned in despatches.

He had gone as far as he could, without blood or background; he grew a neat moustache; but he was not Captain Matthews, or Major Matthews, folderols of achievement so beloved of Blood-Smith the principal shareholder who appropriated to himself the inexplicit portfolio of maintaining the tone of appointments. Realistically then, Bob Matthews did not aspire to management. He married Rose out of cosmetics and bought a house in Roses Avenue.

The heart attacked Blood-Smith as he was perched upon his shooting stick at the coursing and so speedily that he did not have a chance to reach for the hip pocket flask. It happened at the time Bob Matthews was saving every idle penny towards the purchase of a lodge in the West End of Kilkee so that his children might grow up equal to their neighbours. Todds was taken over. The modem tragedy of the honourable firm falling into the hands of the democratic smart men led to the appointment eventually of the best man for the job: Bob Matthews. But by now Bob Matthews did not know whether he was the poor boy making good and intending to do better or the snob that any decent man is sidetracked into wanting to become. He did not have the leisure to contemplate the dichotomy. The democratic smart men were not so offside as to let seep edicts as to the advisability of being seen at the RDS; but a blunt memo *expected* of its executives that Rotary, Chamber of Commerce, the Golf Club (Limerick G.C. *not* Casdetroy), be embraced.

By the time Bob Matthews pushed open the door of the Sarsfield Arms lounge he was the embodiment of everything Billy Whelan ever hated, hated now and ever hoped to hate. Had he known it, it would have struck Billy Whelan as an imbecile irrelevance that Bob Matthews was a nice man, loved by his wife and children and neighbours and commercial peers and clerks and typists and storemen and wrappers (there were no assistant wrappers now and the wrappers themselves could not spell Intermediate Certificate).

On a few occasions, as they broke from a clinch at his approach, Whelan had exchanged good nights with Bob Matthews. He recognised him now as he peered about for his accomplice in rendezvous. Grey suited, grey waistcoated, grey haired, black shiny shoes, inclined to portliness, florid, of clubbable countenance. Whelan, though acknowledging the lack of gambit, was unable to remain unrecognised. He waved. With an unspoken 'ah' Bob Matthews joined him.

'Mr Matthews.'

'Billy. The famous Billy Whelan I've been hearing so much about. What will you have?'

'No. Let me. What would you like?'

'Good of you. Ah, I'll chance a pint.'

'Mr Dufficy, could I have two pints please.' Whelan's own glass was almost three quarters full. He might appear an alcoholic; all he knew was a desire not to be nursing an empty glass when it came the enemy's turn to buy. Bob Matthews cast a weather eye over the seating accommodation.

'Shall we adjourn to a table over there?'

'Breda probably didn't mention this to you. I know it probably sounds daft – but – I can't enjoy a drink unless I'm at the counter. I know. It's mad. But it's a fact.'

'Not at all. I quite understand. Well now. I'll swell your head. Breda says of you that she has never met anyone like you in her life. That you are the nicest, funniest, decentest boy friend she's ever had. And from what I know of my daughter she's well past calf love. You come highly recommended.'

'Mr Matthews, Breda's a dear. But I must be honest. She's overselling me.'

'I don't know. I don't know. I have respect for Breda's opinion. However, where do we start. I don't believe in the heavy father business – as I gather you don't yourself,' Bob Matthews chuckled. 'I liked that touch – neutral territory, and the whole business is easier over a pint. Now, what am I going to say to you?'

Whelan smiled. 'You're going to ask me about my prospects?'

'I suppose I would get around to that. But first, what's the hurry? You know each other three months. What's the big hurry?'

'There isn't any hurry. We're both satisfied that we love each other, that we want to marry. We don't see the point in postponing the pleasure.'

'Marriage isn't all pleasure you know.'

'Which?'

'I said marriage isn't all pleasure you know.'

'Yes, but which marriage? Whose?'

'Marriage in general.'

'Oh. That won't affect us. Ours will be marriage in particular.'

'Breda said it. She said "he'll beat you with words". But you know, smart talk won't always get you everywhere.'

Whelan thought it was an angry sip the man took from his pint. It was far from being a contented swallow. As for the sip, the man was probably out of training, shorts at the nineteenth.

'Mr Matthews, if you think I'm a smart alec, or if what I have said seems like smartalecism, please accept my apology, I'm not a smart alec and I certainly didn't mean to sound like one.'

'Don't get me wrong. What I mean . . . Breda says you're doing very well but so far you're not in a position to raise a mortgage. Now that in itself is not insurmountable. I would not be ungenerous where my daughter's happiness . . .'

'Mr Matthews. Sorry for interrupting. But we must get one thing clear. I would not accept money from you or anyone else as long as I lived. I believe that every penny I have should be every penny I've earned.'

'Yes. It's good to hear a young man speak like that nowadays. When I was a boy, I started in Todds as an assistant wrapper . . .'

'Mr Matthews. Sorry again. But put yourself in my position. If I was sitting here at the counter minding my own business and a stranger sidled up to me slurring out his past, quite honestly I'd move away. Now in that respect you are a stranger to me. I don't feel I know you well enough to have to listen to your bootstrap ascent.'

Bob Matthews shook his head and smiled. Whelan suspected it was classic evidence that the man would gladly choke him. Whelan was not going to wait for the declaration of hostilities. He was already swinging. T. A. Dufficy, at whom Bob Matthews glanced nervously, was on his haunches with a pencil and pad, examining bottles; he might have been taking serial numbers of the bottles. From Whelan's London experience of bar work he could not imagine what a barman would be doing on his haunches with a pencil and pad confronting bottles. Unless that barman happened to be T. A. Dufficy.

'So it is true for Breda. You're a man of words. Now. Where – are – you – going – to – take – my – daughter – to – live?'

'I don't know, Mr Matthews. And that's the truth. I presume we'll start off in a flat. Take it from there,' Whelan could not resist the follow through: 'After the first child we might even qualify for a house in O'Malley Park.'

He managed to meet the man's stare. Bob Matthews coughed in the direction of T. A. Dufficy who was so busy with his bottles that Bob Matthews had to rap the counter with a coin.

'Another pint?'

Whelan nodded and said: Please.

'A pint and a double Jameson please.'

'Certainly, sir.'

Bob Matthews turned to Whelan. 'Over my dead body young man! '

'Pardon?'

'O'Malley Park is not for my daughter.'

'I see. Listen, I wouldn't disagree with you necessarily on that point. Let's shelve that for a moment. Wouldn't it save time and talk if you gave me a list – of the characteristics, financial status and so on you're looking for in a son-in-law?'

'Words, words, words. I can see the obvious attraction for Breda. Now, you're a hawker?'

'No.'

'I was given to understand . . .'

'I'm Billy Whelan. I hawk. That doesn't make me a hawker no more than you yourself are no more than a manager.'

'Can I put it to you this way? Do you think it is morbid curiosity on my part if I enquire in what way you intend to develop – commercially?'

Bob Matthews smiled. He was beginning to get the feel of the part. Whelan wiped the smile off his face. 'Yes. I would consider that morbid curiosity.'

'I see,' Bob Matthews acknowledged deflated. 'I see. I am not to get any good out of you then. That is your tack. You're young, angry, cocksure, without a thought for others including whom you imagine will be your future wife.'

Whelan was genuinely offended and delighted to be so. 'Mr Matthews, the fact that I am going with your daughter and have proposed to her does not entitle you to insult me; you impute that among my vices lurks a disregard for others. That simply is not true. Every waking moment of my life I think of others – including yourself. That is why I say to you now, for *your* own sake, because I don't think you're one hundred per cent compromised, I say to you cop yourself on, it is none of your business what I work at, how much money I have or will have, where I decide is fit residence for your daughter *and* myself. If you are one of those parents who chooses husbands for his daughters and Breda is one of those daughters happy to go along with it then very well. I would like you to know my hat is in the ring.'

'The anger! What are you so angry about? Thank you, thank you.'

Bob Matthews paid hurriedly for the drink on the counter and waited till T. A. Dufficy moved away. He was about to repeat his question when Whelan answered: 'I'll give you some gratuitous information about myself. It's the only type you'll ever get from me. Yes. I'm angry. Now, I'm angry. I respect myself. I *know* I am a *good man*. I don't feel any compulsion to prove it. And I am angry that I should have to account for myself. And for what it's worth, I am not objecting to you as a father-in-law, not because I imagine you're the bees knees in father-in-laws, but because father-in-laws and mother-in-laws and status and money and prospects are ciphers to be hacked away so that the great love Breda and I have for each other can blossom. We will have enough to contend with as it is.'

'And what will you have to contend with?' Bob Matthews spoke almost to himself, he was not looking at Whelan now; he was staring at the beer mat on the counter.

'Impurity!' Whelan let the ghasdy word hang in the air. Bob Matthews slowly turned in disbelief. Unless his ears had been deceiving him he would give the young upstart the benefit of his mature anger.

'What are you saying? If you're saying what I think you're saying I'll put your head through the wall behind you.'

Whelan was genuinely puzzled.

'Mr Matthews, are we at cross purposes by any chance? Such vehemence! '

'Have you taken advantage of my daughter? What do you mean "impurity"?'

'Oh. Oh! That proves my point in many ways, Mr Matthews. I have not taken advantage of your daughter. And I do not feel ashamed to admit that I wouldn't know how to go about it. What I have to contend with – what we'll have to contend with, Breda and I, is impurity. But not the narrow connotation of the word with which you seem obsessed. I am pure – and want to stay pure – free from the shackles of compromise we see all around us, look at yourself – Rotarian, Golfer, Chamber of Commerce disciple, in up to your elbow.'

Bob Matthews detected a glimmer. Mollified, he chuckled: 'I think I have you now. You're beginning to take shape. You have-a-chip-on-your-shoulder! Right?'

'Dreadful expression.'

'That's it. A good old fashioned chip on your shoulder.' He considered the beer mat; pity welled up in him. He said, gently: 'Would you like to talk about it?'

Whelan froze. 'There is no "it" to talk about!' he spat, savagely. Bob Matthews nodded as though the reply verified his suspicions, which it did.

'As you wish. We've had a good discussion. As you said earlier, Breda is over twenty-one. I won't be an impediment to your plans. I've advised Breda to wait; I've advised you. But it's your love affair, your marriage, your future. I wish you luck. If you should ever – please don't misunderstand – Breda told me a thing or two about you, all complimentary as I said, she mentioned the unfortunate accident to your father – I think you know what I'm getting at – I have some years over you – if you ever – you know what I'm saying . . .'

Bob Matthews unwound himself from the stool as he spoke. He drained his glass. 'I have to leave you. Let me get you a drink before I go?'

'That's all right thanks. I'm okay.'

Bob Matthews extended his hand: 'Nice meeting you, Billy.'

Whelan had no option but to shake and say: 'And you, Mr Matthews. Thank you.'

Whelan watched him depart. For the benefit of T. A. Dufficy who creaked erect Whelan muttered: Insufferable bollix.

T. A. Dufficy offered: 'I wouldn't say he's the worst of them.'

Whelan agreed: 'Unfortunately he's not.'

Bob Matthews drove home curiously pleased with himself. He had set out earlier from a very happy household. His eldest daughter, Alice, had called around to see him off. Alice was married one year now to an accountant. Breda was his favourite but he was closer to Alice. Alice loved the musicals, *The Desert Song* and that, that had been Alice in her day; Alice had attended the six months pre-marital course sponsored by the Redemptorists. There had never been any difficulty with Alice. Not that there ever had with Breda. Though only three years younger than Alice, Breda was of a different generation, Breda was better educated, brighter, had a taste in that classical music that pleased yet confounded them all. Chris was a fine boy, spoiled, but he was the youngest, it was a new age now. Chris had cracked a joke: Dad, you want my knife to bring back his scalp? Alice had been tightlipped, depending on him to authoritatively sort the whole business out, bring Breda to her senses. And Rose, whom he had married out of cosmetics, Rose who could be depended upon to have raiment laid out when there was a rush on, see to the dress suit, prepare an excellent dinner when there were guests afoot, looked after the children and himself and the house so well, Rose whom he dearly loved, had watched him set out as though he were a path-finder. For a time back in the Sarsfield Arms he had scented defeat, the prospect of having to return home a redundant father, unable to cope with the headlong passage of time, Breda mutely going to her room set in her determination reacting to his own gentle opposition and the vociferous butting in of Alice.

The boy had a chip on his shoulder. He was a hawker. They did make money, Bob Matthews knew. He had himself started out as an assistant wrapper. The boy had cut him short there. That was part of the chip. He saw the boy in a grocery of his own eventually. And he was quick-witted. Educated too. Bob Matthews rather liked him.

'I must say I rather liked him,' Bob Matthews announced to the assembly. Breda smiled and let her eyelids fall.

'What did you say to him?' Alice demanded menacingly.

'He has an outsize chip on his shoulder though. Savaged me because I'm in Rotary and the Chamber. And golf. He apparently doesn't approve of golf.'

'What did he say when you pointed out it was preposterous for Breda to get married after only three months – if at all – to a hawker?'

'Oh that? Actually he pointed out that that was none of my business.'

'Daddy!'

'Shush, Alice. Bob, you're satisfied?'

'Mammy! '

'Rose. Yes. I still think they should wait. He says he won't. It's up to Breda.'

Mrs Matthews turned to her daughter. Breda ran to where her father reclined on the easy chair. She threw her arms around him and said: 'Oh, Dad.'

Alice rose and barked: 'Daddy. Do you want me to get Simon to see this – this hawker?'

'Now, Alice . . .'

'Mammy, you're as bad. You're all daft. I'm going. Breda you should wake up.'

Chapter Eleven
John Harnett

On leaving the hospital Whelan immediately lit a cigarette. Six months earlier his mother had been operated on for gallstones but they were not the problem. The doctor said, calmly: Six months, maybe nine. A year – at the outside. Whelan drove away from the hospital leaving her shrunken into the bed, starchy nurses swishing up and down. He cried a little but not anything as much as he wanted to: the thought would not leave him that now he would inherit the house in Wellington Avenue, they could move out of the flat and all the talk of suburbia would cease. Hostilities had been suspended from the moment his mother took sick and now that she was back in the hospital, dying, Breda would be more deferential than ever to his whims.

They were married eighteen months and the flat was located in what the agent had called a 'choice area'. The rent testified to the man's selection of adjective. Whelan parked the van and the chip wagon outside the building and thought with solace of the agent calling it a 'choice area' the next time he showed a fool around. Whelan was in irritable humour. It was more than that his mother was dying and that he could feel sorrow without being aware of the benefits of her death; he had returned early that evening from Gowran Park and had to stand around while Breda fried. He had in fact to hold the baby who was crying. Whelan did not understand why the meal was not there on the table the moment he walked in; if she had to post scouts on the road all the way to Gowran Park, Whelan did not care, as long as it was there on the table. His mother had always managed to have it there on the table the moment he walked in. It was not as though he was a man with time on his hands. He had to go to the hospital, he had to see to the van, he had to have a few pints. Everything would change when his mother died. He would weep at that funeral; Bob Matthews would squeeze his arm – Bob Matthews to whom Whelan had been obliged to say: I didn't ask Breda to run and stay with you for the past three days, I didn't ask her to kidnap my child, you have poisoned my wife's mind, you and that dreadful Tupperware Alice daughter, now get out of here, I've done with you.

He would take exactly one week off after the funeral, one week only, at the end of which they would be installed in Wellington Avenue and they would be happy again. No. He would first get some-one to instal a bathroom. He knew where to get the materials cheaply; he knew a plumber; he himself attended by Cyril would lay the bricks. He took Cyril

with him to the Gaelic Athletic Association matches on
Sundays; they manned two stalls. Cyril was growing his
hair. He would no longer let his father cut it. Whelan
was paying Cyril a reasonable couple of pounds and
the eldest brother was sending home from England.
But the eldest brother was not sending home as much
as he would have liked because the cost of living was
high in England and he had met a lovely girl – from
Kerry – and he was thinking of getting married; and
the price of houses was rising all the time. Cyril's
father could not work on account of his bad back and
there was no possibility of saving out of what he drew
in welfare. But Cyril's mother would not let go of her
dream of leaving O'Malley Park; they would never in
the first place have taken the house in O'Malley Park
only that their two rooms in the centre of the city were
in a building that was knocked down.

Whelan could not bring himself to start the van.
He took out another cigarette.

His thoughts went from his mother in the white
bed to Cyril's eldest brother trapped in England and
from him to a card table: Hogan and Mackey and
Martin and Tommy Cook and Maurice of Maurice
and Connie. It was unaccountable the way, from time
to time, Hogan would climb into his thoughts; he felt
guilty at having in some way abandoned Hogan and
then remembered that Hogan had done nothing
to see him fed on Christmas Day. Whelan counted
his blessings: he was not cold and hungry and alone
in the world of hands like shovels and the game of

forty-five and the expatriate faces; the man he had met on Christmas night on the Kilburn High Road haunted him – he could hear the man saying: Yeah, see you Limerick – a man who could not eat crisps in a pub lest he spoil the well fed's recollection of good dinner. Whelan had money and a wife whom he still adored even though he had drawn back his hand and struck her so hard that there was a lump on her forehead and blackness over a closed eye for three days. She had begged him to hit her the way she loomed an inch from his face screaming at him. He put the memory from him. It was quarter to ten. He had changed his clothes while Breda was taking out the frying pan – she had not even taken the frying pan out, the table had not been laid – so he could go direct to the Sarsfield Arms. He started the van.

A sparse mist nestled on the windscreen. He flicked a switch. The remaining wiper fitfully afforded him vision. One of those madmen was jogging on the footpath – the lunatics were everywhere nowadays. No one was willing to die. He pressed the brakes strongly and the van slithered to a halt. It could not be, of course, it was the defective wiper playing tricks, but he may as well satisfy his curiosity. He lowered the left hand window. The jogger caught him up and panted on. It was. Whelan was positive. But it could hardly be. He started the van again and slowed to the jogger's pace. It was. A phrase of Hogan's came back to him from the card table in the Falcon. When the knave was poked into Hogan and he happened to have the five Hogan liked to sort out the cards, gingerly isolate the knave and declare: The Lord has delivered you into my hands. Whelan honked his horn at the jogger delivered into his hands. The jogger, in full livery, running shoes, track suit and face drained of blood, slowed down, clutched a telegraph pole and panted. Whelan bade jovially: 'Mr Harnett!'

The bank manager was not able to respond for some time; he had the palm of his left hand on the pole; his right hand clutched his appendix area; white breath bellowed from his mouth; he coughed and cleared his throat and spat. When he was able to speak he did not speak. He looked at Whelan and remained silent to regain full control of his breathing. Whelan smiled.

'If you want to jog, that's your business; if you want to stop, that's my business.'

John Harnett smiled wanly. He finally managed: 'If it isn't yourself.'

'None other,' agreed Whelan. 'Can I give you a lift?'

'Thanks.'

John Harnett climbed in beside Whelan. Whelan asked: 'Where do you live?'

'Castleroy.'

'What? Castleroy? Did you run all the way out here?'

The bank manager nodded. The question had obviously not been asked out of admiration and the nod had the substance of confession.

Whelan drove off.

'You're taking me out of my way but no matter. Worse, you're cutting into my drinking time. But no matter. I can't afford to lose a considerate bank manager. I haven't told you very much about Fart International. You didn't ask. Understanding of you. But I am at liberty, I find myself deciding, to give you a glimpse. We have a copybook. Full of Non U's I suppose you could call it. Jogging is number two on the list. The only reason it's not number one is because those who go to Tupperware parties was the first on the list and for old time's sake we've left it that way – but jogging! If Fart International was not in existence we would have to invent it to combat jogging. You do see our point of view?'

'I haven't the faintest idea what you are talking about.'

'Of course you do. Of course you do. It's a pity I can't show you the copybook. You'd have such a clear idea. Tupperware, joggers, chaps who catch salmon using silver devon as bait and get their photographs put on the paper; Rotary, Golf, Chamber of Commerce; Toastmasters – boy, are they out – people who don't open letters, chemists who used brand names . . . by the way, I'd like to drop in in the morning to view the accounts. If you're free? Would you be free at around ten? I have to head off to the races.'

'Yes. I'm free. Turn right.'

'Nice area.'

'They've stopped building. We're safe on that side with the College and the river. I don't know about beyond. Just hope all the farmers die intestate and leave twenty children scrambling over the residue. The builders might get impatient. Go elsewhere. Or maybe we should put lambs' blood on the doors.'

'You know, there's a trace of humour in you. Jaundiced, defeatist, but humour.'

'Just here thank you. Thank you very much. I ran too far.'

'You did. Once you put one foot in front of the other you did. In the morning. Tennish. And if there's anything I can do you have only to say the word. But you *must* say the word.'

In the Sarsfield Arms Whelan assassinated the first pint.

T. A. Dufficy said: 'No picking at the food tonight.'

'T.A., I may have news tomorrow that will make the hair stand on your head. I have a nibble.'

'You're not going to tell me now – directly?'

'Of course not. I'm simply trying to ensure that your antennae are concentrated on good ground.'

'How is your good mother tonight?'

'She's dying. The doctor said maybe a week now. It could happen tonight.'

'I'm sorry.'

'I know, T.A. Thank you. The morphine is having less and less effect.'

'That's the worst part. I'll join you in a drink. On me. Finish that.'

'Thanks. I need someone this side of the counter tonight. A man came into my head tonight. Hogan. Did I ever tell you about Hogan? He used to claim he was Wingate's batman . . .'

'Yes. You told me a hundred times.'

'T.A., I didn't?'

'Not a hundred. Five times?'

'Sorry.'

'All right. I don't mind.'

'I told you the history of the dollar?'

'You did.'

'I didn't tell you how I got it back. I went to Mr Ryan's daughter. The night of the funeral. She threw me out. Said I had no respect for the dead. It was six weeks before the bitch yielded it up. Mr Ryan must have been haunting her. T.A., tell me something, honestly, I once told Breda about what Higgins and Murphy and Nicky and Mark Brown did to me the last year at school, my last year, she didn't feel it the way I did, thought I over reacted. What do you think? Did I make a mountain out of a molehill?'

'I wouldn't say it matters much. Where would you be now? Would you have your Breda? Would you have met your Hogan characters? Would you be the Outrageously Suitable Person?'

'T.A., we're not mad, are we? Sure we're not?'

'I'll put it to you this way: I wouldn't care to go around wearing our neuroses on our sleeves.'

'T.A., what do you want? I don't know what I want, but I want something. You're not too old are you? Does it happen with age, I wonder. Have you any longing?'

'No. Nothing that doesn't come and go. How's your child? We didn't have children. Even though Maureen was a barmaid – barmaid stories are exaggerated – I don't think we knew what we were doing in the early days. It wasn't until I started listening in my office that I realised how – how thorough people went about things. There is that come and go longing, if you'll pardon the expression. Drapers were not fiery. I sometimes imagine myself – free – not free of Maureen but free of – of draperhood – without inhibition – oh, isn't drink wonderful – I tipple away during the day – keep the imagination topped up . . .'

Elsewhere – in the flat – Alice was saying: 'I'd better clear off before he comes. Now Breda, I know his mother is dying, but that's beside the point. That child deserves a home – with a decent garden and back.'

'I know, Alice. Let it be for the time being. I know what I'm doing.'

'Do you? A hawker! Ugh! Listen, when are you coming out? I want to show you the fitted presses. We took them in beige to match the floor. And I have a few things put away that might fit Declan.'

'I'll be out soon. Some afternoon I'll drop out.'

'Why don't you come at night. You wouldn't have Declan dragging out of you.'

'Billy is often late getting back. And then he has to go to the hospital and see to the van.'

'You know what I mean now, Breda, I'm not wishing any evil, but if his mother is going to die, I mean when she's gone, he could sell that house, you'd have a deposit on a mortgage. Simon was saying there's a great demand for those compact houses, the rates are low and a lot of single nurses are going in for them . . . you keep at him Breda.'

'I will, Alice. I will. You better go. He'll be here any minute.'

'. . . T.A., I've enough. I want to be fresh in the morning. I can't let Fart down. Can I?'

'No. No. You can't do that.'

'If anything comes of my nibble I might ring Anna and set up a meeting tomorrow night. You'll be at your post? I'll ring during the day and let you know.'

Breda was happy enough in the flat for the time being. She liked the park across the way and the fact that the square was Georgian and contained the medical fraternity. They had looked at so many flats – glorified rooms – she was glad she had held out. She had hunted Alice even though she did not expect Billy for at least another half an hour. It was annoying to have to maintain the fiction that he sometimes came home before closing time. Alice would be outraged if she knew the truth. Breda wondered what Alice would think or what her parents would think if they knew about Fart International. She was three months pregnant with Declan when he told her. He had intended to tell her before they were married but he confessed that he was afraid she might break it off. She had been excited the night he took her into his confidence. He showed her a copy of *Screen Monthly*. She thought the advertisement was hilarious and felt warm because it was typical of him to spot something so unusual. Almost casually he told her how he had replied to the advertisement. He showed her a long letter from a Bill Johnston. He showed her the advertisement in the *Chronicle*. She had never spotted that in the *Chronicle* before. Far Tinternational. Someone neglected to invite him to dinner on Christmas Day, that was it, and he was so lonely that he wrote out of desperation to *Screen Monthly*. It sounded to her at the time like that ridiculous incident with the four boys at school. And then he told her about the fifteen thousand dollars. She had a vision as she listened of a dream home. Only now, fifteen months later, could she accept that he would never touch a penny of that money. But then she built her hopes too quickly and too high. She remembered distinctiy that she was at least six yards away from him and she was not shouting. She was not *shouting*. She had been saying something like: Billy, all I'm asking for is a decent place to live, just one of the new houses, I'm not expecting a Roses Avenue, is that too much to ask, is it? Is that too much to ask, everyone else . . . *He* began to shout, she was positive: I'm not everyone else, how many times did I tell you I'm not everyone else. She had become angry, she remembered, but she would not have been human if she hadn't become angry. She did step a foot nearer to him and she emphasised, she did not shout, she *emphasised:* Do you intend to live in a flat for ever? Think of Declan. What has Declan got to do with it, he shouted. What has he to do with it? she answered calmly. What has he to do with it? Just because you are allergic to suburbia, is he expected, am I expected, are we supposed to live in a way that people will look down . . . People! People! . . . yes ! people ! I want to be able to hold my head up . . . The table knifing into her back checked her and she fell to the floor. She heard the shout: Fuck people and felt the blow across her eyes. She rang Alice after he stormed out of the house. They were gone when he came back. Three days she spent looking in the mirror for a sign that the swelling was easing. And then, drunk, he kicked open the door of the house in Roses Avenue and demanded his wife and child. He made a poet's love to her afterwards. She realised that he was genuinely sorry for hitting her. He would never as long as he lived strike her. But she was never to mention people to him again.

She switched on the Pastoral Symphony and closed her eyes and saw Declan on a swing in the back garden, herself planting flowers while *his* dinner cooked of its own accord supervised by the timer. The cooker in the flat was gas. She did not know how he ate those breast bones. She could never remember offal in her mother's house. And that packet and tripe that he loved. And it was not that she didn't like a fry herself. But rashers and sausages and liver and eggs and black pudding. She rummaged the letter out of her bag, needing to be in touch with someone. Anyone. She had been correct about the Gounod piece:

Dear Mrs Whelan,

Thank you for your letter and reactions to 'Middlebrows'.

The piece by Gounod you are interested in is 'Judex' from his *Mors et Vita.*

If your middlebrow husband would like to give you a middlebrow present, the record label is COLUMBIA two 199! The Royal Liverpool Philharmonic plays and of course there are other items besides the 'Judex'.

I hope you keep listening.

Armed with the imminent death of his mother, Whelan was able to be kind; also, he wanted Breda to make him tea and a fried egg sandwich. Drink gave him a false appetite.

'Hi Breda,' he said, kissing her. 'What's your news? I didn't get a chance to talk to you with the rush.'

'How's your mother?'

'Ah,' Whelan dismissed his grief, 'she's going, Breda. She's going. No point in fighting it. She's going. I'm ravenous. Put on the oul kettle there Breda will you. Thanks.'

'I couldn't go to see her today. With Declan.'

'Breda, she knows that. Don't worry. She understands.'

'If I could get Alice for an hour – or if you were home early some night . . .'

'Yeah. We'll see. Listen, get me up early tomorrow will you.'

'You're up early every day.'

'Earlier. I have to see the bank manager before I shove off.'

'Is there something wrong?'

'No. He has to see me actually. I bumped into him tonight coming back from the hospital. You'll never guess what he was doing.'

'What?'

'Jogging! I caught him jogging!'

'What's wrong with jogging?'

'Breda, Breda! Throw on an egg there and make a sandwich of it. Breda, what hope is there? If my own wife can't see what's wrong with jogging! '

'Oh. In a Fart International context?'

'Of course.'

'Billy – your mother's dying in hospital. How can you think of that ridiculous . . .'

'Not ridiculous. Not ridiculous. There was a letter in the paper today. Some eejit, secretary of nitro. Now what would a man from Mars think NITRO's supposed

to mean. N is National. I forget what the I stands for.
Tax Reform Organisation. They can't even pay tax
now without huddling together. The time I had to get
the tooth out there was a *Time* magazine on the table.
Do you know there's a thing in America called gasp?
Something like Guard Against Smoking Pollution. If
some people had their way I'd have to go and hide to
smoke a fag. Like a kid. They wear stickers on their
lapels. It's true for Ralph Waldo Emerson,' Whelan
continued, making it up as he went along, good old
Ralph was guilty of so much anyway, 'end of a *Reader's
Digest* page: For a conventionally successful marriage,
a man himself must be unconventional.'

'I bet he was single; I bet he was a queer.'

'Ralph? I don't know. If I never got a tooth out
I'd never have heard of him. Kettle's boiling. Don't
let the egg get hard. Whitman. Walt Whitman. You
can't get a tooth out without him either. Breda,
will you stop me talking, will you. Any news? Any
visitors?'

'An insurance man called. He said he'd come
back when you're here.'

'What did he want?'

'As you said once to Chris yourself, he wasn't selling turf.'

'I have you at it now, Breda. A pity, I might have
bought turf from him.'

'Actually, he did have one good idea. I didn't tell
him – I didn't tell him you don't believe in insurance –
that you want to die and leave us all penniless.

He had two good ideas. You need insurance to get a mortgage. Here.'

'Thanks. You're a darlin'. D'you put salt on it?'

'Yes. But his other idea. It's not dear. You could insure Declan and when he's eighteen the insurance would provide for a university education.'

'A university education is something I'd really like for Declan.'

Breda sipped from her cup. His remark was out of character, pleased her, she decided to have a cigarette. It was the best part of marriage so far – having a cigarette and a cup of tea and agreeing with him. He was right about those awful people in America who wanted to stop people smoking.

'There. Insurance isn't the fiend you make out. Right?'

'Wrong. Insurance and a university education have nothing in common. I'll pay through the nose for Declan till he's eighteen. Then, if he wants, he can go to university the proper way – he can dig tunnels in London and pay his way. He'll know the cost. He'll pass his exams. He won't be going around with a scarf down to his ankles, protesting, on strike. And when he's going off to uni I'll ask him one question: Declan, do you believe in God, is there a God there? He'll say: Yeah, Dad. Why? And I'll say: Because if you come in a month and tell me there's no God there I'll thump you, that's why.'

'I should have known better. I should have known. I'm going up. Good night.'

'Hey! What about a peck?'

Breda allowed herself to be kissed. She put nothing into it. Whelan had another cigarette. Ever since the night he struck her they were true to a pact – they did not go to sleep bad friends. Whatever was between them they did away with by making love. Whelan could not rise in anticipation. It seemed like yesterday that he could not wait to take his clothes off. After the honeymoon, before Declan, and when Breda still had her job in the gas company, they made love in bed at night and first thing in the morning, before meals or after meals; one morning they turned to each other and Whelan went through with it although he did not have the heart for intercourse. There had been no forewarning. Suddenly that morning he noticed that Breda had tousled hair, there was flake on her lips, she did not smell of perfume, her teeth needed cleaning. He closed his eyes and imagined her as she was when she was fully clothed and contained a mystery. Now, not wanting to present himself to her limp, he conjured up memories of Breda dressed in the honeymoon hotel and of himself item by item coming closer to the mystery. Risen, he rose and went upstairs. Breda was in bed with the light out. She said: 'Billy, don't forget to leave me five pounds in the morning. I need Ostermilk and tights for myself, and the dinner.'

'Breda, would you ask me have I it? You're supposed to get the dinner out of the housekeeping. I'm not made of money.'

'You don't give me enough. You don't listen. The smallest chicken now, do you know what a small chicken . . .'

'All right, Breda, all right. Shove in there. Lights on?'

'No.'

'What's the matter? We're not committing a crime.'

'I don't like the lights on.'

Whelan did not like the lights on in the early days. Now, he did not want so much to see Breda as expose himself so that she might be so aroused she would agree to do it the other way. They had done it the other way on a Saturday night after he managed to get her to drink more than her quota. And they had done it the other way at Whelan's suggestion; *Forum* magazine had come into his possession at a racecourse. He had not mentioned *Forum* magazine. He behaved as though the other way was something that grew out of their familiarity. Breda had enjoyed it. She had lain on the bed, with the light on, arms and legs outstretched, groaning: Oh. Oh. Ooh. Oh Billy. Billy. Thank you. Thank you. She had reached down and run her fingers through his hair. He rose and put his wet mouth into hers. And then he turned himself about for her to do it. She didn't. She said she thought it was wrong.

Breda was curled up with her back to him. She had from the beginning felt it was unseemly to be seen to be eager. Whelan pressed against her; the leg-nudging began; she turned; they kissed; he brought his mouth down to her chest. Whelan whispered: 'Breda, let's do it the other way.'

'Hmm. No. Hmm. This is grand.'

'It'll pay you.'

Breda could see Declan on the swing in the back garden. She was not aroused. She was in a comfortable, warm position for dreaming – of Declan on a swing in a back garden.

'Do it the real other way. The whole hog. You'll love it. Honestly. I'll pay you. I'll give you six quid instead of the fiver.'

'Hmm. Stop, Billy.'

Whelan progressed netherwards. Breda began heaving.

'Breda – ten pounds. My final offer. Ten pounds.'

'Aaaah.'

Whelan began to turn slowly as he licked her thighs.

'Twenty pounds. I'll give you twenty pounds in the morning. *Dictum meum pactum.*'

Breda did not answer but the co-operative thrust of her body prompted Whelan. He buried his head in her and brought his penis towards her mouth. He made her clutch it with her hand and guide it in. The disentanglement was embarrassing when they finished. They went to the bathroom together and washed their mouths and their teeth. Silently they went back to bed arms around each other. In the dark Breda lay curled away from him planning how to spend twenty pounds and seeing Declan on a swing in a back garden. Whelan girded himself for the confrontation with John Harnett. Both of them were very happy indeed.

'Breda, you can't be serious,' Whelan bluffed in the morning.

'*Dictum meum pactum.* Come on. Hand it over.'

Having paid his wife tweny pounds for sex the other way Whelan felt he had the advantage over John Harnett as he enquired of G. Ellis for the manager.

'Go straight in. He's expecting you.'

Whelan knocked and heard the immediate: 'Come in. Come in.'

'Good morning.'

'Good morning Mr Whelan.'

'Mr Harnett, you may call me Billy. How are the legs?'

'Sore. I'm not used to it.'

'Good. We're only in the nipping in the bud department then.'

John Harnett took three envelopes from a drawer.

'You want to see the statements.'

'Please.'

John Harnett held up the dwindling term loan. Whelan nodded. The manager held up Whelan's deposit account. Again Whelan nodded. The Fart International account was presented. There had been a desultory trickle from the States – apart from Alvin's original fifteen thousand and Paul Tindall's five thousand – cheques and money orders for sums varying between five and one hundred dollars, contributions that were not acknowledged beyond their negotiation. One offering of three dollars in cash reached Whelan unscathed; the donor claimed to be an old lady. She did not receive an acknowledgement. Apart from the single pound note from a box number in the *Chronicle*, the *Chronicle* yielded nothing; enquiries yes, money no. Whelan stared at the balance on the current account: twenty-three thousand pounds and eighty-nine pence. It was the first decimal presentation.

'There seems to be some mistake here.'

'Mistake? Are you sure?'

'Yes. The last statement I saw was for twenty-three thousand pounds, seventeen shillings and sixpence.'

'Oh, well, give or take a half-penny you'll find the conversion accurate.'

'What conversion?'

'Into decimal.'

'That's what I mean. I don't mind the term loan being converted. Or my own account. But Fart International is not going decimal.'

'But – it has to go decimal – the computer.'

'That's something else. No computer. All transactions must be touched by human hand.'

John Harnett let the statement collapse onto his desk.

'I can't help you there. I can't help you there.'

'Could you not fill in a statement in your own handwriting – in old money – and show it to me? What you do behind my back is your own affair?'

John Harnett shook his head slowly – in agreement.

'All right,' he sighed.

He put away the statements, grateful to have something to do.

He joined his hands on his desk and enquired: 'Anything else?'

'I don't know, is it a bit early in the morning for you – it is for me – but once won't kill me – what about a drop from the cupboard?'

John Harnett looked from Whelan to the cabinet.

'Oh, certainly.'

He poured modesdy into two glasses, raised his own and said: 'Luck.'

'The same to you.'

Whelan extended the palm of his left hand expressively:

'Jogging. Jogging?'

The manager shook his head.

'I know. But it's not easy today. *I* laughed at them. But – you're changing after a round of golf, the remarks start. "Harnett, you're getting out of shape." In the clubhouse when you're just settling down, thinking the remark had been of no consequence: "Seriously, John, you are putting on a bit, I was playing the back nine with Doctor Tommy last week, he advised me to stick it – a stone I've lost in three weeks,

he says the blood pressure, the heart, all shipshape –
and you, you were never *heavy*, John." That type of
thing gets to you.'

Whelan merely commented: 'Squash?'

John Harnett nodded: Yes. And that *kills* me. I
prefer jogging to that.'

'Mr Harnett, I might be offside here but I'll risk
it. Mr Harnett, why don't you tell them all to go and
fuck themselves?'

The manager appeared to Whelan to be considering the suggestion seriously. He said, as though
puzzled: 'I don't know.'

The gentle tack was called for, circumlocution,
the search for the underbelly.

'How did you settle for banking? First day?'

'Settle for banking?' John Harnett chuckled, 'I
was educated and masturbated at Rockwell. What
does that prepare you for? My eldest brother was good
on the farm all right. Second eldest read poetry –
the old man packed him off to the diocesan college.
That leaves banking. My father bought me into banking. I graduated up the ladder around the country
via brandy, golf and moneyed father. The tried path.
I have a soft voice, I'm told, and now I have sympathetic grey hair to go with it. Do you know what I
was called? A toff! I gave a chap a term loan – he's
new to business – he had a tiny mortgage on a big
house, insurance policies, I gave him a term loan and
he actually thanked me. Called me a toff. Mr Harnett,

sir, he said, you're a toff. I liked the sound of it, you know? A toff. Anyway, that's how I got into banking.'

'And you like banking.'

'Ah. I don't know. It doesn't matter much now. When I think back, I mean who pauses to worry at that age, I enjoyed Rockwell. Surreptitious smoking, frolicing around – boarding school style – I made a handy scrum half in my last year, reached the final but didn't win – it seemed the most natural thing in the world, he had a big account – he was all go for years – I don't know . . .'

'There was never anything else?'

Mr Harnett reminded himself that he was talking to a man who was in control of an organisation called Fart International. He thought: Why not? If I can't say this to Fart International, who can I say it to?

'This will sound silly because it is silly. It hit me once that I could not go back again throwing stones at my father's cows. What do you do? Grit the teeth and listen politely to the inanity of the pavilion. I sometimes wonder if it would have been any different with a woman – let *that* go too long also . . . set in the ways and choosy . . . suddenly over the top at forty-seven, almost indecent to contemplate it any further, too well known as good sport, no ties, never fail to show up . . . and at the back of it all it's always grigging you – throwing stones at your father's cows . . .'

'. . . you mean you're not married? A bank manager? A manager?'

'The man they wanted at the time crossed over to Allied Irish. The next in line was a bit unrounded for the city – a trifle red in the cheek and to make a clean breast of it more of a Gaelic footballer than not – so Harnett stop-gap Pope – I believe I'm the only one – without the chattels.'

'Could I ask you one question?'

'Yes.'

'Off the cuff, what is it above all that you detest? Clue: I can't bear people who catch the first salmon of the year using a bait of silver devon, whatever that is, and get their photographs printed in the *Chronicle*. Anna Roche-Reilly – she's a member – can't abide Tupperware people. Have you anything on that line? Off the cuff?'

'I can't take people who honk horns going from a church to a wedding breakfast.'

Whelan extended his hand across the desk. The manager accepted and they shook.

'That is A1. A1. Yes. A1. That will go into the book if I have to suggest it myself. It's yours and of course it would be nice if . . . if . . . Mr Harnett, what can I do for you?'

'I don't see that you can do anything for me. I can't see that I *need* anything done for me.'

'Fair enough. What can you do for yourself? No man is an island. Who said that? Was that Ralph Waldo Emerson I wonder? Or was that Walt Whitman? I'll have to get a tooth out and check. But take me. I married above me. A beautiful woman. I wouldn't have

gone within an ass's roar of her on my own. But I had
Fart International.'

'I didn't know you were married.'

'I didn't tell you.'

'I usually know. People come for finance.
Mortgage, furniture. You didn't.'

'I'm going to tell you everything about Fart
International. Everything you don't already know. I'll
begin with a Christmas Day in the Dark Continent of
Kilbum. . .'

Whelan told John Harnett all about Bill Johnston
and Al Guerrini omitting, as instructed by Bill
Johnston, the New York, Los Angeles, London connections. He did not mention that Alvin T. Brine was
a son of a closet Irishman and he did not dwell on
the more horrific information contained in the Paul
Tindall letter. Anna Roche-Reilly was presented as she
was – a tall girl in her mid-thirties, well got and better
connected and without a shadow on her lips thanks to
Removio and Smoothex, products Whelan neglected
to mention. T. A. Dufficy's love of the roundabout,
Whelan saw no harm in revealing, but not its origin.
Whelan concluded mysteriously: 'I could not do anything about Alvin. You were there yourself. A man
travels all the way from the States, I couldn't shut the
door in his face. Of course he's entirely unsuitable.
Paul Tindall is not a man after my own heart either
but he's a witness against Alvin if the need ever arose.
T. A. Dufficy, because of his associate membership, is
no help in the fulfilment of a quorum. It only leaves

Anna and myself. A beautiful woman, Anna. When I think of some of the ugly people going around married and I think of Anna Roche-Reilly it's enough to make me weep. It's just not on that a beautiful woman and myself should be closeted at a meeting in the Blue Room notwithstanding the ghostly duenna of T. A. Dufficy at the hatch. One more acceptable candidate and the membership is closed.'

Whelan had not touched his brandy. He did so now taking the hint of a sip. He was not a spirit man. John Harnett downed the remains of his and offered: 'All very fascinating.'

'Yes.'

'I'm thinking.'

'Yes.'

'I'm thinking – despite the way I ranted on earlier – I don't like squash or jogging but I do like golf. I do. And no more about it.'

'I see.'

'So where does that leave me?'

'Out.'

'Out?'

'Out.'

'But why? What's wrong with a harmless game of golf? What have you to say about Jack Nicklaus? Arnold Palmer, that Spanish chap?'

'Nature's gentlemen for all I know. But they're not golfers, they're businessmen, good businessmen and no bones about it. What's your handicap?'

'Fourteen.'

'And you sit there and admit it. Did you ever hear of a football team going into the nineteenth weekend after weekend *boasting* of having been trounced six nil? My father-in-law Bob Matthews, he's manager of Todds . . .'

'I know Matthews. You married a daughter of Bob Matthews?'

'Yes. And I'm a hawker. He was President of the Chamber of Commerce last year. And he's in Rotary. Goes to a luncheon every Monday. You know what he tried to persuade me? I'm friendly with him actually, he has no choice, I'm his son-in-law, Bob Matthews insisted that Rotary was a gathering of businessmen who performed charitable deeds.'

'And so it is.'

'And so it is my arse. Listen, I have to go to a race meeting. Quorum or no quorum I'm closing the membership today. It's true for Bill Johnston, nobody, *nobody* is worthy of joining Fart International. But I've come so far with you I may as well put the cards on the table. Keep your golf. But repeat after me. Are you ready?'

'Yes.'

'Repeat after me: FUCK THE NEW MONEY.'

A staring contest ensued in which Whelan performed lamentably. He was hopeless at staring contests. His eyes took in the room. When they returned to John Harnett the manager had not blinked. Whelan realised that it had evolved from a staring contest: Harnett was lost. He said out of his trance, weakly: Fuck the new money.

Whelan added: 'AND FUCK THE EEC.'

'And fuck the EEC.'

Whelan rose and took the manager's limp hand in his own: 'I must go. Friday night, Sarsfield Arms Hotel, eight-thirty for nine o'clock. I'll see myself out.'

During the sixty mile drive to the races Whelan did not once think of John Harnett; he tried to think of John Harnett but the man would not stay still. Whelan had come across the letter addressed to his wife earlier that morning. He came across the letter while he was rooting in her handbag looking for any letter that he might come across. He was not afflicted by the T. A. Dufficy syndrome but he discovered that access to Breda's private world gave him a clue to his own standing in her eyes. During the three days that Breda was hors de combat in her parents' house they had sympathetically drawn from her that her husband was involved in an organisation known as Fart International. They couldn't have learned much from Breda because she was as much in the dark as the dumbest front-line troops who do not need to know the overall plan of battle. But they deduced enough to inspire Simon, Alice's accountant husband who wore leather gloves when out walking and a driving jacket when in his car and who did not possess any virtues in Whelan's eyes. Simon was inspired to itemise grounds for having Whelan committed and the marriage annulled. Whelan had come across the crumpled list in Breda's handbag and when they made the love of reconciliation afterwards Breda laughed with him at Simon's straitlaced lunacy. Now, the montage of Breda sitting down to a well earned cigarette while the breast bones sang in the pot, having done her bed making and put Declan for his nap, drawing on her low tar, wondering whether she was coming or going within the ridiculous marriage, while the appropriate *Mors et Vita* seduced her into contentment, swam before his eyes. He could not concentrate on John Harnett. He would get his hands on that record. He would ask for Columbia Two 199 with all the aplomb of a Smoothex purchaser. This was the Breda he had fallen in love with, this was the Breda he had come close to on their wedding night.

Looking back it was something of a miracle, not that he had come close to her, but that there had ben a wedding night. A miracle, yes, and not the wonderful work of Fart International. He had to believe that.

'You're intractable,' Bob Matthews had accused. 'Surely you could be accommodating in the small matter of a dress suit?'

'I'm sorry. I really am sorry, believe it or not. I don't know what it is, to be honest with you, I just don't fancy the idea of getting married in someone else's clothes.'

'They're not someone else's clothes; that's just the way you're looking at it.'

'Whose clothes are they? I have to give them back.'

'If you bought the dress suit it would be yours.'

'To wear for one day?'

'We've gone along with you in every respect. Anyone would think it was a shotgun wedding. It's the biggest day in my daughter's – in Breda's life. You're belittling it. No reception.'

'Every day with me will be the biggest day in Breda's life. I'll see to it. And you yourself saw my point of view about the reception.'

'I know. I know I did. You say you have no friends, no relatives apart from your mother, no neighbours you wish to invite. But we're your friends now.'

'Mr Matthews, please. I bear you no ill will. I bear no one ill will. But don't dump a charabanc load of friends on me just like that. It's too rich. I might not be able for it.'

They were at the bar in the Sarsfield Arms Hotel a week before the wedding. Bob Matthews was on his fourth pint and liking it; it was a long time since he wrote off a night on porter. There was something about porter that encouraged him to loosen his tie and speak from the heart; he associated whiskey with caution and the need to remain alert.

'I don't understand you. That's what it boils down to. I thought I did but I don't. You're happy enough anyway that you'll make money at the hawking. Why not? Why not hawk? Fair enough. Why not your own suit? Fair enough? Why get fleeced for a breakfast? Fair enough. You're well educated, Breda says. Although you were unhappy at school. Some incident or other. I left school after my Inter. Went into Todds as . . . sorry . . .'

'That's all right. You started in Todds as?'

'An assistant wrapper. They had assistant wrappers in those days. I suppose some people would laugh at it nowadays but I remember being pleased as punch the day I wrapped a kettle correctly. There's a forgotten art for you – wrapping kettles . . . Blood-Smith died, he got a heart attack coursing. . .'

'I like the sound of that man; he chose a gentlemanly exit.'

'. . . yes, you could say he did. Rose was very excited about the takeover, I remember refusing to hope myself . . . then, suddenly I'm summoned to a meeting of the board, finish that, two pints please, I'll put it to you this way young man, we're living in a different age now, I was rather proud of rising from an assistant wrapper to become manager, I was and I still am and if you think that makes me an old fogey, then there's nothing can be done about that.'

'Mr Matthews, I want to tell you something. Can I tell you something?'

Bob Matthews nodded disconsolately; the boy was going to insult him again. Nothing moved him. He was bitter. No sense of humour, no appreciation of hard work, merit, a cynic. Bob Matthews nodded.

'My last year at school. It should have been my second last but it was my last. You know traditionally the horse gets a breather in fifth year? I went to two dances. Higgins and Murphy and Nicky and Mark Brown, they went to the dances together, even though Nicky was going to go away to become a priest. I heard them talking about going to the dance and I went home and I shaved for the first time in my life – I nearly cut my throat, most people learn from their fathers or older brothers – I smothered my hair with Brylcreem, shined my shoes; I hung around them under a pillar, they were picking out girls, Higgins was saying: okay Mark's getting up with the one with red hair, Murphy you take the blondie one. I spent the whole night watching them dancing. Well, an hour of it; I went home. They never noticed that I didn't get up dancing. The four of them went into the mineral bar for orange and club milks. While they were inside I tried to pick up the courage to cross the floor and ask someone but I didn't know how; I didn't know what to say. I couldn't dance anyway. Higgins couldn't dance from what I could see but it didn't worry him . . . They used to go downtown to the Café Capri at night. Sit in the cubicles. There was only room for four in the cubicles, comfortably, although I often saw three people sitting at each side. I had to sit at a table near the cubicle. There were girls from the Presentation at a cubicle across the way and Higgins and Murphy and Nicky and Mark Brown were talking about them. Even though Nicky was going away to be a priest. Higgins guffawed into his hand and I said: What was that one? And Higgins says: Mind your own business, Whelan. You've a dirty mind.'

Whelan drank at length from his pint. Bob Matthews saw tears in his eyes. Bob Matthews said: 'I'm sorry.'

'Sorry? For what? That was a night they were being kind. I used to look in the Capri window and if there was only two or three of them there I'd go in and get a seat in the cubicle with them. But if they were all there I wouldn't go in. I went to one more dance but I couldn't get up. I didn't really mind not going dancing; I wasn't even interestted in girls that time. It was only that they were. But in April – it started in April, just after the Easter holidays, they had a meeting around *my* desk, *my* desk. Higgins was saying: "Nicky, you go in with Murphy so and I'll go with Mark."

"What should we bring with us, I wonder?" Murphy said.

"Don't worry about that. I'll make out a list." That was Mark Brown.

"The last two weeks in June. That's settled is it?" Nicky chimes in. Then the Brother came back into the class and they all went back to their seats.'

Bob Matthews was sure he knew what was coming; it was so obvious. He felt genuine pity for the boy. Whelan took another large swallow, licked his lips and said to T. A. Dufficy: 'Two more pints please.'

'They were practically sitting on my desk when Nicky said it was settled, that it was the last two weeks in June and yet that day I sidled up to him going out the yard and when I asked him he said: Tisn't settled yet. I asked him how many were going. He said himself, Mark, Higgins and Murphy. I asked him how much were tents. He said he thought they were about a fiver. Then I said out of the blue: My mother might be buying me a tent for my birthday. He asked me when was my birthday. I said: September, but she says I can get it before then, for the summer. That was in April. When I went home from school I asked my mother if I could get a tent. She was frightened at the idea of me going away in a tent. But she said she'd think about it. After a week I knew. I knew but I wouldn't admit it to myself. The four of them were on the school team and the Harty Cup Final was coming up. They were treated better than greyhounds. Every morning they were allowed to leave the class and join the rest of the team for bovril and egg flips. And when they came back the Brother went over the lesson again because they were on the school team. I couldn't understand Nicky. He was going away to be a priest. I was sure he must have said it to them. If he was never going away to be a priest it would be abnormal not to mention it to them. He could say when they were making their plans – hey, Billy Whelan's getting a tent, will we bring him with us. They didn't talk about it any more. I realised with the final coming up they couldn't think of anything else. They won the cup. They were always winning. They won a shield when they were in the choir when we were only ten. . .'

T. A. Dufficy placed the two pints on the counter. He did not make a token effort to hide the fact that he was listening. He had a right to stand waiting for payment. Absentmindedly Whelan put a pound on the counter. It seemed to Bob Matthews that Whelan was back there at seventeen. T. A. Dufficy changed the pound and began rinsing glasses.

'. . . there was an ad in the *Chronicle* for tents. There was a sale on in the sports store. My mother said twould be better to get it before they went up for the summer. This was early in May. I got the tent. There's no grass in the backyard of my mother's house. There was hardly room for the tent even though twasn't a huge tent. I pitched it using stones to keep it in place instead of pegs. I pitched it in the back yard. I went into it and made my mother throw cans of water over it to see if it leaked. I was trying to figure out Nicky for two whole weeks. I thought he might have forgotten. People going away to be priests are kinda different. I thought he was the wrong person to ask. I should have asked Murphy. The first chance I got I said to Murphy: "Where are ye going away?" I asked him. He said Kilkee. "How many of ye is going?" He said four. Mark, Nicky, Higgins and himself. I told him my mother bought me a tent for my birthday, although my birthday wasn't until September, I said a tent would be no good in September. Murphy owned a tent of his own. He asked me what kind of a tent I got. I told him. He said they were good tents. I told

251

him how I tested it. That was going home from school at four o'clock. Twas a Friday. The whole weekend I couldn't wait for Monday. But on Monday he never said a word to me. I waited for it every day. Nothing . . .'

There had been tears all the time in the back of Whelan's eyes and yet Bob Matthews was surprised when they began to show themselves. Whelan bent his head and put his hand to his forehead. He was trying to choke back his feelings. Slowly he began to shake his head and mutter: Bastards! Bastards! He repeated the word at least ten times. Bob Matthews remained silent. He longed for a sup of his porter but thought it indecent to reach out his hand toward the glass. Bastards, bastards, bastards, Whelan sobbed the word. And then he ran out of the word but continued to sniff. He took out his handkerchief, blew his nose, wiped his eyes, coughed. He drank from his glass.

'Silly of me. It's true for Breda. I made too much out of it.'

'I don't think you did. That would upset any child. I'm surprised at Breda.'

'No, no. Breda understood all right. She thought maybe I would have gotten over it. I should have. It was the bloody tent in the shed in the yard. You know, I waited until the third Saturday in June for a knock on the door. Around four o'clock – my mother was down town shopping – I brought the tent into the kitchen – just to look at it. I did a terrible thing. I knelt down on the ground and clenched my fists and called out to my father. I called him, I called, I said:

Jesus, Mary and Joseph why did you leave me! What world is this that I'm to be walked upon! Then I got vulgar. I cursed and I swore. I cursed my father and I cursed God and I cursed those bastards . . . A week later my mother saw me off with the tent. She thought I was going to Kilkee with friends from school. I left the tent in the toilet at the station. I had a British Rail single ticket . . . when I wrote to her a week later I had a job in a bar in Shepherds Bush . . . bastards . . .'

The descent once more into bitterness aroused Bob Matthew's paternal anxiety for Whelan himself and no longer Breda; he saw an Oliver Twist in Whelan and was human enough to derive satisfaction from seeing himself in the role of a Mr Brownlow – he would let the boy have his way – a simple ceremony attended by the immediate relatives and a subdued breakast in Roses Avenue; his own Rose would cope admirably. Afterwards, with solid in-laws at his back, Whelan would take a respected place in the community.

Columbia Two 199, Whelan memorised; he was half-way to the races and not alone could he not focus on John Harnett, neither could he properly recapture his wedding night – the image that was supposed to be interfering with his desire to dwell on John Harnett. At the breakfast in Roses Avenue, Bob Matthews was railroaded by his family into making a speech. Whelan recollected not having been offended. It was sob stuff about Breda always having been a good girl and Whelan, as far as Bob Matthews was concerned, being a welcome addition to the family. There was a telegram from an aunt of Breda's who lived in Dublin and one from Bob Matthews' Melbourne brother Joe; they were simple, and to the point – wishing happiness and prosperity to the new couple. Simon read the telegrams. He read a third – it had a double meaning. Alice laughed. It was from Simon himself, Simon admitted. There was good-natured laughter. Whelan did not laugh. When Breda went upstairs to change Bob Matthews suggested that Simon and Billy join him for a drink in the Ardhu hotel across the road.

'A man shouldn't overdo it on his wedding day but a pint won't do too much harm.'

'Don't stay long now,' Rose warned. 'They don't want to miss the train.'

Whelan felt they were closing in on him. Telling a dirty joke via telegramese at his wedding breakfast might not have been a solecism in their eyes – for all Whelan knew it might have been part of Alice's and Simon's pre-marriage course – but Whelan had standards to maintain. Two pints and a bottle of lager were on the counter. The Simon merchant did not even drink properly. Whelan circled.

'You know, that's die first wedding I was ever at in my life.'

'That's unusual,' Bob Matthews agreed, 'I must have been at so many I've lost count.'

'Were you at many weddings, Simon?'

'Yes. Although this is the first where the reception was held in the bride's house. I'm not saying anything against it mind. Actually in the olden days the reception was always held in the bride's house. I think. That right, Bob?'

'Aagh,' slipped out of Whelan.

'Pardon?'

'Sorry. Took a mouthful.'

The cretin called his father-in-law Bob. Was that on the pre-marriage course? Whelan had done with circling.

'Yes. In the good old days . . .'

Whelan cut in on Mr Matthews: 'Nice of Breda's uncle to send a telegram all the way from Melbourne. And of course your own telegram. Isn't that unusual? Sending a telegram when you're going to be present yourself? I mean you actually read it yourself. I thought it odd.'

'Not at all. At most weddings you'd have dozens of telegrams. I've heard some priceless telegrams at weddings.'

'Do they all take the form of vulgar jokes?'

Simon was uncertain of himself. The hawker had not smiled.

'I wouldn't go so far as to call them vulgar jokes. A bit of fun. . .'

'I would. I'd call your telegram a dirty joke. Offensive, unclean, not fit for a lady's ears . . .'

'Hold on now. I'm not staying here to be . . .'

MICHAEL CURTIN

'. . . if you wanted to tell a dirty joke why didn't you stand up and say you had a dirty joke to tell in honour of the occasion . . .'

'Billy, Simon didn't mean . . .'

'Did *you* think it was in good taste? '

'Billy, drink up your pint. Simon didn't mean anything. He's sorry. Tell die boy you're sorry.'

'If I caused offence I apologise. I didn't realise people were so sensitive.'

'That's all right. But they are. People are sensitive. People don't realise it but people are sensitive.'

Whelan chuckled on his way to the races. He admitted to himself that he had been a proper bastard to Simon but he was not contrite because he thought that Simon was a proper bastard. It was coming to him now, slowly. They had taken the train to Dublin, a prosaic choice of Whelan's to match the late November time of the year and the inadvisability of travelling by a Pete O'Mara van or a chip wagon. A week's honeymoon was as long as he would allow them justify – he had a wife to keep now. He did not have any objection to a fortnight himself only that they suggested it. He had eaten a fry on the train. They had a drink in the hotel in Dublin. The minutes ticked away. Already the responsibility of married life had begun to pall; it was Whelan's job to ask the porter for directions. They had to stay grimly at the bar until at least half past ten lest they be seen to be hurrying to bed at an hour that was not time honoured for sleep. But they did manage to reach the bedroom that night, Whelan remembered. Breda was dressed in an autumnal going-away outfit. She hung her jacket on a hanger and revealed a white, frilled blouse that contained what would be revealed soon in all its glory. As for what lay beneath her skirt, Whelan sat on the bed, sweating, embarrassed, too sober.

'I'm just going to the bathroom, love.'

'Okay.'

Whelan listened but could hear no sound. He needed to urinate himself and dreaded that she might hear him when it came his turn. He might have been sharing a room with a labourer in Tom Mackey's in Queens Park, so matter of fact had their conversation been, so far away was the atmosphere from a dark night on the red path with houses twinkling in the river. He heard the toilet being flushed. When Breda emerged she sat on the bed beside him and they kissed, passionately, according to the word of that time. They lay on the bed. Breda groaned: Let's go to bed, you go to the bathroom while I undress. Whelan went to the bathroom where he put on his new pyjamas. He hoped she would like the pyjamas. They were not striped. In her nightdress Breda lay under the bedclothes, her long, bare, tanned arms overhanging the spread. Guiltily Whelan put out the light and joined her.

There was no looking that night. Both of them were content kissing and holding each other and would probably have been grateful if an angel appeared with instructions to go no further. In the dark in every sense of the word they tried to make the coupling. Breda knew that it was to enter her in an exact spot and Whelan knew that it was there to make an entry someplace. Shamefully they writhed for an accommodation and when at length they succeeded Whelan immediately began the glory of his release. Breda groaned with pain. A moment later Whelan realised that he was no longer emitting. He stopped. Breda said: 'What's wrong?'

'I think I'm finished.'

He withdrew and lay on his back. He held Breda's hand.

'I'm no good at it. Am I?'

'Don't be silly. Of course you are.'

They lay holding hands without talking. Inexplicably Hogan entered Whelan's head. Before he could come to grips with Hogan Breda said: 'I think we'll have to put on the light. The bed is all wet.'

'Wet? Where? Oh. It is. Put it on so.'

'Billy! You put it on.'

'All right.'

Naked, he switched on the light. Breda rolled down the covers. There was blood on the sheet and on Breda's legs and on Whelan's own legs.

'God,' he said. 'What happened?'

'That's natural. That's meant to happen the first time.'

Breda got out of bed and put on her night dress. Whelan slipped into his pyjamas.

'What will we do?'

'Do?'

'About the sheets.'

'They'll be expecting that. They know we're on honeymoon. We can sleep on the other bed.'

Whelan was sitting on the other bed and stretching his hand out for his cigarettes.

'You knew that would happen?'

'Of course. Didn't you?'

'No. Did it hurt?'

'A little.'

'So you got no fun out of it. God, Breda, I'm sorry. I told you before I was innocent.'

Breda covered the used bed and walked around her husband to climb into the other bed. He remained sitting and smoking with his back to her.

She stroked his back.

'It will be better the next time. Don't worry about it.'

'Breda, I thought it was fantastic – for me. But it didn't last long. I should have had advice.'

'Mammy said the most wonderful thing about sex is the husband and wife learning it together.'

'What! Your mother talked to you about it?'

'Naturally. Come to bed.'

Whelan put out his cigarette. They lay quietly for a time, side by side, Whelan with his hands behind his head.

'Breda.'

'Hmm.'

'Breda, I love you. Do you love me?'

'Hmm.'

'Good. Good.'

He knew now what it was about Hogan that was coming back to him. Actually, it was pre-Hogan, in Whelan's Shepherds Bush barman period but Hogan symbolised all of Whelan's London experience. In his first night sleeping in the bar in Shepherds Bush Whelan could not get used to the idea that outside his bedroom window did not lie Wellington Avenue. And in his wedding bed in a Dublin hotel he closed his eyes and was positive that Wellington Avenue was outside. He had a lovely wife, money, and there was Hogan and Maurice and Corkey and them all, nomads at a forty- five table who could neither go backwards nor forwards. He could not entertain a feeling of guilt; he had not deserted them. Yet some agency was trying to fog his contentment with the picture of Hogan alone putting bacon and cabbage into a pot. He was amazed to wake in the morning and discover that he had slept.

And now in his van on the way to the races eighteen months after his honeymoon Whelan realised that he had given Breda twenty pounds for sex the other way. He was not in the mood to remember what sex was like the other way or any way but he did know that last night he thought it was worth a thousand let alone twenty. No matter how much money he gave her in the early weeks of their marriage she spent it all. She did not budget. He grew to give her as little as she would accept and paying for sex was a joke between them, to hide their lack of confidence in themselves, each other and the fact that they did not possess a unity of ambition; Whelan did not know what he wanted and Breda knew that she wanted Declan on a swing in a back garden with the breast bones cooking themselves on an electric cooker.

CHAPTER TWELVE
THE DINNER

Mark Brown was back with the group when Whelan returned from the bar having purchased for himself with Mark Brown's money. He handed Mark Brown his change. Mark Brown did not query the oddity of Whelan buying his own pint out of the money he entrusted to Higgins. But he did say, 'Thanks Billy,' and continued, 'I don't know, Murph. I haven't seen Cork this year but Cork will be Cork. And I'm not mad about our corner back. A six foot three inch corner back isn't my idea of a corner back.'

'He did all right in the first round against Tipp. He was fast on the turn.'

'I didn't see the first round. I had some people over from London. We put them up. They don't like it dossing in hotels. And they want to see how you live. They went back on the Saturday, I suppose I could have made Thurles but, Murphy, I was jacked. The body was wrecked. And as well –I don't go for the lib shit – but Ann-Marie had had a right few days of it – your wife is as important as yourself at this game –I said I'd throw the kids in the car and take them up the mountains, packed a lunch, told Ann-Marie do nothing, it pays off. You must build up the credits. What do you think, Higgins? Can Limerick do it?'

'No way. No way, Mark. They won't keep the ball pucked out to the Cork forwards.'

'Yeah. I thought so.'

'They were all right against Clare, Mark. Higgins, they were all right against Clare.'

Whelan plunged into his drink. He wished they would change the subject and let him in.

'Clare is not Cork, Murph. You saw them, Nicky. Right?'

'The first match I've seen in eighteen years. It didn't look like hurling to me. No charging the goalie, third man tackle gone . . .'

'It's faster.'

'It's faster all right. But it's not dirty anymore. We were nearly killed in the Harty Cup . . .'

'That was a tough one against North Mon . . .'

Whelan buried his face in the drink again. Mark Brown said: 'You be there, Billy?'

Whelan choked. 'Oh yes. Wouldn't miss it for anything.'

'That must be one of your biggest days. None of my business but, what would you make on a day like that? Is it better than a race meeting is it?'

'It depends,' Whelan sat upright. 'If I sent one of the lads,' he gestured as though plucking a figure from a dusty room full of ledgers, 'I suppose it would

be worth a hundred. If I went myself and got everything set up, went all out, it could be four, five.'

'Wow. In a day? Tony O'Reilly doesn't clear that.
We're in the wrong business.'

'You don't have a Munster final every day, Mark.
Anyway, what's money? I'd prefer to see the game.
Drink up that. What's yours, Mark?'

'A Hennessy. You know you're looking fit Billy.'

At the bar T. A. Dufficy said: 'Your friends know
how to order.'

'Hmm? Ah well. Tisn't often we get together.
They're all right.'

T. A. Dufficy concentrated on filling the drink.
The faraway look on Whelan's face disturbed
him. On the eve of the tenth anniversary of Fart
International, with Bill Johnston due, with Alvin T.
Brine and that new chap Paul Tindall already here,
upstairs in the lounge with John Harnett and Anna,
Whelan's behaviour was odd. Only a fortnight earlier T. A. Dufficy had spent a pleasant night's drinking with Whelan looking forward to the gala event.
Whelan had laughed apropos of nothing and said:
T.A., you won't believe this but the bastards invited
me to a PPU function. Both of them had waxed witty
on the subject of PPU functions. For a time in fact
PPU functions almost displaced Tupperware and
silver devons and joggers. It climbed above chemists
who used brand names, although that was between
themselves, they did not have the heart to mention
it to Anna. Anna Roche-Reilly-Harnett. T. A. Dufficy

had great faith. He persuaded himself that Whelan was working in the field.

Whelan clearly saw them deciding that they would all go in Mark's car. Mark would pick him up on the Thurles road. It would have been bad enough Nicky calling for him to go to the function, Nicky seeing the state of the house in Wellington Avenue, but the idea of Mark Brown knocking at the door was untenable. Whelan would certainly be down a few bob on the day, nothing near the four or five hundred he had wishfully conjured up for them. He would send Cyril along with some dry goods and sandwiches. Cyril might make forty or fifty. He would give Cyril eight. Whelan knew lots of jokes he had picked up from hawkers, jokes and stories, he had a fund. The car journey would be pleasant.

'You're in dreamland.'

'Oh. Sorry, T.A. I was thinking of tomorrow night. Bill Johnston. At last.'

'Yes.'

'I'll see you.'

T. A. Dufficy watched him go. He had never said anything to Whelan. Maybe he should have. But he suspected Whelan would be embarrassed. There had been nights in the cups when he almost told Whelan that he loved him like a son. He had, after all, spoken to him more intimately. He had told him that he liked to open people's letters and listen to them making love. That was a freedom denied him by the world. Admitting that he was T. A. Dufficy. That was a freedom his own wife Maureen was not in a position to convey on him. It was eight years or something now – it seemed like minutes and he did feel younger – since Fart International, and Whelan had come into his life. And the rent of the Blue Room had not risen above three pounds. He told himself not to worry. Tomorrow night he would have his ear cocked at the hatch listening to Bill Johnston. Afterwards T.A. would emerge and they would drink all night, denouncing all round them.

Whelan placed the drinks on the table and said: 'Yes, I wouldn't miss that game for any amount. Tisn't everyday Cork and Limerick are in. . .'

'This is a bit dead lads, isn't it? I have the old guitar outside Murph, will we haul it in and have the crack. Liven them up.'

'Great Mark. I'll get it. Give me the keys. What are you driving these days?'

'Granada. Mind you, I'm not crazy about them. But the Company, image, you know, I can't get a – I can't get a feeling for them somehow. It's in the back seat. Dammit where's the plec. Try the dashboard Murph.'

'Right.'

Whelan took a draught of medicine from his pint.

'Must go to the jacks.'

As he urinated he leant on his arm against the tiles. He would no more be in Thurles the next day in their company than he had been in Kilkee with them camping. In a way he was grateful; he detested hurling and hurlers. He did not mind the followers – they bought sandwiches and milk and lemonade and crisps and chocolate and cigarettes and chips and burgers and ice cream. They could not have given him fairer warning; a guitar, Mark Brown and his guitar. It would not be Over the Sea to Skye but even so. They were going to sing. He hated all singers. Golfers and silver devon and all singers and hurlers and Rotarians and homosexuals and all singers and hurlers and people with the full complement of parents and those who sat around dinner on Christmas Day and all singers. He loved camels. With something of the fatalism of Sidney Carton he zipped and rejoined them in time to hear predictably, seeing as he was not stone deaf, the stage whisper of a one-armed chemist:

'Ha. The lads have a guitar. We'll have a bit of music now. No harm to liven it up. That's the stuff Mark. Tune it in or wind it up and get going. Look, can't ye bring the chairs around. Ye're too scattered. That's it. Bring yer chairs around in a circle.'

The man was obeyed. He had the authority of the disabled. Whelan looked with horror upon his extroversion. In the world of the sensitive that man's remaining hand would be pulled from its socket and he would be clubbed over the head with it.

'Here you are, son. There's a seat here.'

'No, I'm all right thanks,' Whelan pleaded as he grabbed his pint and tried to withdraw to a hovering position on the fringe.

'Nonsense. We don't want to be scattered. Loads of room if they push up. Push up there and make room for the hand that bought.'

The original sixty had dwindled to less than thirty. Most of the older Brothers, fearful of the pace had retired to let the young people get on with it, although Brother Hennigar remained; for Brother Hennigar it was too late in the day for conservation. Whelan was trapped between the old chemist and Higgins. Higgins' foot was stamping the ground even though Mark Brown was merely tinkling with his overture.

> I've been a Wild Rover
> For many a year
> And I've spent all me money
> On whiskey and beer. . .

Higgins pipped Timmy Roberts the chemist, in leading the joining in. Whelan was alarmed at his shrunken status. The heads were thrown back and the mouths open with smiles; this was the life; singing the head off. He met his pint half way up to his face. There was a convivial slap on his thigh.

'Sing up boy. Sing up.'

Whelan opened and closed his mouth and nothing came forth. He thought some people charged the world an awful lot for one hand.

> And it's no, nay, never;
> No, nay, never, no more.
> Will I play the Wild Rover,
> No never no more.

Mark Brown plonked three sharp cords to indicate that that was the last chorus. Everyone applauded, including Whelan.

'Good boy, Mark. Well done. Keep it going now. Don't let it lie down.'

Whelan said: 'Drink up that Higgins,' and escaped to the counter. It galled him to have to buy again but Mark Brown was launching Buddy Holly. Whelan had been unable to share their appreciation of the pop singers of their day. It was worse being tone deaf than stone deaf. If he had been stone deaf he would not, for instance, have heard Timmy Roberts the one-armed chemist.

'I must say your school friends are great to drink,' T. A. Dufficy could not help pointing out.

'T.A., put a sock in it. Please. Oh God, I'm sorry. I'm sorry T.A.'

'All right. Why don't you come upstairs. They're all above.'

'No. As my mother said – or was it Emerson – there's a time and a place for everything. I must do it on my own. Although if Bill Johnston arrived – no. If he comes, don't tell me. Tomorrow night. I've waited ten years. I can wait till tomorrow night. Thurles tomorrow! Normally I look forward to Thurles. They have me upset in there. To hell with them. I'll go back and laugh at them.'

The class of '60 was in full throttle:

> Thereyougoin' baby,
> Here am I-I-we-ell

Upsadaisyhowyou,
Drive me crazy,
Gollygee whathaveyou
Done to me-e-e,
   I guess it doesn't matter any more . . .

Brother Hennigar was tapping a foot; Timmy Roberts was moving his head from side to side, his eyes closed, humming. Whelan handed round the drinks, which they accepted in mid-song. He squashed in beside the chemist and Higgins.

'Grand lads. Grand. Now we'll go round. Who'll give us a song? Mark, ye've all grand voices here. Who'll give us a bar?'

Higgins volunteered: 'Billy Whelan here is a fine singer.' The old chemist drew himself back to benevolently beam on Whelan for corroboration. Whelan panicked: 'I don't sing at all, sir.'

'Of course you sing. My sister can't play the piano but she does, said the man. Come on now. We'll all join in.'

'I could swear. I don't sing. Father Nicky has a lovely voice.'

'Well, Father. Will you give us something?'

'I have hay fever. What about Murphy?'

'Here, why pick on me. What about Higgins?'

'Ah, ye're no good at all. I'll have to oblige myself.'

Listening to the old chemist Whelan concluded that he had spoken the literal truth; he could only have been obliging himself. Lonely as a Desert Breeze,

he began, and before there were five execrable intro-
ductory lines out of his mouth he had by dint of his
all-embracing one hand inveigled the assembly to
join him in 'One Alone'.

'Now,' the old chemist declared triumphantly, 'if
an old frog like me can sing there's no excuse for the
young thrushes around me.'

There was no excuse. Mark Brown said, firmly:
'Come on Higgins. Sing. From now on it's singer's
choice.'

The old chemist was relegated to titular MC.
Higgins leaned forward, supped from his large Hen
and sang to his knee with great concentration:

> Far across deep blue water.
> Lived an old German's daughter,
> On the banks of the old river Rhine. . .

The cavalry chorus joined in. Higgins was not that
great a singer, Whelan deduced.

> Fraulein, Frau-uh-li-ine. . .

Whelan was undecided. To join in was to admit to a
voice; to refrain was to convey that he was selecting
from his own repertoire for the next song. And there
was no doubt about the next singer. It was singer's
choice by decree of Mark Brown and Higgins would
not be the bastard Higgins if he deviated from his
one paced dependability to wound.

'Now ye're hurling. Singer's choice. I bet Brother Hennigar would oblige if called upon.'

Whelan could have kissed the old chemist. Higgins said grimly: 'Billy Whelan.'

'I really can't sing. Honestly. I could never sing. Ask any of the lads. Nicky, sure I don't sing?'

'Ah, go on Billy.'

'Singer's choice. Singer's choice,' the chemist repeated and was struck by a happy refrain:

> Why was he born so beautiful,
> Why was he born at all,
> He's no bloody use to anyone. . .

Every voice joined in and every good natured smile was turned upon Whelan, including the voice and the smile of Brother Hennigar. They repeated the lines; Whelan put up a hand to stay the baying; they cheered the success of the chestnut. If he had been strategically placed at the back where they could not see his face; the round robins would notice every tic and see the hue spread from his collar up over the arteries till it met at the top of his head. But anything was better than the sea of vulgarity chanting 'Why was he born at all?'

He began:

> Alone, all alone,
> By a wave-washed strand

'Sshh, sshh, sshh, sshh, easy, this is lovely, good man,' the old chemist interjected. It was not lovely. How could it be lovely when he had taken one breath to sing 'Alone' and another breath to sing 'All alone' and had paused and swallowed and drawn dry breath and licked his lips to sing 'By a wave-washed strand' not even getting the 'd' in 'strand'. Whelan felt it must have taken him a minute to sing 'All alone in a crowded hall', a minute during which Higgins let his hand climb slowly to his mouth to cover a snigger.

Whelan ploughed on:

The hall it is gay. . .

He stopped and swallowed and licked his lips and saw Murphy glance at Nicky who looked at the floor. Mark Brown sat evenly attentive as though Whelan was not naked save for Queen Victoria's knickers. Whelan was grateful for Mark Brown's command of command. It might spread.

His eyes beginning to close with tears Whelan ploughed on:

The waves they are grand . . .

Mark Brown's gaze flickered in the direction of Higgins who appeared to be rapidly getting out of control. Higgins coughed and took out his hankie to lend verisimilitude to the notion that he was not laughing. Whelan saw Mark Brown smile, control the smile, and become evenly attentive again.

> But my heart is not there at all.

His head was bent in a mist; he could not climb up to the next line. He tried:

> It flies . . . it flies . . . it flies . . .

No more would come. The old chemist sang:

> It flies far away,
> By night and by day,
> To the times and the joys that are gone;
> BUT I NEVER WILL FORGET
> THE SWEET MAIDEN I MET
> IN THE VALLEY OF SLIEVENAMON.

Whelan raised his head to the applause; it was for his one-armed voice. Like Timmy Roberts' putative sister, Whelan could not sing but he had to and the reward was applause in inverse proportion to his talent. He did not care if they saw him acknowledging applause through a mist. The worst was over. He croaked in response to demands: 'Brother Hennigar.'

He scarcely heard Brother Hennigar recite Father O'Flynn. This was why Brother Hennigar was born beautiful – to recite Father O'Flynn. It was a bitter thought to nourish about an old, old man who had never harmed anyone apart from pucking a bit of education into people but Whelan nourished the thought. The wet about his eyes was beginning to dry and his eyes were tired from the smoke and the drink and the false hopes of being invited to Thurles. He applauded Brother Hennigar and then excused himself past the old chemist; his pint was half full, a testimony to his going to the toilet. But he did not go to the toilet.

He lurched down O'Connell Street to meet Cyril in the Wimpy. The Wimpy had replaced the Café Capri where he had used to sit catching the crumbs from the Higgins cubicle. He passed a queue of stragglers at the Kentucky Chicken shop; looking younger than Dorian Gray, Colonel Sanders was on genial advertising duty, beaming from his placard outside the door for all the world like a man who would not dream of organising a nigger-shoot. He passed Burton's, where once an august T. A. Dufficy in striped trousers and black coat and tape measure around the neck had used to encourage: But it's a beautiful piece of cloth, madam, and where now Italian suits at one fifty a week and no deposit peered out the window. He turned to enter Cruises Hotel, a great haunt of nighthawks in search of free urination but the management, he now discovered, had executed the legerdemain of moving the dance box office in front of the toilets and converted free urination into the price of the dance. He could not complain; he himself gave away free milk at racecourses. He relieved himself down a lane around the corner from the Capri and was grateful to the alert management of Cruises Hotel – it was unnatural to piss elsewhere than down a lane. Put that into the book – toilets out. Colonel Sanders was definitely in. John Harnett and his wife, the former Anna Roche-Reilly had objected; indeed afterwards T. A. Dufficy wondered out loud what was coming over Whelan. But Whelan was adamant; any man who sold pigeons in batter and called them Kentucky Chicken deserved the palm.

The chairs were stacked on tables but in a cubicle Cyril sat smoking over coffee.

'They're just about to throw me out. You pissed?'

'No. Not too bad. Are they finished? Any chance of a coffee?'

'Angela! Two more cups.'

'At this hour. No. The till is closed.'

Whelan watched Cyril put his hand up under her uniform. She protested coquettishly.

'Come on now, Angela. You never know your luck. Two more. Good girl.'

Whelan smiled. He was often reminded of Hogan when he listened to Cyril telling his tales of conquests. But Cyril told the truth. With his own eyes Whelan watched Cyril put his hand up her uniform and clutch. There was no need for him to say: Now, you see my problem? He knew Whelan understood.

Whelan said: 'Bastards.'

'What?'

'I'm talking to myself. Nothing.'

'Good night?'

'Terrible. Well, it wasn't too bad, really. You know the crowd. Never did a real day's work in their lives. Sit on their arses in government jobs chancing their one arm at the weather.'

It was a mistake to speak disparagingly of civil servants, he realised, as Cyril smiled and mentally added the remark to his armour. Lest he actually bring the subject up now, the interminable request to be allowed leave school, Whelan asked: 'How did you get on?'

Cyril shook his head. He was now going on seventeen, a casual six-footer with hair no longer cut by his father, or anyone else, Whelan mused; but it was clean hair and Cyril was clean, a good boy, good to his mother, he was determined to realise her dream of getting away from O'Malley Park yet no matter how much they saved they made little headway against the rising cost of houses.

'Cyril, sometimes I think you exaggerate; it can't be that bad at dances. Surely you must come across someone.'

They had the conversation regularly. No matter how many times he listened to Cyril on the subject he was never bored; he loved it and dismissed any suggestion that he was a voyeur, which he certainly was.

'Nope. Not one. And Billy, they're not dances, they're discos. I just wish they were dances like you say they were in your day. Although – I thought – I had a feeling tonight was going to be the night.

There was one girl. There was something about the way she walked, the way she looked at me, kinda shy. I thought, this is it.'

'What happened?'

Cyril turned his thumb down.

'I bought her a drink. Ah, I forget what we talked about. The records. Then I said-in-my-inimitable-style. I said, Let's blow. She nods. Then I said: You safe? She nods. I excused myself to go to the toilet. I had no notion of going back. I realised you mightn't turn up for another hour so I said to hell with it. I took her down the docks and fucked her.'

Whelan, rising to the occasion, prompted: 'Many people would call that a successful night.'

Cyril nodded.

'Billy, there must be someone, someplace? Someone like Breda? God, I often he awake at night dreaming of someone like Breda. Tell me about the red path ye used go out with the lights from the houses in the water. I love the bit where you take half an hour to hold her hand.'

Once he had come to realise that Cyril was not having him on, Whelan had looked forward to the occasional outburst that always culminated in Cyril's dream of a Breda like vision who not alone did not fuck at the drop of a suggestion but did not allow herself to be kissed on her first date and did not smoke on the street. Cyril gaped at him as though Whelan conjured up a Victorian age rather than nineteen sixty-nine. Whelan had come to know

Cyril's own story gradually; at fourteen a neighbour of Cyril's, also fourteen, had invited his pals to share his fifteen-year-old sister and not against her will. She had not been too popular with her own girl friends on account of her lack of experience. Whelan had listened in horror. He had spoken like a father. And now at the approach of seventeen, Cyril despaired of finding a girl like die girls of Breda's time.

The voyeur continued: 'You exaggerate, Cyril. I know you do. Remember this is Limerick, the City of Churches. I see girls your age sitting on the pavement outside Todds fasting for the Third World.'

'Yes. They fast for the Third World. And the Fourth when it appears. I wouldn't take it away from them. But all I have to say is: You want to fuck? And they want to fuck! It's fucking awful I'm telling you.'

'They made me sing tonight and they laughed at me.'

'What? Who? You mean that bunch of weirdos you're always talking about? How?'

'I said I couldn't sing and then they all started singing "Why was he born so beautiful why was he born at all, he's no bloody use to anyone, no bloody use at all". So I sang to stop them singing. And they laughed.'

'Why did they laugh?'

'Because I can't sing.'

'What did you sing anyway?'

'Slievenamon.'

'Oh. You should have told them it was the anthem of Fart International. Really give them a laugh. How is the good old F.I. these days? And when can I join? If I can't leave school at least let me join up.'

'You don't need Fart International and Fart International doesn't need you. Let's go.'

Cyril paid Angela for the coffee. He put his arm around her, squeezed her breast and kissed her. The behaviour embarrassed Whelan. He thought it inconsistent with Cyril's desire for a girl like Breda. He did not know whether he was glad or sorry that he had told Cyril about his delicate courtship of Breda. It was good that Cyril wanted an escape from random fornication; Whelan did not know if girls like Breda had been were rare nowadays but he did know that Breda was not now anything like Breda was then. There had been one trouble after another and Whelan had always come out on top of the unequal struggle. He had said to Breda a month after the funeral: 'Breda, don't ask me to promise anything. I'm not over her death fully. I'll get a bathroom put in and then get the house valued and then we'll see. Okay?'

'All right.'

Breda claimed afterwards that the only possible construction of his remarks led to her justifiable assumption that he would sell the house and use all or a portion of the proceeds for a mortgage on a house of Breda's dreams.

'It's a good job. I'm not saying it isn't,' Breda said touring the new bathroom.

'Right. Then what are we paying rent for a flat for? Let's move in. While we're taking our bearings.'

'Can't we sell it now? Why move in when we'll have to move out again?'

'These things take time. Look, we'll move in, save rent, and we can be looking around. You might even get to like it.'

'No fear.'

'What do you mean? It's not a slum.'

'I didn't say it was a slum. I'm talking about a simple thing like a garden. A bit of privacy.'

They moved in. The house was in impeccable condition apart from the odd scrape due to the bathroom installation. The bathroom itself had yet to be decorated. It was the only room in the house with new, flush walls but there was no hurry in doing it up. Who would see it bar themselves? A length of carpet came Whelan's way at a race meeting. It was no more than an inch at the most short all round but it did the bathroom floor just nicely. It was a good, thick dark brown carpet.

'So the bathroom suite is green. That doesn't mean you can't have a brown carpet on the floor.'

'Billy, it just doesn't match.'

'Who says so? Who makes the laws about what matches what? Gangsters! The same people who come out and say skirts are up this year or skirts are down and everyone copies them. You know I'm hopeless at wallpapering. Couldn't you get a tin of nice sky blue paint and have a go at the walls? I haven't a minute.'

'Sky blue? Sky blue? Green? Brown?'

'Breda, whatever colour you want.'

'There isn't a colour. There's no colour to match brown and green.'

But there was. It was pink. That was the colour of the wallpaper that Whelan got his hands on at the races.

Little things, stupid things like colours, where to live, how to live, where to go on holidays came between them. And somewhere during the years Breda had given up. She plonked herself down at night now with a magazine and did not notice or point out any more that the skirting needed painting, that the wallpaper was faded and hanging in strips from the walls; the children's depredation went uncured; the furniture was tattered; the house was a shambles; there was no knowing where to begin. Ten years, two children, a house falling apart; she did not wash die cups properly any more. She rinsed them idly in the sink as she listened to the Enigma Variations of Elgar on her record player. Her tights were slack when she wore them; her denim was baggy and out of date, she wore no make up and her hair – God, when he remembered her hair that first day in Roses Avenue – and yet Cyril thought she was beautiful. If he could only have seen her when she was buying cones in Roses Avenue. And she had lost her snobbery; the holiday in Kilkee had hammered that. Whelan had no snobbery to rail against. He was sorry about Kilkee. But he did not see what else he could have done.

'What is so awful about accepting the use of my father's lodge for two weeks? Is that compromising yourself?'

'It is, Breda. It is. I'll find a place. A place of our own. I'll drive down today.'

When he returned that night and told her of his coup in renting half a house from a Mrs Kelly, Breda said: 'Billy, that's the East End.'

'I don't follow you.'

'Nothing. It's useless.'

'What do you mean Breda? The East End? I suppose it is the East End as you look at the bay. But what about it?'

'It – it's common!'

'You're joking.'

'No, I'm not joking. Factory workers and pork butchers and carpenters and labourers – they all stay in the East End.'

'And hawkers. Don't forget hawkers, Breda.'

Declan was four years old then and Eddie still in Breda's womb; she had two months to go and the heat and the two months to go made her irritable. It was to be Whelan's first and triumphant visit to Kilkee and it was the first holiday of their married life. Whelan could not afford to go in other years; he could not afford to go now. Breda had gone every year taking Declan and staying with her mother in the lodge. Whelan complained that a true wife would forego a holiday that did not include her husband. Breda maintained that a true husband would curtail his drinking and be able to afford a holiday with his family. They nagged each other into a holiday in Kilkee. A friend advised Whelan that plastic sacks were handier for packing than cases; cases were on the way out. Whelan was delighted to believe this. It saved him the spiritual expense of having to borrow cases that might not turn out to be modern. He delivered Breda and Declan in the dark. He dropped them at the rented half house and left Breda to unpack the plastic sacks while he drove the van back to Limerick and hitched to Kilkee the following day. Breda had agreed that the van would not be the thing in Kilkee.

Kilkee was new to Whelan and Whelan was new to Kilkee. After the breakfast Breda led them forth to the rocks on the West End; it was form to lie on the rocks in the West End; it was vulgar to sunbathe on the steps in the East End. Whelan did not enjoy his first day in Kilkee. He tired easily of playing with Declan at the sand; his life style would not allow him lie down and do nothing. Whelan had heard – from a friend – that the Sea View Guest House was notorious for after hours. It was fifty yards from the rented half house. That was why Whelan rented the half house. They would not need a babysitter.

'The Sea View? The Sea View?'

'Yes. I heard they give you a break there.'

'You would. That's exactly the type of thing you'd hear. Ah well, I may as well make the best of it.'

'What are you saying, Breda? Make the best of what?'

'Ugh! They sing songs there all night.'

'I thought you were the musical member of the family.' 'Musical! They sing like people who never had a holiday in their lives. I was there once. "And now we'll have Maisie O'Brien to sing The Sunshine of Your Smile. Come on now Maisie, don't let us down, Maisie." Ugh! Common!'

But they went to the Sea View, a reconciliation having been affected on the floor of Mrs Kelly's kitchen in the rented half a house, a reconciliation that cost Whelan five pounds – a straightforward reconciliation – not the other way. In the Sea View Whelan learned from a pork butcher that only a lunatic stayed on the beach in Kilkee. Everyone swam in the Pollock Holes when the tide was out and in Burns's Cove when the tide was in. Burns's Cove and the Pollock Holes were for Men Only.

Towards the end of the first week a system had evolved.

At night while Breda tidied the rented half house and put Declan to bed and got herself ready, Whelan had a pint here and a pint there until it was time to settle down to after hours drinking in the Sea View with his good wife, listening to the sing-songs and praising the weather. In the morning while Breda cleaned up after the breakfast and saw to Declan, Whelan leaned on the wall of the prom and watched the vacationing Christian Brothers hurling on the beach, where the thought struck him that he would love to be feeding them. Then he returned to the room – they no longer called it a half a house because it was a room with a kitchenette off and the use of Mrs Kelly's bathroom upstairs – and spoke words of encouragement to Breda as she filled her beach bag with appurtenances and then he led the way to the beach and laid out the rug and made a few token castles for Declan. And then the battle began.

'Breda, I think I'll go for a dip in Burns's.'

'Why can't you go in here?'

'Can't get a dive. Will you be okay? I'll only be about an hour.'

'And I'm supposed to amuse Declan on my own? What if I wanted to go in? What should I do with him?'

'Go on in so and I'll mind him.'

'You'd mind him would you? You'd mind your own son while I went for a swim? Is there a brass band in town I wonder, or a shop where I could buy a medal for you.'

'Ah, come on, Breda. Don't start.'

'You build one sandcastle and then you lie down and even that won't do you. You want to desert us. Look at all the other men digging tunnels . . .'

'All right. I'll stay here. I'll stay here every minute of every day digging tunnels. I'll make the dinner. I'll wash up. I'll put Declan to bed. Will that suit you?'

Breda snorted. Whelan took the shovel and bucket and made ten sand castles in a frenzied circular pattern. Declan was thrilled but Breda did not relent and beg Whelan to go for his swim in

Burns's Cove as Whelan expected. He tried a second approach. Taking his swimming trunks and towel from the beach bag he stood up and said: 'See you.'

'Yeah.'

He paused and enquired with stilted tone: 'What time is the dinner?'

'When it suits me.'

'I'll just have the one pint after the swim. I'll be up at half one.'

'Give my love to the pork butchers.'

In Burns's Cove after his swim Whelan was talking to a man, who as it happened, was a pork butcher. The pork butcher said: 'Do you know what would go down well now?'

Whelan expected the man to say a pint.

'Do you know what'd be lovely now? A feed of breast bones. Even in this weather. A feed of breast bones after a swim.'

'Yes,' agreed Whelan, 'can't get them here though.'

'You like breast bones?'

'I'd eat nothing else if I had my way.'

'The missus brought down a rake of 'em. I'll give you a few if you like.'

Breda was tired. Carrying Eddie and dragging Declan, the heat, the glorified bedsitter, the fact that her parents' commodious lodge clung tantalisingly to the West End foreground, all combined to make her weary. Staying in the East End was not as bad as she had imagined; it was worse. The pork butchers did not know how to tan themselves; they threw themselves flat down without oils and at night their red faces burned with drink. They had a reptilian fascination for her. Billy loved them. She watched him in the Sea View jostling for drink at the counter and listened to his familiar 'how's-it-goin' ' with strangers. He was worse than any of them; at least they had been coming to Kilkee for generations; a man's first time in Kilkee. It was inconceivable that she had married a man who thought Kilkee exotic. And the East End of it at that. But then it was just as implausible that she had married a hawker, a man who thought living was a poky house within a minute of a betting shop; what constituted an amenity in his mind led to a drop in real estate values in the opinion of gentle folk. She would not let it go with him; though she knew in her heart that he would never buy her a house with a garden, she would not let go. At least she had only to put on the kettle. They had agreed on that – salads, leaving plenty of time for die outdoors. God, that sounded like him already. She jumped up and began to fill the kettle. A gas cooker – of course. It would take ages to boil.

'Hi.'

'Enjoy your swim?'

'Lovely. Listen, I passed that novelty shop and I thought of you. Is this little bracelet any good?'

It was not.

'Billy, that's nice of you. What have you in the bag?'

'Breda, this is going to give you a right laugh. You're right about this place. Full of pork butchers. I had a swim with one of them. I walked back with him. He said he had something for me in his house. Guess what?'

'What?'

'Breast bones.'

'Oh Jesus no.'

She sat down on the sofa that was convertible into a bed at night; she began to shake her head and cry silently. Whelan said: 'I'm sorry Breda. It was my fault. I'll ditch them. It's too hot for breast bones anyway. I didn't like to insult the man. It's not right to throw away food I know. I wonder would Mrs Kelly like them. We could give them to her as a present. She might go easy on the rent.'

Breda began to laugh. It frightened Whelan. The laughter was as silent as her tears.

'A convertible sofa. That's the ultimate East Endism. And having to read your own meter when you come and when you leave. Do you know what that woman said to me the other day? She said the people here before us were very good, they left the place spick and span. Did you see the notice she has in the bathroom? "Please do not flush soiled nappies down toilet". That woman looks at me and sees a wife that would flush soiled nappies down a toilet and who would leave this place without cleaning it and who counts every atom of electricity. Look at me. I'm gross. It's sinful going on holiday seven months gone. And you really thought I was going swimming this morning. That's how much of a woman's world you live in.'

'Breda, I swear to you, only for I know you're pregnant I wouldn't know you're pregnant. You have the carriage, some women look terrible after a month, but honest, no one would knew you were pregnant.'

'There's the kettle. Switch it off will you.'

'Breda, you relax. I'll do the rest.'

'The rest. Put three spoons of tea in the pot and pour the water.'

'Breda, I have an idea. After dinner, why don't you take Declan and go to the lodge for the afternoon? You could sit out in front with your feet up and take it easy. Your mam will play with Declan. And stay there for your tea. Don't worry about me. I'll look after myself.'

'We – you made a deal before we came. No contact with the lodge, you said. It wouldn't be *our* holiday otherwise.'

'I can't hold you to that deal when you could do with a rest and attention. You'd love to go to your mother. Be honest.'

'How could I leave you, Billy? No one to make your tea. How would you pass the time without me?'

'I suppose I'd stroll out to the Pollock Holes.'

'I suppose you would too. *Diving* in with the pork butchers. You might be lucky. You might get more breast bones.'

'Breda, don't be snide.'

'You're planning to get rid of me in front of my eyes. Do you think I'm blind? You bring in a bracelet that Woolworths can't get people to rob and then you have the cheek. . .'

'Hold it. Hold it there. I'm not a judge of jewellery and I don't pretend to be. If you don't like the bracelet give it back. I thought it was the thought that counts.'

Breda shook her head, smiling wanly.

'I wish you weren't so thoughtful. I haven't a washing machine because you think so much of me. You're afraid I'll end up like all the other women. All the zombies. Electric cookers are dangerous, gas is cheaper. You wouldn't have me live in a place depending on supermarkets. You protect me from the antiseptic life. You intend to stay hawking so I can be proud to be the wife of an independent man. You . . .'

'Shut up. Just shut up,' Whelan knelt on the floor in front of her, taking her hands in his. 'Breda, I don't mind what you're saying, it's what it's doing to you I mind. I'm kneeling here in front of you and all I want to tell you is that I love you. It doesn't mean much nowadays, it's cheapened, but I love you. Oh God, Breda, let's convert the sofa, hmm.'

'Billy, I'm not recovered from this morning. I'm too big.'

'Hmm. I can go in the back way. Hmm. Declan, play out in the front.'

'No Billy. The dinner.'

'How much?'

'It's not that, Billy.'

'Two pounds for a quickie. You can't turn that down,

Breda. You could buy your mother a present. Oh God, Breda, hmm.'

'A fiver.'

They did not need to collapse the sofa. Breda lay on her stomach while Whelan stripped her sufficiently to penetrate from the rear. Far from not being conscious of her seven months bulk he had to conjure memories of books passed around by his fellow hawkers at the races. The disentanglement effected in Breda the belief that she was married to a pork butcher who was the king of the East End. Yet she was feeling happy. She had a fiver of her own, she would be in her mother's lodge for the afternoon and somebody did not find her seven months state repulsive.

'Cyril,' Whelan said as they walked back up O'Connell Street, 'did I ever tell you about the time we went on holiday to Kilkee?'

'I don't think so.'

'Somebody advised me – I forget who – that people weren't using cases any more. They were putting all their stuff in plastic sacks. I drove down in the middle of the night and brought the van home and thumbed back down myself. But when the holiday was over we decided to go back by bus. The bus stopped in the square, about two hundred yards from where we were staying. It's amazing the amount of stuff you'd bring with you on a holiday. We had seven plastic sacks – there was only one of them mine, I packed my stuff in five minutes – but you know women, Breda had two sacks full of Declan's stuff and four full of her own. That was going. Coming back everything was mixed up but we still had seven sacks *plus* a cot, a go-kart, a net we bought Dec for fishing, a bucket and shovel, our own knives and forks, you have to bring your own knives and forks to these places, and our own sheets for the bed. It wasn't even a bed, it was a glorified sofa. Actually I took Declan for a last look at the beach while Breda was packing. But when I saw the lot lined up in the hall. I had to make six trips carrying the stuff up to the square and of course we're a half hour early for the bus. The bus driver wrinkled his nose – all the other passengers had a pair of meticulous suitcases. The clothes were bursting out of the sacks. He told us to take them on the bus. I think he was ashamed of the notion of plastic sacks on the top of his bus. A pair of underpants fell out of one of the sacks on to the floor of the bus. Mine. A passenger diffidently picked it up and handed it to me. It was full of shit. Declan was a bad traveller. He still is. But then he was hopeless. We could see him getting white. He threw up. There was lowering of windows. All the way back to Limerick Breda didn't say a word. She was mortified, red. I was embarrassed myself . . .'

'I'd say.'

'I was, Cyril. I didn't want to be but I was. What do you think?'

'What do I think of what?'

'Of what I'm telling you.'

'I suppose it is an embarrassing situation to be in. If you had suitcases.'

'Cyril, did I drag Breda down? You think Breda is a nice woman now?'

'I think she's wonderful.'

'Cyril, you should have seen her. You should have seen her before she met me. She looked like a girl who never had to carry a suitcase in her life. She's living for me to buy a house with a garden in the suburbs. That's what your mother wants. A house with a garden in the suburbs. Ye have a garden in O'Malley Park?'

'My mother wants to get out of O'Malley Park and she doesn't care where we go. It has nothing to do with gardens.'

'The neighbours.'

'Fuck the neighbours.'

'But they're all God's creatures?'

'He's welcome to them. Fuck them.'

'That's not a charitable observation.'

'Admittedly. It's not meant to be. Fuck them. Every single one of them. Drunks, criminals, dog owners. We had two rooms in the city centre. Thrown out. Just because we were homeless they housed us with the rest of the homeless. I'm particular about whose homeless company I'm in when I'm homeless.'

They turned into Barrington Street and then off Barrington Street where a lane housed Whelan's fleet. Whelan said again: 'You don't think now I dragged Breda down by making her live in Wellington Avenue?'

He sat down in the shed on a butter box and offered Cyril a cigarette. 'A ten minute break before we start. We'll pretend we're in Government jobs.'

Cyril took the cigarette but began to work. He did not answer Whelan's question. Whelan repeated: 'Did I drag her down?'

'I don't know. It sounds like it. Why *don't* you buy her a house with a garden if that's all she wants?'

Whelan smoked and stared at the ground. 'I don't know, Cyril. I don't know.' His hands were shaking.

'Cyril, the mineral industry portfolio is yours. I'm not steady enough for the delicate alloy.'

He began making sandwiches and drew from Cyril the observation: 'You must be in a good mood.'

'Why?'

'You're putting a fair bit of butter in with the marge, aren't you?'

The very act of working, at his own job, revived Whelan.

'Cyril, it's Limerick and Cork tomorrow. The Cork crowd are a decent bunch, good spenders, and we don't want to do our own, do we? Twenty-five per cent water will do there, Cyril. They're not apes either.'

It was three o'clock when he reached home. They arranged to set off at half seven to be sure of good stands. Four hours sleep. The drink was wearing off. Breda was asleep. He was too considerate to wake her, as he had once done, and say: 'Breda, just hold on to me. Tell me you care a little bit about me. Tell you'd notice if I dropped dead.'

'What's wrong,' Breda had asked. He had tried to explain to her that he felt alone but she had not properly understood him because he had not properly understood himself. He told her that he missed Mr Ryan; that he missed his mother, that he missed Hogan, that he missed his father. Breda was sleepy and put her arms around him to comfort him. She fell asleep as he was saying: The butt of a cigarette, there's no meaning to that, what plan is that part of?

Once was enough to carry on like that. He made a cup of tea to accompany a fag. The wallpaper was stained over the gas cooker, torn around the skirting. Eddie was a destroyer. The ceiling wasn't painted in years. He could not bear to look at the window sashes. He was no good with his hands. He had often thought of paying a man out of his money in the bank but he was afraid the neighbours would start: too lazy to paint his own door, now we know who has the money. Pays good money to a painter to slap up a bit of paint. Dirty bugger anyway. You'd think he'd put on a decent suit of clothes. God be with his poor mother. Spotless she used to keep that house. No help from him. Did all the wallpapering herself. They say she's a dirty housekeeper too A lovely girl when she came here first, from a good family, but no good at the back of it. Whelan realised that if he did hire a man, the man would want him to provide the paint. He would not mind providing the paint, he would not mind paying for it in a shop if necessary, but he could not imagine himself going into a paint shop with pricks behind the counter saying: Yessir. Why had he not thought of that before? Into the book. He should have thought of bringing Nicky to the door to call for him. He could have brought Nicky in and given him a seat on the tattered easy chair and then told Nicky at the last minute: Actually I don't think I'll bother, I think PPU functions are juvenile, you know, for those who never grew up.

He was in the mood now to write to Bill Johnston and would have done so only that Bill Johnston was expected, if he had not already arrived. He had written regularly to Bill Johnston and admitted in his letters aspects of his own character that he would not admit to himself. His only defence in life outside Fart International was his line of bullshit that had enabled him to land Breda and that Breda no longer believed in but pretended to believe in to justify their union. He saw himself as an old fashioned cad where his wife was concerned. *He did love her.* But that was not enough for her. It should have been enough for her because she had everything else before she met him. It was certainly not enough for him that she should love him because he had nothing before he met her. He had had to go and create his own world to survive. He had brought happiness to people and they had brought nothing to him except the fact that he had. T. A. Dufficy could do nothing for him; the Paul Tindall creep, whom he would meet at the meeting after the match, had nothing to offer except his evidence against a bigger creep, Alvin T. Brine, alias Fonsie O'Brien; it was some consolation to have a bank manager singing 'Slievenamon' at the behest of a hawker with a dollar bill suspended from a piece of twine around his neck and to have been instrumental in bringing the bank manager and the neurotic issue of proselytised aristocratic blood together. John Harnett had moved into Barrington Street with her; they had engaged a couple of servants; they called in the decorators and began to entertain. Whelan and T. A. Dufficy had been invited. T. A. Dufficy declined on the grounds that he would have to stand behind the curtains in danger of his feet being spotted and being unmasked by a large Hen. Whelan had gone with Breda and withdrew disgracefully after half an hour, Breda not even having the blood for the occasion. Whelan consoled Breda and himself by maintaining it was not a question of blood but of neck. John and Anna Harnett put little into Fart International gatherings from then on. They attended out of a sense of fear of blackmail, made token offerings to the book – people who watch television, John Harnett had offered lamely – and left early.

There was always that wonderful man, Bill Johnston.

He climbed the stairs to get a few hours in. He had not bothered folding the suit and putting it on a hanger. He threw it on the floor in a ball.

Breda was snoring. The clothes on his side of the bed were tossed and revealed the mattress gaping foam. He leaned over and prodded Breda.

'Stop snoring.'

She was fast asleep and stopped snoring. He lay beside her and prayed himself to sleep:

Why do they have to ground me into the ground? Have they no sensitivity? Jesus help me. Breda help me. My dead mother and Mr Ryan come back and help me. I was an altar boy. My father come back to me. Mind me. I'll work morning, noon and night and I'll spend all my earnings on cigarettes for you. I'll build a house made out of cigarettes and a garden made out of cigarettes if you take me on your lap and read the Hopalong Cassidy strip out of the Independent to me. . .

CHAPTER THIRTEEN
THE MATCH

There was more in the air when Whelan woke than his sick head or the memory of insensitive guffaws; he trilled to its identity: *Limerick v Cork*.

A token of its magic was that when Eddie woke in the cot demanding to be transferred to the bed of his parents, Whelan nipped out and rocked him back to sleep so that Breda could have a lie in. There was that in the air: *Limerick v Cork* and it filled him with consideration for others. It was bumper day, licence to print money day. If all died belonging to him he would be enticed to be pleasant on Munster Final day. All had, as a matter of fact, died belonging to him. He unfurled his suit and wore it to attend mass. Downstairs he took from the fridge the dregs of Breda's pint bottle of orange, marketed for in front of the television consumption; it effected the detachment of his tongue from the roof of his mouth. His cough warned him that he was far from a condition to smoke. He went out to church.

There was more consideration in the air at mass. The celebrant declared that it was penance enough for the congregation to rise so early and that he would spare them a sermon beyond invoking God's intercession to help Limerick win. They had not beaten Cork in over thirty years. Outside the church Whelan lingered over his first cigarette. It was traditional to linger outside a church, smoking. When people were cured of smoking the religion would die out. Optimistic children already wore green and white hats and hopped from one foot to another while their parents said to each other: Will we win? *Limerick v Cork.*

It was in the air. Crowds, happy, hungry, thirsty. Spenders; not a bootboy, mugger, skinhead, angst-mad, cross-grained whelp among them; unadulterated spenders, he hoped. He was obliged to maintain an ambivalent view of the proceedings. It was all very well and good to have the County at last in the Final, but would they spend? Would he make as much as if it was *Cork v Tipperary*?

At any rate it was good to be up early on such a day. It was good to be nobbing his cigarette and starting to walk home to breakfast. He put the butt of the cigarette in his top pocket. He was hungry. He planned to sling at random on to the pan and toodle up the stairs to Breda with a laden tray to give her a treat. But of course, notwithstanding the pus in her eyes, the hair in curlers, the strealing dressing gown, the slippered feet, she was already up and wielding the pan herself.

'Breda, why didn't you stay in bed?' he cried, trying not to look at her. She had disappointed him in not turning out to be a television mum. 'I was going to bring it up to you.'

'Heard it before, Joe. It must have been all hours when you got home. How did it go?'

'Pleasant night. Dinner, a few jars, the sing-song. You know.'

'Will I throw on a bit of black pudding as well?'

'Ah, no. I think I'll spare the black pudding. It mightn't go down too well.'

'I'd say it's how fast it would come up is what's worrying you. I suppose you got legless?'

'No, no. Quite civilised. No, to tell you the truth, it was torture. They made me sing and then they laughed at me. You know I don't sing, Breda.'

'What did you sing for then?'

'I had no choice, Breda. They were singing "Why was I born so beautiful, why was I born at all", and it occurred to me that I might be better off singing. So I sang and they laughed at me and it was all over faster rhan you could get a tooth out. Anyway, it's a minor detail. One can't be over-sensitive. What's being laughed at? With the big problems going around these days.'

Breda stopped prodding the sausages.

'It was bad, was it?'

'It was fucking terrible, Breda. Forgive my language but they are a shower of bastards and fuck them and all belonging to them. Breda, I don't know how long more I can carry this burden through life! '

'Billy, I'm sorry for you. But I have burdens of my own,' Breda paused expectantly and concluded, 'and you don't want to know about them.'

'All right, Breda. Truce.'

'Did you get the papers?'

'I forgot.'

'You always forget the day you have to go to a match. I suppose I'm expected to pay for them now myself am I?'

'I won't be reading them, Breda. Anyway, why do we have to get four newspapers on a Sunday?'

'Because you want three of them. You want the *Express* to keep you in blimpish touch with London and the two Irish ones to keep you abreast of events – wherever there might be two or three gathered in your name, as you put it. I'd be happy with just the *Sunday Times.*'

'Yeah, look at the price of it. And you'd want to be on a three day week to finish it.'

'It's about time you took notice of the cost of living. When are my wages going up? I can hardly buy a pair of tights for myself and Alice can't manage on four times what I get.'

'Breda, you'll bring my head at me. Look at the time. Throw it up there while I change into me duds.'

'Do you want another cup of tea?'

'Half a cup.'

'Make sure you bring them back something now mind.'

'Yeah.'

'Don't forget now.'

'Breda, would I forget my own children?'

'You would. And no fruit. Or chocolate. None of your leftovers. You'd want to start taking an interest in the children. They never see you. Declan is nine and he hardly knows you. You're out all day and night.'

'Breda, here's a pound. Give us a kiss. There's the cost of living for you. A pound a kiss. You should think of my expenses, Breda. See you.'

'Be careful.'

They did not bring the convertible. Cyril sat in the back of the van ready to pounce on anything that might rattle or roll or threaten to spill or break. Whelan concentrated on avoiding bumps in the road. It seemed that Higgins was about to be correct in his forecast of rain.

Whelan was at the wheel. Whelan was at work. The remnants of drink-sodden, confused emotions were shaken off by keeping the van steady.

'All right, Cyril?'

'Yeah.'

In the mirror Whelan could see both Cyril's hands occupied.

'Light me a fag, Cyril.'

'You light me.'

Whelan chuckled. Expertly he lit two cigarettes and with his eyes on the road he passed one slowly back over his shoulder. Cyril took it carefully. Outside roadway cottages gnarled, peak-capped men waved.

It was the day of the match. There was good will in the air. Whelan banished all thoughts of the excitement in store for him that night in the Sarsfield Arms. It was heady enough to be a hawker on Munster Final Day. He chugged into Thurles at ten o'clock and early as it was there were groups pawing at the door of pubs looking for cures. In another two hours there would be bedlam; continuous orders; short-staffed; pints pulled not by the Queensberry Rules.

A phalanx of collectors for 'Northern Aid' were spread out inside the main gate; Whelan set up shop twenty yards behind them; the psychology of offering those who came through the phalanx something for their money was not lost on him. They had two tables, one with sandwiches and free milk which Whelan manned himself, and Cyril's sweets, chocolate, apples, oranges, pears, ripe bananas and cigarettes stall. Under both tables they placed boxes of reinforcements, homemade lemonade. Whelan bought his milk in Thurles from a fella he knew and at a price that discouraged him from asking where the fella got it.

A man blind since birth sat on the grass with his overcoat spread out to receive. Around his neck hung a piece of cardboard. On the cardboard was written: Blind Since Birth. Whelan knew him from the race meetings. He threw two pence on the coat for luck.

'There's ten p to start you off.'

The man blind since birth smiled.

'Thank you, anyway.'

It was not Higgins' fault that the sun began to burst through and the clouds scurried away in dread. God, no more than Higgins, had no control of the weather on Munster Final Day. The early arrivals were in their shirt sleeves and thirsting for lemonade and lemonade alloys. A weatherbeaten man with a raincoat slung over his shoulders and a pint bottle of Guinness in each pocket approached Whelan.

'Free milk, sir. A free pint of milk with every quality sandwich purchased.'

The man wore a red and white rosette.

'White bread and red ham for Cork, sir. Up the blood and bandage. Free milk sir with every sandwich.'

'Matches. Have you matches?'

'I'm very sorry, sir. Matches is the one thing we haven't got. But hold on a minute. Here, take my own box and the best of luck to Cork.'

Whelan held out one of the dozen boxes of matches he had secreted about his person.

'Free milk with every quality sandwich. Real ham, not the shiny stuff. And creamery butter.'

'Gimme two.'

'Good man, sir. Two and two pints of milk.'

'No milk. Don't want milk.'

'God bless you, sir. Up Cork.'

Green and white, red and white, they were all buying like mad. Whelan did not know what hat to wear. He was not missing Tipperary. It was almost half past one. The minor match was due to start. Whelan had no more than a dozen sandwiches left and Cyril had the last of his reinforcements on display. Whelan saw that the stand side was almost full. And then he saw Higgins.

The met officer was wearing an anorak, faithful to his forecast, although the sun was melting down on top of him. They were fifty yards away progressing in a direction that did not include Whelan's stall. Nicky was wearing his clerical grey. Whelan stood exposed, waiting for them to capture him in all his shoddiness; but they did not see him. To Cyril's astonishment, and his own afterwards, he began to shout: 'Higgins! Higgins! Nicky! Murph! Mark! Over here! Higgins, over here! '

Cyril was familiar with the names over the years. The four animals seemed to him human as they made their puzzled way towards the stall.

'Hey lads. I've been keeping a dozen sandwiches for you all day. Everything sold out. I knew ye'd be hungry. Thirty p a sandwich and a free pint of milk to wash it down.'

'We've just had our lunch in the hotel.'

'Higgins, you'll be starving before the match is over. Think of it at half-time, you'll look around you and see people guzzling; your tongue will hang out.'

'Billy, after the blue steak I've had I couldn't look at food for a month.'

'You only think that, Murph. Nicky, I bet you'll be ravenous later on. There's real ham in these sandwiches. And one hundred per cent butter. Well, nearly a hundred per cent. Hi, Mark.'

'You had a good day, Billy?'

'Fantastic. Of course I'm joking about the thirty p. How could I charge you? There was a chap a minute ago wanted to give me fifty pence for a sandwich. I said no. They're booked. I knew ye'd be along. Will I wrap them in something for you?'

'Billy, I'll just take one. We're really after a good dinner. Just one sandwich in case.'

'Are you sure, Mark, now? I kept them for ye.'

'One is fine. We'll take one each. You're right. I'm often hungry at half-time.'

'And a pint of milk. Ye'll take a pint of milk.'

'Not at all. Billy, we don't want to look as if we're up for the day.'

'Ha, ha. Here so. I'll wrap the four of them together.'

'Thanks Billy. Higgins, you bring them.'

'All right. Come on lads. The minor is started. See you, Whelan.'

'Good luck, lads.'

'See you, Billy.'

Whelan did not want to do it in front of Cyril; he did not want to do it in front of anyone; he did not want to do it alone; but tears came. They were moving further and further away from him, shrinking wetly out of sight. He thought he saw something drop. Slowly he walked after them till he reached where he thought something dropped. He bent down and picked up the parcel with the four sandwiches and walked back to the stall. As Cyril watched him, he carefully opened the parcel and took out the sandwiches and laid them out on the table. Whelan blew his nose and said: 'Cyril, I'm going to sit on the grass for a while and have a smoke. Look after the two tables will you?'

'Okay.'

He sat with his back against a butter box and smoked. Those who had hung on to the death in the pubs were now staggering into the ground. Cyril would have no problem selling out. For almost an hour he sat smoking, cigarette after cigarette. Occasionally his thoughts were interrupted by Cyril's cry: 'FREE MILK! FREE MILK! With every ham sandwich, FREE MILK.'

They would have good seats in the stand, somewhere near the reserved enclosure. Mark would probably acknowledge a wave from the mayor. Mark would have said to Higgins: Get a programme in case we need it. And after acknowledging the wave from the mayor, Mark would say: Higgins, where's the programme, who's that corner forward, he's a promising youngfella.

They threw his sandwiches on the ground. Blue steaks. Tonight, before the meeting, blue steaks would streak from nowhere, toppling Tupperware. The sun shone down on the colourful fifty thousand of them cheering their heads off at the minor match. The minor match was almost over. Limerick, in their inexperience, took the field first to a mighty cheer. Whelan knew the sounds without ever attending. The

comparative hush now attended the mentors round-
ing up the team to be photographed. Half of the
team would sit on a long stool and half would stand
behind. The mighty cheer had been for Limerick,
so long in the wilderness. Cyril was dismantling the
stalls and loading them into the van. It was quiet now.
Almost unnatural. Whelan waited. There it went.
Cork had taken the field.

'Jesus, what a racket,' Whelan muttered.

'Yeah,' Cyril answered, 'all of Cork must be at the
match.'

All of Cork was always at the match and not a bit
shy of being there. They were still cheering, although
the Cork team must be getting photographed now.
Whelan rose, slowly straightening his back. At least
Limerick would be hammered. There was that
consolation.

'How is it going, Cyril?'

'Ready. Who's driving?'

'You are.'

Whelan counted the money on the floor of the
back of the van. It was a habit he had no love for,
counting his money in front of anybody, even Cyril.
He would have preferred to count it at home on the
bed. But it was a habit he could not shake; he could
not wait to count his money. Cyril was blessed with
an amiable reticence and never asked Whelan how
much he made. So Whelan always told him. Whelan
cleared two hundred and ten pounds odd.

'Cyril, made a hundred and ten today.'

Cyril whisded appreciatively and when Whelan handed him fifteen pounds he had to remind Cyril to keep his eyes on the road. It was three pounds more than Whelan should have given him and it took in Cyril's Saturday performance of seeing to the van and loading up after the dance.

Whelan took over the wheel and Cyril sat beside him. For a moment Whelan relaxed in the contentment of his riches and Cyril was quiet thinking of – Whelan knew what he was thinking. Cyril usually broached the subject on the first cigarette but today he contained himself more than ever. He was preparing his case with more than usual ammunition; he had seen them with his own eyes. They had thrown away the present of sandwiches. Whelan's thoughts flitted; he had to be prepared to do battle with Cyril; he imagined the four of them cheering knowledgeably from the stand. Donal O'Sullivan was among the crowd someplace; and that one-armed chemist.

'Billy, take me on full time.'

Whelan was grateful; this was a familiar part of the road. He thought of not even answering Cyril but he was afraid Cyril might have false hopes in the silence.

'No.'

'Ah, Billy.'

'No.'

'Why?'

'You know why. How many times do I have to tell you?'

What was not familiar was Cyril snorting and looking out the passenger window. He took out his cigarettes and lit one without offering the packet to Whelan. Not offering his cigarette packet was a crime Whelan had not supposed Cyril capable of. A glance was rewarded with Cyril's jaw in a pout.

'Come on, Cyril. Pack it in.'

There was no response. Whelan drove a few miles before he said firmly: 'Cyril.'

'What?'

'I don't want to pull rank but you're working for me. Right?'

'Yeah.'

'And I'm not having a silent van. Do you understand? So snap out of it and stop sulking or you can walk home. Okay?'

'All right.'

'Good. Another thing I demand in my van is smiles. So what about a smile now, Cyril. Come on now. Give us a big laugh.'

Cyril did his best and laughed but Whelan knew there was more to be done.

'Cyril, do you want to talk about it?'

'What's the point? You always give me the same answers.'

'You ask the same questions.'

Now they both laughed.

'You left school yourself at seventeen.'

'You're not seventeen yet.'

'What's the difference? You still didn't do your Leaving. Why must I waste my time in doing the Leaving?'

'I told you. You finish your schooling and I'll have a job for you. Get the nine honours in the Leaving Cert. Nine subjects ! There weren't nine subjects in my day. We might even go into partnership eventually. I told you that before and *Dictum Meum Pactum*.'

'What does that mean?'

'Nine subjects ! And no *Dictum Meum Pactum*. My word is my bond, Cyril. But you might feel different after you get your nine honours. You might feel inclined to do something else.'

'Like what?'

'Get a government job. Finish at five and go home and forget about it. Enjoy yourself. Sit on your backside all day and when you grow old you'll be looked after.'

'Great. You're even making fun of it yourself.'

'You'll see.'

'All I know is I could be making a bomb and bringing good money home. Mam might be dead before we get out of O'Malley Park. And you want me to end up like that bollix, Higgins.'

'Higgins is all right.'

'All right! He threw your sandwiches away! '

'He wasn't hungry. He was just after a blue steak.'

'Billy, they had a committee meeting before they threw the sandwiches on the ground. Higgins

313

wouldn't do that without permission, from what you told me. They were all in on it. A bloody priest. You'd think *he'd* keep them for the third world. Billy, in another year, I'll have my honours. And I don't want to work in an office. I want to make good money. Like you. I'll be wasting a year.'

'Cyril, Cyril -*I* might have thrown the sandwiches on the ground. It's the type of thing I might have done. I'm an integrated member of society, I meet a smelly hawker, a solecist, he forces his damn sandwiches on me, I don't want them, what's more natural than to dump them? You're too hard on the lads because you don't know. You're green. Young. Impetuous. Idealistic. Now you get your nine honours. Get to know the world. If you become a hawker, become a hawker because you want to become a hawker, you *have* to become a hawker. You follow?'

'No. I don't follow. You wouldn't have thrown those sandwiches on the ground if you were an integrated member of an asylum. You said they made you sing and then they laughed at you. They went on holidays and they didn't let you go with them. You told me. They're a shower of cunts and stop pretending they're not.'

'Ah, Cyril. I made a mistake with you. I didn't mean to, but I must have poisoned your mind against the world. There are so many things you could do with your life. More edifying than dressing in rags and shouting free milk. You could become a doctor, a teacher, a solicitor. You could become anything,

Cyril. Broaden your oudook. A hawker! My God, a hawker! '

'*You* became a hawker. If my mother let me. Supposing I asked my mother.'

'You already asked your mother.'

'I did not. I never mentioned it to my mother.'

'Yes you did.'

'How do you know?'

'She told me. You tried before and she said no. And now you want to go along and say I'm willing if your mother is. Anyway, even if you fooled your mother, No. Come to me when you get your Leaving. Nine honours. If you don't get nine honours – don't come near me. But when you do, come to me. Okay?'

'It's no good talking to you. You don't understand how badly my mother wants to get out of O'Malley Park.'

'I do. Better than you do. And she'd hate to get out of O'Malley Park at the expense of nine honours I can tell you. Cyril, what do you think of a country where you'd need nine honours to become a hawker's assistant?'

'I'm not laughing.'

'Cyril, I can tell you the country is in grave need of hawker's assistants festooned with honours.'

Cyril was surprised at the change in tone. Whelan had switched from whimsy to bitterness.

'I'm going to put the boot into Fonsie O'Brien tonight. Prick!'

'Who?'

'Alvin. Alvin T. Brine. His father changed his name and he carried it on.'

Cyril had never heard him bitter about Fart International.

'I thought you said to me once you forgave him that.'

'I do. I do. I admire his old man. I mean look at our image. Bombs, drunkenness, Litter. Athletes with personal best times that are still short of what Long John Silver achieved. Who wants to be Irish? We can't even talk. I asked a lady for a packet of cigarettes in a London kiosk once and you know what she said? She said: "Youwah- dearie?" Thought I was Chinese or something. No. But that bastard Alvin did something else.'

'What did he do?'

'I'll tell you some other time. I'll give him a hearing first. I might even get Bill Johnston to deal with him. You'd love Bill Johnston, Cyril. I haven't met him but you'd love him. A man after my heart. Cyril? Cyril, you asleep?'

'No. Trying to figure you out. You go from one thing to another.'

'You've just figured me out. I'm incontinent of thought. Because I don't know where I'm going or why. And I don't want you to end up that way. You get nine honours and know where you're going. Bastards! Bastards! Fucking bastards! '

He slowed the van to a halt. Without a word Cyril took the wheel. Neither of them spoke till they reached home. Whelan dropped Cyril up to O'Malley Park. Cyril said: 'Good luck tonight.'

'Thank you, Cyril. And Cyril?'

'Yeah?'

'A year won't kill you.'

'Yeah.'

Cyril was reasonably persuaded to finish his studies, reasonably persuaded until the next time, when he would have to be reasonably persuaded all over again. It was only ten past five. If Whelan went home he would have to watch Breda making the tea; worse, she might ask him to help lay the table or amuse Eddie. Eddie! Declan! He had forgotten to buy them a present. He drove to Davis Street opposite the station. It was a street that catered for those who forgot their children. He thanked God for the street. Breda would give him a withering look and, by the time she rounded into her peroration, the spectre of a house with a garden and a swing would have been raised. In the window of a huckster shop golliwogs stood erect under guitars; dolls were laid out in boxes, arms outstretched and eyes ready to roll independent of rigor mortis. There was one of those thingumajigs that, when blown, unfurls about a foot and startles the audience. That would do fine for Eddie. Declan was a problem. It was as hard for Whelan to choose a toy for his eldest son as it had once been for himself when he used to dream before Lil Dwyer's window until Mr Ryan hauled him off to be an acolyte. Lil Dwyer was dead. Her premises now belonged to a turf accountant who had restricted limits pasted up on his wall. There was a six hundred piece jigsaw puzzle that might suit but Whelan did not want to have to help Declan make it. He wanted something that Declan would play with by himself, something that would keep him out from under people's feet. The guitar. Declan would break the string of the guitar and Whelan would have to mend it. The dulcimer. The dulcimer was the very thing.

He was putting the presents behind him in the van when the mad sensation struck him to get something for Breda. He settled on a pair of footmen for the mantelpiece. If Eddie asked: What's them, Dad? Whelan could say to him: Long ago before we came down in the world. . .

He went into the pub next door to the huckster shop to reward himself with a pint and to make sure that he would not be too early for the tea. He stood at the counter while the drink was being filled because he found it advisable always to stand at the counter while the drink was being filled on the grounds that if there was juggling he may as well admire the performance. He overheard a droplet of conversation:

'. . . the radio said it was one of the best matches ever. I was glued to it. I never thought they'd hold on. The way Cork were pressing . . .'

He sat with his pint at the counter, eavesdropping on two old men discussing the match. They had won again. If Mark Brown did not go directly back to Dublin they would stop in various pubs coming home from Thurles. The four of them would have large Hens in their hands as they analysed every smithereen of the match. They would listen to each other and then they would listen to Mark Brown. And at some stage, during a lull, Mark Brown would ask Father Nicky how long he would be in Ireland; he would invite Father Nicky to visit him in Dublin. Father Nicky would accept, not realising the agony he would suffer as he watched Mark Brown's children and Mark Brown's wife and Mark Brown's life style being paraded. Father Nicky would be delighted to return to the Congo or whatever it was called but Father Nicky would never know why he wanted to return to the Congo. This was a happy train of thought for Whelan to pursue. Poor Murphy would return to his rural bank where Fart International did not have its account. Higgins would flower any place; how discontentment could ever penetrate a man who thought he could forecast the weather was a mystery Whelan would not try to solve.

The Angelus rang out from the television. The two old men rose and doffed their hats; foolishly, Whelan was on his feet, silent for the duration the Angelus supposedly took to say. He finished his pint and left for home.

There was cheering for Daddy bearing gifts. Breda said she was pleased with the footmen though she looked at them suspiciously on the mantelpiece. Whelan assured her. 'They didn't come from the North, Breda. Look,' he brandished the underside of

one of the footmen and quoted the bonafides: 'Made
in Japan. Okay?'

'I didn't say a word, Billy.'

Whelan did not say a word about the complete
absence of tea on the table. He did say: 'I'll run up
and change for the meeting. I'll hardly have time for
tea, unless you can make it while I'm up.'

While he shaved he could smell the sound of
rashers on the pan. But when he did come down
to tea the hunger was gone off him; it was replaced
with excitement. His mind was free of everything but
Fart International. Technically, he could remember
not eating on Christmas Day ten years earlier. But
he could not recapture the pain of not eating on
Christmas Day. He knew that he had been slighted in
the Sarsfield Arms the night before yet the salty sting
of rejection eluded him now. He was conscious of
power, of the Fart International money in the bank,
of the *capture* of a bank manager and a lady with a
double-barrelled name, triple-barrelled now if she so
chose.

'Breda, I'll rush. See everything's so so.'

'Give my love to Bill Johnston. Tell him it's from
a Fart International widow.'

Whelan smiled.

'Breda, I'll be a new man after tonight. I promise
you. You'll see.'

Breda fingered one of the footmen. She might
indeed have known them before a hawker brought
her down in the world. Whelan could see she was

pleased yet he did not expect her to say, huskily: 'I've time for a quickie. Only cost you four. Guineas.'

'Breda, guineas? Guineas went out with the gun-boats, Breda. I have to rush, anyway. I might see you tonight. The whole hog – everything – twenty quid. To hell with it. Twenty guineas! '

'Bye.'

'See you. Hey kids, what about a kiss for Daddy. Now Eddie, don't blow that thing in my face. Go down and blow it in Mr Ryan's daughter's, bitch tried to hang on to my dollar.'

CHAPTER FOURTEEN
BILL JOHNSTON

There were no more than half a dozen people scattered about the lounge of the Sarsfield Arms at twenty to seven. The meeting was timed for eight o'clock. One man sat at the counter talking to T. A. Dufficy. He was too young to be Bill Johnston. The cut of him was American, Whelan deduced as he opened the door into the lounge. It had to be Paul Tindall. Though seated, the American was obviously tall; he was slender; his hair was neatly cropped; he wore a grey suit and a wine tie, the combination of colours that Whelan had found irresistible on Breda. And yet Whelan would have preferred someone in a ten gallon hat or bearded and unkempt and wearing sneakers.

'T.A.'

'Ah, Billy – Mr Paul Tindall, Des Moines, Iowa. Mr Tindall, Mr Whelan.'

'It sure is a pleasure, Bill,' Paul Tindall unwound himself and stood a foot taller than Whelan, 'I've been looking forward to meeting you.'

Whelan accepted the firm handshake, recalling nervously that he had once entered firm handshakes into the book.

'Paul Tindall. Welcome. T.A., any sign of . . .?'

T. A. Dufficy shook his head. 'I thought the man over in the corner with the white hair might be him. But I doubt it. He's made no effort to reveal himself. He's there an hour and a half. On his fifth pint. I was tempted to ask him.'

'Why didn't you?'

'I resisted the temptation.'

All Whelan could see of the man in the corner was his white hair. He was reading a newspaper. The newspaper was not folded. The man gripped the newspaper with the thumb and forefinger of each hand allowing the paper to reveal his white hair gradually as he read down the page. This method of reading a newspaper struck a chord in Whelan. The man's hand emerged regularly and drew his pint inside the newspaper and replaced the pint less a swallow. The size of the swallow fitted in with the method of reading the newspaper. At a fair distance Whelan thought the shiny object on the table near the man's pint was a case for spectacles. Only the white hair jarred. Whelan began to walk slowly towards the man. Ten yards off he could see over the newspaper, see the face behind the black horn rimmed glasses.

'Wingate!'

The man lifted his eyes over the rims of the glasses and the newspaper and then resumed reading.

'Wingate! You flogpot.'

Hogan put down his newspaper and enquired: 'Who have I?'

'Billy Whelan. Ten years ago in the Falcon in Queens Park. I stayed with Tom Mackey. Jesus, Hogan!'

'Whelan, Whelan. Ah, yes. Yes. I remember. You upset Mackey.'

'How do you mean I upset Mackey?'

'Go and take long and immediate steps to the bar and purchase the porter. And we'll talk.'

'Oh. All right. I'll only be a minute.'

'T.A., two pints please. You know who that is? Hogan! You remember I told you about Hogan? That's him. T.A., bring over the two pints. I must talk to him, I'll see ye later. Let me know if Bill Johnston turns up.'

Whelan sat on a stool to render humble audience to Hogan. He was the same old Hogan apart from the grey hair turned white.

'What are you doing here? How did I upset Tom Mackey?'

'You left without proper ceremony.'

'What do you mean? We had a night in the Falcon. I stood ye all drink.'

'You did, fair play to you. Mackey kept your room idle for a month. You paid him the rent and you didn't rifle the meter. He thought you were coming back.'

'But I told him I was going home for good.'

'You were the only lodger he ever had who didn't rob the meter. He budgets for it.'

Hogan was smiling.

'Hogan, I could kick myself. You never lost it. I was believing you again.'

Hogan chuckled.

'O ye of little faith. And what are you doing with yourself? Married? Family?'

'Yes. Two boys. Are you on holidays?'

'I'm on the half-pay list. The flak above the heart is pressing downwards. They don't think I'm capable of decision. I protested. Said I'd join the ranks.'

'Hogan, please. Talk normal. I'm a man now. I've a wife and children. Are you retired?'

Hogan nodded. 'In the best tradition. I have John Bull's pension to find a room someplace and talk to myself for the rest of my days. What are you at yourself?'

'I'm a hawker.'

'What's that? I'm out of touch with the technology of business administration.'

'I'm a hawker.'

'Really?'

'Yeah.'

'Here's mine host.'

T. A. Dufficy lifted the drink from the tray and hovered. Whelan could not resist: 'If a Mr Bill Johnston of Des Moines, Ohio enquires for me will you have me paged please?'

325

'Certainly, sir.' T. A. Dufficy interpreted the request as an instruction not to hover.

'You sound like a cosmopolitan hawker. Good luck who stood.'

'Hogan, tell me. How are they all in the Falcon? How's Mackey? Tommy Cook? Martin? Maurice of Maurice and Connie?'

'Aahh. Good porter. Not schemery porter. My compliments to the chef. Mackey is dead.'

'Dead? What happened him?'

'Nothing. He just died. Two years ago. He was due to retire last year. He was going to come home. The family are grown up and married. He talked about nothing else. We were playing forty-five and he crashed his fist on the table to take a trick and kept going. I can see his head striking the floor. The five of trumps was still in his hand. The excitement killed him. Of going home. We had to prise the five out of his hand to finish the game.'

'Ah, Hogan!'

'No. We didn't finish the game. In fact we didn't play since. Mackey and myself were the last of the old school. Martin went to Southampton. Tommy Cook went home. I must look him up. And of course you heard about Maurice.'

'What about him?'

'You didn't hear? About his book.'

'You're not going to tell me he wrote a book?'

'I am. Where do you hide? Don't you read your *TLS*?'

'What's that?'

'Never mind. Maurice wrote a bestseller. *Subtleties of the Albigensian Heresy: a Hindsight View.* It's the rage of France. I read in the *Standard* that he was to sign copies in Foyle's of a Saturday. I went along and dutifully purchased. And your name, sir? Maurice says in a grand accent. We hadn't seen him in the Falcon in three years. I said, Maurice you flogpot, what about all the money you owe me from forty-five. I don't know whether you heard of her – Lady Antonia Fraser, she was standing beside him. He said: Ah, Hogan, I remember. Toni, this is an interesting study from my past. . .'

'Hogan!'

'. . . afterwards, the three of us . . .'

'Hogan! Stop. Please now. Is this supposed to be true?'

'True? What has true got to do with it? You asked after Maurice. I have no idea where he is. He stopped coming into the Falcon years ago. There was much speculation.'

Whelan glanced at the bar and saw Alvin T. Brine in attendance.

'Finish that,' Hogan said and rose. Whelan planned feverishly while Hogan was at the counter. He had in his inside pocket the original letter from Bill Johnston. He thought of giving it to Hogan to read; it would explain all. He could then fill Hogan in with sketches of Anna, John Harnett, T. A. Dufficy, Alvin, Tindall. Some way or another he must enlist Hogan in Fart International.

'I like the cut of mine host,' Hogan declared as he put the pints on the table. 'Not often one sees wooden buttons nowadays. And you're a hawker.'

'Yes. Tell me something. Out of curiosity. Are there restaurants or caffs open on Christmas Day these times? In the High Road?'

'No. Not a chink nor an eyetie with the frying pan out. Why do you ask?'

'Where do you go? With Mackey dead and every-one scattered?'

'I haven't dined out on Christmas Day in years. Years. It's not fair to people. I dine alone as befits a crusty old bachelor. Tell me about this hawking. You go to matches and that?'

'Yes. I was at Thurles today for the Munster Final.'

Anna and John Harnett were pulling up stools. All of them were looking in his direction.

'And you make a good living?'

Whelan was impatient with ludicrous talk of mak-ing livings. He could contain himself no longer.

'Hogan, I've something fabulous to tell you. It's about an organisation I founded. I didn't exactly found it. It's like this . . . excuse me a minute . . .'

A gentleman carrying a suitcase and a light rain-coat entered and made his way to the bar. Whelan watched him put his belongings on the floor and call for a drink. Whelan rushed up to the counter and stood expectantly beside the man. Whelan said: 'Excuse me. Would you by any chance be Bill Johnston?'

'Sorry, old chap. Hodges. Fred Hodges.'

'I'm sorry. My mistake.'

Rather embarrassed, Whelan avoided eye contact with the Fart International horde and returned to Hogan. He pulled out the letter.

'Read that. This is a letter I received in answer to an enquiry I sent to a box number in *Screen Monthly*. Read that and I'll tell you the rest. This is right up your alley. The advertisement simply said: Fart International, Box 13, Send No Money. Read the letter and I'll fill you in.'

Hogan's reaction was more encouraging than Whelan expected. Every few lines Hogan chuckled, occasionally raking off his glasses and wiping his eyes. When he finished he let the pages slip out of his hands on to the table and sat back heaving his stomach.

'Beautiful. Beautiful.'

'Wait till you hear the rest of it.'

'. . . and so here I am. That's why I'm waiting for Bill Johnston to appear. Listen, Hogan. From what you've heard. Tell me you'll join. Will you? Will you become a member?'

Hogan was shaking his head but not in refusal to join.

'Whelan, Whelan, you're an awful man.'

'Will you join? Just tell me you'll join. Hogan, we'll have a ball the two of us.'

'Will you purchase the porter, will you. A man could die of the drought listening to you.'

'Sorry. Don't go away.'

At the counter Whelan asked John Harnett the time.

'Nearly half seven. We'd want to be getting ready.'

'I won't be five minutes. No sign of Bill Johnston.'

'It doesn't look like he's going to show.'

'He'll be here. If he doesn't come until a minute to eight he'll be here. He knows what we think of punctuality.'

Punctuality had gone into the book. It had an otherwise smooth passage apart from Anna's quaint notion that it was aristocratic to disregard the clock. But Whelan had been eloquent about the ramifications of letting people down. He was a little tipsy walking back with the drink. Hogan still had a mouth like a shorehole.

'Which of those people at the counter is the Alvin T. Brine you mentioned?'

'Of the two Americans, he's the squat chap.'

'You're not to spare him.'

'Pardon?'

'What you said the other American told you in a letter. About the Success Motivation Institute. I would have thought that's something Fart International could not possibly stand for.'

'I know. I want to consult Bill Johnston first. I don't believe in lightly putting the boot in. Even the likes of Alvin has feelings.'

'You flogpot. It's always kind to camels week with you.'

Whelan had not mentioned his camel story. He looked sharply at Hogan who was wiping the swallow froth from his lips. Hogan said: 'Not schemery porter, thank God. Good old Dufficy.' And then Hogan began to tap his own chest emphatically and say: 'Bill Johnston.'

Confused for a moment, Whelan looked around the lounge and back again at Hogan who simply nodded and stabbed his chest again.

'No. Hogan, stop now. No. No Hogan.'

Hogan nodded: 'Yes. Yes, Billy.'

There followed a brief mime. Whelan shook his head from side to side while Hogan nodded his head just as emphatically. Whelan picked up the letter and searched to find reference to a camel; reference there was none. He decided he must have told Hogan the camel story while they drank in the Falcon; he was always telling someone the camel story. But why would Hogan – even Hogan – pretend he was Bill Johnston and expect to get away with it?

'Hogan, what are you sitting there pretending you're Bill Johnston for? Do you never give up?'

Hogan slipped his hand into his inside pocket and drew out a letter. He held it out for Whelan to take; Whelan looked at it suspiciously, knowing what it was and not wanting to acknowledge it. He recognised his own handwriting. It was his original letter to Fart International.

He read with embarrassment the appreciative comments he made about Hogan to the box number in Los Angeles. He looked from the letter to Hogan. Hogan was not grinning triumphantly; far from it, he was ticking his lips with concern. Whelan did not know where to begin.

'Hogan, it's a bit of a nightmare knowing you. I wrote to *Screen Monthly,* a box number in Los Angeles. Are you telling me I was writing to you?'

Hogan nodded. He might have been a doctor confirming malignancy so graven did he manage to look.

'But how? Why? Explain. Who's Bill Johnston and Al Guerrini?'

Hogan tapped the side of his head with a finger.

'You made them up? Sweet Jesus look down on us. You made them up?'

'Yes. I didn't keep a copy of the letter I sent you. Tonight is the first time I've seen it in ten years. Do you know, it wasn't a bad effort at all. It had nice touches. Would you think?'

Whelan glanced through the letter.

'Hogan, all this Russian hug bit from your father before you went off to war – all right I can see that's vintage Hogan – but this Al Guerrini, you invented him?'

Whelan almost winced at the nod.

'Your own agency, Jack Daniels, singing the White Cliffs of Dover, Hemingway and Fitzgerald, how did you think all that up?'

'I'm as amazed as you are. It was the only time I ever put a fantasy down on paper. You know, the day your letter arrived, I was working late at the hotel, a matter of ball-cocks, and I went straight to the Falcon instead of going to my flat. You were there that night. I went home afterwards and there was the letter. I thought I was finally going round the bend. I thought it might have been a judgement on me for not getting you invited to dinner at Christmas. I stayed up all night – trying to find a meaning. The Lord had delivered you into my hands. It was more than coincidence, for reasons that would not be apparent to you at the moment – if I get drunk enough I might tell you the reasons – but I knew it was not coincidence. Your misery at going hungry and alone on Christmas Day, your anger, a fine anger, all that did in fact make me cry. Yes, I cried for you that night. But it did not bother me as much as you might imagine. You see, I had been through it all, was still going through it all. I must say that Higgins, Murphy, Nicky and Mark Brown intrigued me. Your later epistles explained all that. It was a great comfort to me to hear about your Mr Ryan. Anyway, I had to do something about your letter. You did enclose NO MONEY. I couldn't take the money out and throw your letter away even if I wanted to. I toyed with the notion of bringing your letter in to you the following night and talking about it. But I realised how much I needed you. You have no idea how much I needed you. I'll come to that, if I get drunk enough. With that end in mind you might purchase more porter.'

Hogan's glasses were off again and he was mopping his eyes.

'Blasted cataract. Should have had that seen to too. Years ago.'

Whelan could not but admire Hogan now; old-fashioned tears would not do the man; he had to invent a disease of the eye. Whelan lurched towards the bar, placed the two empty glasses on the counter (he had a full pint of his own untouched apart from natural sinkage back on the table) and motioned to T. A. Dufficy: 'Two more, T.A. Send them over.' Without a word to the curious, Whelan returned to his seat.

'Hogan, I'll be pissed if I try to keep up with you. From here on in I'm on half pints. What am I going to do? I'll have to start the meeting.'

'Of course it was your Fart International when I handed it over but I didn't quite fathom some of your decisions. I'd never have gone along with punctuality for instance. But never mind. Start your meeting.'

'Are you coming in? Do I tell them who you are?'

'No. Certainly not Alvin T. Brine. After you deal with him you won't be hearing from him any more. And that Tindall chap sounds worse. There's no need to enlighten them. You wrote that the bank manager and his wife were beginning to lose the faith?'

'Yes. Once they had each other they didn't put the same – feeling into Fart. I opposed the match. Mentally. Imagine how ludicrous it would be to have Breda a member. Or T. A. Dufficy's good wife. But I couldn't speak my mind. They're very happy. But it's not fitting.'

'Keep them in the dark too. What are you going to do about an Outrageously Suitable Person now?'

'I intended to try and hand back to Bill Johnston. That's you. You tell me.'

Hogan shook his head. 'No. It's your organisation. What about Dufficy?'

'No. A certain self-effacement is desirable I agree. But I can't very well elect the invisible man.'

'He's a beautiful character.'

'You think so? So do I.'

'The bank manager.'

'John Harnett? I thought you didn't approve of his lack of zeal.'

'No, no. *You* didn't. I think you're all mad. Including you. But have you no sense of occasion? You may not have founded the Argentinian navy, as I seem to recall once persuading myself an ancestor of mine did, you may not have made an obvious mark yet; but I think if you could usher a bank manager to the throne of an organisation such as Fart International that it would be something of an achievement. The money *is* safe? In *your* hands? No one can get at it?'

'The money is safe. It's all mine. If I want it.'

'No interest. Just lying there. I've never understood that. You make me feel mercenary.'

'Hogan, how did you come to start the whole business? They're getting restless.'

'Later. We'll have that later. When I'm drunk. Now doesn't this Dufficy have a spy hole for meetings?'

'Yes. It's a hatch at the end of the bar. He can see and not be seen. Hear and not be heard.'

'Good. You can declare me to Dufficy. I want to listen at his hatch. You go on in and have your meeting. Elect the bank manager.'

'Alvin fancies himself in the position.'

'All the more reason to be merciless with the man.'

'I don't know if I can do it.'

'What are you going to do? Make him president?'

'I'll see what I can do. I'd better go. I'll take them in and come back out and speak to T.A. He'll look after you.'

'All right.'

Hogan remained at his post waiting for a sign from Dufficy. He sipped his drink now, not because he had reached or passed his quota, but because of absent-mindedness. He removed his glasses and dabbed at his eyes from time to time. Years earlier, when the nightmare had taken to following him into pubs and driving him to tears in public, he had invented cataracts. He would reproach his glasses, drink, the smoky atmosphere individually or as a job lot and he never came across a doubting Thomas. The only place he had difficulty was on the tube where he could not lean over and accost strangers with tales of a cataract but where strangers could sit impassively and pretend there was not a stranger opposite them, crying. Knowing that what haunted him should not haunt an imbecile let alone an intelligent man like himself was of little consolation. Had he been an American of means a psychiatrist might have been the man to call in; there was solace in that realisation, that his complaint would go down big in America. He cleaned his glasses with the crafty end of shirt that had detached itself from his trousers. T. A. Dufficy was behind his counter, neck craned with invitation. Hogan rose.

'Mr Hogan.'

Hogan accepted the hand.

'Mr Dufficy, sir.'

'This way.'

Off the lounge bar, screened by a curtain, a chair nestled in what was not much bigger than a closet. Hogan sat down. Ahead of him was the curtain screening the bar; to his right coats were hung up; on his left was the hatch that gazed out upon the Blue Room. Dufficy pointed a finger at Hogan's glass and raised an eyebrow. Hogan said: 'Please.'

Hogan watched Billy Whelan stride to the top of the room and stand behind a table. The bank manager and his wife were seated directly in front of him; behind them Paul Tindall, behind Tindall, Alvin T. Brine. Whelan carefully placed the twine around his neck; although Hogan could not see its condition he supposed the dollar to be possessed of fatigue. Whelan began to sing:

> Alone, all alone,
> By a wave-washed strand,
> All alone in a crowded hall;

> The hall it is gay,
> The waves they are grand,
> But my heart is not there at all.

He did not have a bad voice, Hogan thought, in the way that one would shrink from noticing a deficiency in the tone of a priest trying to lead a congregation in 'Faith of our Fathers'. Anna Roche-Reilly-Harnett's falsetto was singularly feeble. The Americans' effort were lost among the photocopies of the ballad on the desks in front of them. The bank manager struggled bravely in a lower register. All in all, had he been at peace with himself, Hogan would have declared it an auspicious beginning to the prospect of people making fucking apes of themselves. But he was far from at peace. He dabbed his eyes. T. A. Dufficy – the man had a sense of timing – was beside him, quietly offering the pint.

Hogan nodded and swallowed. Dufficy remained, looking out at the Blue Room over Hogan's shoulder.

'To begin,' Whelan began, 'with the first item on the agenda, if we had an agenda, and of course we certainly do not have any such thing as an agenda, God forbid, the first item on the non-agenda is the election of officers. And thanks be to God we do not have any such thing as officers or elections for that matter. I had intended to step down; I had fond hopes of handing over to Bill Johnston; unfortunately, Bill Johnston is late, gravely late, if you all follow me.

I would like to ask you to stand for one minute's silence in honour of the late Bill Johnston.'

Hogan eyed T. A. Dufficy who blinked in acknowledgement. Hogan was warming to Dufficy. The unspoken message they traded was that both of them were warming to the Outrageously Suitable Person in the Blue Room. T. A. Dufficy took a Baby Power from his inside pocket, uncapped and held it out to Hogan who shook his head and indicated his contentment with the black brew. Dufficy sipped and licked his lips dry. In the Blue Room Whelan raised his hand and dropped it; the minute's silence had nm its course.

'Bill Johnston or no Bill Johnston, I'm stepping down. The notion of the succession stakes not running smoothly is anathema to Fart International I'm sure you agree. So I propose nomination and acclamation. I nominate and you acclaim Nomination must, unfortunately, be with the consent of the nominee. I can think of no way out of that. So it's over to the nominees.'

The Harnetts whispered to each other. Paul Tindall turned and smiled at Alvin T. Brine. Alvin raised his hand.

'Yes, Alvin?'

'I'm willing to stand, Bill.'

'No, Alvin.'

'Bill?'

'Billy! Billy! You're stained, Alvin. I'll say no more about it if you sit down and acclaim *my* nominee.'

'Hey, what's goin' on here? Stained? I've been in from the start. I flew four thousand miles to see you ten years ago. Fifteen thousand bucks I shelled out. Hey, look what I gave up. Yeah, you made me go back and work from the inside but you know I gave it up. I gave it up in here,' Alvin's left fist patted his heart. 'Rotary, Elks, why at that time I had it made, I was so much the American Dream, why I used to screw my best friends' wives in the locker room of the Country Club. I'm not stained Bill – Billy. Billy, I'm not stained.'

'Alvin, was your father's name O'Brien?'

'Howsat?'

'Was your father an O'Brien who was not unaware of the hostile climate towards the Irish of his day?'

The Harnetts turned to look back at Alvin. Alvin directed his appeal to them.

'Okay. I can't deny it. And you might think it's late in the day to say it now, but I did intend to change back to O'Brien. Someday. But you know how it is. That takes time. A decision like that takes time. But if it never took time – I don't have to pay for my father's sins. Is that right? This is Fart International, right?'

The Harnetts turned back to look at the Outrageously Suitable Person.

'A good answer, Alvin. A good answer. It was not the taint I had in mind. Now, Alvin, before I call on Paul Tindall to say a few words, I want to ask you: Will you stand down? Will you stand down from unworthiness?'

Alvin consulted Paul Tindall's pate. Yeah, he remembered the prick. He examined his conscience haphazardly. Yeah, he had masturbated at school. Couldn't be that. There was a stenographer and an abort here and there. Only two. No. Fart International was above that. Non-political and non-sectarian. Bill Whelan himself said so. Political? Sure, he had sung Happy Days Are Here Again. But they knew all that. That was part of what he had given up. In his heart. Sectarian? Never. There was that black doctor tried to move into the neighbourhood – but that was part of it. Couldn't be that. Rotary, Elks, Country Club, Chamber of Commerce, Toastmaster. Gave up the lot. In his heart.

'Gee, I dunno what to say to you guys. I'm clean, I know I'm clean. So I got ambition, want to do good for Fart. Is that a crime for Chrissakes?'

Whelan shook his head.

'I believe you do believe you're clean. That's tragic. But innocence is no excuse. All right, Paul Tindall. The floor is yours.'

Hogan felt constrained to speak. Dufficy was the type of man who would forgive him, speaking.

'Do you know the Paid Tindall Story?'

'No.'

'It's the type of thing that would have killed Al Guerrini.'

'One of nature's gentleman, Mr Guerrini.'

Hogan chuckled.

Whelan sat down beside Alvin as Paul Tindall rounded upon his audience. Tindall smiled in the

friendly tradition of the sociable American and
began formally: 'Hi. I guess I better say Ladies and
Gentlemen. Well, hi Ladies and Gentlemen. My
name's Paul Tindall. I come from Des Moines, Iowa
. . .'

Whelan used his knee to nudge Alvin's leg. He
whispered: 'Alvin, let's you and I nip outside for a jar.
I want to hear you tell me about Tindall.'

'. . . I guess you could say I flunked college. Yeah,
why hide it. I flunked. Mom and Dad couldn't take it.
It wasn't Mom and Dad's fault. No sir. Dad hadn't my
start. Not to hear Dad tell it. Dad got up off his butt
and went out there and hung in swingin'. A great guy
my dad. And that's what got me. Hurtin' Dad like that.
I'll tell you, once, there was talk once of Dad runnin'
for mayor. I wasn't no more than a kid. I listened at the
keyhole the night they tried to talk him round. But no
way. He put his arm around Mom's shoulders and he
told them he was a family man. They told Dad how well
thought of he was, the charities, the boards – they said
they needed Dad, the town needed Dad. Dad thanked
them. He called them Gentlemen. Gentlemen, my
Dad said, yes it's true I did pull myself up by my boot-
straps and I did work hard – for my family. I'm sorry
but I'm not your man. They didn't give up easily but
they gave up. Mom caught me on the stairs but all she
did was let me stay up. They were all being shown out
and I heard one guy say – under his breath – but I
heard him, he said: "Cocksucker". He said that about
my dad. And then I go and flunk college . . .'

Hogan and T. A. Dufficy watched Whelan and Alvin leave the Blue Room and arrive at the bar. Dufficy emerged from the curtain to serve them. While Whelan's pint was settling Dufficy joined Hogan behind the curtain. They scarcely breathed trying to listen to two sides of the same story.

'You remember Paul Tindall, Alvin?'

'Yeah. Of course I remember him. What's he gonna say?'

'. . . he hated doin' it. I realised it even then, but I was his son and he did have buddies and Mom was in there rootin' for me. Well, I gave it a go. I'd go out there and sell the sonsabitches out of sight, I'd do it for Dad. But I hadn't it, you know? I just did not have it! Every day I'd hit a bar and grab one with the other salesmen and we'd say: After lunch we're goin' out there and slay 'em. But you guessed it, after lunch we'd be back in that bar and we'd say: Tomorrow. Really get down to it tomorrow . . . I flunked. Who wants to lose a buddy? But Dad had other buddies. I flunked again . . .'

'How did you happen to meet him in the first place, Alvin?'

'That guy gatecrashed into my office. Got past Miss Pratsche and no one gets past Miss Pratsche. But he did. I looked up from my desk and there he was in front of me. All nine feet of him, thin as a match and grinning at me. No appointment. Grinning at me. I said: Who the hell are you? He just grins and says: I know who I am but do you know who you are?

Well, I said, I dunno what I said, but I must have said something like of course I know who the fuck I am. I dunno. I don't remember. Anyway, next thing he has his case open and he flashes one of these colour pictures of Ted Kennedy's kid runnin' or jumpin' after been left for dead or what and he says: Isn't that inspiring? Then he starts flashing charts in front of my face and asking questions – personal questions – and you wanna know what, I was answering him . . .'

'. . . I think Dad was just about at the end of his rope. And then it happened. I heard about Norman Vincent Peale. Saw an ad in a movie magazine for the Success Motivation Institute. SMI. Well, I'll just put it this way. I did that course and – well, let's just say I began to realise my potential. Sales began to zoom! The vice-president called me in, you know. Tindall, how do you do it? I didn't tell him. I threw him a line and next thing I'm holding teach-ins for the other salesmen. Took ten years off Dad. I reported back to SMI. Even they were impressed. So impressed they asked me to flog SMI. Which I naturally jumped at. I knew this was for me. It was zoom all the way. That's how I met Alvin. Alvin was all screwed up. Sure, Alvin had it made. But he didn't know why he had it made. He didn't know did he want to have it made. I had some big sessions with Alvin . . .'

'. . . actually I kept Tindall on for therapy. I mean, what could he give me? I had it all. And there's this young prick trying to motivate me. But I played along. You know he used to get me up with a gang of other deficients for seven o'clock breakfast meetings! Seven o'clock in the *morning*! I got a kick out of it though. Sure, I knew he was a rip-off artist but so what. He used to set me exercises, targets. That Kennedy kid's picture that he hawked around, that was supposed to be his inspiration. You didn't have to go for the Kennedy kid. You could get a picture of your dream house and put it on the wall over the bed and see it first thing in the morning and go out inspired and achieve towards that goal. One guy at the breakfasts told us he had a picture of Cassius Clay; he was a scrapper on the fringe. Thirty years of age if he was a day. He saw himself champ. Anyway, I used to report back to the group at that hour of the morning. I was supposed to cut down the handicap. "Well, Alvin, how did you get on?" I mighta shot ninety-four that weekend, I'd tell 'em I got round in seventy-seven.

'Then I saw the ad: Fart International, Box 13, Send No Money. And I knew. I felt it in my gut. This was it. You know the rest. You know I wanted to give it all up. You sent me back. But to give it all up it turned out I *needed* Tindall. No disrespect to Fart International but d'you think I could give it all up just like that? I needed Tindall to motivate me out. De-motivate me. I mean Tindall's line works. I seen it work for guys. You take Norman Vincent Peale himself. And other guys. The scrapper didn't make it but Tindall showed him he had the wrong goal. The scrapper really wanted to help old folks only he

didn't know it. Tindall knew. The scrapper gives aU
his time to charity nowadays. After I came over here
and met you and Anna I needed Tindall . . .'

'. . . Alvin became my first SMI client to be
attended at his own residence. The group sessions
were out, charts not worth a curse. SMI rate went
by the board. Alvin paid me a retainer. I wasn't supposed to but I took Alvin as my own client. How did
I do it? How did I de-motivate Alvin? I dunno. I did
it. You see Alvin today. You know better than I if I did
good with Alvin . . .'

'. . . Tindall was one hell of a confidant. Yeah, I
couldn'ta done it without him. I reached the stage
where I was going to chuck everything in and come to
Ireland whether you liked it or not, whether Sookie
liked it. I wrote you, remember? And then Tindall
disappears! Just like that. He had some bucks to come
but he disappears. I'm there in Des Moines and sure
as hell nearly cracked up without him. But I managed
to wind back to where I was before he gatecrashed
Miss Pratsche. And I hung on. When you wrote me
that he was about to become one of us and he'd be
here and you were standing down and Bill Johnston
was coming I said: Pratsche, get me a plane ticket.
What happened to Johnston?'

'He's dead.'

'Yeah, but what happened?'

'I don't know. I've known for some time but I
thought I'd keep it for tonight.'

'. . . and then Dad popped off. I'm over Dad now. But then it near broke me up. You see, I found him. Dad was great to work out. He keeled over off the exercise bike in his study. With Dad gone, my motivation was gone. I was back to being a flunker. Truth was I never wanted to work for SMI. But it was in my blood. You know it's a funny thing? I couldn't kick the habit. I'd try to lie in bed in the morning and I couldn't do it. "Tomorrow, I'll lie in, tomorrow I won't shave, tomorrow at the therapy breakfast I'll tell everyone to go home." But tomorrow wouldn't come. And, you've guessed it. I remembered Alvin. If SMI could help Alvin join Fart International, then Fart International could help me chuck SMI. So I wrote to Box 13. And I knew enough from listening to Alvin to enclose money. Alvin had told me how hard it was to get into Fart . . .'

'Johnston's dead, okay. You want to step down and you tell me I'm tainted. Now how am I tainted, that's all I want to know?'

'Alvin, I'll be with you in one second. I have to go back in there and see that everything's okay. Okay?'

'Yeah.'

Whelan entered the Blue Room as Paul Tindall was saying, 'I guess that's it.'

He walked directly to the Harnetts.

'You heard?'

'Yes. Anna and I have been – entertained?'

'Yes, I know. I want you to stay here with Paul for a time. I'll get T.A. to send in drinks. Hold the fort. I'll be back.'

Hogan and Dufficy emerged from behind the curtain. Hogan went to where he had been sitting earlier in the night. Whelan joined him.

'You heard the man. He doesn't know.'

'Tell him.'

'But how will I put it?'

'You'll think of something. And while you're at it would you take long and immediate . . .'

'I know. I know.'

'Alvin. Alvin, Alvin, Alvin. What am I going to do with you?'

Alvin smiled.

'Alvin, you're so fucking tainted there's a smell off you!'

'Hey!'

'SMI. The Success Motivation Institute. Success! Motivation! Institute! Define Fart International, Alvin.'

'We've been through that ten years now. You said yourself there's no definition.'

'I couldn't have defined it Alvin but I knew what it was. It was something holy. You can't describe holiness. But you can come near it. When you're given a little help you can come near it. I knew when Paul Tindall wrote me enclosing money, I knew I had been given a glimpse. If there's a smell off you Alvin, there's a stink off Tindall. I didn't take his money and run. I kept him on the line. I told him drop you or I'd drop him and that I'd send for him when I needed him. There are three divine persons in Fart International, Alvin. Anti-Success the Father, Anti-Motivation the Son and Anti-Institute the Holy Ghost. That, Alvin, is the nearest definition we have yet.'

Alvin ran his tongue over his lips.

'You are unclean, Alvin. You're not going to become the Outrageously Suitable Person. Alvin, do you remember the story of the camel?'

'Yeah, I remember.'

'Well, I'll do as much for you, Alvin, as some people wouldn't do for their camels. I'll give you your fifteen thousand dollars back and you leave here in ten seconds and I never want to hear or see you again; or, I don't give you your fifteen thou back but I make you a proposition?'

'I don't want the money, you know that, I don't want the money.'

'Alvin, there's work to be done and you can do it. You and Tindall. The Success Motivation Institute must be defeated. You can begin in Des Moines. Paul Tindall must get his job back with SMI. But he must preach the Fart International gospel. Continue the breakfasts – at seven o'clock *at night*. I'll leave you to work out the details, you know the sort of thing, the chap at the therapy session who sold all round him that day, he gets the horse's laugh, and whoever got out of bed at ten to seven *at night* and turns up unshaven and borrows a fag, he's got it made. You can have charts. You could have JFK with his head shot off. No. JFK was all right. Banged all round him. But you know the idea. Maybe Wallace in the wheel-chair? A photo of Rocky in a bad mood with all his dough? What do you say Alvin?'

'I dunno.'

'I do. You've two choices. And ten seconds to make up your mind and get out of here. And take Tindall with you. I don't even want to talk to him. Which is it Alvin? Your money back or tilt your lance at SMI?'

'It's so sudden.'

'Alvin, take him down to the Hotel Percy *now*. Get him out of here. Get yourself out of here. Get him a woman at the Percy. Get yourself one.'

'I don't know. Is the Percy that kind of a hotel?'

'Yes, you do know the Percy is that kind of hotel. The place is unionised. Who'd stay at a unionised hotel if he wasn't getting his change upstairs? Do you take me for a fool, Alvin?'

'All right.'

'Go now. Now. Go on. Now, Alvin. I'm count-ing three. Take him with you. And report back in a month's time. And good luck.'

After the Americans had left Whelan joined the Harnetts in the Blue Room. He went to the head of the room and waved his fingers downwards; the Harnetts took their seats.

'The Hun is at the gate. You heard Paul Tindall, you know about Alvin. I've sent them both packing back to the States. I think between them they have brought home to us the enormity of what Fart International is up against. It may be too late to save America – certainly Tindall and Alvin will have a job saving themselves. Too late to save America and England can go and fuck itself, but we must protect our own shores. Bill Johnston where are you when we need you. I must tell you about Bill Johnston. He never did exist. You saw me out-side talking to Hogan whom I told you so much about? Well, believe it or not, Hogan founded Fart International. I have to hear further from him on that score. But Hogan is our founder. He invented a Bill Johnston to keep a Bill Johnston between him and ourselves. But the Hum is at the gate and Hogan has declared himself. I told Hogan I am stepping down as OSP and he thinks it is fitting. He further agrees with me on the succession: John Harnett, will you accept?'

'I don't see myself as quite an effective OSP as you have been.'

'Of course. That is why you are such a worthy OSP candidate. Enough of formality. Come here till I invest you.'

Whelan put the dollar and the twine around John Harnett's neck; he then applauded, drawing Anna out to join him.

'Now. All I know is that Hogan is our founder. I don't know how or why but I'll find out tonight. Suppose we leave it at that. I might give you a shout tomorrow or during the week and fill you in. After that you're in control. All right? All right Anna?'

'Billy . . .'

'Yes, Anna?'

'Billy . . .'

'Yes?'

'Oh. Nothing.'

'Are you sure? John?'

'I was content among the congregation.'

'What you mean by that is you don't feel you need Fart International any more. And that further translates to there being no need for Fart International. Right?'

'I'm not saying that.'

'I'm not blaming you if you are saying that. I'm saying it myself. I don't need Fart International. Anna doesn't need it any more. You have each other. But I knew the both of you, I knew the three of us when Anna was so confused she thought she was in love with her cousin, when you were out on the wet streets running yourself into an early grave to satisfy the more passremarkable of your business colleagues, and I was, what was I? My God I was nobody. I thought I was nobody. If we feel we don't need Fart International then all the more reason to put it at the disposal of those who do. Would you leave the people of Ireland defenceless? The Success Motivation Institute is going to land in Ireland with all its colours showing. We must defeat it. We must . . . but you know. You *do* know?'

'Yes.'

'Anna?'

'Yes.'

'Good. We'll sort it out during the week. All right?'

Whelan escorted them to their car. He was tucking his prisoners in for the night and so that they would sleep peacefully he said: 'Both of you have been very good for me. I thank you.'

'You've been good for us, Billy.'

'Thank you, Anna. John, you know what the dollar means to me. Treat it gently. Don't ever let a computer see it.'

John Harnett smiled: 'I'd say a computer would react violently to it.'

'Good night.'

'Good night.'

It was five minutes to ten as Whelan reported back to Hogan. Sunday night closing time approached. The bar counter was crowded for last orders.

'Now, Mr Hogan. Enlighten me. How in God's name did you start this mad business?'

Whelan was in the throes of the empty excitement that fills the void after a burden of responsibility is lifted. He was satisfied, within the context of insanity that necessarily prevailed in Fart International, that he had dealt successfully with Alvin and Tindall *and* the bank manager. Here was Hogan after all the years sitting beside him in the Sarsfield Arms. Hogan was a man who had understood him when Whelan had not understood himself. If he had only met Hogan once and had not met him again for fifty years, he felt that he would immediately feel at home with him. Two is no company among the same sex and Hogan and T. A. Dufficy bore Whelan's soul gently on either side and carried it over the hydra threat of the Higgins's and Murphys and Nickys and Mark Browns who were successful, motivated but unfortunately not institutionalised.

'Hogan. You flogpot. Are you all right?'

The cataract was leaping in all its glory.

'Hogan, what's wrong?'

There was no pretence about the activity. Hogan was crying. It was not the tears that flew out of the eyes rather the sadness in the eyes and the gaping wound of misery on his face that alarmed Whelan.

'Hogan.'

Hogan shook his head and waved Whelan away. Whelan remained. He noticed Hogan's glass half empty which in Hogan's case constituted drought. He went to the bar and bought two pints as the guillotine came down. T. A. Dufficy said: 'Will you be staying on?'

'Yes. Something's wrong. Hogan is crying. Seriously. He's upset. I don't know what to do.'

'time now gentlemen. I'll join you after I clear the house.'

Hogan was somewhat recovered when Whelan brought the drink.

'Ah, you've taken the long and immediate steps my good fellow. Excellent. Excellent.'

'Hogan, what's wrong? Can I do anything? You were crying.'

'Yes. I was crying. I was crying. You dealt with Alvin?' 'Yes. I was gentle. . .'

Whatever it was that had driven Hogan to tears was dissipated as Whelan narrated his treatment of Alvin and his abdication in favour of the bank manager. The Sarsfield Arms was quaint in that the bar cleared itself by ten fifteen prompted by T. A. Duffcy's follow up to TIME GENTLEMEN PLEASE. He walked from table to table pounding the brush on each table, on the wall behind each table, on the floor under each table; he pounded every inch of the counter. When he had completed a clrcuit of the lounge he began again.

'Has Duffcy gone mad? I mean madder?'

'He always does that. He's impatient to join us after hours.'

'Oh. I thought he might have thought the Hun was at the gate. Ho ho.'

'You've recovered your spirits.'

The remark checked Hogan's mirth and puzzled Whelan. They took their drinks to the counter; Duffcy raised the guillotine, poured himself a large Hen and drew up a stool between and facing them.

'T.A., Hogan is about to enlighten us.'

'Perhaps I should go behind the counter?'

'That won't be necessary,' Hogan said rather stiffly. 'I need a witness, an official witness.'

Whelan rearranged his posture on the stool; he might have been back in class when a story was about to be told.

Hogan rocked him: 'Years ago – as part of my job – I reversed a wagon out in the cement factory and crushed a man to death.'

Whelan saw a hateful old man to whom nothing was sacred.

'Hogan, for Jesus Christ's sake, don't start that!'

'The date was the fourth of September, nineteen forty-nine. Three o'clock in the afternoon.'

Whelan tugged at his inside pocket. Since the day missals became redundant he had taken to carrying the In Memo-riam card in his good suit. His father looked younger now in the photograph than Whelan himself was. He read: In Loving Memory of Patrick Whelan, who died 4/9/49.

'Hogan, how did you find out the date?'

'Now you stop that! Credit me with sensitivity. I would not make this up.'

'You're seriously trying to tell me you were driving the wagon that killed my father?'

'I heard voices shouting: Drive back, drive back. I climbed down. Can I see that?'

Whelan handed him the In Memoriam card. Hogan stared at it long enough to have to dab at his eyes.

'He was not recognisable. The priest came. And the ambulance. When they took him away everyone continued to stand around. I was the centre of attraction. I don't know how I felt. Shock, I suppose. But everyone kept coming up to me and saying: It wasn't your fault anyway, Hogan. They squeezed my arm: There was nothing you could do about it. I was told to take the rest of the week off to get over it. I went to the funeral and felt terrible. I didn't know your father. The firm decided that there had been contributory negligence on your father's part. It was true that I could have done nothing about it, that I was not in the least to blame. And it was true that your father was one hundred per cent negligent. Everyone saw it. They awarded damages where they might not have awarded a penny. Everything was not as cut and dried in those days as it is today. I lived eighteen miles out in the country. Cycled to work every day. I went back on the Monday. Putting my bicycle in the shed, a chap I was friendly with, always chatted with, he looked at me, as though I was a different man. I thought it was my imagination. All morning at work I had the feeling. In the canteen at lunch, there were four to a table. Four of us always sat at the same table. That Monday, one of the four was a bit late coming in, and a man who usually sat at another table asked if we minded if he sat down. It was odd. It wasn't as if where he usually sat was taken. There was a tacit conspiracy to show that I was not a leper. And when the usual fourth did come in he brought a chair from another table and drew it up to make five. This went on for two months. This type of thing. I might have to go to the stores with a requisition. Instead of an endearing: Now Hogan fuck off to the end of the queue, there was an opening of ranks and the store-keeper bypassing a head to take my requisition. I'd cycle home at night and for eighteen miles in the road I'd see faces. Faces. All looking at me when I wasn't looking, wondering how I was taking it. Gradually it began to seep in. I had killed a man. I began to look at it that way myself but I reasoned that it was ridicu-lous. I felt no guilt, no remorse. It might have been a wagon driven in Russia as far as I was involved. I'd go to work determined not to allow the Faces treat me as though I should be suffering remorse. A group might be chatting and I'd approach. End of laughter. Forced concern and interest in my affairs. I'd snap: Why don't ye say what ye were saying before I came along? What was the joke? They might tell me the joke but registered wonder that I hadn't been driven from the world of the joke . . .'

Dufficy took advantage of the pause to go behind the counter and draw porter. Whelan's mind was blank except that he was standing ten yards off Hogan in the clinker covered cement yard watching the workmen looking at Hogan. Hogan's spectacles were on the counter, his handkerchief mopping his eyes.

'I went to England. Where else? I didn't want to go. You couldn't move from one job to another in Ireland. I went not as a man looking for work, I went as a freak. I was already a man settled in my ways. I was a quiet man. I did my job and cycled home and had

THE SELF-MADE MEN

a drink at night and played twenty-one. I was thirty-eight years old. We had a small house in the main street of the village, there was only my mother and myself, my father was dead, I had one brother married back in the west. I was gone beyond marriage and that. You know, I was – I was nearly looked up to in the village. For people like us who were not farmers, had no land, it was something to have a secure job in the cement factory. The foreman tried to talk me out of it. But no. I went over in the boat. I was thirty-eight years old but my heart was pounding with loneliness the same as if I was seventeen. And terror . . . terror.'

Hogan put his hand out for the pint T. A. Dufficy placed near him. Dufficy remained behind the counter. Grateful for Dufficy to look at behind the counter while Hogan recharged, Whelan examined Dufficy to keep his own mind blank. The proprietor had exhumed herring-bone tweed from his wardrobe in honour of the occasion. He was stiffer than usual within the suit, it was probably of a cut and quality threatened with extinction long before the girls took to noughts and crosses in Burton's.

'. . . it's inaccurate to say that the Faces haunted me. There would not be the remotest sign of them until I conjured them up. I got into a factory as a storeman and the day would pass reasonably; I'd listen to them talking about bleeding sods and you-whamayt? and the rest and to shut them out I'd go back and think of them all looking at me after the body had gone off in the ambulance. And at night in bed even after a rake of beer I couldn't sleep, the brain would keep ticking over. I'd read the newspapers and do the crosswords. I joined the library and used to take four books out a week, books on *anything*, as long as they had pages and words. I went to the second-hand bookshops. I read and I read and I read and I read and I read. I went into another factory where there was better money and I left there with another chap who was going on the buildings for the summer, he got me on as tea boy. And somehow I came to get over the accident, I mean to get over *their* getting over the accident. I'd wrestle with the problem night after night, I'd summon the Faces and I'd spot one man whom I knew to be of sound judgement and yet he'd be looking at me as though I should hide. This was a man I knew and was friendly with and if he was stopped in the street and asked his opinion of capital punishment he would probably think and give a careful, considerate answer. I reasoned and reasoned until I figured it out. I had to *reject* that man. And reject all the Faces. Either reject them or feel guilt. I had no guilt to feel. And they were all – decent people, they were humanity. I had to reject humanity. I was thirty-eight, moderately educated, although a moderate education in those days was equivalent to a lot today . . .'

Hogan's voice now, comparatively dry eye and warmth of narrative encouraged Whelan to further defuse: 'My wife's father had a job as assistant wrapper in those days, on the strength of an Intermediate Certificate . . .'

'Exactly. I was afraid to grapple with the problem. I thought that if I rejected the whole army to keep myself in step then I would be declaring myself a madman. I let it rest. Life went on in my case as predictably as in any other thirty-eight year old first time emigrant. I got over the terror of the English, their strange language, I got over being amiably addressed: Youwahcock? I read and I read and I began to broaden. What I dismissed in Ireland as not being destined for me – marriage – I didn't expect it in England but the other desires surfaced, where I was known to no one. In short, I had a prostitute. I settled down in all ways like my peers, a rather belated, red-faced, unwanted spoil of Empire. Trying to find an early morning taxi from Soho back to my room, trying to recapture the desperate hunger that had launched me earlier in the night to approach old newsboys for an address, that type of thing. You end up looking at yourself, wondering about your destiny, a tea boy travelling across London to relieve himself into the gaping mechanism of a whore's fanny in a dirty Soho room, all because a man threw himself under the wheels of a wagon to pick up a cigarette end. As I mentioned, I read and I read. I picked the brains of the written word and I grew in confidence. I would conjure up the Faces and say out loud in my room: Fuck you, you fools, un-rounded robots, fools.

'Quite deliberately, I dwelt in an alternative world; I might be in a public house that had a television, a programme, say, about New York. I would turn to my neighbour and say: New York's changed since my day, we'll pay for Roosevelt's sins yet. Or some such rot. I could do that type of thing from my voracious reading. Go so far, I discovered, and people will believe anything. If they could believe it. For happy moments in a bar, I was an expatriate New Yorker. Of course one came a cropper. Take New York again for the sake of argument. My neighbour might say: Oh, what part? I was there forty-eight to fifty-two. Nothing for it then but to bluff: All over. And dive into the pint and out the door. I saw an ad for this maintenance man's job in a hotel in Swiss Cottage. I was a tea boy on the buildings. I didn't know a washer from a three eight lock nut. I presented myself to the guvnor as a man who could strip a rawmill before breakfast. I had to send letters home to my mother and get her to post them back to me. References. The guvnor said he couldn't understand how they ever let me out of Ireland. It was this business of getting people to believe things, getting myself to believe them, it led me to search for some way to enshrine the whole business. I had read somewhere that statistics suggested that if any given individual announced that he was God that one hundred people in America would follow him. It led eventually to the Fart International stroke. I tell you when I received a cheque for ten dollars I was afraid I might be in need of an exorcist.

But the replies were so regular – not all containing money – that I knew there was nothing wrong with *me*. I grew and grew in omniscience. There was no doubt about it – the whole *army* was out of step . . .'

Hogan brought his handkerchief to his nose, blew and finished: 'There you are.'

T. A. Dufficy had his hands spread out on the counter, leaning on them. No part of him moved save his eyes which darted from Whelan to Hogan and back again; he realised this was a moment of *moment*; Whelan stared at the floor contemplating the magnificent coincidence that surely had been ordained; Hogan was composed now, free of demons. Dufficy felt privileged to be a witness. Whelan showed the first sign of life. He took his drink from the counter, shook the glass to resurrect the neglected head and looked frankly at Hogan. He stood up and walked to the window over-looking the back lawn where wedding couples were photographed. He thought of Dufficy listening to the wedding couples at night. He thought of Hogan presenting himself to the guvnor as 'a man who could strip a rawmill before breakfast'. He thought back to the day his father brought him on an educational tour of the cement factory. Whelan had, at seven years of age, been bored by the event. But he had nodded dutifully as his father began at the quarry and told him how they blasted the rock – there was no blasting that day so blasting a rock did not have the glamour it should have had for a seven year old. Carefully he climbed up in front of his father on the iron ladder to watch the slurry basins. He had been through the rawmills and the cement mills, the skin of his face contracting from the heat. It was a day he had not enjoyed, a day he had never thought of again since his father was killed; until now. He thought of it now because Hogan had mentioned 'strip a rawmill before breakfast'. Was it possible that Hogan had come across rawmill as he had come across the New Deal, Wingate, and so on?

No. Unfortunately, it did not seem possible. A rawmill was unlikely to crop up in the library of the most indiscriminate reader. Whelan felt a sense of desolation now that he had never known before, not even at the death of his father. This was adult disenchantment. Gone was Hogan the forty-five player, the fellow traveller of joyless Christmas Days, the cosy fibber, the Fart International Grand Puppeteer. At the counter sat an old man who had been associated with the death of Whelan's father, an old man shorn of picaresque senility and tainted with careless driving. Not alone had Whelan's father not been negligent, it had been his duty to lunge after falling cigarette ends; that was the age that was in it. Whelan could not bring himself to turn around and go back to the counter with his face gleaming with hatred for the absurd partner in grotesque coincidence. Whelan had been momentarily appalled to discover that Hogan and not the solid Bill Johnston was at the back of Fart International; but he had bowed to the weight of evidence. He had written to a box number in Los Angeles and the letter had reached Hogan in London. He had written subsequently to a London accommodation number and those letters had reached Hogan. There was no point in being appalled. In fact only a half hour earlier he was delighted with the intelligence. He tried to find an accommodation within himself to stomach the notion of Hogan driving the wagon but he was unsuccessful. That was not coincidence or destiny; it was a sick joke. 'A man who could strip a rawmill before breakfast.' It was curious, he thought, that the phrase should come back to him. Hogan had used another phrase that had made him smile, something about the prostitute, 'the gaping mechanism of a whore's fanny in a dirty Soho room'. A man who could strip a rawmill before breakfast, the gaping mechanism of a whore's fanny in a dirty Soho room. Whelan did not want to go back to the counter and yet it was ludicrous to remain looking out at the lawn marrying two totally disconnected phrases in his thoughts. 'Travelling across London to relieve myself.' *Across?* Bleeding sods, youwahmayt? Youwahcock? Whelan himself had been through that, going into a kiosk for a packet of Embassy and been received with Youwahdearie? He yawned. He was tired and at the point of drinking himself sober. He longed to go home and be with his wife. The night had turned sour. There was that about his father, the young man now in the In Memoriam card that rejected association with a Hogan, a man who travelled across

London to relieve himself in the gaping mechanism of a whore's fanny in a dirty Soho room. Whelan had never seen a prostitute in his life. He was able to conjure up such a lady – green eye shadow, a class of a black corset, red lips, black mesh tights, red high heels and brocade appointments overhead the saloon. Certainly not a dirty room. Dirty? Did it necessarily follow that because of the nature of the profession the room would be dirty? Any dirtier than the room of a Paddy bachelor who used it as a launching pad to the pubs and a place to throw the weary frame at night? *Across London.* Not across. Whelan had never thought of himself as crossing London when he took the Queens Park tube to Piccadilly. Across London, dirty Soho room. Hogan was telling lies. He had never been within an ass's roar of a prostitute. Had he been with prostitutes, an ex-thirty-eight year old Irish virgin, his heart would pound too fast to think of gaping mechanisms. He would blubber and ask her to marry him, thinking the gaping mechanism fitted him like a sheath. Whelan went over as much of Hogan's phraseology as he could remember. Youwahmayt? Hogan had never been a man to mimic the Londoner when Whelan knew him in the Falcon. In his original letter to Bill Johnston – the letter Hogan produced earlier to short circuit any unnecessary demands for proof – Whelan had written of the Youwahdearie incident in the kiosk – the reaction to a young man asking for Embassy who had supposedly left home to become an actor. That was where Hogan got his Youwahcock and Youwahmayt. And the bleeding sod was unworthy of Hogan or Whelan or anyone else. That was out of the tame 'cor chase me round the mulberry bush' school. Hogan was telling lies. There were no prostitutes and no Irishman ever really was taken aback by the youwah-cocks or dearies – except in retrospect. What else did he lie about? He lived in the main street of the village with his mother; his father was dead and his brother married back in the west. A quiet man who cycled home and had a pint and played twenty-one. Twenty-one? They didn't play twenty-one in that village: in Kerry they played twenty-one or possibly back in the west where his brother was married. But they did not play twenty-one in the village; they played forty-five. Another lie. A silly lie. They were all silly lies. It was a pity his driving the wagon that killed Patrick Whelan was not a silly lie. 'Credit me with sensitivity, I would not make this up,' Hogan had declared angrily and Whelan had sat and listened respectfully. There was a ring about Hogan's account of tie accident: Drive back, drive back. It was not the ring of lies.

It was the ring of Hoganism!

Wingate, flogpot, New Deal, across London, Maurice, Lady Antonia Fraser, long and immedi-ate steps to the bar, My Dear Fellow, Al Guerrini, Bill Johnston and his wife cailed Honey (and if I'm admitting it I gotta be telling the truth) – Hoganism! Whelan was sure in his heart that Hogan no more drove the wagon than T. A. Dufficy or Al Guerrini.

But knowledge in his heart had not ever served him well. His heart knew that he was the type of citizen who should have been sought out by Higgins, Murphy, Nicky and Mark Brown; his head acknowledged that such had not been the case. Even today, when she was not at her best, he *felt* he was not a fit companion for Breda yet the sordid fact was that she found him acceptable. He *felt* that Hogan had not killed his father yet he knew that generally among Hogan's tissue of lies lay buried a germ of truth.

He drained his glass and turned to rejoin the pair at the counter. Hogan would have made a comical sight in his driver's hat and . . . Driver's hat, train-driver's hat. Train driver's hat, driver's hat, come to me, there was something odd about Hogan in a train driver's hat. That day, on their return to the packing plant after the educational tour, he had watched the wagons being loaded. Of course! Suddenly he could not understand how Hogan managed to gloss over such an obvious contradiction. The night was beautiful again. The sour taste was gone from his mouth, he could face another pint while Hogan scraped the bottom of his barrel.

'. . . a thorough gentleman, the guvnor. Hogan, let's the two of us break open a bottle, he would say when he felt the need of quality conversation . . .'

Whelan thought he detected in T. A. Dufficy's welcoming smile a trace of relief that the cavalry had arrived.

'He's still at it, T.A.? Fill up a pair of pints there and a drop for yourself. Hogan, you're a terrible man.'

'Why so?'

'You cycled to work in the morning; you put your bike in the shed. You sensed atmosphere. In the canteen where four sat at a table. In the stores where you out-requisitioned all round you. How do you think them up?'

'You persist. I will not have aspersions. . .'

'Hogan, employees of the cement factory do not drive wagons. Men with caps on them drive wagons. Caps with the legend CIE, Coras Iompar Eireann, or in the language of the foreigner, Irish Transport Company. You can't have it both ways. Now. Did you work for the cement factory or did you work for CIE when you were reversing wagons knocking people down?'

'Ah ! When CIE were short staffed. . .'

'No. No. No. No. No. Never, never, never has CIE been short staffed. Not when the Asian flu was around, not when the All Blacks play at Thomond Park. There's a superfluity of man power traditionally idle in CIE. Hogan, why? For what possible reason did you make that up?'

Hogan's eyes did not fill with tears as Whelan expected. He concentrated for perhaps a minute and then allowed a grin appear.

'I don't know.' He shook his head as though confronted with the problem for the first time. 'I honestly don't know.'

MICHAEL CURTIN

'Well, I'm glad you weren't driving the wagon.
Those faces you claimed haunted you. They wouldn't
be in it with my face. Tell me, to pass away the last
pint, why *did* you go to England? Now that faces have
nothing to do with it.'

While Hogan composed another pack of lies,
Whelan was sine, T. A. Dufficy placed the drink on
the counter with his own brand of composure.

'T.A., do you find nothing remarkable? What do
you think of this man? Can he make them up or can
he make them up?'

'Thinking is dangerous. I don't like thinking.'

'I went to London . . .'

'Hogan, one moment.' Whelan extended his
hand. 'Truce. Shake on it. Truce, no fibs. The truth.
I've had enough of the other thing.'

'This is, unfortunately, the truth. Nothing excep-
tional about it. I went to London at seventeen or eighteen. There were no jobs to be had. I went to London
for nothing more complicated than a job . . .'

'Yes?'

'That's it.'

'How do you mean "that's it"? Continue.'

'That's it. I can adorn it or adulterate it, just as
you like. But that's it. A job. Come back home with
money in my pocket, the pocket of a suit, and make
an exhibition of myself. Stand drinks in the pub and
tell them about money. I did that. I came home year
after year, sometimes twice a year, and I bought drink
in the pub and told them about London and how I

370

didn't know how they survived. They didn't know how they survived themselves. But survive they did. They not alone survived but they married and survived. I was thirty-eight before I realised that. I was thirty-eight, standing in the bar, and they actually bought rounds back. And someone said: Hogan, you'll be bringin' one of them black women home with you one of the days, ha ha. My God. It comes as an awful shock to realise that you're no longer the conquering hero. I hadn't been living in a fool's paradise. It was always a wrench to go back, from Dun Laoghaire on, on deck looking at Dublin fading and Holyhead and Euston and your room approaching. But at least you had always that two weeks. Hogan will be home one of the days, they say Hogan is landed, there'll be great sport tonight, Hogan's home. Yes. Suddenly, they were not pinched faces any more, standing at corners with no ties on, only the stud keeping out the wind, hands in the pockets and foot shoved against the wall. They were buying back in the pub and their shoes were polished and they wanted to know when I was going to settle down. And I'm not making it up because it's not worth making up, it's an old, old sad story without a tit of drama or romance. You were part of it. I'm part of it. I'm the whole and I'm the part. I had very conventional desires. Didn't we all? Didn't everyone? A job, a wife, a family, a place to live among your own. People are marrying each other every day, having families, living in places, among their own. But it was denied us, a lot of us.

The likes of Mackey who thought he had succeeded only make it tragic. Two English daughters and the end – he follows the five of trumps till his head hits the ground. Adorn it, adulterate it. With what? With a playwright's sleight of hand? How do you clothe the unwanted?'

Hogan's inclusion of Whelan as part of the old, old story was no ploy on Hogan's side to recruit a sympathetic audience; it was the simple truth Whelan recognised and he was humble and cut down to size in the presence of truth. He had never listened to anybody talk in that way about emigration before. Certainly no emigrant ever spoke of emigration as such. It was a forbidden subject. Shop. He saw Hogan now in a there-but-for-the-grace-of-God-go-I light and almost wished he was home counting his blessings, beginning with his wife.

'It's rough,' Whelan volunteered.

Hogan considered and then shook his head. 'You don't know. You can't know. You've had a glimpse. You were too young. I'm only back a week and I've seen them still coming. They'll get the wild hair tamed to a trendy cut and at the weekends the boys will be on the town again. And in thirty years time they'll be putting money in juke boxes to hear "Lovely Leitrim". I can't cry, would you believe that?'

Whelan timidly looked at Hogan's face. There was no sign of a tear. The voice was steady, the tone ironic.

'I practically trained myself to switch on the old ducts for effect. Sometimes in the room when there did not seem to be any consolation in going out drinking I would summon tears and then I'd feel better and go out and enjoy the night's drinking. But I tell you now, and if I never spoke the truth I'm speaking it now, I tell you my heart is fit to burst and a tear won't come. I'm close on fifty years in England and I've made no mark. The mother died long ago. The brother's dead. I have a few nephews in the west and that's it. To die mourned by nephews. To have had my throat cut by the Dane or the Norman, there was dignity in that, but to die mourned by nephews who do not know me. I have often wondered, who will forgive England?'

Whelan immediately spotted the relapse into Hoganism. He countered: 'You mean: Who will forgive Ireland?'

To his surprise Hogan nodded, and caressed the bridge of his nose with thumb and forefinger and muttered: Yes. He rose from the stool, cleared his throat.

'Mr Dufficy, sir, I think I'll inspect your lavatorial appointments.'

'Straight out. First left.'

Whelan thought the line a pathetic effort on Hogan's part to pull himself together. Hogan was a beaten man. Whelan thought of one thing and said another: 'He must have amazing kidneys. His first visit tonight.'

'I noticed.'

In the silence they could hear the sound of flushing water. Whelan left the bar and stood ten yards away from the exit door, his hands in his pockets, his eyes on the pattern of the carpet. As Hogan sailed steadily by on his way back to the counter, Whelan put out his hand and checked his progress.

'Hogan.'

'Yes?'

Staring at the carpet Whelan continued: 'Will you do something for me?'

'My dear fellow. Ask and you shall receive. Knock. . .'

'Hogan. I can't even bring myself to ask.'

'Nonsense.' Hogan put his arm on Whelan's shoulder. 'Ask. Ask away.'

'Hogan. . .'

'Yes?'

'Hogan, will you be my father?'

The hand slid from Whelan's shoulder. Whelan raised his eyes and forced himself to look at Hogan. From behind the counter Dufficy watched as they stared at each other. Whelan took his hands from his pockets and quickly put them around Hogan's neck. The immobile embrace was more eloquent and valid than a king's seal. They parted, Whelan resting his palms on Hogan's shoulders.

'T.A. Put this old flogpot up for the night. Where have you been staying?'

'I have a room.'

'A room. I can't do anything about rooms. I can't swing a cat in my place and there's Breda. A lovely woman but I can't spring a father on her. Hogan I love you. You're a lovely man. Don't speak. You are.'

'Gentlemen, I couldn't help overhearing.' Father and son turned towards the proprietor. 'This hotel lacks that certain touch of class, in a word, a maintenance man. The salary is not great. It, in fact, does not exist, but there is room and board. . .'

Whelan walked to the counter and shook Dufficy's hand.

'I'm off. There's a woman with a rolling pin waiting for me. We must all rise refreshed and carry the battle to the Success Motivation Institute. Good night T.A. Good night Hogan.'

'Good night – Billy.'

Hogan had always called him Whelan.

CHAPTER FIFTEEN
THE WHOLE SECRET

The house was in darkness save for the eternal vigil of the test card. On the rare occasion Whelan watched television he did not switch off the lights considering such action redolent of premeditation. Breda pulled curtains, put her feet up and had a table with a bottle of orange, her cigarettes and a magazine or knitting at the ready when she looked at the box. She was asleep now with her feet up, the bottle empty and a magazine on her lap. Her mouth was ajar as she breathed through her nose rhythmically snoring. Whelan followed his nose to the kitchen.

Cooking in advance was a habit of Breda's he had often scorned but tonight he was grateful; breast bones were simmering. They were for Monday's dinner, there being no racing on Monday. Whelan fetched a large, deep plate. He lifted a breast bone from the pot with two spoons and ladled soup into an island around the bone on the plate. It was a meaty bone that fell away in large slivers to the slightest prod from a fork. There would be war if Breda woke up now. Whelan's porter appetite was insatiable; he took a second and a third bone. He poured the remaining soup into a jug and drank. He would not have her giving out to him for eating tomorrow's dinner. It was his own dinner. She did not eat breast bones. It would be punishment enough to have cold ham put in front of him as she would certainly do to illustrate her lack of intention to cook the same dinner twice. His hands were sticky from holding the bones to gnaw the meat from the recesses out of reach of the fork. He ran cold water over them from the tap in the sink.

He put his own feet up and had a cigarette. The lino on the kitchen floor was in a shocking state but it was easier on his head to look at it and easier on the eye from the point of view that nothing could be worse than the condition of the wallpaper. It was utter selfishness and laziness not to have the house in good repair and he could not tell himself now, as he often told Breda, that he would not be sucked into the herd of decorators who began with a paintbrush and before they knew where they were they were in the clutches of finance companies who lent them money for triple glazed windows and beauty board.

He heard Breda stirring. She entered the kitchen tapping a yawn after the fashion of youngsters simulating the war cries of Red Indians.

'I must have fallen asleep.'

She examined the empty breast bone pot and shook her head.

'Now, Breda, we will not have breast bones coming between us.'

She took the pot and filled it with water to steep. It was a gesture of resignation with which he was familiar but it frightened him now, now that Fart International had lost the mystique of Bill Johnston, now that Bill Johnston was no more than Hogan and Hogan was no more than a Paddy. She was not about to remonstrate with him for eating Monday's breast bones on a Sunday; she had not, yet, asked him how the tenth anniversary meeting at Fart International had gone; she was not curious to hear of Bill Johnston. She was in a world of her own, a world into which he had driven her, the world of steeping a breast bone pot and no longer railing against the world into which she had been dragged. He did not find her attractive now and yet he knew that five minutes monkeying about in front of a mirror would yield her glamorous, desirable.

'Breda, I have good news for you.'

She did not hear him.

'Breda? Breda, I said I have good news for you.'

'What? Oh. Sorry, I was in a brown study. Did you have a good meeting?'

Whelan had a vague idea of the good news he would announce but he would only announce the good news if the good news came out of his mouth of its own accord. It had always been good for him, saying the first thing that came into his head.

'Bill Johnston never turned up.'

'Oh. I suppose – maybe he couldn't make it.'

She was not interested. It was not her fault. There were people – and he thought he understood them – who were congenitally uninterested in off the track movements such as Fart International; they were afraid for the good of their mental processes to stray.

'He doesn't exist. He never did. No such person as Bill Johnston.'

'But didn't you write letters to him? Didn't he write to you and say he was coming?'

'Breda, do you remember Hogan?'

'Who?'

'I must have told you a thousand times. Hogan. The man I knew in London. He used to make up stories, you remember, he killed a hundred yellow men with the jawbone of an ass?'

'Oh, yes. I know who you mean now. What about him?'

'Hogan turned up in the hotel tonight. It turns out he invented Fart International and invented Bill Johnston so that I wouldn't know he was behind it.'

'Isn't that a bit of a coincidence? I mean you knew him in London.'

'Yes. It's too much of a coincidence. I don't know how I should react to it. Do you know something, Breda? You know Higgins, Murphy, Nicky and Mark Brown? I think I'm over them. I don't know why. It's a feeling I have. I can think about them now with equanimity. Isn't that odd?'

'Good. I'm delighted to hear that. I always said you took them too much to heart.'

'But I don't know that I'm happy thinking of them that way. I might be losing my touch. For instance, I said

I have good news for you and you don't seem curious to know what it is.'

'Well, I'm all ears.'

'What would you think of us buying a house in suburbia, with a garden front and back. This place is a shambles.'

Breda ceased her absentminded pot scouring.

'You're losing your touch all right.'

'I was expecting you to cheer. Throw your arms around me and say: Oh, Billy! '

'Hip hip hooray. My hands are dirty. Oh, Billy! '

'I have it all figured out. We could get eleven thousand for this place if we dickeyed it up. There's the money I have in the bank and there's the Fart International money. Nearly forty thousand Fart International money. Just think how much it would be if I'd let it gain interest. There's no doubt about it but I was a right nut. We could buy one of those food markets and live overhead. Nothing to it. Yes, madam, and a very good morning to you, madam.'

'Billy, why do you tease me? Is that what you learned at your meeting tonight? A new trick to tease the wife. They must have elected you president again. You're celebrating.' 'No. John Harnett is the new Outrageously Suitable Person. That's the bank manager in case you don't remember. And I'm not a sadist. I mean it. You want a house you have a house.'

'You said you'd never touch a penny of that money?'

'Well, I've changed my mind. It's my money. People sent it to me. I have a right to do what I want with it. I have a wife and children to think of. Declan is at an age when teachers start asking what does your father do for a living.'

'You know that money isn't yours.'

'Breda, I don't understand this. Only yesterday it seems you wanted me to buy a washing machine out of it. How do you make out it isn't mine?'

'You told me often enough. You said you had a sacred trust minding that money. You implied it was on a par with a priest dipping into the poor box.'

'And you said I was suffering from delusions of grandeur. Do you not feel that way about it now?'

'I don't know how I feel. After ten years you spring the prospect of a house on me. What got into you tonight? What happened at your meeting?'

'You're not interested in what happens at Fart meetings.'

'I'm interestsed in what happened at this one. Come on.'

Whelan went through the meeting with the discovery of Hogan in the lounge and ending with the embrace and his request to Hogan that Hogan become his father.

'You asked the man to be your father? Seriously?'

'Yes.'

'But why?'

'Because – because I felt he needed a son.'

'You didn't feel I needed a father-in-law?'

'Breda, I love that about you. You never lose your sense of humour.'

'You're serious about getting a new house?'

'Dictum Meum Pactum.'

'Dictum – Meum – Pactum,' Breda repeated slowly and just as slowly began to cry. She left her breast bone pot and threw herself onto Whelan's lap. She put her arms around him and sobbed into his jaw. Sitting on him and with her chest pressed against his he became aroused. She was crying the words: 'Thank you, thank you, thank you. Oh, Billy, I love you. Love you.'

She sat erect on his lap and clutched his hair gently with both hands. 'I won't let you. Do you hear me? I won't let you. I'll help you. The notion of you in suburbia is enough to give me a stroke. And I'll tell Declan, when the first teacher asks him what his father does he's to stand up and say: My Daddy is a hawker, and I'll tell him to shout it out and shout it out with pride. A great big wonderful hawker.'

'Breda, what's got in to you?'

'You're frightened.'

'I beg your pardon?'

Breda disengaged herself from his lap. She stood in front of the mirror near the sink and idly brushed her hair. She began to laugh as though at a private joke.

'Breda?'

She put down the brush and turned to him.

'Would you really buy a house?'

'I said I would. My word . . .'

'It's too late. Billy, I often sat and thought about you. When you're off at the races I'd sit and imagine you. I'd experience a mad pride that you were shouting your head off even though I'm mortified when someone asks me what you do. I haven't been able to get a word in edgeways in ten years. You were too cute for me. I'd wonder how it would have been married to Norman. I'd have a lovely house and little niche in little society. I'd go over every word you said. And I'd agree. But it was no consolation. No one else would agree with you. If everyone stopped me in the street and said I envy you married to a hawker who fights the great battle against washing machines it would have been marvellous. But they didn't. And now tonight you march in and want to throw ten years away. Because you're frightened. You have no letter of credence anymore from Bill Johnston to lend authority to your actions. You tell me you have a Paddy standing four square behind you. For the first time you can see everything through everyone else's eyes. Everyone else's compromised vision. And you're frightened. You want to run away, out to the suburbs, to a foodmarket. You see Higgins and his friends no longer a nightmare. Good for Billy Whelan. With you one recipe is no longer in so it's out. Start again with new ingredients out in the suburbs. That won't do me, my friend. I've had ten years of this, know-ing what I've had ten years of. While you didn't know anything or care less, just went on your merry way. Well, I'm not going to make a mockery of ten years of my life. It's ridiculous. I can see it now for the first time just when you are losing sight of it. You were right. Right all the time but you didn't really know it. If you did you mightn't have had the courage. My beloved hawker, outrageously, suitable person, what did you say that dreadful American chap used to do? You're going to hang in there swinging. Hawking, Fart Internationalling, black-balling for all you're worth. And you're going to have company.'

Fascinated, Whelan saw her tap her chest.

'I'm joining Fart International. My own. I'm not going to worry about prising the money for a blouse or a skirt out of you any more. I'll wear anything that's clean. I'll act the bohemian. I'll wear my tights as a belt and my panties for a hat if the mood takes me, I'll go naked, I'll. . .'

Whelan stood up and went to her. He took her in his arms to control her sobbing.

'Breda, take it easy. Hysterics. Easy.'

'There's only been one life in this house. Yours. Your wife, the children, bit players. You make every-thing revolve around you.'

'Is there another way, Breda? You a libber now?'

'See? I can't talk to you.'

'Breda, I said I'd buy the house. What more do you want? With a garden. We'll get a swing in it.'

'Declan is too old for a swing. I don't know what I want. I don't know what I want.'

'There. Now you're learning. Let's go up. You don't know what you want and that's the right way to have it. I would have bought you the house, Breda. I want you to know that. But you don't want it and you never did want it. No one wants it. And you hit me under the belt there with Bill Johnston. I am a little afraid. Now, dry your tears and we'll go up and make old fashioned love. I see the problem now. You were a closet hawker's wife all the time. But now you're coming out. We'll instal babysitters. You'll come with me to the Sarsfield Arms and make your contribution. You might come up with a gem: people who think washing machines are a threat to purity. That's better. I like it when you giggle.

My God, Breda, you have a lovely bottom. What's the rate tonight? It's after midnight.'

'Every ninety-ninth customer gets it free.'

'No no. None of that. What'll you give me for a quid?'

'I'll give you the lot. The other way. But not for money. For a certain thing.'

'Half my kingdom.'

'It's not money so you'll have to give me your word.'

'Dictum Meum Pactum.'

Breda gave out a triumphant laugh.

'The whole works – for a washing machine.'

'You said it's not money. You know how much a washing machine costs?'

'You don't have to buy it. It can come like a thief in the night. Like the cot. Oh, Billy, I love you. It isn't every husband will buy his wife a washing machine for a little old fashioned dose of the other way. Come on.'

At four o'clock in the morning Whelan lay awake debating whether or not to invite Hogan to dinner on Christmas Day. It was not the cut and dried issue he had supposed. There was the state of the house. Eddie began to wail. Rocking the cot Whelan noticed that it too needed a lick of paint. A lick of paint was the phrase, a clue to the proper way to go about it. It would be difficult to paint a cot. A small gabled end wall – progress could be reported – but a cot. The man in the shop would never believe that he was nervous of painting. He would advise Whelan not to take too much on the brush. The whole secret was not to take too much on the brush. As an antidote to having promised Breda a washing machine and admitting the house was in need of maintenance, Whelan promised himself that whatever else he did, he would certainly take too much on the brush.

Printed in Great Britain
by Amazon